The Romance of Lust, which was first published in four volumes between 1873 and 1876, introduces Charles Roberts, a quivering lad of fifteen, who is taken in hand by a married woman, Mrs. Benson, visiting at his mother's house. She becomes his full initiator-instructress and launches him on an amorous career that spans a lifetime.

Sent away to school at the house of an uncle, he again falls into sympathetic hands. Here, too, he draws about him a tight little circle of like-minded friends, until he goes up to King's College, where he further indulges his fancy for intricate *tableaux ensembles*. He rejoins his beloved Mrs. Benson, and together with his new friends the Count and Mrs. Egerton they form a secret society much given to *la double jouissance*.

Now a wealthy man by dint of several inheritances, Charlie retires before the age of thirty, and marries the divine Miss Frankland, who had been one of his childhood governesses. The two go off to tour the continent, rejoining the Count and meeting a host of friends both new and old, with whom they make "merry" in mirrored bawdy houses, ruined castles, and other fanciful places.

An Addenda to the book contains twelve letters which figured in the divorce scandal of the Count de la Rochefoucault, in 1859. The letters seem to have been included for the sole purpose of demonstrating that married women are as charming in their way as the freshest young creatures.

The Romance of Lust

or Earlier Experiences

BOOK-OF-THE-MONTH CLUB
NEW YORK

Contents

ADDENDA

Volume I
The Romance of Lust

*T*here were three of us—Mary, Eliza, and myself. I was approaching fifteen, Mary was about a year younger, and Eliza between twelve and thirteen years of age. Mamma treated us all as children, and was blind to the fact that I was no longer what I had been. Although not tall for my age, nor outwardly presenting a manly appearance, my passions were awakening, and the distinctive feature of my sex, although in repose it looked magnificent enough, was very sufficiently developed when under the influence of feminine excitement.

As yet, I had absolutely no knowledge of the uses of the different organs of sex. My sisters and I all slept in the same room. They together in one bed, I alone in another. When no one was present, we had often mutually examined the different formations of our sexes.

We had discovered that mutual handlings gave a certain amount of pleasing sensation; and, latterly, my eldest sister had discovered that the hooding and unhooding of my doodle, as she called it, instantly caused it to swell up and stiffen as hard as a piece of wood. My feeling her little pinky slit gave rise in her to nice sensations, but on the slightest attempt to insert even my finger, the pain was too great. We had made so little progress in these *attouchements* that not the slightest inkling of what could be done in that way dawned upon

3

us. I had begun to develope a slight growth of moss-like curls round the root of my cock; and then, to our surprise, Mary began to show a similar tendency. As yet, Eliza was as bald as her hand, but both were prettily formed, with wonderfully full and fat mounts of Venus. We were perfectly innocent of guile and quite habituated to let each other look at all our naked bodies without the slightest hesitation; and when playing in the garden, if one wanted to relieve the pressure on the bladder, we all squatted down together, and crossed waters, each trying who could piddle fastest. Notwithstanding these symptoms of passion when excited, in a state of calm I might have passed for a boy of ten or eleven.

My father had left us but moderately provided for, and mamma, wishing to live comfortably, preferred giving me lessons along with my sisters at home to sending me to school; but her health beginning to fail, she inserted an advertisement in the *Times* for a governess. Out of a large number of applicants, a young lady, of the name of Evelyn, was selected. Some ten days afterwards she arrived, and became one of the family.

We did not see much of her the first evening, but after breakfast the following morning, mamma accompanied her to what was considered our school-room, and said, "Now, my dears, I place you under Miss Evelyn's care; you must obey her in all things; she will teach you your lessons, as I am unable to do so any longer." Then, turning to our new governess, "I fear you will find them somewhat spoiled, and unruly; but there is a horse, and Susan will make you excellent birch rods whenever you require them. If you spare their bottoms when they deserve whipping, you will seriously offend me." As mamma said this, I observed Miss Evelyn's eyes appeared to dilate with a sort of joy, and I felt certain that, severely as mamma had often whipped us, if we should now deserve it, Miss Evelyn would administer it much more severely. She looked amiability itself, and was truly beautiful in face and person, twenty-two years of age, full and finely formed, and dressed always with the most studied neatness. She was, in truth, a seductive creature. She made an instantaneous impression on my senses. There was, however, somewhat of a sternness of expression, and a dignity of carriage, which caused us at once to fear and respect her. Of course, at first, all went smoothly enough, and seeing that mamma treated me precisely as she did my sisters, I came to be regarded as quite a child by Miss Evelyn. She found that she had to sleep in the same room with my sisters and myself. I fancied that on the first night Miss Evelyn did not approve of this arrangement, but gradually became familiarized with it, and seemed to think no more about it.

When bedtime came, we all kissed mamma and retired early, as usual. Miss Evelyn followed some hours later. When she came in, she carefully locked the door, then looked at me to see if I was asleep. Why, I know not, but I was instinctively prompted to feign sleep. I did so successfully, notwithstanding the passing of the candle before my eyes. So she at once commenced undressing. When her back was turned, I opened my eyes, and greedily devoured her naked charms as they were gradually exhibited before me. The moment she turned round, I was again as if asleep. I have said that my passions had begun to develope themselves, but as yet I did not understand their force or direction. I well remember this first night, when a fine ripe woman gradually removed every particle of dress within a couple of yards of me—the effect of each succeeding charm, from her lovely and beautifully formed bubbies to the taking off her shoes and stockings from her well-formed legs and small feet and ankles, caused my prick to swell and stiffen to a painful extent. When all but her chemise was removed, she stooped to pick up her petticoats that she had allowed to fall to her feet, and in lifting them, raised also her chemise, and exposed to my view a most glorious bottom—dazzlingly white and shining like satin.

As the light was full upon it, and she was still in a stooping position, I could see that below her slit she was well covered with dark hair. Turning round, to put her petticoats on a chair, and to take up her night-gown, she slipped her chemise from her arm, and letting it fall to the ground while she lifted the night-gown over her head, I had for some seconds a view of her beautiful belly, thickly covered with dark curly hair over the mount of Venus. So voluptuous was the sight, I almost shuddered, so intense was my excitement. She now sat down on the bed to take off her shoes and stockings. Oh! what beautiful thighs, legs, ankles, and feet she had!

I am now advanced in life, and have had many handsome and well-formed women, but I never saw limbs more voluptuously formed.

In a few minutes the light was extinguished, and a rushing rill flowed into the night vase; very different from the gentle tricklings from myself and sisters as we often squatted down opposite each other and crossed water, laughing at the different sources from which they flowed. My sisters often envied me the power of directing the spurt where I pleased, so little were we from dreaming of the real intent of that projecting little instrument.

I heard the charming creature get into bed, and shortly breathe hard. As for me, I could not sleep. I lay awake the greater part of the night, afraid to be restless, lest I should disturb Miss Evelyn and give her reason to think I had been observant of her undressing. When at last I dozed off, it was but to dream of all the charms I had seen.

About a month passed thus. Every night Miss Evelyn became more and more at her ease, and confident of my mere childishness, often gave me glorious and lengthened glimpses of her beautifully developed charms: although it was only about every other night that I could enjoy them, for, as they always produced sleeplessness afterwards, the following night nature assured her rights, and I usually slept profoundly when

I would infinitely have preferred continued gazing on the charms of my lovely governess. But, doubtless, those exhausting sleeps helped to throw her off her guard, and gave me better opportunities than I should otherwise have had. Once or twice she used the night ware before putting on her night-gown, and I could see the rosy-lipped opening embosomed in exquisite dark curls, pouring out its full measure of water; showing a fine force of nature, and driving me wild with excitement. Yet it is singular that I never once thought of applying to my fingers for relief from the painful stiffness that nearly burst my prick asunder.

Whether mamma had observed my very frequent projection of my trousers, or began to think it better I should not sleep in the same room as Miss Evelyn, I cannot say, but she had my bed removed into her own. However, I was so thoroughly treated as a mere boy by every one in the house, that Miss Evelyn seemed to forget my sex; and there was at all times a freedom of carriage and an *abandon* in her attitudes that she certainly would not have indulged in if she had felt any restraint from considering herself in the presence of a youth of the age of puberty.

In cold weather I used to sit on a low stool by the fire—Miss Evelyn was seated in front, I had my lesson book on my knee, and she herself would place her beautiful feet on the high school fender, with her work in her lap, while she heard my sisters repeat their lesson, totally unconscious that for half an hour at a time she was exposing her beautiful legs and thighs to my ardent gaze; for sitting much below her, and bending my head as if intent on my lesson, my eyes were below her raised petticoats. Her close and tight-fitting white stockings displayed her well-formed legs, for while confined to the house during our morning lessons she did not wear drawers; so that in the position she sat in, with her knees higher than her feet on the already high fender, and her legs somewhat apart to hold her work in her lap more easily, the whole glorious underswell of both thighs, and the lower part of her fine large bottom, with the pinky slit quite visible, nestled in a rich profusion of dark curls, were fully exposed to my view. The light from the fire glancing under her raised petticoats tinged the whole with a glow, and set me equally in a blaze of desire until I was almost ready to faint. I could have rushed headlong under her petticoats, and kissed and fondled that delicious opening and all its surroundings. Oh, how little she thought of the passion she was raising. Oh! dear Miss Evelyn, how I did love you from the dainty kid slipper and tight glossy silk stocking, up to the glorious swell of the beautiful bubbies, that were so fully exposed to me nearly every night, and the lovely lips of all that I longed to lovingly embrace.

Thus day after day passed away, and Miss Evelyn became to me a goddess, a creature whom, in my heart of hearts, I literally worshiped. When she left the school-room, and I was alone, I kissed that part of the fender her feet had pressed, and the seat on which she sat, and even the air an inch above, imagination placing there her lovely cunt. I craved for something beyond this without knowing exactly what I wanted; for, as yet, I really was utterly ignorant of anything appertaining to the conjunction of the sexes.

One day I had gone up to my sisters' bedroom where the governess slept, that I might throw myself on her bed, and in imagination embrace her beautiful body. I heard some one approaching, and knowing that I had no business there, I hid myself under the bed. The next moment Miss Evelyn herself entered, and locked the door. It was about an hour before dinner. Taking off her dress, and hanging it on the wardrobe, she drew out a piece of furniture, which had been bought for her, the use of which had often puzzled me; she took off the lid, poured water into its basin, and placed a sponge near it. She then took off her gown, drew her petticoats and chemise up to her waist and fastened them there, straddled across it, and seated herself upon it.

I thus had the intoxicating delight of gazing on all her beautiful charms, for when she tucked up her clothes she stood before her glass, presenting to my devouring glance her glorious white bottom in all its fullness, turning to approach the bidet, she equally exposed her lower belly and beautiful mount, with all its wealth of hair. While straddling over the bidet before she sat down, the whole of her pinky-lipped cunt broke on my enraptured sight. Never shall I forget the wild excitement of the moment. It was almost too much for my excited senses; fortunately, when seated, the immediate cause of my almost madness vanished. She sponged herself well between the thighs for about five minutes. She then raised herself off the bidet, and for a moment again displayed the pouting lips of her cunt—then stood fronting me for two or three minutes while she removed, with the rinsed sponge, the trickling drops of water which still gathered on the rich bush of curls around her quim. Thus her belly, mount and thighs, whose massy-fleshed and most voluptuous shape were more fully seen by me than they had heretofore been, and it may easily be conceived into what a state such a deliberate view threw me.

Oh, Miss Evelyn, dear, delicious Miss Evelyn! what would you have thought had you known that I was gazing on all your angelic charms, and that my eager eyes had been straining themselves to penetrate the richness of those charming pouting lips which lay so snugly in that rich mass of dark curling hair. Oh! how I did long to kiss them; for at that time I had no other idea of embracing and still less of penetrating them.

When her ablutions were completed, she sat down and drew off her stockings, displaying her beautiful white calves and charming little feet. I believe it was this first admiration of the really exquisitely formed legs, ankles and feet, which were extraordinarily perfect in make, that first awakened my passion for those objects, which have since always exercised a peculiar charm over me. She was also so particularly neat in her shoes—little dark ones—that were *bijoux* to look at, I often took them up and kissed them, when left in the room. Then her silk stockings, always drawn up tight and fitting like a glove, set off to the greatest advantage the remarkable fine shape of her legs.

Putting on silk for cotton stockings, she took down a low-bodiced dress, finished her toilet, and left the room. I crawled out from under the bed, washed my face and hands in the water of her bidet, and even drank some in my excitement.

Some six weeks had now elapsed since the arrival of Miss Evelyn. The passion that had seized me for her had so far kept me most obedient to her slightest command, or even wish, and, from the same cause, attentive to my lessons, when not distracted by the circumstances already detailed. My example had also had the effect of keeping my sisters much in the same groove, but it was impossible this could last—it was not nature. As long as all went smoothly, Miss Evelyn seemed to be all amiability. We fancied we could do as we liked, and we grew more careless.

Miss Evelyn became more reserved, and cautioned us at first, and then threatened us with the rod. We did not think she would make use of it. Mary grew impertinent, and one afternoon turned sulky over her lessons, and set our teacher at defiance. Miss Evelyn, who had been growing more and more angry, had her rise from her seat. She obeyed with an impudent leer. Seizing her by the arm, Miss Evelyn dragged the struggling girl to the horse. My sister was strong and fought hard, using both teeth and nails, but it was to no purpose. The anger of our governess was fully roused, and raising her in her arms, she carried her forcibly to the horse, placed her on it, held her firmly with one hand while she put the noose round her with the other, which, when drawn, secured her body; other nooses secured each ankle to rings in the floor, keeping her legs apart by the projection of the horse, and also forcing the knees to bend a little, by which the most complete exposure of the bottom, and, in fact, of all her private parts too, was obtained.

Miss Evelyn then left her, and went to mamma for a rod. In a few minutes she returned, evidently flushed with passion, and proceeded to tie Mary's petticoats well up to her waist, leaving her bottom and her pinky slit quite bare and exposed directly before my eyes. It was quite two months since I had seen her private parts, and I was well surprised to observe the lips more pouting and swelled out, as well as the symptoms of a mossy covering of the mount much more developed. Indeed, it was in itself more exciting than I had expected, for my thoughts had so long dwelt only on the riper beauties of Miss Evelyn that I had quite ceased to have any toying with Mary.

This full view of all her private parts reawakened former sensations and strengthened them. Miss Evelyn first removed her own scarf, laying bare her plump ivory shoulders, and showing the upper halves of her beautiful bubbies, which were heaving with the excitement of her anger. She bared her fine right arm, and grasping the rod, stepped back and raised her arm; her eyes glistened in a peculiar way. She was indeed beautiful to see.

I shall never forget that moment—it was but a moment. The rod whistled through the air and fell with a cruel cut on poor Mary's plump little bottom. The flesh quivered again, and Mary, who had resolved not to cry, flushed in her face, and bit the damask with which the horse was covered.

Again the arm was raised, and again, with a sharp whistle, it fell on the palpitating buttocks below it. Still her stubborn temper bore her up, and although we saw how she winced, not a sound escaped from her lips. Drawing back a step, Miss Evelyn again raised her hand and arm, and this time her aim was so true that the longer points of the rod doubled between the buttocks and concentrated themselves between the lips of Mary's privates. So agonising was the pain that she screamed out dreadfully. Again the rod fell precisely on the same spot.

"Oh! oh! oh! Dear, dear Miss Evelyn. I will never, no, never, do so again."

Her shrieks were of no avail. Cut succeeded cut, yell succeeded yell—until the rod was worn to a stump, and poor Mary's bottom was one mass of weals and red as raw beef. It was fearful to see, and yet such is our nature that to see it was, at the same time, exciting. I could not keep my eyes from her pouting quim, the swelling lips of which, under the severity of the punishment it was undergoing, not only seemed to thicken, but actually opened and shut, and evidently throbbed with agony. But all this was highly exciting for me to witness. I then and there resolved to have a closer inspection at a more convenient opportunity, which did not fail me in the end.

Meanwhile, her spirit was completely cowed, or rather, crushed. Indeed, we were all fully frightened, and now knew what we had to expect, if we did not behave ourselves. There was now no fear of any manifestation of temper, and we felt we must indeed obey implicitly whatever our governess chose to order. We instinctively learned to fear her.

A very few days after this memorable whipping, some visitors arrived—a gentleman and lady. The gentleman was an old friend of mamma's, who had lately married, and mamma had asked them to visit her on their wedding tour and spend a short time with us.

The gentleman was a fine-looking man, tall and powerfully built; the lady rather delicate looking, but well shaped, with good breasts and shoulders, small waist, and spreading haunches, well-formed arms, small hands and feet, and very brilliant eyes.

I think it was about three days after their arrival that one afternoon I went into the spare room, which was occupied by these visitors; while there, I heard them coming upstairs.

The lady entered first, and I had just time to slip into a closet and draw the door to; it was not quite closed, but nearly so. In a minute the gentleman followed, and gently shutting the door, locked it. Mrs. Benson smiled, and said—

"Well, my love, you are a sad teaser; you let me have no rest. Surely, you had enough last night and this morning without wanting it again so soon?"

"Indeed, I had not," he said, "I never can have enough of your delicious person. So come, we must not be long about it, or our absence will be observed."

He seized her round the waist, and drew her lips to his, and gave her a long, long kiss; squeezing her to him, and moving himself against her. Then seating himself, he pulled her on his knee, and thrust his hands up her petticoats, their mouths being glued together for some time.

"We must be quick, dear," she murmured.

He got up, and lifted her on the edge of the bed, threw her back, and taking her legs under his arms, exposed everything to my view. She had not so much hair on her mount of Venus as Miss Evelyn, but her slit showed more pouting lips, and appeared more open. Judge of my excitement when I saw Mr. Benson unbutton his trousers and pull out an immense cock. Oh, dear, how large it looked; it almost frightened me. With his fingers he placed the head between the lips of Mrs. Benson's sheath, and then letting go his hold, and placing both arms so as to support her legs, he pushed it all right into her to the hilt at once. I was thunderstruck that Mrs. Benson did not shriek with agony, it did seem such a large thing to thrust right into her belly. However, far from screaming with pain, she appeared to enjoy it. Her eyes glistened, her face flushed, and she smiled most graciously on Mr. B. The two appeared very happy. His large cock slipped in and out quite smoothly, and his hands pressed the large glossy buttocks and pulled them to him at each home thrust. This lasted nearly five minutes, when all at once Mr. B. stopped

short, and then followed one or two convulsive shoves—he
grinning in a very absurd way at her. He remained quiet for
a few minutes, and then drew out his cock, all soft, with
slimy drops falling from it onto the carpet. Taking a towel, he
wiped up the carpet, and wrapping it round his cock, went
to the basin and washed it.

Mrs. Benson lay for a few minutes longer all exposed, her
quim more open than before, and I could see a white slime
oozing from it.

You can hardly imagine the wild excitement this scene
occasioned me. First, the grand mystery was at once explained to me, and my ignorant longings now knew to what
they tended. After giving me plenty of time to realise all the
beauties of her private parts, she slipped down on the floor,
adjusted her petticoats, and smoothed the disordered counterpane, and then went to the glass to arrange her hair. This
done, she quietly unlocked the door, and Mr. Benson went
out. The door was then relocked, and Mrs. B. went to the
basin, emptied and filled it, then raised up her petticoats,
and bathed the parts between her legs with a sponge, and
then rubbed all dry with a towel; all this time exposing everything to my ardent gaze. But, horror of horrors! she after
this came straight to the closet where I lay hid—opened the
door, and gave a slight scream on discovering me there. I
blushed up to the ears, and tried to stammer out an excuse.
She stared at me at first in silent amasement; but at last said—

"How came you here, sir, tell me?"

"I was here when you came up; I wanted my football,
which was in this closet, and when I heard you coming, I
hid myself, I don't know why."

For some minutes she seemed to consider and examine me
attentively. She then said—

"Can you be discreet?"

"Oh, yes, ma'am."

"You will never tell any one what you have seen?"

"No ma'am."

"Well, keep this promise, and I shall try what I can do to reward you. Now, go downstairs."

I went to the school-room, but I was greatly agitated, I scarcely knew what I was doing. The scene I had witnessed had complete possession of my thoughts. In years but a boy, the mystery now practically explained to me had awakened all the passions of a man. Instead of studying my lessons, my thoughts wandered to Mrs. B., thrown back on the bed with her fine legs and thighs fully exposed; above all, the sight of the pinky gash, with its fleecy hair at the bottom of her belly, which I had seen for some minutes all open and oozing out the slimy juice that followed the amorous encounter they had been indulging in. It seemed so much more developed than Miss Evelyn's. I felt sure that Miss Evelyn could never take in such a thick long thing as Mr. B. had thrust into his wife, and yet it appeared to go in so easily, and moved about so smoothly, and so evidently to the satisfaction and utmost delight of both, as was proved by their ardent embracings, fond murmurs, and voluptuous movements, especially just before they both ceased together all movement whatever.

Then I thought, how delicious it would be to treat Miss Evelyn in the same way, and to revel with my stiff-standing prick in her delicious quim, which in my mind's eye I saw before me as I had viewed it on her rising from the bidet, when I lay hid under the bed. Then I thought of my sister Mary's smaller, although very attractive little quim, and I resolved, as that was the easiest to get hold of, to initiate her in all the newly discovered mysteries. I fully determined that my own first lesson, as well as hers, should be taken on her little fat chubby cunt. Then the recollection of its pouting and throbbing lips under the fearful flagellation she had undergone, began to excite me, and made my cock stand stiff and throb again. All the weeks of excitement I had now constantly been under had produced a wonderful effect on my pego, which had become considerably more developed when in a state of erection. As you may suppose, with such distracting thoughts, I did not get on with my lessons. Miss Evelyn, for some reason or other, was out of humour that morning, and more than once spoke crossly to me for my evident inattention. At length she called me to her, and finding that I had scarcely done anything, she said—

"Now, Charles, I give you ten minutes longer to finish that sum, if not done in that time I shall whip you; you are exhibiting the mere spirit of idleness. I do not know what has come over you, but if persisted in, you shall certainly be punished."

The idea of the beautiful Miss Evelyn whipping my bare bottom did not tend to calm my excitement, on the contrary, it turned my lewd thoughts upon the beauties of her person, which I had so often furtively gazed upon.

It was close upon four o'clock, at which hour we always broke up for a run in the garden for an hour, and during this period I had resolved to begin instructing Mary in the secret mysteries I had so lately been a witness to. But fate had ordered it otherwise, and I was to receive my first practical lesson and be initiated on the person of a riper and more beautiful woman; but of this hereafter. At four o'clock I had done nothing with my task—Miss Evelyn looked grave:

"Mary and Eliza, you may go out, Charles will remain here."

My sisters, simply imagining that I was kept in to finish my lessons, ran into the garden. Miss Evelyn turned the key in the door, opened a cupboard, and withdrew a birch rod neatly tied up with blue ribbons. Now my blood coursed through my veins, and my fingers trembled so that I could hardly hold my pencil.

"Put down your slate, Charles, and come to me."

I obeyed, and stood before my beautiful governess, with a strange commixture of fear and desire.

"Unfasten your braces, and pull down your trousers."

I commenced doing this, though but very slowly. Angry at my delay her delicate fingers speedily accomplished the work. My trousers fell to my feet.

"Place yourself across my knees."

Tremblingly, with the same commixture of feeling, I obeyed. Her silk dress was drawn up to prevent its being creased—my naked flesh pressed against her snowy white petticoats. A delicate perfume of violet and vervain assailed my nerves. As I felt her soft and delicate fingers drawing up my shirt, and passing over my bare posteriors, while the warmth of her pulpy form beneath me penetrated my flesh, nature exerted her power, and my prick began to swell out to a most painful extent. I had but little time, however, to notice this before a rapid succession of the most cruel cuts lacerated my bottom.

"Oh, dear! Oh, dear! Oh, dear! Oh, Miss Evelyn. I will do the sum if you will only forgive me. Oh, oh, oh, &c."

Holding me firmly with her left arm, Miss Evelyn used the rod most unmercifully. At first, the pain was excruciating, and I roared out as loud as I could, but gradually the pain ceased to be so acute, and was succeeded by the most delicious tickling sensation. My struggles at first had been so violent as to greatly disorder Miss Evelyn's petticoats, and to raise them up so as to expose to my delighted eyes her beautifully formed silk-clad legs up to the knees, and even an inch or two of naked thigh above.

This, together with the intense tickling irritation communicated to my bottom, as well as to the friction of my cock against the person of Miss Evelyn in my struggles, rendered me almost delirious, and I tossed and pushed myself about on her knees in a state of perfect frenzy as the blows continued to be showered down upon my poor bottom. At last the rod was worn to a stump, and I was pushed off her knees. As I rose before her, with my cheeks streaming with tears, my shirt was jutting out considerably in front in an unmistakeable and most prominent manner, and my prick was at the same time throbbing beneath it with convulsive jerks, which I could by no means restrain.

Miss Evelyn glared at the projection in marked astonishment, and her open eyes were fixed upon it as I stood rubbing my bottom and crying, without attempting to move or button up my trousers. She continued for a minute or two to stare at the object of attraction, flushing scarlet up to the forehead, and then she suddenly seemed to recollect herself, drew a heavy breath, and rapidly left room. She did not return until after my sisters came back from the garden, and seemed still confused, and avoided fixing her eye upon me.

In two days afterwards, all disagreeable marks of this very severe whipping had disappeared. On the following day we were invited to pass the afternoon at the grange, a beautiful place about two miles from us. The afternoon was fine and warm; we walked there, and arrived about four o'clock. Mr. and Mrs. Robinson were in the drawing-room, but at once desired us to go in the garden and amuse ourselves with their three daughters, whom we would find there. We went at once, and found them amusing themselves on a swing. Sophia, the eldest, about nineteen, was swinging a sister about two years younger, a very fine, fully developed young woman. Indeed, all three sisters were finer women and more beautiful than the average of young ladies.

Another sister, Agnes, was not seated, but standing on the board between the ropes. Sophia was making both mount as high as possible. They were laughing loudly, when we found them, at the exposure each made—one in advancing, the other retiring. Agnes's light dress of muslin and single petticoat, as she retired and the wind came up from behind, was bulged out in front, and exposed her limbs up to her belly, so that one could see that her mount was already well furnished. The other, in advancing, threw her legs up, and exposed all the underside of her thighs and a part of her bottom, and you could just discern that there was dark hair between the lower thighs and bottom.

As they considered me but a child, I was no check to their mirth and sport. On the contrary, they gave me a long rope to pull down the swing when at its highest, and I sat down on the grass in front for greater convenience. The fine limbs and hairy quims exposed freely before me from moment to moment excited my passions. None of them wore more than one petticoat, and they had no drawers, so that when they mounted to the highest point from me, I had the fullest possible view of all. My cock soon rose to a painful extent, which I really believe was noticed and enjoyed by them. I observed, too, that I was an object of attention to Miss Evelyn, who shortly seated herself in the swing, and allowed me to swing her with the end of the rope. I even fancied that she threw up her legs more than was at all necessary; at all events, she naturally, with the strong feelings I had towards her, excited me more than all the rest.

We all were as merry as could be, and we passed a delightful evening until eight o'clock, when it began to rain. As it continued, and became very heavy, Mr. Robinson ordered out the closed carriage to take us home. It was a brougham, only seated for two. Mary took Eliza on her knee, Miss Evelyn took me upon hers. I know not how it happened, but her lovely arm soon passed round my body as if to hold me on her knee, and her hand fell, apparently by accident, exactly on my cock—the touch was electric. In an instant, my member stood stiff and strong beneath her hand. Still Miss Evelyn, who must have felt the movement going on beneath her fingers, did not remove her hand, but rather seemed to press more upon it. In my boyish ignorance, I imagined she was not aware of what was happening. The motion and jolting of the carriage over rough road caused her hand to rub up and down upon my erected and throbbing member. I was almost beside myself, and to conceal my condition I feigned sleep. I let my head fall on Miss Evelyn's shoulder and neck—she allowed this.

Whether she thought I had really fallen asleep I know not, but I was quite sensible that her fingers pressed my swollen and throbbing cock, and I fancied she was measuring its size.

The tight grasp she managed to gain, and the continued jolting of the carriage, brought me up at last to such a pitch state that a greater jolt than usual, repeated two or three times in succession, each followed by a firmer pressure of her charming fingers, caused me such an excess of excitement that I actually swooned away with the most delicious sensation I had ever experienced in my life. I was some time before I knew where I was, or what I was about, and was only made conscious of our arrival at home by Miss Evelyn shaking me to rouse me up. I stumbled up, but though partially stupefied, I fancied Miss Evelyn's eyes shone with a brilliancy I had never before observed, and that there was a bright hectic flush on her cheek. She refused to go into the parlour, but hurried to bed on pretence of a headache.

When I retired to bed, and took off my shirt, I found it all sticky and wet in front.

It was thus I paid down my first tribute to Venus. I thought long over this evident approach to familiarity on the part of Miss Evelyn, and went to sleep with a lively hope of a more private interview with her, when I trusted that her evident passion would initiate me in the pleasures to be derived from her beauteous body.

But again fate intervened, and another, not less beautiful, more experienced, and more inclined for the sport, was to be my charming mistress in love's revels.

Two days after this, Mr. Benson was unexpectedly called away on pressing affairs, which he feared might detain him three weeks. He left Mrs. B. with us. As he had to be driven about nine miles to the town where the coach passed, mamma took the opportunity of going to the town with him. Mrs B. complained of not being equal to the fatigue, and mamma told Miss Evelyn she would like her company, and as the two girls wanted new shoes, they could go also; I was to remain at home, and mamma desired me to be quiet and attentive to Mrs. Benson, and keep her company. This arrangement was made when we were at breakfast. On leaving the room I was followed by Mrs. Benson, who, observing no one, said to me, with a peculiar look:

"I shall want you to hold my skeins, Charlie, so don't go out of the way, but be ready for me as soon as they are gone."

She then went up to her bedroom, where Mr. B. immediately joined her, no doubt to re-enact the scene I had already witnessed from the closet on a previous day. They were fully half an hour occupied together. At length, all was ready, and off they went, leaving me to a fate I had little dreamt of.

Mrs. B. proposed we should go up to the drawing-room, which looked out to the garden, and was nowhere overlooked. I followed her, and could not help admiring her fine figure as she preceded me in going upstairs. Although pale in complexion, she was well made, and very elegant in her carriage, and sat down on a low easy chair, throwing herself completely back, and crossing one leg over the other, apparently without being aware that she carried her petticoats up with the action, and exhibited the beautiful underleg up to the garter.

I had never forgotten the day, when secreted in the closet, I had seen them completely exposed, and how charming they were. Her present negligent attitude, although far from the same exposure I speak of, was still, with the former recollection running in my head, enough to set my whole blood on fire. I have before remarked what a power beautiful and well-stockinged legs, and ankles and small feet, had upon my nervous system, and so it was now. As I gazed upon her handsome legs, ankles, and feet, I felt my prick swell and throb in a manner that could not fail to be perceptible to Mrs. B, especially as her head lay on a level with that part of my person as I stood before her.

Although she continued knitting, I could see that her eyes

were directed to that part of my person, and fixed upon the increasing distention of my trousers. In a few minutes she gave me a skein of worsted to hold, and desired me to kneel in front of her, so as to bring my hands down to the level of the low chair on which she was seated.

I knelt close to the footstool on which her foot rested; it was raised up, and a very slight movement brought it against my person, at first rather below where my throbbing prick was distending my trousers. As she commenced to wind her ball, she gradually pushed her foot further forward, until the toe actually touched the knob of my cock, and occasionally moved it right and left, exciting me beyond measure.

I flushed up to the very ears, and trembled so violently that I thought I should have dropped the skein.

"My dear boy, what is the matter with you, that you blush and tremble so, are you unwell?"

I could not answer, but blushed more than ever. The skein at length was finished.

"Charles," she said, "get up, and come here."

I rose and stood by her side.

"What have you got in your trousers that is moving?"

And here her busy fingers commenced unbuttoning them. Released from confinement, out started my prick—stiff as iron, and as large as that of a youth of eighteen. Indeed, I was better hung than one boy selected out of five hundred of that age. Mrs. B., who had pretended to be perfectly astonished, exclaimed—

"Good gracious, what a pego! Why Charles, my darling, you are a man not a boy. What a size to be sure!" and she gently handled it. "Is it often in this state?"

"Yes, ma'am."

"For how long?"

"Ever since Miss Evelyn came."

"And pray, sir, what has Miss Evelyn's coming had to do with it?"

"I—I—I—I—"

"Come now, Charles, be candid with me; what is it you mean where you say Miss Evelyn has caused you to be in such a state, have you shown her this, and has she handled it?"

"Oh! dear no; never, never!"

"Is it her face, her bosom, or her legs that have captivated you?"

"It was her feet and ankles, ma'am, with her beautiful legs, which she sometimes exhibited without knowing."

"And do all ladies' legs and ankles produce this effect upon you?"

"Oh, yes, ma'am, if they are neat and pretty!"

"And what makes you so excited now?"

"It was the sight of your beautiful legs just now, and the recollection of what I saw the other day, ma'am," I stammered out, blushing more than ever.

While this conversation was going on, her soft hand grasped my distended prick, and had commenced slowly slipping the loose skin over the swollen head, and allowing it to slip back again.

"I suppose, Charles, after what you saw in the closet, you know what this is meant to do."

I muttered out an indistinct reply that I did, and I hung down my blushing face.

"You have never put it into a lady, have you?"

"Oh! dear no, ma'am."

"Would you like to do so?"

I did not answer, but sheepishly held down my head.

"Did you see what I had in the same place, when you were in the closet?"

I muttered, "Yes, ma'am."

"Would it afford you any pleasure to see it again?"

"Oh, yes; so much!"

Mrs. B. rose, went to the window, drew down the blind, then gently turned the key in the door. Returning to the chair, and drawing well up her dress, petticoats and chemise, she exposed all her person up to the middle of her belly; and sat down stretching herself backwards, and opening her thighs well.

"Well, my dear boy, look at it if you wish."

I was no longer shy. Nature prompted me to an act of gallantry that gratified the lady immensely. Falling on my knees, I glued my lips to the delicious spot, pushed my tongue in as far as I could, and sucked it. It was quite spunky; I had no doubt but that Mr. B. had fucked her two or three times just before leaving. This, however, made no difference to me. The attack was as unexpected as it was delightful to the lady. She placed both hands on my head and pressed my face against her throbbing cunt. She was evidently hotly excited, not only by what I was then doing, but by the scene, the conversation, and the handling of my prick, which she had been indulging in. She wriggled her bottom nervously below me, I continued to greedily lick her moist and juicy cunt.

"Oh! oh! dear Charles, what exquisite delight you are giving me. Oh! oh!"

And she pressed my face more fully into the gaping sheath, and thrusting her bottom up at the same time, spent right into my mouth, over my cheeks, chin, and neck. Her thighs closed convulsively round my head, and for some moments she remained still. I continued to lick away, and swallowed the delicious spunk that still flowed from her. At last she spoke again—

"Oh! you darling Charles, I love you for ever; but get up, it is now my turn to give you a taste of the exquisite pleasure you have given me."

I raised myself, and she drew me to her, and gave me a long kiss, licking her own sperm from off my lips and cheek; and desiring me to thrust my tongue into her mouth, she sucked it deliciously, while her soft hand and gentle fingers had again sought, found, and caressed my stiff-standing prick.

She then desired me to lay myself on the floor, with three pillows to raise my head, and lifting up all her petticoats, and striding across me, with her back to my face, she knelt down, then stooping forward, she took my standing prick in her mouth, and at the same time lowering her buttocks, brought her beautiful cunt right over and down upon my mouth, the pillows exactly supporting my head at the proper level, to command a thorough enjoyment of the whole, which now I had completely before my eyes.

In the former sucking my own position hid everything from view beyond the rich mass of hair adorning her splendid mount of Venus, which I found to be much more abundant than it had appeared to me when I had seen it from the closet. When I applied my lips to the delicious gap, I found that she had the most beautiful silky light curls running up to and around her charming pink bottom-hole, and losing themselves in the chink between the buttocks. I applied myself furiously to the delicious gash, and sucked and thrust my tongue in alternately. I could see by the nervous twitching of her buttocks, and the bearing down of her whole bottom on my face, how much she was enjoying it. I, too, was in an extasy of delight. One hand gently frigged the lower portion of my prick, while the other played with my balls, and her beautiful mouth, lips, and tongue sucked, pressed, and tickled the head of my excited prick. The more furiously I sucked her cunt, the more her lips compressed the head of my pego, and her tongue sought to enter the urethra, giving me almost overpowering delight. Such reciprocal efforts soon brought on the extatic crisis. I cried out:

"Oh, lady! oh, dear lady! let me go; I am dying!"

She knew well enough what was coming, but she had her own way, and at the instant that she again poured down upon my mouth and face a plenteous discharge, her own rosy mouth received a torrent of my sperm.

For some minutes we lay mutually breathless and exhausted. Then Mrs. B. rose, shook down her clothes, assisted me to rise, and taking me in her arms, and pressing me lovingly to her bosom, told me I was a dear charming fellow, and had enraptured her beyond measure. She then embraced me fondly, kissing my mouth and eyes, and desiring me to give her my tongue, sucked it so sweetly.

"Now, fasten up your trousers, my darling boy."

When I had done so, the blind was drawn up, and the door unlocked.

We sat down, I by her side with one arm round her lovely neck, and the other clasped in her hand.

"I am sure I can depend upon your prudence, my dear Charles, to keep all this a profound secret from every one. Your mamma thinks you a child, and will suspect nothing. I shall take an opportunity of suggesting that you shall sleep in the small room adjoining my bedroom, and with which there is a door of communication. When every one is gone to bed, I shall open the door, and you shall come and sleep with me, and I will let you enjoy me as you saw Mr. B. do the other day. Will you like that?"

"Oh! above all things, oh, yes. But you must also allow me to kiss that delicious spot again that has just given me such pleasure. Will you not, ma'am?"

"Oh, yes, my darling boy, whenever we can do so safely, and unobserved; but I must impress upon you never to seem very familiar with me before any one, or to take the slightest liberty unless I invite you to do so. Anything of the sort would certainly draw attention, and lead to our detection, and at once put an end to what I mean shall be a delightful connection for you as well as myself."

I, of course, promised the most perfect obedience to her very prudent directions. The ice was broken, and we allowed no ceremony to stand between us. I grew again very excited, and would fain have proceeded at once to try again to fuck her as well as suck her, but she was inexorable, and told me I should only spoil the pleasure we should afterwards have in bed. The day passed like an hour in her charming society.

The carriage brought mamma and party to dinner. Mamma hoped I had behaved well, and been attentive to Mrs. B. in her absence. She answered nothing could be better, and that I was quite a model youth—so gentle and so obedient.

My mother found that she had caught cold, and had febrile symptoms after dinner. Mrs. B. persuaded her to retire to bed, and accompanied her. When in her room, she apparently noticed, for the first time, my little bed. She took the opportunity of suggesting that it would be much better to remove it to the small room, so as to leave my mother in perfect quiet, which my coming to bed might disturb.

This was said in such an innocent natural manner, that no suspicion was excited on the part of mamma or anybody else. Mamma only making the objection that my early rising might by my noise disturb Mrs. B. in the next room.

"Oh, no; I am not so easily disturbed, besides he has been so well behaved all day, that I am sure, if I tell him to be quiet in the morning, he will not fail to do so."

So it was settled, and my bed was at once removed to the little room.

I know not what Miss Evelyn thought of this; at any rate, she made no remark, and I went to bed early. It will easily be conceived that I did not go to sleep. The hours struck one after the other, and no appearance of my amiable instructress. The remembrance of all her charms was ever present to my mind's eye, and I longed once more to dart my tongue into her moist and juicy cunt, as well as to try the new method that was to initiate me into the real secrets of Venus.

The long delay of her coming put me in a perfect fever. I tossed and tumbled in bed; my prick throbbed almost to bursting. Fortunately, I had never frigged myself, and that resource never occurred to me, or I might have rendered myself quite incapable of enjoying the raptures my beautiful benefactress afterwards entranced me with. At last I heard voices and footsteps on the stairs. Mrs. B. bid Miss Evelyn good night, and the next minute her door was opened, closed again, and the key turned in the lock. I had taken the precaution to do so with my door. I heard her use the night vase, and then she opened my door, at once coming up to my bed side. Seeing me wide awake and quite flushed, she kissed me, and whispered—

"Have you not been to sleep, Charles?"

"No, ma'am," I answered, in the same subdued tone, "I could not sleep."

"Why, my dear boy?"

"Because I was going to sleep with you."

Her lips pressed mine, and her soft hand, thrust under the clothes; sought for and caressed my stiff-standing prick—it was as hard as iron.

"Poor boy, I am afraid you have been suffering. How long has it been in this state?"

"All the evening, ma'am, and I did think you were such a long time in coming."

"Well, Charles, I could not come sooner without causing suspicion—I thought Miss Evelyn was suspicious, so I pretended to have no desire to go to bed; and even when she showed evident symptoms of drowsiness after her long ride, I rallied her upon it, and begged her to sit up with me yet a little; until at last she could hold out no longer, and begged me to let her retire. I grumblingly complied, and she is thrown completely off any scent on our account, as she could never suppose I was as impatient as you to come here. I shall undress as fast as possible, and then do my best to relieve you of this painful stiffness. Get up, shut this door, and come to my bed. My room has an inner baize door, and we shall there be certain of not being overheard."

I instantly complied, and she commenced undressing. Every detail of her charming toilet was devoured by my greedy eyes. Her smooth, glossy, and abundant hair, arranged in braids, was neatly fastened in under a coquettish lace cap with pretty blue ribbons. Her *chemise de nuit* of the finest, almost transparent cambric was edged with fine openwork. She looked divine. The drawers of the commode contained scent bags of that peculiar odour which is generally found to perfume the persons of the most seductive women. In another moment she was in bed, clasping me in her arms.

"Now, Charles, you must be a good boy, and make no noise, and allow me to teach you your first love lesson, see I will lay myself down on my back, thus—do you place yourself on your knees between my out-spread thighs—there, that is a darling—now let me lay hold of your dear instrument. Now lay yourself down on me."

I placed myself on her beautiful smooth and white belly and pressed against the hair of her mount. With her long taper fingers she guided my prick—I trembled in every limb and almost felt sick with excitement—but when I felt the delicious sensation caused by the insertion of my skinned pintle between the smooth warm oily folds of the lady's cunt—I gave but one shove which carried me up so that I swooned away on her belly and milk-white bosom.

When I came to myself I still lay on her belly, enfolded in her lovely arms, my prick sheathed up to the cods in her delicious cunt, which was throbbing in the most extatic way and pressing and closing with every fold on my prick—which had hardly lost any of its pristine stiffness; as my eyes began to discern her features, an exquisite smile played upon my darling companion's lips.

"You sad rogue," she whispered, "you have given me a baby; what have you been doing to make you spend so soon, and in such a quantity. Did you like it?"

"Oh, dearest madam, I have been in heaven—surely no joy can be greater than you have given me."

"But you do not know as yet everything that is to be done,

and to how much greater an extent the pleasure may be enhanced by mutual efforts; move your instrument gently in and out—there, that is delicious, but not so fast. Good, is it not nice!"

And she moved in unison with me, meeting each slow thrust down by an equal movement upwards, and squeezing my prick in the most delicious manner internally, as she retired again to meet succeeding thrusts in the same way.

Oh! it was extatic—my prick, swollen to its utmost size, seemed to fill her exquisite vagina, which although capable of easily accommodating the larger prick of Mr. B., appeared to be sufficiently contracted to embrace tightly with its smooth and slippery folds my stiff throbbing prick. So we continued, I shoving myself into her, and she upheaving her beautiful bottom to meet me. My hands removed everywhere, and my mouth sucked her lips and tongue, or wandered over her pulpy breasts sucking their tiny nipples. It was a long bout indeed, prolonged by Mrs. Benson's instructions, and she enjoyed it thoroughly, encouraged me by every endearing epithet, and by the most voluptuous manœuvres. I was quite beside myself. The consciousness that I was thrusting my most private part into that part of a lady's person which is regarded with such sacred delicacy caused me to experience the most enraptured pleasure. Maddened by the intensity of my feeling I at length quickened my pace. My charming companion did the same, and we together yielded down a most copious and delicious discharge.

Although I retained sufficient rigidity to keep him in his place, Mrs. B. would not allow any further connection with her, and she made me withdraw, and bade me go to sleep like a good boy, and she would give me a further lesson in the morning.

Finding that she was determined on this point, and that she disposed herself to slumber, I felt I was obliged to follow her example, and at last fell fast asleep. It might be about five in the morning, quite light at that time of year, when I awoke, and instead of finding myself, as usual, in my own little bed—I found my arms round the person of a charming woman, whose large plump smooth bottom lay in my lap, pressing against my belly and thigh. I found my prick already in a rampant state, and it at once began throbbing and forcing its way between the delicious cheeks of her immense bottom, seeking the delightful sheath it had so enjoyed the previous part of the night. Whether Mrs. B. was asleep or not, I do not know, but am inclined to think she really was so, from the muttered mistake she made in waking. She was probably dreaming, for she mechanically raised her thighs. I pressed my prick stoutly forward against her luxurious body, knowing that the entrance to the temple of pleasure which had so entranced me the night before lay in that direction. I found more difficulties than I expected, but at length began to penetrate, although the orifice appeared much tighter than on the previous evening. Excited by the difficulties of entrance, I clasped the lady firmly round the waist and pushed forcibly and steadily forward. I felt the folds give way to the iron stiffness of my prick, and one-half of it was fairly imbedded in my extremely tight sheath. I put down my hand to press my prick a little downwards to facilitate the further entrance; you may imagine my astonishment when on so doing I found myself in the lady's bottom-hole, instead of her cunt. This at once explained the difficulty of entrance. I was about to withdraw and place it in the proper orifice when a convulsive pressure of the sphincter caused me such exquisite satisfaction by the pressure of the folds on the more sensitive upper half of my prick, which was so delicious, and so much tighter, and more exciting than my previous experience of the cunt that I could not resist the temptation of carrying the experiment to the end. Therefore, thrusting my two fingers into her cunt, I pressed my belly forwards with all my might, and sheathed my prick in her bottom-hole to its full extent. Mrs. B. at this awoke, and exclaimed, "Good Heavens! Fred, you hurt me cruelly. I wish you would be content with my cunt, I shall be unable to walk to-morrow. You know it always has that effect. It is downright cruel of you—but since you are in, stay quiet a little, and then continue to frig me with your fingers, as you know that eventually gives me great pleasure."

She calls me Fred, what can she mean? I was, however, too agreeably situated to speculate on anything, but as I was now buried within her bottom-hole, I lay quiet for a few minutes as she had requested; and as her complaints subsided, and I felt a slight reciprocating movement, I, too, moved within her, working at the same time my two fingers in her cunt. By this time she was wide awake, and became conscious of who was her bed-fellow.

"What are you about, Charles?" she exclaimed, "do you know where you are?"

"I did not know I was doing anything wrong."

"Doing wrong, indeed! My, a lady's bottom-hole was never intended for a pego. How came you to put it in there?"

"I cannot tell; I did not do it on purpose. I thought I was going into the same delightful place I was in last night."

All this time I was moving my prick in and out of one aperture, and my fingers were working away in the other. The tightness of the sheath round my prick was delicious beyond anything I could conceive, and I think, from the way the lady conducted herself, she liked it as much as I did. At any rate, she permitted me to go on until I had a delicious discharge; and she herself spent all over my hand.

When the bout was over, she jumped out of bed, went to the basin, and with a sponge purified herself. After which, she said—

"My dear boy, you had better come and wash yourself, too; and take care not to make a mistake of this kind again, as it is sometimes attended with disagreeable consequences."

It was now perfect sunny daylight, and my enchanting

mistress looked so lovely in her almost transparent cambric night-shift that I was emboldened to ask her to let me see her perfectly naked in all her glorious beauty of form. She gratified me at once; but, laughingly, pulled off my night-shirt, and said—

"I, too, must have the pleasure not only of contemplating your promising youthful charms, but of embracing your dear form disencumbered of all the superfluities of dress."

We clasped each other in a most enrapturing embrace, and then my lovely and engaging companion allowed me to turn her in every direction so as to see, admire, and devour every charm of her exquisitely formed body. Oh! she was indeed beautiful—shoulders broad, bosom, or rather upper neck, flat, not showing any projection of the collar bone; bubbies firm, well separated and round, with most exquisite rosy nipples not much developed; a perfect waist, small naturally, with charming swelling hips, and an immense bottom—it was almost out of proportion, large, but oh, how beautiful. Then her belly, undulating so excitingly, and swelling out, the lowest part into a very fine and prominent mons Veneris, covered with a thick crop of silky and curly light hair; then the entrance to the grotto of Venus had such delicious pouting lips, rosy, but with hair still thick on each side, which is often not the case even with women who have a sufficient tuft above, how beautiful where it exists as it did in this charming and perfect woman, continuing in beautiful little curls not only down to but around her lovely pinky and puckered little bottom-hole, the delights of which I had already, in this infancy of my love education, tasted and enjoyed. Her two alabaster thighs, worthily supporting by their large well-rounded fleshy forms, the exquisite perfections of the upper body, I have already described. How beautiful, elegant, and elongated her legs were, rising from well-turned ankles and most tiny beautiful feet. Her skin was white as milk, and dazzlingly fair and smooth. To my young eyes she was a perfect goddess of beauty. Even now, in advanced life, I can remember nothing that, as a whole surpassed her, although I have met many with points unsurpassingly beauti-. ful—some carry it in the bosom, some in the general carriage, some in the mount of Venus and bottom combined, for these two are generally prominent together, and some in legs and thighs; but this divine creature, without having the appearance of it when dressed, was, when stripped, perfect in all her parts as well as beautiful in face—caressing and voluptuous by nature, and lending herself, with the most enchanting graces to instruct me in all the mysteries of love, and let me say, of *lust* also.

We caressed each other with such mutual satisfaction that nature soon drove us to a closer and more active union of the bodies. Fondly embracing one another, we approached the bed, and being equally excited threw ourselves upon it, and, in the exquisite contact of our naked flesh, enjoyed a long, long bout of love, in which my most charming companion exhibited all the resources of amorous enjoyment. Never shall I forget the luxury of that embrace. She checked my natural tendency to rush at once to a completion. I think we must have enjoyed the raptures of that embrace fully half an hour before bringing on the grand finale, in which my active companion showed the extraordinary suppleness of her delicious body by throwing her legs over my back, pushing my bottom forward with her heels, and raising and sinking her bottom in unison with each thrust of my terribly stiff prick, which seemed to swell and become thicker and harder than ever. In retiring from each thrust, her cunt seemed to close upon my prick with the force of a pair of pincers. We both came to the extatic moment at the same time, and both actually screamed with delight; my ardent mistress in her fury of excitement actually bit my shoulder and drew blood; but I felt it not—I was in the seventh heaven of delight, and lay for long almost insensible on her beauteous body, clasped in her loving arms. On coming to our senses:

"Oh, my beloved boy," she said, "never, never, have I experienced such pleasure. You are a perfect angel. I only fear I shall come to love you too much."

We turned on our sides without dislodging the dear instrument of our enjoyment, and my lovely friend prattled on and delighted me with her toying, embracing, and gaiety. My prick had once more swelled up, and I wished to quietly enjoy a fuck in the luxurious position in which we lay; but my lovely friend said—

"That must not be, my dear Charles, I must consider your health. You have already done more than your age warrants, and you must rise and go to your bed to recover, by a sound sleep, your strength."

"But feel how strong I am," and I gave a forcible thrust into her glowing and well-moistened sheath. But, though she certainly was greatly excited, she suddenly turned round and unseated me, and drew away from me, refusing to take it again. As she was quite naked, the movements of her beauteous form were most graceful and enchanting, and one leg being thrown backwards left her lovely cunt full in view, and actually gaping open before me. Seized with the strongest desire to suck and kiss it, as I had done the night before, I begged that at least she would grant me that last favour, as it could not in any way do me harm. To this she readly consented, and lay down on her back, opening her glorious thighs, and with a pillow under her bottom so as to raise up her cunt into a better position for me to gamahuche her, as she called it. Before letting me begin, she said—

"My dear Charles, do you see that little projection at the upper part of my quim, that is my clitoris, and is the site of the most exquisite sensation; you see it is rather hard, even now, but you will find as you titillate it with your tongue or suck it, that it will become harder and more projecting, so apply your lips there."

I did as my lovely mistress desired, and soon found it stiffen and stand up nearly an inch into my mouth.

The convulsive twitches of her buttocks, the pressure forward of her hand on my head, all proved the exquisite felicity my lovely friend was enjoying. I slipped my hand under my chin—the position was awkward, but I managed to thrust my thumb into her cunt. My forefinger was somewhat in the way—but finding it exactly opposite the rosy hole of her bottom, and all being very moist there, I pushed it forward and it easily entered. I could not move my hand very actively, but I continued to gently draw my finger and thumb a little back together, and then thrust forward again. It seemed to add immensely to the pleasure I was giving her; her whole body quivered with excessive excitement. My head was pressed so firmly against her cunt that I had difficulty in breathing, but I managed to keep up the action of tongue and fingers until I brought on the exquisite crisis—her buttocks rose, her hand pressed hard on my head and her two powerful and fleshy thighs closed on my cheeks on each side and fixed me as if in a vice, while she poured down into my mouth and all over my chin, neck, and hand a perfect rush of sperm, and then lay in convulsive movements of enjoyment, hardly knowing what she was doing. As she held me so fast in every way, I continued to lick up the delicious discharge, and continued at the same time to pass my tongue over her clitoris. This, by producing a new excitement, brought her senses round. So relaxing her hold of me with her thighs she said—

"Oh, my darling Charles, come up to my arms that I may kiss you for the exquisite delight you have given me." I did so, but took care, in drawing myself up, to engroove my stiff-standing prick in the well-moistened open cunt that lay raised on a pillow so conveniently in the way.

"Oh, you sad traitor," cried my sweet companion. "No, I cannot, I must not allow it," but I held her tight round the waist, and her position was too favourable for me to be easily unhorsed.

"Ah! you must not, my dear boy. If you will not consider yourself, consider me. I shall be quite exhausted." I shut her mouth with my kisses and tongue, and soon the active movements I was making within her charming vagina exercised their usual influence on her lubricity, so as to make her as eager for the fray as myself.

"Stop, my dear Charles, and you shall have it in a new position, which will give you as much more pleasure as it will me."

"You are not going to cheat me, are you?"

"Oh, no! my darling, I am now as much on fire as you are—withdraw."

I obeyed, half in fear. My fair mistress turned herself round, and getting on her hands and knees, presented to my ardent gaze her magnificent bottom. I thought she meant me to once more put it into the rosy little orifice, and said so.

"Oh! no," she replied, "not there"; but putting her hand under her belly, and projecting it backwards between her thighs, she said—

"Give it me and I will guide it into the proper place."

Before doing so I stooped forward and pushing my face between the glorious cheeks on her bottom, sought and found the lovely little orifice, kissed it, and thrust my tongue in.

"Oh! don't Charles, dear, you tickle me so," then flinching, and squeezing her buttocks together, I had nothing for it but to put my prick in her hand. She immediately guided it to and engulphed it in her burning cunt up to the very hair. I found I apparently got in fully an inch further this way—the position also gave my beautiful instructress more power of pressure on my prick—then her glorious buttocks, heaving under my movements, and exposed in all their immensity, was most exciting and beautiful. I seized her below the waist with a hand upon each hip, pressing her magnificent backside against me each time that I thrust forward. Oh! it

was indeed glorious to see. I was beside myself, and furious
with the excitement the view of all these charms produced
upon me. My charming mistress seemed equally to enjoy it,
as was evinced by the splendid movements of her body; till
at last overcome by the grand finale, she sank forward on
her belly, and I followed on her back, without losing the
position of my throbbing prick within her. We both lay for
some time incapable of movement, but the internal squeezing and convulsive pressure of her cunt on my softened, but
still enlarged prick, were exquisite beyond imagining. At last
she begged me to relieve her. Getting out of bed, she sighed
deeply, kissed me tenderly, and said, "My dear Charles, we
must not be so extravagant in future, it will destroy us both—
come, let me see you to your bed." The sight of my lovely
mistress standing naked in all the glory of her beauty and
perfection of form began to have its usual effect upon my
prick, which showed symptoms of raising his head again;
she gave it a pat, stooped down, and for a moment plunged
its head into her beautiful mouth, then seizing my night-
shirt, she threw it over my head and conducted me to my
own bed, put me in, tucked me up, and tenderly kissing me,
left the room, first unlocking my door and then locking the
door of communication between the two rooms. Thus passed
the first glorious night of my initiation into all the rites of
Venus, and at the hands of a lovely, fresh and beautiful
woman, who had only been married long enough to make her
a perfect adept in the art. Never, oh never! have I passed
such a night. Many and many a fine woman, perfect too in
the art of fucking, have I enjoyed, but the novelty and the
charm, the variety and the superiority of the teacher, all
combined to make this night the *ne plus ultra* of erotic
pleasure.

It need not be said that, exhausted by the numerous
encounters I had had in love's battlefield, I fell into a deep
and sound sleep, until aroused by being rudely shaked up.

I opened my eyes in astonishment. It was my sister Mary. She threw her arms round my neck, and kissing me, said—

"You lazy boy, do you know they are *all* down at breakfast, and you still asleep. What has come over you?"

"Oh!" I said, "I got frightened with a horrible dream, and lay awake so long afterwards that when I did sleep, I overslept myself."

"Well, get up at once," and pulling the clothes quite off me, she laid bare my whole private parts, with my cock, as usual in youth on waking, at full stand.

"Oh! Charlie," said Mary, fixing her eyes upon it in astonishment at its thickness and length. "How your doodle has grown," and she laid hold of it. "Why it is as hard as wood, and see how red its head is." Without her knowing why, it evidently had its natural effect on her senses, and she flushed as she squeezed it.

"Ah! my dear Mary, I have learnt a great secret about that thing, which I will tell you the first time we can be quite alone and secure from interruption. Just now there is no time, but before you go downstairs, let me see how your poor little Fanny is."

We had been used to these infantile expressions when in our ignorance and innocence we had mutual examinations of the difference of our sexes, and my sister was still as ignorant and innocent as ever. So when I said that I had not seen it since it was so ill-treated in the terrible whipping she had received from Miss Evelyn, she at once pulled up all her petticoats for me to look at it.

"Lie back for a moment on the bed."

She complied. I was delighted. The prominence her mons Veneris had assumed, the increased growth of moss-like little curls, and the pouting lips of her tiny slit—all was most promising and charming. I stooped and kissed it, licking her little prominent clitoris with my tongue; it instantly hardened, and she gave a convulsive twitch of her loins.

"Oh! Charlie, how nice that is! What is it you are doing? Oh, how nice! Oh, pray go on."

But I stopped, and said—

"Not at present, my darling sister, but when we can get away together I will do that and something much better, all connected with the great secret I have got to tell you. So run downstairs, and tell them why I had overslept myself, but not a word to any one about what I have told you. I will be down in a trice."

She went away, saying—

"Oh, Charlie, dear, what you did just now was so nice, and has made me feel so queer; do find an early opportunity of telling me all about it."

Very few minutes sufficed to finish my toilet and bring me to the breakfast table.

"Why, Charlie," broke out my mother, "what is this horrid dream?"

"I can hardly tell you, my dear mother, it was so confused; but I was threatened to be murdered by horrid-looking men, and at last taken to high rocks and thrown down. The agony and fright awoke me, screaming, and all over perspiration. I could not sleep for hours after, even though I hid my head under the clothes."

"Poor child," said Mrs. Benson, who was quietly eating her breakfast. "What a fright you must have had."

"Yes, ma'am, and at the same time, as I awoke with a scream, I was afraid I might have disturbed you, for all at once I remembered I was no longer in mamma's room, but next door to you. I hope I did not awake you?"

"Oh, no, my dear boy; I never heard you, or I should have got up to see what was the matter."

So it passed off, and no further observation was made about it, but I once caught Mrs. Benson's eye, and the expression and a slight nod was a sign of approval of my story. After breakfast we went as usual to the school-room. I thought

Miss Evelyn was kinder in her manner to me than usual. She made me stand close to her when saying my lessons, occasionally letting her left arm fall round my neck, while she pointed to my book with the finger of the right, and there was always a certain pressure before raising her arm again. These little caresses were frequently repeated, as if she were wishing either to accustom me or herself to a habit of it, so as, doubtless, gradually to increase them to something more definite. I could not help feeling what a different effect these endearments would have had twenty-four hours earlier; but now, momentarily satisfied passions, and the new love that had seized me for Mrs. B., prevented at first the inevitable cockstand that would otherwise have been produced by these approaches of Miss Evelyn. Not that I had given up all desire to possess her. On the contrary, my last night's instruction only made me more anxious to have Miss Evelyn too. Therefore, I by no means repulsed her present caresses, but looked up innocently in her face, and smiled affectionately. In the afternoon she was more expansive, and drew me to her by her arm round my waist, and pressed me gently to her person, saying how well I was attending to my lessons, and how sorry she was to have been obliged to punish me so severely the week before.

"You will be a good boy in future, will you not, dear Charlie?"

"Oh, yes; as long as you are so kind to me. I love you so much, and you are so beautiful when you speak so kindly to me."

"Oh, you little flatterer."

And she drew me to her lips and gave me a sweet kiss, which I returned with eagerness. I felt my prick had raised itself up to its full extent as these caresses were exchanged, and as Miss Evelyn held me tight pressed against her thigh, she must have felt it throbbing against her. That she did so, I have no doubt, as her face flushed, and she said—

"There, now, that will do, go to your seat."

I obeyed; she rose in an agitated manner, left the room, and was absent for a quarter of an hour. I had no doubt but that she was overcome by her feelings, and I thought to myself she will manage to have me some of these days. I could afford to leave it to her own discretion, as my charming mistress of last night was there to keep me in exercise and cool the effervescence of passion under which I should otherwise have laboured. Nothing particular occurred during the day; Mrs. B. was apparently indifferent about me, and never sought to approach or be in any way familiar; I studied her looks and followed her example. Mamma sent me early to bed, as she feared I had not had sleep enough the previous night by reason of my bad dream, and hoped I should have no more of the kind. This time my beautiful mistress found me sound asleep when she came to bed. She did not awake me until she had completed her night toilet, and was all ready to receive me in her arms. I sprung up, and in an instant, without a word being said, had her on her back, and was into her delicious cunt as far as I could drive my stiff-standing prick. My energy and fury seemed to please and stimulate the lady, for she replied to every eager thrust with as eager a spring forward. In such haste matters were very speedily brought to a crisis—with mutual sighs, and "oh's" and "ah's," we sank exhausted, and lay for a very short time, when charming Mrs. B. said—

"Why, Charles, you are quite wild to me; what a hurry you have been in, but it was very nice, and I forgive you, but you must be more rational in future."

"Oh, my beloved mistress, how can I help it; you are so beautiful, and so good to me; I quite adore and love every part of your charming body. I know I was too impetuous, but I must make it up by kissing and fondling the dear source of all my joys."

She did not resist, but let me do as I liked. Pushing myself down the bed, I applied my lips and tongue to her lovely cunt, all wet with our mutual discharge, which was so sweet to the taste that I first began licking between the lips, and then applied myself to her excited clitoris, and with my finger and thumb working as on the previous morning I threw her into an extasy of delight, until again she had a delicious discharge. Then creeping up, I thrust my prick into her well-moistened and velvety cunt—as you may imagine it was rampant as ever after my mouth contact with the exquisite quim I had been sucking.

"Stop, Charles, darling, I will show you another position, where you can lie easily with your dear delightful prick up to the hilt in the sheath you have so charmingly excited. Here, lie down by my right side—on your side."

She lay down on her back, and throwing her right leg over my hips, told me to bend my knees forward and open my legs, or rather lift up my right leg. She placed her left thigh between my thighs, then slightly twisting her bottom up towards me brought the lips of her cunt directly before my prick, which she seized with her delicate fingers, and guided safely into Venus's grotto. I gave one or two shoves, and she a heave or two, to house him comfortably.

"And now," she said, "we will take it reasonably in this way; we can go on, or stay occasionally; embrace, cuddle, or talk, just as we please. Are you quite comfortable?"

"Oh! deliciously so!" I replied, as my hand wandered all over her beautiful belly and bubbies, and then my mouth sucked the last.

"There, darling, that will do for the moment; I want to have some talk with you, First, let me thank you for your very discreet behaviour this day, it quite justifies the confidence I had in you. Your story of the dream was capital, and just suited the purpose. I hope, my dear Charlie, that under my auspices you will become a model lover—your aptitude has been already proved in several ways. First and best, with all the appearance of a boy, you are quite a man, and even superior to many. You have already shown great discretion and ready wit, and there is no reason to fear that you will become a general favourite with our sex, who soon find out who is discreet and who otherwise—discretion is the trump card of success with us. Alas! few of your sex understand this. Let me impress one lesson on you, my dear Charles. You and I cannot continue long on our present footing. My husband will return and carry me away, and although circumstances will throw us at intervals into each other's arms—for you may be sure you will be always welcome to me—yet my very absence will force you to seek other outlets to the passions I have awakened and taught their power. I have one piece of advice to give you as to your conduct to newer lovers—for have them you must, my dear Charles, however much you may fancy yourself now attached to me; with these, let them all for some time imagine that each possesses you for the first time. First of all, it doubles their satisfaction, and so increases your pleasure. Your early discretion causes me to think that you will see all the advantages of this conduct. I may add that if they suppose you have had previous instruction, they, if they are women, will never rest until they have drawn from you the secret of your first instructress. You might, of course, tell some tale of a 'cock and a bull,' but in searching for the truth and cross-questioning you when you are least aware of it, they will lead you into contradictions, and the truth will at last be ferreted out. Now this would be unjust to me, who have risked a good deal to give you the delightful instructions of last night, and, as I hope, of many more. So you see, my dear Charles, in all early cases you must enact the part of an ignoramus *seeking* for instruction, with vague ideas of how to set about it. I hope, while I am near you," she added, "no such occasion will arise, but I feel certain, with your

passions and your power, dear, darling fellow—push away—I!
—I!—I feel for cer-certain they will ar-arise."

Thus ended the very wise and excellent advise this charming woman was giving me. Do not imagine that I did not pay
great attention, and, indeed, her very reasonable maxims
became the guide of my after-life, and I owe to them a
success with women rarely otherwise obtained. Her sensible
remarks had been drawn out to such a length, that my prick
had so far rebelled that he had throbbed inside of her delicious cunt so forcibly as to produce a happy movement of
her body that interrupted and cut short her words.

"Charlie, my darling, pass your middle finger down and
rub it on my clitoris, and then suck the nipple of my bubby
next you, and work away with your glorious prick."

I did as desired. She seconded me with an art quite
peculiar to herself, and at last we both died away in that
love's death which is so overpowering and so delicious. The
glorious position we were in rendered it almost impossible to
lose ground, spend as often as you please; but if my prick
had been one that would have shrunk to nothing, the wonderful power of retaining it within her possessed by my
delicious mistress would have prevented the possibility of exit.

In after-nights I have often fallen sound asleep with it
entirely engulphed within her, and awoke hours afterwards
to find her extraordinary power of retention had held him
firm, notwithstanding his having shrunk up to a mere piece of
doughy flesh. In this instance, after recovering our senses, I
still retained my place, and we recommenced our conversation; my lovely instructress giving me many and most useful
hints for my after-life. I have often since dwelt on the wisdom
of all she so charmingly taught me, and wondered how so
young a woman could have so thorough a knowledge of her
sex and the world. I suppose love is a great master and
inspired her on this occasion. I may here remark that for
forty years afterwards this charming woman and I remained

the fastest of friends after being the most ardent of lovers. She was the depository of all my erotic extravagancies, and never showed any jealousy, but really enjoyed the recital of my wildest love combats with others.

Alas! death at last took her from me, and I lost the main-stay of my existence. Forgive this digression, but I am writing long after these events, and sorrows will have their vent. Woe is me!

To return to present joys. We continued talking and toying, until I was again anxious to commence love's combat. My prudent mistress wished me to finish for the time, and to sleep and refresh ourselves for renewed efforts; but youth and strength nerved me for the fight, and being securely fixed, I held her as in a vice, with my thighs around only one of hers that could have allowed her to escape. Passing my finger down on her stiffened clitoris I so excited her that she had no wish but to bring matters to a crisis.

"Stop, my dear," she said, "and we will renew our plea-sure in another attitude."

So withdrawing her leg off my loins, she turned on her side, so as to present her glorious buttocks before me, and pressed them into my belly and against my thighs, which seemed to introduce my prick even further than he was within before. Besides, in all these positions, where a woman presents her splendid backside to you, it is always more exciting, and has a greater hold of you than any other way. We did both most thoroughly enjoy this splendid fuck, and without withdrawing, both fell into the sweetest imaginable slumber. This was one of those occasions in which, having fallen asleep engulphed, I awoke some five hours later, to find my prick still lightly held within the velvety folds of one of the most delicious cunts ever created for the felicity of man, or of, I may say, woman either. You may easily imagine how soon my prick swelled to his wonted size on finding himself still in such charming quarters. I let him lay quite still, barring the involuntary throbs he could not avoid making, and bending my body away from my lovely mistress, I admired her breadth of shoulders, the beauty of her upper arm, the exquisite *chute* of her loins, the swell of her hips, and the glorious projection and rotundity of her immense buttocks. I slowly and gently pushed in and out of her juicy sheath, until, awakened by the exquisite sensations of my slow movements, all her lubricity was excited, and we ended one of our most delicious encounters, finishing, as usual, with a death-like exhaustion. She declared I had done enough for one night, and jumping out of bed, compelled me to betake myself to my own room, where, I must confess, I very shortly slept as sound as could be, without at the same time over-sleeping myself.

Thus passed several successive nights, until the fall of the moon, when one day Mrs. B. complained of headache and feeling unwell. I was very much alarmed, but she took occasion to tell me it was quite natural, and she would explain to me how it was so at night. I was obliged to be content with this. At night, she came and sat on my bed, and told me all the mysteries of the case. How women, not with child, had these bleedings monthly, which, so far from being hurtful, were a relief to the system, and that they happened at the full or the new moon, generally at the former. Further, that all connection with men must cease at such a time. I was in despair, for my prick was stiff enough to burst. However, my kind and darling mistress, to relieve me from the pain of such distention, took my prick in her mouth, and performed a new manœuvre. Wetting her middle finger with her saliva, she thrust it up my bottom-hole, and worked in unison with the suction of the knob, and the frigging of the root of my prick with the other hand. I had a most exquisite and copious discharge, the pleasure being greatly enhanced by the action of the finger up my fundament. My charming mistress swallowed all I could give her, and did not cease sucking until the last drop had exuded from my throbbing prick.

I was obliged to be satisfied with this, and my mistress informed me I could have no more enjoyment for four or five days; which, to my then impatience, was like condemning me to as many ages of hope deferred. I observed, while she was kissing me, that her breath had a peculiar odour, and I asked her what she had been eating.

"Why do you ask, my dear boy?"

"Because of the difference of your breath, generally so sweet and fragrant."

She smiled and said it was all from the same cause she had just been explaining to me, and was very generally so with women at that period. I mention this because it was the means of my discovering that Miss Evelyn was exactly in the same state. She had continued her endearing caresses without proceeding much further than I have already described, excepting more frequently kissing me. She now always did so on first entering the school-room, and also when we were dismissed. I suppose to prevent an observation or inference, she had adopted the same habit with my sisters. On this day, having drawn me with her arm round my waist close to her, when she kissed me I felt the very same odour of breath that I had observed in Mrs. Benson. She too was languid that day and complained of headache. I also observed a dark line under her eyes, and on afterwards observing Mrs. B., saw precisely the same—so I became convinced they were unwell from the same cause. Mrs. B. had told me that most women were so at the full of the moon—which was then the case.

The next day my mother proposed to drive to town, and probably knowing the state of the case, asked Mrs. B. and Miss Evelyn to accompany her, as she thought the airing would be beneficial. They at once accepted—my younger sister cried out, "Oh, mamma, let me go with you also."

Mary interposed, and thought she had the best right—but Lizzie said she had spoken first. I managed to give Mary a wink and a shake of the head, which she instantly comprehended, so gracefully giving way, although with apparent reluctance, it was arranged that Eliza should accompany the ladies. I now felt my opportunity was at hand to initiate my darling sister into the delightful mysteries that I had just been myself instructed in.

At eleven o'clock the carriage drove up, and we stood looking after them until they were lost to sight. Then returning into the parlour, Mary threw her arms round my neck, and kissing me, said—

"Oh! I am glad, Charlie, you winked to me, for now you know we can do as we like, and you can tell me all about this secret, and you must kiss my little Fanny as you did before, it was so nice. I have thought of nothing else, but how to have it done again."

"Well, my darling, I shall do all that, and more, but we cannot do so here. I tell you what we will do—we will pretend to go for a long walk in the country, but instead of that, we will pass through the shrubbery into the orchard and hazelwood, and so gain the little remote summer house, of which I have secured the key; there we shall be safe from all observation."

This little summer house was at some distance from the house, and in a lonely corner of the orchard, raised on an artificial mount, so that its windows should command a lovely view beyond the walls of the grounds. It was about ten feet square—was beautifully sheltered, and the ladies in summer took their work there, and occupied it for hours every fine day; so it was furnished with tables and chairs, and on one side a long couch without a back. It had already entered into my idea that this was the spot I should contrive to get to with Mary—little thinking how chance would throw so glorious an opportunity in my way so soon. It was always kept locked to prevent it being used by the servants, gardeners, or others. I knew where the key was kept, and secured it when the ladies were dressing for their drive—so after staying sufficiently long to prevent any suspicion, and saying then we were going for a long walk in the country, so as to prevent them seeking for us at the summer house if any visitors should chance to call, we sallied out, but re-entered the grounds where we could not be observed, and speedily gained the spot we had in view—entered and locked the door. Then I drew down the blinds, threw off my coat and waistcoat, and told Mary to take off her shawl and bonnet, and outer gown.

"But why all this, Charlie, dear?"

"First, my darling—all those are in the way of kissing and toying with your charming little Fanny, and next, I don't want anything to appear tumbled when we go back."

This was enough, and she did everything as I desired, indeed, more, for she took off her petticoat and little corset, saying she would be cooler thus. So, following her example, I took off my trousers, saying she would be better able to see and play with my doodle. When these preliminaries were accomplished, I drew her on my knees—first pulling up her shift and my own shirt, so that our naked flesh should be in contact. Seeing that her chemise fell off from her bosom, I first felt her little bubbies, which were beginning to develope themselves, and had the tiniest little pink nipples that even my lips could hardly get hold of. She had pulled up my shirt to look again at the great change that had occurred to my prick—of course, our preliminaries had already excited it to a stiff-standing position.

"Oh, Charlie, what a size it is to be sure; and how nice to pull this skin over its head; look how it runs back again. Oh! how funny!"

It was time to stop this, or she would have soon made me discharge.

"Well, then, what is this great secret, and what has it to do with your doodle and my Fanny?"

"I will tell you, but you must never say a word to a soul—not even to Eliza, she is too young yet."

"Well, go on."

"I was one day seeking something in the closet in Mrs. Benson's room, when I heard them coming, and had only the time to slip into the closet. They entered, locked the door, and Mr. B. laid her on the bed, and lifted up all her petticoats so that I saw her Fanny quite surrounded with hairs, as yours will be by and by. Mr. B. stooped down, and applied his tongue as I did to you the other morning."

"Oh, yes; and it was so nice, Charlie!"

"That is exactly what Mrs. B. said when he had done. Then he pulled out his doodle, such a size, much bigger than mine, and whipped it into her Fanny. I was quite frightened, and thought he must have killed her. But no, it went in quite easy; and she hugged and kissed him while he pushed it up and down for some time, till they both stopped all at once. He then drew it out, hanging down all wet, and asked if it had not given her great pleasure. 'Delightful,' she said. 'I have now got used to it, but you know you hurt me, and made me so sore the first time you did it.' After this they left the room, and I got away without being discovered. But I found out what our two things were made for, we will do as they did, so lie down on the couch whilst I kneel at the end, and begin in the way I kissed it the other morning."

"Oh, Charlie, if it is all like that, I shall be so pleased with it."

Down she squatted, drawing up her chemise. My hand wandered all over her charming belly and mount. Then kneeling down, and putting her legs over my shoulders, and my hands under her thighs and bottoms, I applied my tongue at once to her little clitoris, which I found was already stiff, and showing its head at the upper part of her pinky slit. The action of my agile tongue produced an instantaneous effect—her loins and thighs heaved up her bottom to press her little pouting cunt against my face. Mechanically she put her hand on my head, and muttered terms of endearment.

"Oh, darling Charlie, how delicious! Oh! do go on! it is so nice, &c."

I wanted no stimulant, but licked away until, with shortened breath, and greater heavings of her body, she began to stammer—

"Oh! oh! I feel so queer—ah, stop; I am going to faint—I, I, I, can't—can't bear it any longer—oh!—oh!" Her limbs relaxed, and she died away in her first discharge, which was very glutinous and nice, but only scanty in quantity. I let her quiet until she came to; then looking in her face, and smiling, I asked her how she liked it.

"Oh! I was in heaven, dear Charlie, but I thought it was killing me—it was almost too much to bear—nothing could be more delicious."

"Oh, yes!" I replied, "there is something more delicious still, but, I must kiss you in this way again before we try the other; the more moist the inside is the easier I shall get in."

"But, Charlie, you don't mean to say you will ever get in your doodle, now that it has grown so big."

"Well, we will try, and if it hurts you too much we can stop."

So I began again to gamahuche her; this time it took a longer effort to produce the ultimate result; but apparently with still greater effect, and a more copious discharge. Her little cunt being now relaxed, and well moistened with her own discharge and my saliva, and well inclined to recieve my prick, I spat upon it and lubricated it from head to root. Then rising from my knees, I stretched myself over Mary's belly, and gently directing my prick, and rubbing it up and

down first between the lips, and exciting her clitoris by the
same action, I gently and gradually inserted its head between
the lips of her charming little cunt. There was less difficulty
than might have been expected, the gamahuching and double spending had relaxed the muscles, and her passions being
excited also acted on her organs of generation; at all events,
I got in the head, and about two inches of its length without
her murmuring anything beyond—

"How big it feels—it seems to stretch me so."

All this was exciting me dreadfully, and it was only by the
greatest effort that I did not thrust rudely forward. I now
felt I was pushing against some obstacle, I thrust hard and
hurt her. She cried out, begged me to stop. I was so near the
finale that I felt I must go on. So, plunging forward, I
rushed at the impediment, and made her cry out most lustily.
Probably another push would have decided my position,
but nature could hold out no longer, and I yielded down my
erotic tribute to her virginal charms, without having actually
deflowered her. So far, perhaps, it was fortunate, because I
poured into her a torrent of sperm which was not only balm
to her partially wounded hymen, but so relaxed and lubricated the interior of her cunt as greatly to facilitate my
after-efforts.

I lay quiet still for some time, and the gradual swelling
out and throbbing of my prick reawakened her young passions. She said—

"Charlie, my dear, you said that it would prove delicious in
the end, and I can feel it is becoming so. I have no more
pain, and you shall go on just as you like."

As my prick stiffened at her endearing words and involuntary pressures, and as I had it completely under control, since
I had taken the edge off its immediate appetite by the last
discharge, I held it literally well in hand; and as I had lost no
ground by withdrawing, I started with the advantage of possession. First I slipped my hand down between our two bellies

and began frigging her clitoris, which immediately excited her passions to the highest pitch.

"Oh! Charlie, dear, now push it all in—I do so long for it —and I don't care how it hurts me."

I had been giving short thrusts more to stimulate her passions than to alleviate my own; and as she was totally unaware of what was going to happen, she widened her thighs and heaved up her bottom, expanding her vagina in the act. I gathered my strength together, and as my cock was standing as stiff as iron, I suddenly drove it forward, and felt that I broke through something, and gained two inches more insertion at least. The effect on my poor sister was most painful, she shrieked out lustily; strove hard to unsheath me, wriggled her body in all directions to effect this; but I was too securely engulphed for that, and all her struggles only enabled me the more easily to sheathe him up to the very hairs. So excited was I by her tears and screams, that I was no sooner there than a torrent of sperm burst from me, and I lay like a corpse on her body, but perfectly maintaining the ground I possessed. This death-like quiet lasted some minutes, and, to a certain extent, assuaged the violence of the pain I put poor Mary to. Doubtless, also, the balmy nature of the ample quantity of sperm I had shot up to her womb helped to soothe her suffering. At all events, when we were both able again to converse, she unbraided me with the agony I had caused her, and wished me to get off her at once; but retaining the advantageous possession of her very tight and delicious sheath, I told her all was now over, and we might look forward to nothing but enrapturing pleasure.

Some minutes had elapsed in these remonstrances on one side; and coaxings on the other, when I suddenly felt her charming little cunt actually throb upon and give an involuntary squeeze to my prick, which was still throbbing her. He was far too ready to stand at any time, still more when engulphed in the exquisite young cunt he had just initiated into love's mysteries—*bref*—he stood stiff as ever, and Mary, at first

with a shudder of fright, then with all the energy of awakened
passion, began to move her body under me. I held off from any
interference, feeling certain that if the desire came naturally
to her it would doubly enhance my own pleasure. My foresight did not fail me. Mary's passions became fully aroused,
and when so, the trifling soreness passed out of mind, and we
actually had a most delicious fuck, in which my prick appeared as if in a vice, and Mary wriggled her backside almost
as well as the more artistic movements of Mrs. Benson. All
things must come to an end, but this did so amid screams of
delight on both sides. This single bout began and finished the
education of my darling sister. She hugged and fondled me
afterwards, declaring I was quite right in telling her pleasure
followed pain; for nothing could exceed the enrapturing nature of the sensation my prick had produced. She thought now
that it was not a bit too big, but just made to give the utmost
satisfaction. We remained locked in each other's arms, my
prick still engulphed in its tight and exciting sheath. We
fondled and prattled, until it became again in a state of violent
erection, equally stimulating her tight little cunt, so that we
were forced to recommence our love encounter. I found that
my dear little sister possessed naturally the power of throbbing on or nipping a prick, which the French call *casse-
noisette*. It is a great gift and adds immensely to the man's
pleasure, and I should think to the woman's too. In my sister's
case it began from the very first complete insertion of my
prick and the years that I afterwards continued to fuck her
added nothing to this delicious accomplishment, except in
the variety of positions in which it could be exercised.

The dear girl was in extasies at the pleasure she had received, and at the pain which seemed to be past. Oh! she was
so sweetly caressing that I could not withdraw from her, and
we fondled and toyed until again my cock rose to his first
vigour, and she nothing loath, began her new and naturally
taught gift of bottom upheavings and cunt pressures until
again we sank exhausted in the death-like ending of love's

battles. On recovering our senses, I was obliged to withdraw and relieve my sister of the dead weight of my body on her person.

It has always struck me as extraordinary how the most delicate women will support a heavy man on their persons, not only without flinching, but even with ease and pleasure—but so it is. On rising and withdrawing, we were both alarmed to see that my prick was all bloody, and that blood and semen were oozing from her cunt. We had no idea this would be the case, and at first I was as frightened as she was. A moment's reflection showed me that it was only the natural result of forcing my way in, and that the pleasure since enjoyed proved it to be of no consequence. I soon convinced and calmed my sister on the point—fortunately the sofa covering was red, and applying my handkerchief, I wiped up all the semen mixture, and, in fact, no marks remained; the same handkerchief wiped all results from Mary's dear little cunt, and as her shift had been kept well up, fortunately no stains appeared upon that.

We now ate some luncheon and drank some wine that we had prudently brought with us. We then began playing and romping together—she wanting always to get hold of my prick, and I to pull her about in every way. It was gloriously warm weather, so I proposed we should off with every thing. In a trice we were as naked as we were born, and flew into each other's arms in a frenzy of delight, then we had a mutual thorough inspection. My darling sister gave every promise of becoming a magnificent woman—her shoulders were already wide—her arms well shaped, although still thin—her waist small—the swell of the hips already well developed—as to her bottom, it stuck out well and hard behind, quite charming to see, and giving promise of very ample dimensions hereafter. I made her kneel on the low couch, with her head well up and her thighs open; kneeling behind, I gamahuched her until she spent; then rising, shoved my prick into her cunt, in her then position, and had a downright good poke, which she, too, found was a way that gave her extra excitement. We passed thus some hours in mutual delights. I taught her the side fuck which had so charmed me with my delightful instructress, and I found dear Mary even an apter scholar than myself had proved. The afternoon advancing, we dressed, and eradicating all signs of what we had been doing, returned to the house, mutually promising to keep thoroughly secret all that had passed and agreeing that no sign of unusual familiarity should escape us. I strongly advised Mary to get some warm water and bathe her cunt well, for, as may be supposed, I had taken the opportunity of teaching her the true erotic language as applied to the organs of generation of both sexes, and the name of the connection itself, "fucking."

Thus delightfully ended the first lesson in love taught to my sister, and such was my first triumph over a maidenhead, double enhanced by the idea of the close ties of parentage between us. In after-life, I have always found the nearer we are related, the more this idea of incest stimulates our passions and stiffens our pricks, so that if even we be in the wane of life, fresh vigour is imparted by reason of the very fact of our evasion of conventional laws.

We had both returned to the drawing-room for more than an hour before the arrival of the ladies. Dear Mary complained of feeling sore and stiff in every limb. I had advised her to lie down on the sofa and try to sleep. I did the same, and happily we both dozed off, and never awoke until the loud rat-tat of arrival at the house door roused us up. I told Mary to hide all appearance of pain, and only to say, as an excuse for going early to bed, that we had gone further afield than we at first intended, and that she was very tired. We were both sent early to bed, for I was still treated as quite a boy, and I was sound asleep when my charming Mrs. B. woke me up by her warm caresses. I could well have spared them that night, but when did one of my years not respond to the endearments of the woman he loved, and who yielded all to him. She sucked me dry as usual, and I slept soundly till morning.

The next three days passed without anything to record. Mary did not allow her real soreness to appear, but heroically went through her sufferings, for she told me afterwards she felt very severe pains all over, doubtless her whole nervous system had been overexcited, and this was the natural reaction; it was so far fortunate that not a shadow of a chance of our having fresh connection occurred, so she had time to perfectly recover from the ill effects of her first initiation into the erotic raptures. I continued to have the relief each night of the charming mouth of my loved and beautiful instructress. At last, the adominable *menses,* as she called them, were past and gone. For a full twenty-four hours after, she would not allow me to reassume all the privileges she had previously granted, and admit me to share her bed. She told me this was necessary to prevent any recurrence, and also that in some cases a virulent white discharge occasionally followed for some hours, sufficiently acrid to affect my local health, and "that," she added, "was now too precious in her estimation to risk it in any way." I thought it hard at the time, but it was only another proof of the thoughtful wisdom of this estimable woman. At last, I was again in full possession of her charming person. Oh! how we did revel in all the luxuries and lubricity; almost every night my enchanting friend found some new position to vary and enhance our erotic raptures. One new dose was laying me down flat on my back, then straddling over me, she sank on her knees, and with body erect, lifted up or rather bent back my stiff-standing prick, until he was fairly below her open cunt, then guiding it exactly to the proper entrance, she sank her body slowly down upon it until fully engulphed, hair crushed hair, then as slowly raising again, she drew off until all but the nut was uncovered, to again sink down. In this position we could both see the whole process. At length, becoming too excited, she sank on my bosom, then one arm and hand pressed her splendid buttocks down on my throbbing prick after every elevation of her magnificent back-side while my other hand, doubling round behind her, introduced the middle finger up her charming bottom-hole, and worked in and out in unison with both our heaving movements, until stopped by the grand crisis, when death-like langour overcame us both almost at the same moment. I must not forget to mention that from time to time I paid a visit to the small and rosy orifice that lay so near to the more legitimate altar of Venus. It was a variety of enjoyment that my lovely mistress acknowledged to me she at times felt much inclined to enjoy, but only after having the front path of pleasure well fucked and lubricated with sperm, which alone caused the other mucous membrane to feel inclined that way.

I will here insert a characteristic letter from my loved mistress to her intimate and bosom school friend, with the reply thereto. It was several years before they were shown to me, and some time after I had possessed *both* the charming writers, for we all three became fast friends; indeed, I may call myself or rather my prick, the pivot on which their friendship turned, yet there never was the shade of jealousy on either part, but in these remarks I am anticipating what I may, perhaps, be hereafter tempted to describe more fully. I give these letters now, because they immediately refer to the events I am at present relating. They show the secret working of my loved mistress's mind, and the voluptuous nature of her temperament, and the satisfaction that my delicious initiation had given. Her affectionate and flattering remarks, relating to myself, are greater than I deserved. The following is the first letter addressed to her friend:

MRS. BENSON TO THE HON. MRS. EGERTON.

Dear Carry,

I am about to keep my promise, and give you an account of our honeymoon. You, my dear, must be equally faithful, and reply as frankly as I am now about to write to you.

Two giddier girls than you and I never entered the bonds
of matrimony, or more earnestly longed for the sights connected with it. Well, after the usual breakfast, we left by rail
for Leamington, where we were to pass our first night. We had
a *coupé* to ourselves; and beyond seating me on his knee, and
kissing me, Fred behaved with much decency and propriety.
We arrived and dined. The hour between tea and bedtime was
sufficiently tedious, as both of us were naturally much preoccupied. My husband wrote a letter to mamma, telling her of
our safe arrival, and of his intense happiness. After which he
asked me if I would go to bed, in the most matter-of-fact way
imaginable. I murmured an affirmative, scarcely knowing what
to say. He rang for a candle, and told me he would follow
shortly. It seemed like a dream to me. The maid showed me to
a room containing a large four-post bedstead, heavily hung
with curtains, and provided with old-fashioned furniture.

I seated myself on the edge of the bed and began to medi-
tate. I sat thus, for, I dare say, ten minutes, and then commenced undressing, I had put on my night-gown, and removed everything but my stockings, when I heard footsteps
approach the door. I opened, and my husband entered, closed
it, and turned the key. Oh! Carry, I did feel so funny. I was
undressed in a bedroom with a man, and that man had a
right to my person. He seated himself in an armchair, and
drew me on his knee. Nothing but my thin night-gown separated my bottom from his bare knee, for he had quite undressed in an adjoining room and had nothing on but his
shirt under his dressing-gown, which flew open as he sat
down. He drew my lips to his, and kissing me, thrust his
tongue between them, while his hand first caressed and
squeezed my bosom, which, you know, is pretty full and well
developed; it then wandered down upon my thigh, pressed
and felt the fleshy form. Little by little he approached my
belly, and for a moment pressed my mount. These preliminaries are at all times exciting, but now they made me almost

ill, so great was my confusion. Seeing this, he drew up my
night-gown, and placed his hand, first on my naked thigh,
then he felt my mount, and you know, Carry dear, what a
forest I have got there. He seemed delighted with it. His
fingers played with the silky curls, drawing them out to their
full length, so long that it appeared to surprise him, and his
eyes sparkled, and his face showed much excitement.

"Open your thighs, dearest," he whispered.

I obeyed mechanically, and his middle finger forced itself
between the lips of my cunt, and commenced rubbing my
clitoris. You know, by experience, what an excitable one it is
and to what a size it developes itself when excited. Again Fred
seemed delighted with his discovery.

"Does that please you, my darling?"

"Yes," I faltered out.

He thrust his finger up my cunt, then rose up, threw off his
dressing-gown, took me in his arms, and lifted me on the bed,
placing a pillow under my head. Then letting my legs fall
over the sides, he knelt on the floor, and separating my thighs
with his arms, stooped and kissed my quim. He did more, he
sucked and then licked with his tongue my already excited
clitoris. It set me on fire, and I could not avoid showing it by
the convulsive twitchings of my loins and buttocks.

"Do you like that, my love?"

"Oh! yes; so much!—so very much!"

I was nearly mad with the excitement he was putting me
into. He again stood up, and lifting my legs, his hands pressed
them again and again.

"What delicious legs," he exclaimed.

I could see his shirt bulging out. He leant forward, and
with his arms under my legs, lifted them well up, and I felt a
stiff thick thing pressing against my cunt. His left hand opened
the lips, his right hand guided it between them, and a cruel
push lodged its great head completely within. Neither you, or
I, Carry, were strictly virgins, our fingers and other means

had opened our vaginas to a certain extent. We had played too many tricks together to have left our maidenheads quite intact, so that the passage was less difficult than it might have been. Nevertheless, it had never been penetrated by the male organ, and that of my husband was of the largest. I experienced, therefore, a great deal of pain, and cried out—

"Oh, my dear Fred, you hurt me dreadfully, what are you doing?"

"Doing, my darling! why, I am getting into you. Have a little patience, and I will make you mad with pleasure."

Another determined thrust sent him halfway, and then with another, still more violent, he lodged himself up to the hilt within. I screamed with real pain, and struggled to free myself.

"Good heavens, sir, you are killing me; I will not endure such treatment."

He heeded me not, but holding me fast by the thighs commenced shoving in and out furiously. A sensitive woman never receives an insertion of this kind with impunity. The friction began to excite feelings that first deadened the pain of entrance, and then began to awaken the delicious sensations of lubricity. The enjoyment I began to experience was delicious, and I could not refrain from heaving up to meet his thrusts.

"That is right, my angel; was I not correct in saying it would soon turn from pain to pleasure? Do you not enjoy it now?"

"Yes; but you make me feel so funny. I don't know what—it—is."

His increased and rapid movement filled me with delight; I bounded up and down in response to his thrusts, and felt so queer when, all of a sudden, he gasped for breath, stopped, and I felt a greater and stiffer swelling of his instrument, and then a gush of hot liquid dashed against my womb, which continued running for some seconds. This, Carry, was my first experience of what a man can do for us.

Withdrawing his huge affair—for he since admits he is larger than most men—letting go my thighs—he pressed down upon me, and tenderly embraced me, and said that I had behaved admirably; in future there would be no more pain, and from what he had already experienced he felt sure I was made for the fullest enjoyment that husband and wife could indulge in. After a little fondling, he rose, drew off my stockings, and helped me into bed, immediately following me. On throwing back the clothes to enter the bed, he said he must kiss the dear little hairy thing that had given him such pleasure. He kissed and toyed with it, admiring the profusion of hair on my mount, the whiteness and beauty of my belly, and then, baring my breasts, admired, kissed, and sucked them. All this not only excited me, but I could see very well it had again caused his affair to stick out. Seeing that I was timidly glancing at it, he seized my hand, and made me lay hold of it, showed me how the skin covered and uncovered its head; then becoming rampageous, he got on my belly and between my thighs, and again introduced his cock to where it had already given such pleasure. He still rather hurt me, and made me smart for a little while, but as the interior was well lubricated by his former discharge, the penetration was easily accomplished. When up to the hilt, and the two hairs were closely joined, he paused and said—

"We will take it less impatiently this time, that my darling Bessie may enter into all the joys of fucking, for that is what we call it, my dear; so I shall go slowly to work until my darling's passions awake and urgently call for more rapid movements."

He did so, and gradually produced the most lascivious excitement in my whole body. I writhed beneath him in the utmost extasy, threw my arms round his body, and hugged him to me.

"Oh! you are an angel," he cried, "and made for enjoyment. Throw your legs also over my back—there, that is it—and now

I will hasten my movements, and we will die away together."

Oh, the delight he gave me was inexpressibly delicious; his rapid and eager thrusts were as eagerly met by the upheaving of my bottom to reciprocate them. The grand crisis seized us simultaneously, and we sank momentarily exhausted in each other's arms, leaving the dear exciter of such joys soaking within. My dear husband was so pleased, he kissed and fondled me in the sweetest manner, telling me that never woman before had yielded him such intense pleasure, that nature had prompted me to as much enjoyment as if I had been already married a month.

We were locked closely in the warmest embrace; his tenderness and fondling began to have its effect on my passions, and involuntarily I made some internal convulsive twitchings.

"I feel you, my darling, calling on my instrument for renewed efforts; he will soon respond."

And, in fact, I felt it swelling and swelling so deliciously that I could not help continuing the interior pressures, although feeling confusedly ashamed of the notice my husband took of it.

"Don't be afraid, my sweetest love, but give way to whatever your passions dictate, and thus you will best please me, and give to yourself double enjoyment. I mean to initiate you into every secret that the rites of Venus possess, and wish that my loved wife should become a devoted votary, and I will do my best that she may revel in all the luxuries of perfect coition."

We completed this course with even greater *abandon* than before, and I began to enjoy his embraces beyond anything our imaginations used to suggest. This time he withdrew and lay down by my side, and taking me within both his arms, continued his charming endearments. I never slept that night; I was in a fever of restless excitement. My husband fucked me five times before he dozed off. Towards morning I tossed and tumbled, and could not sleep. Daylight soon came, my restlessness had shaken all the bed clothes off, except a part of the sheet, and turning towards my husband, I perceived that the sheet stuck up over the lower part of his body. Curiosity seized me—I looked at him, and saw he was evidently sleeping. So gently removing the sheet, I beheld the dear instrument of all my last night's joys as well as pains. You know how we used to long to see man's cock when we were at school, and how, when we did sometimes see a boy's limp thing hanging down, we used to wonder what change would come over it, and how. Well, here was an opportunity of examining, at my ease, the wonderful curiosity that had so puzzled us. The last edge of the sheet passing over it touched its ruby head; it throbbed and pulsated to the view. I was afraid this had awakened Fred, but no, he slept as sound as ever. So I gently raised myself on my bottom, and gazed on the dear object I had so longed to see and feel. There it stood up like a pillar, rather bending towards his belly: and what surprised me much was to see a dark strongly wrinkled bag at its roots, with apparently two large balls inside; the hair on its roots spread in dark mass up to his navel, and beautifully bright and curling it was. I approached my lips, and made the action of kissing, without touching it. Whether it felt my warm breath, I know not, but it actually throbbed a response. What a great big thing it was, equally long as it was thick. I did not think I could encircle it with my hand; I longed to try, but was afraid I should waken Fred, and what would he think of me, I blushed at the very idea; but my passions became excited, and too strong to resist the temptation. So first lying gently down again, I very quietly dropped my arm over him and touched his cock, it throbbed at the touch, but Fred slept on. So raising myself again, I very gently laid hold of it. It was as much as I could grasp below the head, but was beyond my grasp at the root; I found it took three of my hands to measure its length from the root to the nut, which stood out in all its redness above. I was almost breathless with excitement, and lost some of my caution. Stooping down, I gently kissed the ruby head, when, before I knew where I was, it was pushed up into my mouth, and my husband's voice said—

"Oh, you dear darling creature! how kind of you to waken me so luxuriously!"

I was horrified at being discovered; and blushing up to the eyes, I hid my face in his bosom.

"Do not be ashamed, my angel, it is now as much yours as mine, and have you not as much right to see, kiss, and handle it? come, don't be ashamed."

However, I could not face him, and when he tried to raise my head I turned my back. He seized me round the waist, and, before I knew where I was, passed a hand between my thighs, and guided his huge cock to the lips of my cunt, and was in me, I thought further than ever, in a moment. It is true the previous toying with his instrument had terribly excited me, and I had felt that my cunt had become very moist, but I had no idea that anything could be accomplished in that position. I was most delightfully undeceived, for not only did it feel tighter in it, but transferring his fingers from guiding his prick, he touched and played with my clitoris, and produced such excessive lubricity that I went off and spent with a scream of delight before he was ready; but continuing with finger and cock to ravish me inside and out, he soon brought me again to such a pitch of lewdness that I was quite ready to spend with him when the grand crisis arrived. Nothing could exceed the pleasure; my internal pressures, he declared, were the most exquisite he had ever experienced. My clitoris, too, he declared was quite unique. You remember how it used to stick out when excited as far as the first thumb joint, and how, when sometimes I played the husband on your belly, you declared that it actually entered between the lips of our cunt, rubbed against your smaller development, and gave you great pleasure, as indeed it gave me. My husband has often examined and sucked it, and admires it beyond measure. At present he did not withdraw, declaring that I held him so tight he did not think he could pull it out if he tried. In fact, it was involuntary on my part, and I could not help clinging to his dear instrument for the life of me.

Oh, how he fondled and embraced me, making me partially turn my body so that he might kiss and tongue me, and then suck my bubbies; his busy finger all the time tickling and frigging my clitoris. I soon felt his cock swelling so deliciously within me, and he shortly recommenced his rapturous pushings in and out. We made a long, long bout of it, and I am sure that I spent twice before joining him at the last moment, when he died away in a shout of joy that I feared must have been heard by the servants in the house, who long before this had been on the move. After this we lay soaking and enjoying it for more than half an hour, when my husband declared he felt as if a wolf was at his stomach, and that he must have some breakfast. He got up and quickly dressed, desiring me to lie still, and he would bring me some breakfast in bed, and that, while it was getting ready, he would order some warm water to bathe myself with. I felt his delicacy, and loved him for it. The water came, I was much refreshed after using it, and got into bed again, but I felt awfully stiff and done up all that and next day.

My darling husband waited on me himself at breakfast, stimulating me to eat freely as a means of restoring my lost strength; which he very soon put to the test again, for he fucked me three times during the day, and each time he gave me greater pleasure than before. He was just as active at night. And the whole three weeks we stayed at Leamington, he never fucked me less than four times a night, declaring that I had become most perfect in the exercise.

We then came here, our old friend, Mrs. Roberts, having kindly insisted upon our paying her a long visit. Fred has been called away suddenly and will not return for a month. I am sure you will pity me, as you know my temperament is too hot to keep chaste so long. You remember Charlie Roberts; you would consider him a child, but he is not so. One afternoon Fred followed me into my bedroom, as was usual, and gama-huched and fucked me on the edge of the bed. I was about to leave the room after he was gone, when on opening a closet, in which my dresses were hung, who should I discover but this same Charlie. I was in a fix.

There was no doubt the lad had seen everything. I spoke kindly to him, and he promised secrecy. In order to ensure it, I determined to have his maidenhead. A few days afterwards my husband left me, and the girls with their mamma and the governess went to town with him, leaving Charlie to keep me company. I went upstairs with him to the drawing-room, and seating myself in a low chair, crossed my legs carelessly, ex-posing them, and letting the garter and part of the bare skin of one thigh be visible. The effect was what I expected. I saw Charlie's eyes fixed on the exposure, he blushed scarlet, and I could distinctly see his cock swell out under his trousers. In a little while I had unbuttoned them, and, oh, Carry, would you imagine it, I found he had the cock of a man. I could scarcely believe my eyes. He is not quite fifteen, and yet he is almost as large as Fred. Here was a godsend, indeed! I drew up my petticoats, and the gallant little fellow instantly fell on his knees, kissed and sucked my cunt. To reward him, I placed him on his back on the couch, and got on the top of him. I took his pego into my mouth, and pressed my cunt against his face, we devoured each other with our luxurious caresses until we both spent copiously. Nothing was lost, we both greedily swallowed all we could get.

At home he is looked upon as still a child, and I had little difficulty in arranging for him to sleep in a little dressing-room adjoining my bedroom, with which there is a door of com-munication. He was sent early to bed, but when I came I found him still awake, expecting me, and I had the delicious treat of initiating him into the pleasures of fucking. If you ever wish to enjoy *par excellence* this pleasure, get hold of a vigorous boy who has never had a woman. My good fortune threw into my hands a wonderfully provided youth, whose aptitude, as well as size and powers, it would be very difficult to match. I had already given him several lessons in the enrapturing art when we fell asleep, and now I must mention a little episode, which it would not do to omit.

In the morning I was dreaming of Fred, when I became conscious that something was entering me. I was in that half-dreaming state when it is difficult to be quite certain what is happening, but gradually I became aware that although there was no doubt I was being entered, it was not in the usual way. My husband had frequently of late pushed his prick up my bottom-hole, and as he told me that all husbands did so, I could make no objections. I, therefore, at first took it for granted that Fred, finding my naked bottom in his lap, could not resist the temptation of entering it. I, therefore, humoured him, and so moved my bottom as to facilitate his complete entrance, and began to feel myself the excitement it occasioned, but as I became wider awake, I gradually called to mind that Fred had left me, and that Charlie was my bed-fellow. The audacity of the young rogue paralysed me, but his delicious movements had become too nice for me to think of dislodging him. He insisted that he was quite unconscious of his mistake, and that he believed himself buried in the delicious grotto of the night before. It probably was so, for so perfect an ignoramus as he is, although ever so apt a scholar in Venus's rites, he could hardly have imagined there could be any entrance in the smaller orifice. I let him go on, and with his well hung cock in my bottom, and two or three fingers in my cunt, he fucked and frigged me most deliciously, until we both spent in an agony of pleasure. If, Carry, you have not tried this route I strongly recommend you to do so without delay, but you must be well fucked in the first instance, to stimulate a desire in those parts, and your lover must be up to the art of frigging you at the same time, or you can pass your hand under your belly, and rub your clitoris, which was the plan I adopted with Charlie, until I taught him the art of rubbing the clitoris properly. As there is always more excitement when this is done by a male, it is better to have them when one can, but, *faute de mieux*—one can do it oneself with much additional lascivious satisfaction.

To give you an instance of the precocious aptitude of this dear little fellow, I mounted upon him one morning, keeping my body erect, that we might see the delicious instrument in its action of being engulphed and then withdrawn, a most exciting pose which I recommend you to try, if your husband has not already taught it to you.

At last, overcome by the lascivious movements, I sank on his bosom. He pressed my bottom down with one hand, and with the other embracing the nearer buttock, introduced his middle finger up the rosy orifice of my bottom, and frigged me in unison with our ups and downs of fucking, giving me the most delicious additional sensations.

What do you think of that for a *tyro*? His discretion, too, is extraordinary. The first night after I sent him to his own bed, he overslept himself. I had not thought of that, and had not looked into his little room before descending to breakfast. His sister was sent to call him. He at once excused himself by saying he had had a bad dream; she came down and told us. In a few minutes he followed, and in the most natural way possible, told a tale of fright, declared he had awoke screaming and afterwards had been so frightened that he could not sleep, and turning to me in the most natural way, hoped his scream had not disturbed me. He never came near me, or appeared in any way attracted by me—a discretion worthy of a man of the world. Oh! my dear Carry, I shall make a great deal of this boy. We have had several delicious nights since, and he improves wonderfully. Splendidly as my husband fucks, Charley already beats him. He is quite as often ready, indeed, oftener, and it is I that hold him back, but there is something still so charmingly infantine in his way of caressing me, and then the lascivious idea he is all my own, and that I initiated him in love's mysteries, adds an inexpressible charm to our lascivious encounters. I feel that I shall almost regret my husband's return, as it will force me to give up this delicious indulgence. Not the slightest shadow of suspicion of our doings is excited in the family, thanks to the very guarded and admirable conduct of Charlie, which is above all praise.

Write to me soon, my dear Carry, and be sure you are as candid as this long, long letter is to you, for the life of me I could not make it shorter. I only hope you will give me one as long, and have as much delicious intelligence for me. I know you too well to suppose that you have not found means as I have done, to try what other men are made of, although you can scarcely have had such wonderful luck as mine. Write then, and write without reserve. Our mutual affection is too sincere to allow of any concealment whatever between two such loving and lewd lascivious friends.

Ever your affectionate friend,
E. BENSON.

Such was the long letter my adored mistress wrote at the time to her school companion. It will be seen that their attachment had led to something more than the usual fingerings and caressings of school girls, indeed, had led them on to the lewdest and most lascivious indulgences that two girls could practise in common, and had first excited their passions and given them the delicious power of pleasing coition they were both so perfect in, for, as I before said, about two years after this time, I was the possessor of both and many and many an orgy we three had together, without the shadow of jealousy on any side. It will be seen that Mrs. Egerton, in her reply, even looks forward to the delicious indulgence, which in the end was happily effected and long continued. The following is her reply—

THE HON. MRS. EGERTON TO MRS. BENSON.

How can I ever sufficiently thank my darling Lizzie for her delicious letter. I have devoured its delightful details a dozen times already. I keep it in my bosom, and renew the pleasure of its perusal at every spare moment. *Too long?* Oh! with such a charming power of description, why did you not cover fifty more pages. Never in my life have I enjoyed such an exquisite description of those dear lascivious encounters. How delighted I am at your good fortune in meeting with such a miracle of a boy as that dear Charlie Roberts. Why, he has every quality of a man, united to the charm of extreme youth. What a splendid man he will become, the very perfection of a lover, and already possessing so lewd and lascivious a lubricity. Oh! how I envy you his possession. What luck for him too, to have fallen into the hands of so delicious a teacher as my beloved Lizzie is. Am I not myself her pupil, and were you not my own delicious instructress in all that one of our sex could teach each the other.

You will remember a long-standing engagement entered into, between us made, when we were both so lewd and so longing for the real knowledge of man, and how we pledged ourselves that if either got possession of a lover, we should manage after a while to share him between us. Your description of Charlie Roberts has brought this pledge most vividly to my recollection. I am sure my dear Lizzie will not be angry or jealous when I avow that I long to participate with her in the possession of that darling boy; and if my Lizzie is as of old, I feel certain she will rather indulge and cultivate this propensity than otherwise. Think how easy it will be for us both to arrange the meeting of all three together, because I wish to possess him *in common*, certain that it will increase the lascivious pleasure of coition. No one will suspect us when we drive out, two women with one man. It will naturally be supposed that one fears the other, and so there will be no danger. See, here I am at once anticipating future scenes, but it is all owing to the extremely exciting and lascivious details you have so vividly given me.

I have no such delicious scenes to depict as those you have so delightfully described to me. My honeymoon passed off in a much more common-place way than yours. Our marriage, which was performed within a day of your own, went off as such events do. My husband was loving, without being very warm. I felt very much as you describe on going to bed the first night, but the discretion or delicacy of my husband, which I could well have pardoned him for dispensing with, left me time not only to get into bed, but kept me waiting there some time. He entered like yours in his dressing-gown, but immediately put out the light and found his way into bed, as best he could. He crept to my side and embraced me tenderly enough, and began to fondle and kiss me, telling me how dearly he loved me, etc., but for some time he avoided any indecent liberties. I suppose he thought it necessary to gain my confidence and quiet any alarm I might be in. He might have saved himself the trouble, for in reality I was longing for and at the same time somewhat dreading an attack on my maiden charms. At last, little by little, he approached the object of delight, and eventually begging me not to be alarmed, he mounted upon me and effected the object of his desires. He did not hurt me much, not nearly as much as I expected, nor so much as you seem to have suffered. I deemed it politic to affect more suffering than he really inflicted. Towards the end I had slight scintilations of pleasure, but not worth mentioning; it is true my husband is not so well-armed as yours and Charlie appear to be, and he is also much colder in his passions; for instance, he did not attempt to fuck me again, although I would have been gratified if he had done so; perhaps it was considerate towards me in his idea, but, merely embracing me in his arms, he talked himself and me to sleep.

In the morning he again fucked me, this time giving me something like pleasure, but I was altogether disappointed with my night's experience. It was not such as you or I, my dear Lizzie, had pictured to ourselves, in our anticipations of the marriage night. My husband since has never exceeded twice a night, but he has become more exciting, and has generally made me spend twice to his once, first exciting my passions by feeling all my private parts, and frigging my clitoris, so that I generally have lubricated the passage by my own discharge before he attempts to make an entrance. I find he likes this, and so far it pleases me, because only one discharge would leave me in a state of excitement unbearable. He has never attempted any of those lewder and more lascivious methods, of which you have had such delicious experience. Altogether, I cannot but say I am disappointed. My husband is loving, and very anxious that I should improve my mind in every way. You know I was rather more proficient than usual at school in Italian. My husband speaks it fluently, and as we mean to spend a winter at Rome, was anxious that I should have further instruction. He asked me if my school teacher was a good one, but I did not encourage that idea. You may remember our former master was a Count Fortunio, so handsome and so enterprising that you and I had both formed the plan of having him, and had already put over some of the preliminaries when, unfortunately, he was caught with that impudent Miss Peace, with whom, doubtless, he had accomplished everything. Of course, he was instantly changed for another, and we saw no more of him, to the sad disappointment of our then libidinous hopes. My husband proposed advertising for a master, when I had the happy instinct to tell him that schoolmistresses generally applied to Rolandi, of Berner's Street, for language masters, and that, if he would write or call, he would be sure to get every information. That evening, after dinner, as we sat dozing over the fire in the library—very imperfectly lighted—my husband informed me that he had seen Rolandi, who had most strongly recommended a very gentlemanly man, moving in good society, namely, the Count Fortunio. I started in amazement; fortunately, owing to the half-light we were in, my surprise and confusion were unnoticed by my husband. He said that he had been referred to one or two gentlemen of standing as to the Count's character, that he called upon them, and felt satisfied that I could not be in better hands. You may imagine what an effect this information had upon me. All night long I could think of nothing else. What seemed most difficult to me was the hiding from my husband our previous knowledge of each other. I feared the Count would at once recognise me and claim acquaintance, which was what I most wished to avoid; to you, from whom I have no secrets, I may own it immediately occurred to me that this would be an opportunity (for which I had in heart been longing) of obtaining the services of a lover I could trust. How to manage it I knew not, but chance, that favourer of all wrongdoers, stood me in good stead.

My husband had intended to be present to receive the Count. Fortunately, a letter arrived in the morning requiring his instant attendance in the City about the sale of some stock, of which he was trustee. He begged me to see the Count, and arranged as to hours of attendance, &c., the more frequently the better. I felt my embarrassment was at an end; the next thing was to avoid letting the servants, those domestic spies on our conduct, see the first meeting. There was a small room off our drawing-room that had no door but the opening into the drawing-room; this was fitted up as a sort of boudoir writing-room, and my husband had pointed it out as a convenient place for me to take my lessons in.

Here, therefore, I posted myself, and awaited the hour of arrival, to which he was punctual. He was announced and I told the servants to show him in. I sat purposely with my back to the entrance, apparently engaged in writing, as if I did not know he had approached, until I heard the door of the drawing-room shut. I then rose, turned, and smilingly held out my hand. He started with surprise, but immediately and gallantly kissed the hand held out to him.

"I hope you are not disappointed in finding who is going to be your pupil."

"Oh, no, certainly not; I did not know you under your married name; but I am so happy to renew an acquaintance which at one time had such charming promise."

"Stop, signor, I am now married, and it is necessary to be very cautious. I do not wish to deny that I am much pleased to renew acquaintance with you, but it must be with great reserve. Sit down by my side, and be reasonable."

"Reasonable! and by the side of one whom I so much loved, and from whom I had such hope. Oh! dear Mrs. Egerton, you are surely not going to treat me as a mere master. You would render me miserable if you did so. How can I help admiring one whom I so fondly loved, and with whom I hoped for such happiness long ago."

Here, having possession of my hand, his other arm was passed round my waist, and he drew me to his lips, and I must own, I reciprocated the ardent kiss he gave me. You remember how handsome he is, and how soft and loving was the expression of his eyes. Well, my dear, to cut matters short, I was so excited that I hardly observed that he had passed his hand up to my petticoats, until I found he had got it on my mount. My passions being excited, and knowing that my husband could not return, and also that he had given strict orders that I was not to be disturbed in my Italian lessons, I gave way unreservedly to the excitement the Count raised. Before I well knew where I was, he was on his knees in front of the low chair on which I was seated. He had thrown up my petticoats, and I felt a long and extremely hard prick rush up my cunt, and begin the most lively action. In fact, he carried me (not unwillingly I must avow) by storm, and made haste to secure the fortress at once, so that I had a very quick fuck, that did not assuage the fire he had raised within me. He has since apologised for his haste, saying that he wished to secure possession of me before I could think of resistance, so as to ensure more facilities of connection hereafter. We had no lesson in language that day, but another bout of love, in which he did his utmost, and with perfect success, to give me the most delicious enjoyment.

In fact, my dear Lizzie, I may say it was the first fuck that thoroughly realised *my*, or rather our, anticipations of the act. We arranged the line of conduct necessary to be followed so as neither to compromise me or him either. In a short time we had again a delicious fuck. Seated, with outstretched legs, on a chair, he got me to straddle over him, and sink down on his stiff upstanding prick. I have tried this position kneeling, with my husband on his back; but it does not equal the chair fuck. One has so much better a spring from one's feet than from one's knees, besides, the man is brought more face to face, and there is more facility for mutual embracings; but both ways have their charm. I had repeatedly observed that the Count apparently lost his place, and on recovering it, partially penetrated the smaller orifice, which you so picturesquely describe. I thought it accident, and as it hurt, I always put him back, and joked him on his awkwardness. But after I read your dear delightful letter, I became convinced that he had a wish to penetrate there, without the courage to tell me so.

I must confess to you, that our stolen embraces at home had become too unsatisfactory, and the Count had arranged for a private house to be at our disposal. Of an afternoon I drove out shopping, called at Swan and Edgar's in Regent Street, leaving the carriage at the door, walked upstairs, made some trifling purchase, paid for and left it until I should call in an hour; then descending by another staircase, left by the Piccadilly entrance, and taking a cab, joined my expectant lover, where he was waiting for me. There stripping perfectly naked, we enjoyed each other most lasciviously, and practised every act of lubricity. When satiated with our efforts, a second cab conducted me to St. James's passage, in Jermyn Street, from whence I gained on foot Swan and Edgar's in Piccadilly, received my parcel, and rejoined my carriage. Thus no suspicions were excited, either in the household or otherwise.

We have met thrice since your dear delicious letter fired my imagination, and I have seized the occasion to taste the sweets of the neighbouring altar to Venus's legitimate one. After the Count had fucked me twice I turned my back as if wishing it in a way we often enjoyed it, but took care to place my bottom in such a position that the smaller orifice was nearest to his standing prick. Whether he saw my drift I know not, but finding with his finger how conveniently it lay, he plunged boldly forward, and half sheathed himself at the first push. I started with the sudden pain, and should have disengaged myself at once, notwithstanding that I purposely placed myself to receive his prick in my bottom-hole, but with his arms round my waist I was perfectly powerless, and another thrust sent him up to the hilt, but really hurting me most sensitively; I begged him to desist and withdraw, but he said—

"I will remain quite quiet for a time, and you will see that your pain will diminish, and then you will like it."

I could not help myself, and sure enough he was right. Shortly I felt no pain; slipping one hand down, he began to frig my clitoris, and in a little time, finding by the involuntary movements of my loins that my passions were excited, he began to move very slightly and slowly. I soon found a strange excitement seize me, which increased to such a degree that I almost fainted, when my nature gave down its divinest essence. We have since repeated the new experience, but I quite agree with you in thinking that we must be well fucked first.

The Count is a master of his weapon, which, neither quite so long as you describe your husband's nor nearly so thick at the point, is very much so at the root, and as stiff and hard as iron. I assure you, the wild excess of passion he drives me into is indescribable. You shall experience the delight of his fucking, for, with you and me, there must be no difficulty, diversion, nor jealousy, Nay, I shall try to seduce your husband, with a view to cover our delinquencies. I would offer you mine, but, truly, he is not worth having to a woman who can find better, as my dear Lizzie so charmingly does. We have managed matters so prudently that my husband has taken a great fancy to the Count, and he dines frequently at our house.

We have often talked of you. I told him of your marriage, and of a probability of your eventually settling in London. I marked the sparkle of his eyes at the news, but was silent as to your letter and adventures. It is better we should manage the affair between us when you are here.

So you see, after all, I have not come off so badly, although, I must say, tamely in comparison with the delicious adventures of my dear and charming Lizzie. I think, when we meet, we shall be able to get up parties of the most delightful kind. I even hope we may induce the Count to join you and Charlie in a *partie carrée;* what fun and pleasure we should have, and then the delight of exchanging lovers at each bout. Oh! the very idea has set me on fire; fortunately, I am expecting my lover at every moment. I will close my letter with this lascivious picture, and in hopes of some day realizing it with my loved Lizzie,

Whose most affectionate and attached friend,

I shall ever remain,
CARRY EGERTON.

Such were these two charming letters, and I may immediately mention now that the lascivious picture dear Carry drew of a *partie carrée*—we four the actors—was afterwards realised to the utmost extent of every salacious enjoyment that the most experienced lubricity could suggest.

The Count and I often sandwiched them between us, which they declared to be the *ne plus ultra* of pleasure, while the upper operator gamahuched the unoccupied quim. Nay, these giddy delicious creatures were not satisfied until they had induced us to alternate the joys of coition with each other; but that was rarely the case. These enchanting women were so exquisitely seductive that, while we had them at our disposal, we sought no other source of delight. But I am digressing, and talking of events that occurred long after the period which I am more particularly describing.

The three weeks' absence of Mr. Benson terminated, alas, far too soon; in fact, time flew so quick that it hardly appeared three days when a letter arrived announcing his return for the next day. My heart was ready to burst, but I managed to make no show or mention when Mrs. B. told the news at breakfast. Mrs. B. observed that I turned pale, but no one else remarked anything. We contrived to meet for a short time in the middle of the day, and she embraced me tenderly, with tears in her eyes, and looking so loving that my passions became overexcited, and hers too. Notwithstanding, the imprudence of the risk, we there and then had a most delightful and salacious fuck; and at night this charming woman allowed me full liberty to do anything I liked; and as often as nature would support us we revelled in a sea of lubricity. How often I cannot say, although my loved mistress declared that I had spent ten times. I am certain she did oftener than that, for neither closed an eye, nor ceased from the most loving embraces. She exerted all the wonderful powers of seduction for which she was so distinguished. Never mortal man could have passed a more intoxicating night of pleasure.

We heard movements in the house before we parted with mutual tears coursing down our cheeks.

It was with difficulty I tore myself from her; indeed, I could not have done so if she had not herself risen, and tenderly embracing me, told me to have courage and hope, for, some how or other, we should manage an occasional interview. Particularly cautioning me to be perfectly on my guard when her husband came, she said it would be better if I kept out of the way until after the first interview was over, as it might be too much for me to see him embrace her. I did as she desired. No one noticed me in the confusion of his arrival.

Mamma had insisted upon my returning to my bed in her room, as she was sure Mr. Benson would require the dressing-room. Mrs. B., from policy, objected, saying that there was no occasion, that I had been so quiet she had never once been concious of my being there, &c., but mamma had her own way, and I really believe very much to the satisfaction of Mrs. B. herself; for I doubt, if Mr. B. had been aware of my close proximity, whether he would altogether have liked it. Nevertheless, he so completely treated me as little more than a child that I am quite sure he had no suspicion of my having occupied his place so continuously during his absence.

Mr. and Mrs. B. retired shortly after his arrival, doubtless to plunge into all the joys of venery after his long absence, and his wife's supposed privation of them. The idea of that being the case did not so much annoy me as I expected; on the contrary, imagination portrayed them in all the agonies of delight, and actually excited me extremely. All at once, the idea struck me that I might be purposely hid in the closet, behold all their delicious encounters, and when he had left his wife to put herself to rights, and the key was turned upon him, I might then in my turn, fly into my enchanting mistress's arms, and revel in all the joys her well moistened and juicy cunt could give. I determined to propose this to dear

Mrs. Benson the first moment I could get her apart from all observation.

I was a little *distrait* in the school-room that day, but an appeal from Miss Evelyn recalled me to my senses. She asked me what I could be thinking of; I held down my head and blushed. Already an adept in dissimulation, I faltered out that it was of herself and of her endearing caresses the day before, which had made me feel so queer all over. In fact, the previous day she had hugged me rather close to her, and kissed me more lovingly than usual, which really had, at the time, inflamed my desires, and given me great hope of matters coming to a more satisfactory termination with her. She patted my cheek, and kissed me again, saying I was a naughty boy to have any such thoughts, and I must not indulge in them, or she would not love me any more. But there was a sparkle in her eye, and a flush on her cheek, which showed me she was anything but displeased.

At our usual break-up at four o'clock, I went to the parlour to see if, by chance, I could get a secret word with Mrs. B., but found that she and her husband had again retired. I knew what that meant; it set me too on fire, and I flew to the garden where my sisters had gone to play. I gave Mary a hint, which she readily understood, and proposed a game of hide and seek. To prevent Eliza interrupting us, I took up a stone, which I furtively dropped again, and proposed that Eliza should guess first, in which hand I had got it, and if she guessed wrong she was to be the seeker. Of course, she guessed wrong. So we bound up her eyes, and she was to stand behind a tree and count one hundred before she attempted to look for or seek us. We made a detour, and as fast as we could run reached the summer house, which, as all the ladies were in the house occupied, I knew to be untenanted. We entered and locked the door, in an instant I had Mary down on her back on the sofa, my head between her thighs, and my tongue in her cunt, and then on her

clitoris. She was as eager for it as myself. A week had passed
since the happy day of giving up her maidenhead to me. She
had thoroughly got over all the pains and inconveniences of
that day, and was as ready for a renewal of what could only
be joys now as I was. She spent in my mouth almost as soon
as I began to gamahuche her clitoris. Waiting an instant to
lick up and swallow the soft and delicious young discharge,
I rose, pulled out my bursting prick, and engulphed it
in her well-moistened sheath with one rapturous shove up to
the hilt, positively taking away her breath by the energy of
the attack. I was almost as rapid in coming to a conclusion
as she had been. Nevertheless, she died away a second time,
the moment she felt the warm gush of my raging discharge.
We lay some minutes rapt in the lascivious lap of lubricity.
But in our young and unbroken energies, nature soon reas-
serted her power. I must give my sister the palm. It was the
internal pressures of the inner folds of her deliciously tight
cunt that first awakened my vigour. Somewhat more slowly
we began another love encounter, which speedily became
much more rapid and energetic, ending as usual in an extasy
of delight, and closing with actual cries of intense pleasure.

It was well we had completed our second course, for we
heard the footsteps of Eliza, who, after in vain searching
for us near to where we had left her, had at last sought us in
the summer house. I had just time to arrange my trousers and
unlock the door when she arrived and burst in upon us. She
said it was unfair to go so far away, but we only laughed, and
proposed that Mary should now seek us. We were standing
outside below the mound, tying on the handkerchief, when
Miss Evelyn was seen approaching. She came up and noticed
the flush still on Mary's cheeks, but we at once told her that
we had been playing at hide and seek, and had had a good
run, and that it was now Mary's turn to be the seeker. However, Miss Evelyn said she thought we had had enough exercise for the time, and that it would be better to walk gently

about to get cool, as it only wanted a few minutes of the hour for renewing our lessons, so we all demurely returned to the house. A reflection struck me that it would be necessary to initiate my sister Eliza in our secrets, and although she might be too young for the complete insertion of my increasingly large cock, I might gamahuche her while fucking Mary, and give her intense pleasure. In this way we could retire without difficulty to spots where we should be quite in safety, and even when such was not the case, we could employ Eliza as a watch, to give us early notice of any one approaching. It will be seen that this idea was afterwards most successfully carried out to the immense increase of my pleasure.

It was a lovely summer evening. After dinner Mr. B., who, doubtless, had no longer any amorous longing, after having twice retired during the day, challenged Miss Evelyn to a game at chess, of which she was a great proficient. Mamma, Mrs. B., and the two girls stepped out into the flower garden, to enjoy the beauty of the evening. Fortunately mamma fancied she felt chilly, and shortly went back again, taking the two girls with her, and setting Mary down to the piano. I seized the happy moment, and drew Mrs. B. to a seat, far removed beyond the hearing of any listeners, but in sight of the windows. There I unfolded to her the plan I had proposed to myself; she smiled at my precocious ingenuity, but added it would not be safe to leave the closet door open, even partially, as by chance Mr. B. might open it, and that would never do; but she might lock me in—or rather I might do so from the inside.

"Ahh! but then I want to see it all—it is so exciting to see Mr. B. working into that divine body of yours."

She laughed heartily at my remark, and said I was a lewd lascivious young rascal—adding:

"But are you not jealous to see another in possession of me?"

I admitted that that was my first impression, but on

thinking over it, I had become convinced I should like her and enjoy her all the more lasciviously if I were a witness to their love contests, but I must be able to see them.

"Well! can you not bore a couple of holes an inch and a half apart, below the middle panel, and cut a narrow slit from hole to hole? I will take care to place myself in a proper position, and do my best to gratify your premature lubricity. My darling boy, you progress wonderfully, and make me proud of my pupil."

Seeing she took it thus kindly, I said—

"Do tell me, my beloved mistress, how often he has fucked you to-day?"

"Will it please you really, my dear Charlie, to know that?"

"Oh! yes, so much."

"Well, then, six times in the morning, and four before dinner. He was bursting with desire, and could not hold. He spent twice before giving me time to come once, but then you know, my dear Charlie, how actively you had been employing your time all the previous night, you sad rogue that you are."

"Did you enjoy it much, my dear Mrs. B.?"

"Why, if I must tell you, you little curiosity box, I did; you know how powerfully my husband is hung, and loving him as I do, it is impossible to undergo his powerful and lascivious embraces without feeling all one's libidinous passions stirred up within me, but even while in his possession, my dear boy, I thought of your young charms, and the fierce delights we had enjoyed together last night. My husband little imagined it was of you, not him, that I was thinking and stimulating myself to wild upheavings of voluptuous movements, while he was revelling in all the lubricity of his own passions, and fucking me to my heart's content."

"Oh! how delicious! my angelic mistress," I cried, "the pleasure of your vivid description almost makes me faint with desire—oh! that I could possess you at once."

"You must not think of that, my dear darling boy, we must

manage it to-morrow; I shall go into the house at once, and occupy your mother's attention, do you get a gimlet and chisel, slip up at once to my bedroom, and prepare a peep-hole for to-morrow; be careful to put it low down, below the projection of the middle panel of the door in which the lock is placed, and take care to remove the pieces of wood you take out. I shall put the key inside of the door. Your sisters always take two hours at the piano after your midday meal, our luncheon is served at the same time. Mr. B. is sure to require my attendance in my room after that, but I shall detain him by some excuse till I observe that you have dis-appeared, and after giving you sufficient time, we shall fol-low, and you shall have the extraordinary satisfaction you require; but above all remember—not a movement to betray yourself until my husband leaves and I have locked the door behind him." So saying, she pressed her lovely hand on my stiffly excited member, rose and joined mamma. I lost no time in following her advice, and happily executed all I wanted, and returned unconcernedly to the drawing-room, without my absence having occasioned any remark. Next day I got safely to my hiding-room, and had comfortably stowed myself away in such a position that the opening I had made was on a level with my eyes, before they arrived. She, dear creature, anticipating my vista, had merely slipped on a dress, without a corset, and told her husband that he was so insati-ate that she was obliged to be ready at a moment's notice to satisfy his inordinate passion, so she had only to take off her gown to be at her ease. "Most admirable, my darling wife, but drop off every thing, and let me contemplate, at my ease, all the beauties of your exquisite body."

No sooner said than done, and my lovely mistress stood in all the glory of her magnificent and beautiful naked form. He kissed and fondled her from head to foot, laid her on the bed and gamahúched her till she squealed again with plea-sure. Then pulling out his magnificent prick, he plunged it into her delicious cunt at a single bound, evidently giving her the most exquisite delight, as was evidenced by the instantaneous clasping of him with her arms and legs, and the rapid wriggling of her backside. They soon ran a first course, but Mr. B. remained engulphed in the closely fitting sheath of his salacious wife. She evidently exerted herself more than usual, both for her own pleasure as well as to give satisfaction to me, for once when she turned her head in my direction I caught her eyes, and she smiled, giving a still more vigorous heave than usual, and showing me all her cunt at full stretch with the noble prick in it. I was ready to burst. At last their bout was over for the present; Mr. B. withdrew his prick, all slimy from its sheath, pendant, but still full of size.

Most extraordinary! I would have given a good deal to have dared to rush out, put it in my mouth and suck it dry, I can hardly describe how strongly this desire took possession of me. It was the first promptings of a passion I have since often indulged in, where I have met with companions with whom I could join in orgies of both sexes. Mrs. B. professed to be dead beaten by the constant and frequent renewals of these interviews in addition to night work and lay perfectly still, while he performed his ablutions and readjusted his habiliments.

"Fasten the door after me," said he, as he ardently pressed her form in his arms and kissed her. She had continued stretched on the bed, exactly facing me, with legs widely extended, so as to show me the whole of her lovely cunt, which I could see still panted under its late excitement. My charming mistress told me it was palpitating not for what had passed, but for what it was waiting for. She rose at last and closed the door, turning the key upon her husband. She then approached the bidet to purify herself, but I bounded from the closet, seized her in my arms, dashed her back on the bed and immediately glued my lips to her glowing and foaming cunt, with all the froth and spending of her husband

oozing out. I greedily devoured it, and raised her to such a
frenzy of lewdness that she dragged me up and cried, fran-
tically—

"For God's sake fuck me—fuck me!"

Of course my cock was bursting to do so; with one shove
he was sheathed to the cods; my loved mistress spent with
that alone, so highly was she excited, not only by the preparations, but as she herself acknowledged to me, by the idea
of the instantaneous infidelity to her husband, at the moment
after he had just fucked her—such is the wild imagination
of women when they give way to every libidinous thought. It
would have been exactly the same if some equally fortunate
lover had been awaiting my retiring from the field. The idea
of success in deception is a passion with them, and they
would almost sacrifice any thing to obtain it. Before I could
arrive at the grand crisis, she was again ready, and we died
away in an agony of blissful lubricity—she held me, as usual,
so tight that I never thought of withdrawing from the folds
of her delicious cunt, but lay still enjoying the never ceasing
compressions of its velvety folds, which sometimes really had
almost the force of a vice. I was rapidly ready for a second
bout, which, like the first, ended in extatic joys, beyond the
power of description. My charming mistress thought I ought
now to desist, but pleading my forty hours' fast (for, of course,
she knew nothing of my fucking Mary), I begged her to
allow me to run one more course.

"Then, my darling Charlie, you must let me turn on my
side, for I am so heated with your weight and my husband's
that I must have some relief, but there is no occasion for you
to withdraw, leave me to manage it."

With an art quite her own, she accomplished her object,
her splendid buttocks' pressing before my eyes against my
belly fired me immediately. My cock swelled and stood firm as
ever. Then passing an arm round her body, I used my fingers
on her excited and stiffly projecting clitoris. We had a much

longer and more voluptuous fuck than before; nothing could exceed the delicious movements of my divine mistress; she twisted her body so, that I could suck one of her bubbies, while I fucked and frigged her; she spent with such a scream of delight that I am sure she must have been heard in the house, had it not been for the inner baize door to the room. She continued throbbing so deliciously on my prick that I began to flatter myself I should obtain a fourth favour, but she suddenly bolted out of my arms and out of bed. Turning round, and taking my whole prick into her mouth, and giving it a voluptuous suck, she said—

"No, my loved boy, we must be prudent if we mean to have a repetition of these most exquisite interviews. You have given me most extatic pleasure, and by moderation, and running no risk in too long indulgence of our passions, we may safely manage to enjoy similar interviews every day. Get into the dressing-room, remain there until I leave my room and pass your door. After I have seen that no one is near, I will cough twice, wait a minute longer, then quietly leave and descend by the back stairs."

All was happily effected, and for the week longer they remained with us, I found means to repeat the charming lesson every day, without raising suspicion in any one's mind.

At last this admirable woman departed. It was with difficulty I could bear the scene, but I gulphed down my feelings as best I could. She had become a universal favourite, and all regretted her leaving, so that my distress was not noticed in the general regret. It was more than two years before fortune favoured me in again meeting with this charming woman. And then we saw very much of each other, both alone and with other congenial spirits, of which, perhaps, I may hereafter write a detail; but at present I have got events to relate that followed fast on her departure.

I have said that Miss Evelyn had been gradually growing more familiar in her manner of partially caressing me. She drew me closer to her, almost invariably placing her arm round my waist, frequently kissing and pressing me against her firm and well-formed bosom. This had frequently an evident effect on my lower person, even while I was kept less excitable by the constant relief my passions were obtaining in the arms of my adored Mrs. B. Now I no longer had that vent, for the little relief I could get at rare intervals from my sister Mary was as nothing, after the constant exercise I had been provided with for a whole month. Ever since I had practised that little deception on Miss Evelyn by attributing to her embraces the evident distraction I was in on the day of Mr. Benson's return, she had increased her pressures of my person, and could not but feel my stiff prick throbbing against her thigh, while she closely pressed my body against it with her arm. I often noted the increased sparkle of her eyes and changes of colour on her face when she kissed me, and I put up my hand and caressed her cheek. At times she would push me suddenly away, and beg me to resume my seat; frequently she would quit the room in an agitated manner, till this led me to suppose that an internal conflict was going on, and that passion urged one course, reason another. Remembering the sage advice given to me by my loved and beautiful mistress, Mrs. B., I resolved to play the part of an innocent ignoramus, and let her own passions develope and produce the result I so longed for. I doubt if I could have held out but for the relief I found in dear Mary's embraces, who, each time we could manage to meet, became more and more attractive, and more capable of giving and receiving pleasure. We had some difficulty in keeping Eliza blind to our doings. At last Mary agreed to initiate her into gamahuching, and to tell her I did so to her when we shut ourselves up together, and that if she would keep the secret, I would do the same to her; but that it was necessary that one should keep watch while the other amused herself with me, for fear Miss Evelyn should chance to come. Mary proceeded to gamahuche her, which delighted

Eliza beyond measure; indeed, although a year and a half younger, she speedily showed a developement of passion superior to Mary. At first I only gamahuched her, letting her play with my prick as I did so, but not attempting to instruct her in the art of insertion into her charming little quim, which already showed symptoms of a hairy growth on her well-formed and very prominent mount. When I had done enough in this way, Mary, who had previously been fucked by me, returned, and Eliza took up the watch, while I appeased in Mary's deliciously tight cunt the thirst that gamahuching Eliza had raised.

It was thus I could more coolly await the gradual approximation that Miss Evelyn's evident passion for me was bringing about. That she struggled against it was evident, but passion was gaining the advantage, as was shown by her nervous tremblings and sudden clutches, drawing me up to her parched lips, and sometimes pushing me away with a shudder that shook her frame and paled her lovely cheeks. I fancied that nature had been too much for her on these occasions, and that in reality the sudden clutching was the approach of love's crisis, and that when she shuddered, and suddenly repulsed me, she was discharging. It was evident this could not continue. At last the happy day for which I so longed arrived. Mamma was going to go to the town, and taking my two sisters with her, to get something or other for them. She invited Miss Evelyn to accompany her, but the latter declined, on the excuse of an alleged headache. In truth, the violent nature of the conflict going on between her passions and her prudence had visibly affected her health; she had become pale and anxious-looking, and my mother was somewhat uneasy about her. She told her not to occupy herself too much with my lessons that day, and only give me work for an hour in the morning and an hour in the afternoon, and begged her to take a quiet stroll in the garden, and rest as much as possible.

On leaving us, she cautioned me to be as gentle and obedient as possible, as Miss Evelyn was poorly and out of spirits. Mamma and the girls departed. Miss Evelyn, almost as pale as death, and quite visibly trembling, falteringly begged me to go to our school-room and study the lesson she had given me the previous evening, saying she would join me shortly. I went, but no lesson could I do that day. The evident agitation and apparent illness of Miss Evelyn distressed if not alarmed me; I was still too inexperienced in her mind. It was a phase of woman's nature which I had as yet no knowledge of. I had merely a vague kind of idea that it all tended to the ultimate gratification of my libidinous hopes, and I only held off to a certain extent in obedience to the counsel my loved Mrs. Benson had so wisely impressed upon me, and was waiting in lively hopes of the result I so ardently wished for.

At last Miss Evelyn joined me, her eyes were swollen and red as if she had been weeping; my own filled with tears when I saw her, and I approached, hesitatingly, and said—

"Oh, my dear governess, I am so grieved to see you look so poorly. Oh, do nothing to-day, and I promise to work twice as hard to-morrow."

At the moment I really felt quite distressed at the sad expression of her features. For an instant she smiled languidly, then, by some compulsion of feeling, she seized me in both arms and drawing me to her bosom, covered me with kisses; her eyes became almost perfectly brilliant.

"Oh, you dear, dear, darling boy, I love you beyond expression. Kiss, oh, kiss me! my darling! and comfort me, because I love you all too well."

Then, again, there was a change, she seemed to fear she had said too much, and turned away her head and tears started to her eyes, but her arms did not relax the embrace in which she held me. I was deeply moved at her evident agitation. I thought she was really ill, and suffering greatly;

so I threw my arms round her neck, kissing her tenderly, and weeping myself, tried to comfort her in my inexperienced way, sobbing out—

"Oh, dear, dear Miss Evelyn, do be comforted, I so dearly love you that it makes my heart bleed to see you so unhappy. Oh, let me see you smile, and do try not to cry so. Why are you so unhappy and low spirited? Oh, that I could do anything to make you happy?" And redoubling my endearments, she again turned her lovely face to me. Again there was the unnatural fire in her eyes, and a hectic glow flushed her cheek.

"You darling angel of a boy; it is *you* that makes me so unhappy."

I started back in surprise.

"*I* make *you* unhappy! Oh! Miss Evelyn, how can that be, when I adore the very ground you stand on, and love (*sobbing*)—love (*sob*)—love you more than anything in the world."

She seized my head in her two hands, glued her lips to mine, gave me a long, long kiss of love; then, pressing me to her bosom—

"Oh, say that again, my loved, my darling boy; it is the love I feel for you that is breaking my heart, but I can resist it no longer. Will my Charlie love his Evelyn always as he does now?"

"Oh, how could I do otherwise? I have worshipped you from the first moment of your arrival, and have had no other idea. What can I do to prove it—try, oh, try me. I have never breathed a syllable of my love for you, even to yourself, let alone other people."

Her eyes, sparkling with passion, were searching the depths of mine, as if to fathom my thoughts. I, too, began to feel my amorous passions excited by her warm embraces and kisses. She held me tight to her body, and could not help feeling the hard substance that jutted out against her.

"I believe you, my Charlie, and will trust you with my life—with more, with my honour! I can no longer resist my fate. But, oh! Charlie, love me always, for I run a fearful risk in loving you as I do."

She again drew me to her lips, my hands clasped her neck in a close embrace. Her hands wandered—pressed upon my throbbing prick. With trembling and hasty fingers she unbuttoned, or rather tore open, my trousers, and her soft fingers clasped my naked instrument.

"Oh, I shall die, dear Miss Evelyn; what must I do to make you happy?"

My apparent ignorance could not but please her. She sank back on the long low chair on which she was seated, apparently accidentally drawing up her petticoats with her hand in falling back. I threw myself on my knees, and pushing her petticoats further up disclosed the rich, dark, curly beauty of her mount. She covered her burning face with her hand, while, pressing my head forward, I began pressing her beauteous cunt, sucking it without daring to lick her clitoris. She tried to push me away—"No! no! I must not."

But I suppose my proceedings fired her passions still more, for she was quite moist and juicy, and I have no doubt had already had one discharge while embracing me so warmly. She suddenly said—

"Come then, my loved boy, and I will be all in all to you."

Drawing me up—nothing loath—I was soon extended on her belly, with my stiff-standing cock pressing against her cunt. I had still the prudence not to show any knowledge of the act. I sighed deeply—

"Oh! my loved Miss Evelyn, do help me, I know not what to do."

Her hand glided down between us, she guided my glowing instrument between the longing lips of her delicious cunt. I pushed, and buried the head and two inches of its body at the first thrust. The second brought it against an unexpected obstacle, for it never had struck me that Miss Evelyn was a virgin. I pushed hard at it.

"Oh, Charlie, love, be gentle, you are hurting me very much."

Knowing that the best way would be to excite her by short shoves, without at first trying to go further, I did so, and she began to feel all the raging desires that so formidable a prick as mine must excite, when moving between the soft velvety folds of her tight and juicy quim. I held myself in, and continued my proceedings until the convulsive movements of her loins, and the increased pressure of the folds of her cunt, showed me that the crisis was approaching, and she was about to spend. She hugged me close in her arms, and at the moment of spending involuntarily heaved up her bottom. This was the very moment I was with difficulty waiting for. I retired a little and plunged forward with irresistible force. I burst my way through every barrier, up to the very roots of my prick. The attack was as painful as unexpected. Miss Evelyn gave a shriek of agony and swooned away. I at once improved the opportunity, and thrusting in and out with the utmost vigour, broke down every obstacle, and enlarged the opening by side movements as much as possible, while she was insensible to the pain. I then died away myself in an agony of delight. I lay soaking within the delicious sheath until her convulsive shudders and short sobs showed that my now fully deflowered mistress was recovering her senses. The thought of the unexpected victory I had won had already begun to make my cock stand again, although it was still comparatively soft. I could feel an involuntary pressure on it, as she came to a full consciousness of our position. She threw her arms round my neck, gave me a most impassioned kiss, and then sobbed and cried as if her heart would break.

It is a curious idiosyncracy of my nature to be most libidinously excited by a woman's tears, and although I really suffered to see her in such grief, it stiffened my prick to its utmost dimensions. I tried to comfort her with words, but she sobbed, sobbed on. I suddenly thought that a renewal of action might bring about a revulsion of feeling, and began vigorous movements. She sighed deeply, but I could tell by the nervous twitchings of her loins that her passions were being excited. They soon decided the contest. She threw her arms round my waist, and pressed me to her, devouring my mouth with her kisses. Nature prompted her movements, and in a very few minutes we both poured down a plenteous offering on Venus's altar. She shook and trembled as she felt the warm gush within her, and squeezed me with all her might to her bosom. We lay in a trance for some ten minutes, my charming governess fainting with love, and giving my delighted prick the most luscious pressure, which speedily fired him to new efforts. Miss Evelyn herself was most amorously excited, and we again dashed on love's delicious path—to end, as usual, in the death-like swoon of satiated passion. When we came to our senses, my loved mistress, embracing me tenderly, and throwing her eyes up to heaven, said—

"Oh, my dear darling boy, you made me suffer horribly at first, but I have been in heaven since. Oh, how I love and adore you. But we must rise, my Charlie, we may be discovered. We have, in fact, run great risk, as the door has not been fastened.

I rose, and withdrew my prick from her reeking quim, which seemed by its close pressure to let me go with regret. I found it was all bloody.

"Stop, Charles, let me wipe it with my handkerchief, lest it stain your shirt."

She did so, and folding it up and placing it in her bosom, said—

"I shall keep this precious relic as a memorial of the sacrifice I have made to you, my loved boy. Ah! Charlie, you cannot yet understand the value of that sacrifice and the risk of ruin I have run for your sake. I love you as I never loved anyone before, or can ever love again. My honour and happiness are now in your hands, and it is on your discretion they rest. Be careful never to exhibit any liberty of conduct towards me or to mention to anyone what has occurred."

It may readily be imagined I gave her every assurance on that head, and told her I loved her too dearly, and was too grateful for the extatic happiness she had taught me how to enjoy, for any chance of betrayal to take place through my indiscretion. She embraced me tenderly, told me to go straight to the garden, that she must seek some repose after all that had happened, and we should meet again at midday meal.

I did as desired, full of sweet thoughts at the exquisite delights she had afforded me, and already longing for the afternoon school hour to renew the enrapturing union of our souls and bodies. Miss Evelyn did not come down to her luncheon, but had something sent up to her room. However, she joined me in the school-room at two o'clock, as usual. She was very pale, but embraced me tenderly, and was very endearing. Of course, I immediately became excited, and very enterprising, but she gently repulsed me, and requested that I would leave her quiet that day, as she felt not only exhausted, but in pain, and would be all the better for perfect repose. I begged hard to be allowed some slight favours, if not all, but she was inexorable. Finding that I could neither do any lessons nor be quiet, she said—

"Then we must go into the garden, I think the fresh air and a gentle walk will do me good."

It instantly occurred to me that if I could draw her away to the summer house, I should have a better chance of succeeding in again enjoying her delicious embraces. Accordingly, when she went up to her room to put on her bonnet and shawl, I possessed myself of the key, to be prepared for any chance of success.

We walked about the flower garden for a time, Miss Evelyn

taking my arm, and most lovingly conversing with me. She walked somewhat stiffly. We sat down for a rest, shortly she felt the heat of the sun too great, so I proposed a walk in the shaded shrubbery. I kept prattling on, so as not to let her see how far I was leading her away, she appeared surprised that we had got so far, when we came in sight of the summer house.

"Oh! Charlie, my dear, I am afraid it will fatigue me too much to walk all the way back without rest and we have not the key."

"Sometimes it is left in the door, I will run and see." Off I bounded, slipped the key in the lock, and ran back to say it was there, she followed me in, and sank on the long backless sofa, which had already served me so often. I begged her to extend herself at length. I placed pillows for her head, and drew a chair for myself near her. She did not appear to have any suspicion of any act on my part, but lay down on her side. She took my hand in hers, and we began a conversation, very interesting, in as much as it was how we should regulate our conduct, so as not to raise any suspicion of our amorous connection, and also of how we should manage to meet from time to time.

"You, dear boy," she said, "I cannot now live without the comfort of your embraces, but you must remember, in my dependent position, discovery would be my ruin. I rely on your silence and discretion, and if I am as dear to you as you, my adored Charlie, are to me, I may safely trust to you." I threw my arms round her neck, and told her I loved her all too dearly, and longed too much to return to her endearing and delicious embraces, for her to have any fear of my committing either her or myself. She fondly embraced and kissed me. I became fired with passion. My hand wandered, her position only enabled her to make a feeble resistance, I reached her beauteously covered mount, she murmured supplications to be left alone, and held her thighs close together.

She was not aware of my knowledge of the parts, so inserting my finger into the upper part of the lips, I reached her clitoris, and began rubbing in and out, purposely, in an awkward way, but taking care to hit the right point.

"Charlie, my Charlie, you must not do that—I—I cannot bear it."

At the same time she threw her arm round my neck and drew me to her lips, which glued themselves to mine. I felt her thighs yield and open. I immediately improved the occasion, and began frigging her with my middle finger up her quim. Her passions became inflamed.

"Come then, my darling boy, to my arms, I cannot resist you longer."

In an instant I was unbuttoned and had my trousers down, and was between her legs almost before she had concluded her sentence. The excitement of my caresses had moistened her juicy cunt, and the head of my prick entered without any difficulty. In my ardour I was about to rush on with a vigorous shove, when she implored me to be more gentle, as she still smarted from our morning encounter. Moderating my movements, and gently insinuating my stiff instrument, I gradually made my way up to its utmost limits, and hardly occasioned even a grimace of pain. Here I stopped, leaving it sheathed up to the root, and making it throb from instant to instant. Then seeking my loved Miss Evelyn's mouth, our lips and tongues met. Her arms round my waist became tighter in their embrace. The delicious folds of her luscious juicy quim began to throb and press on my excited member. Allowing her to become thoroughly excited, I waited until she actually quite unexpectedly yielded down her nature, and spent profusely, to the exquisite pleasure of my saturated organ. I still held all off, to give her time after the delight of that spend, which was probably the first of unalloyed extatic pleasure she enjoyed; for as I was an inactive participator, there was nothing to cause any action on the still raw edges of her

broken maidenhead. Her internal pressures were most exquisite. Our embraces with tongues and lips were like the
billing and cooing of doves, and very rapidly brought her
again to a raging point of desire. I then began with slow and
gentle movements, drawing my prick slowly nearly all the
way out, and then as slowly driving it up to the hilt. Her
previous very copious discharge had so oiled the delicious
folds of her cunt, that no pain was felt, only the intense
pleasure. At last it became overpowering; her arms were
thrown round my waist, and her legs were involuntary cast
over my hips. Nature prompted her to the most delicious
movements of her bottom; she met my forward thrusts, and
responded to them in the most libidinous manner.

"Go on, go on, dear Charlie—faster!—faster!"

I wanted no spur. Fast and furious grew our movements,
until at last, with a mutual cry of delight, we sank in each
other's arms in the blissful extasy of the most complete enjoyment. It was several minutes before we regained our
senses, and both our organs of generation were pulsating, the
one within the other, in all the luxury of satiated passion.
With her beauteous legs still thrown over mine, she moved
her arms to my neck, kissed me voluptuously, and mingled
the sweetest accents of gratification with the most endearing
caresses and flatteries. I lay, as it were, in the paphian bower
of bliss, in a state of exquisite sensations quite impossible
to describe. It seemed even a greater pleasure than the more
active state of delight we had been to. I could have lain so
for hours, but for that excitable prick of mine, whose sensibilities were far too rapidly set in motion by the luscious
pressures of that most delightful cunt in which it lay engulphed. It had gradually resumed its pristine firmness, and
was now at full stand, throbbing impatiently for further
combats. I began to move. Miss Evelyn said—

"Oh, my Charlie, you must cease, my dear boy; we must

not only be prudent, but consider your youth and health. Do, oh! do! my dear boy. Oh!—pray cease."

Her words were cut short by the increasing passion that the vigorous movements of my prick occasioned to her whole system. She could resist no longer, but with arms and legs closely embracing me, and devouring me with kisses, she threw herself into the fight, and with body and soul so seconded me that we died away in screams of delight, and sank quite insensible in each other's arms.

It was many minutes before we recovered speech. I still lay entirely embedded in her most exquisite cunt, and would have liked to have continued in her delicious embrace. But Miss Evelyn so imploringly beseeched me to cease for this time, and pointed out how necessary prudency was, if we ever wished to meet again, that I felt compelled to raise myself from her body. But, in doing so, I slid off downwards, and before she could prevent me, I glued my lips to the open pouters below me, and greedily devoured all her delicious discharge, and did not desist until I had so licked her clitoris as to make her spend most copiously again. At first she had tried to resist, saying—

"Charlie, what on earth are you at? You must not, my dear boy, it is dreadful."

But, as I roused her passions, her hand, instead of trying to draw away my head, held it firm and pushed it well against her throbbing and delicious quim, her thighs closed against the sides of my head, and she almost swooned away with the extasy of her discharge. I greedily swallowed it and rising completely, took her in my arms, and placing her on her bottom, sweetly kissed her.

"Oh, what a charming creature you are, my beloved Miss Evelyn, I adore you from the sole of your feet to the crown of your head."

"But you, my beloved Charlie, have more than justified my imprudence. You have given me a joy which I could never have dreamt of. I am yours, body and soul; do with me as you like. I, too, adore the very ground you tread on."

We continued exchanging the sweetest vows of affection, until, seeing my prick rising to its usual stiffness, she said—

"Oh, my darling, you must put this away; it would be most imprudent to continue any longer. Now, let me button it up."

First stooping and kissing it, she put it into my trousers with some difficulty, buttoned me up, and we strolled towards the house.

Our conversation turned on our chance of fresh encounters. She begged I would not think of attempting anything of the kind next day, and she would try and arrange for the day after, although my sisters were terribly in the way.

I suggested she should keep me in as when she flogged me, nay, indeed, she should flog me in reality if she liked.

She laughed at my idea, but said something might be done in that way as a blind. So I said—

"I will neglect my lesson on purpose to furnish an excuse."

"We shall see—we shall see. Meanwhile, remember to be very prudent."

We reached the house; she retired to her room until mamma returned. Very kind inquiries were made, she said she had suffered severely from headache, but, on the whole, felt better and hoped that a good night's rest would put her all to rights. We all retired early, both mamma and the girls were tired with their drive and shopping. I had resumed my bed in the little dressing-room, and went to sleep with thoughts of my delicious day's doings, to dream of re-enacting them with every amorous excess that the utmost lubricity could suggest.

The next day Miss Evelyn began to resume her former looks—the struggle was at an end. She was very gentle in her manner, and seemed even more affectionate than usual to my sisters, who, fancying she was not very well, were attentive, rather trying to anticipate her wishes than following them.

There was rather a greater appearance of reserve than previously in her manner to me, but when I went up to her to repeat my lessons, there was a warmer clasping of my waist and a suppressed manner that showed she was restraining her desire to press me to her bosom. Her face slightly flushed, and she turned her beautiful eyes upon me with such an endearing expression of affection that I could have thrown myself into her arms but for the check upon my ardour which her own reserve imposed upon me.

Nothing more took place between us that day. At our usual hour of recreation, from four till five, Miss Evelyn retired to her room to repose after the efforts of restraint that she had put upon herself all day, and left us to ourselves. I need not say an immediate resort to the summer house followed. There, first deliciously fucking Mary, and then gamahuching Eliza, with the addition of gently introducing, at the same time, a finger a short distance up her quim, I finished off with another voluptuous fuck with Mary. I thus was enabled to bear the bridle Miss Evelyn put upon the indulgence of my appetite in her person, and was apparently more reasonable than in reality. She again, on the second day, failed to give me the opportunity I so longed for. Thinking she might hesitate, from fear of discovery, and the fact of having no apparently reasonable excuse of being alone with me, I determined to play the idler next day in the afternoon. On being called up, I had done nothing. Miss Evelyn looked grave, but blushed deeply at the same time.

"What do you mean, Charlie, by this idleness? Go, do your lesson, or I shall be obliged to punish you."

She took me by the arm, and gently pressed it as she told me to resume my seat. At four o'clock, of course, my lesson was as far as before from being done.

"Mary and Eliza, you can go into the garden. Charles will remain until he finishes his lesson, or is punished for his idleness."

They left and Miss Evelyn locked the door after them. Then we flew into each other's arms, and indulged in the most endearing caresses for a very few seconds. I had been in a state of most violent erection for some time, so that my hand was up her petticoats immediately. I gently pushed her back on her low long easy chair, and kneeling in front, first thrust my head between her thighs, and taking a glance at her beautifully haired cunt, already all moist and juicy, showing that she was as ready as myself, I gamahuched her until she spent in my mouth, and sucked the delicious liquid most greedily. There was something peculiarly sweet in her spend, and my tongue sought the innermost lining of her delicious quim as far as its limited length would admit, that I might not lose a drop of her exquisite nectar, worthy indeed of the gods. The excitement I occasioned her was almost too much for her to bear, she drew me up, saying—

"Oh! Charlie, my angel of a boy, come, oh, come to my arms." I raised myself up, threw myself into her arms, and in a moment I was engulphed up to the cods in her exquisite and throbbing cunt; she closed upon me with arms and legs, we were both too violently excited to pause for any of the more voluptuous movements of less violent desires, but rushed on in passion's wildest extasy, both far too eager to think of any restraint, and with the utmost vigour on both our parts, we ran our first course with great rapidity. My adored Miss Evelyn had quite got over every feeling of pain, and could not but be delighted with the heat and vigour of my attack. We both died away together, at the extatic moment pouring down a mutual flood of spunk to cool the inflamed members that had the instant before been in such tumultuous action. Darling Miss Evelyn hugged me close to her bosom, and threw her beautiful eyes, screaming with passion, up to the ceiling, as if to thank heaven for the joys she had felt. Our lips then met and glued themselves together in one long, long kiss of love, which quickly lighted up our lust; she was as eager as myself, and we had another vigorous encounter, ending in all the agonies of delight, as before. Then after a longer interval of the most endearing caresses and fond accents of murmured love, we ran our third course, with more *abandon*—lengthening out our exquisite sensations, by slower and quicker movements and pauses between—in which my beautiful governess began to develope an art in which she shortly became even superior to the more experienced Mrs. Benson, who had so charmingly initiated me into love's mysteries.

There was a peculiar charming and endearing softness in the manner of Miss Evelyn most winning and most exquisitely attractive. It was evidenced even in her mode of handling my prick; without grasping it, her hand appeared to pass over it hardly touching it, but in so exciting a manner that after any number of encounters, she could raise it by her fairy touch in a moment. Our third encounter lasted quite half an hour, and when we sank in the death-like luxury of discharge, our whole souls seemed to exude with the exquisite distillation of our seed. We had long before regained our senses. I was still engluphed in her delicious cunt, but she begged me to relieve her of my weight. We rose, she shook her petticoats down, and assisted me to arrange my trousers. I then sat down and took her on my knee. Our lips met in a mutual warm kiss of gratified passion. She thanked me for the joys of paradise I had given her—and for my discretion in procuring an excuse for our meeting. She acknowledged that she had been as impatient as myself, but was obliged to take every precaution against raising the slightest suspicion in the house.

"You must always remember, my darling boy, that for me discovery would be my ruin for ever. I risk every thing to possess you, my beloved boy, I would care little for discovery, if it would not also separate us for ever. That idea, my adored Charlie, is insupportable, I can no longer exist without you." Here she threw her arms round my neck, and burst into tears.

I have already described the effect of tears on my unruly member, which, while I was consoling and vowing eternal attachment to my loved mistress, burst from its bonds and stood out in all its glory. I took her soft and beautiful little hand, and laid it on it. She grasped it tightly, and looking at it, while smiling through her tears, said—

"My Charlie, what a great big thing it is. I wonder how it could ever get into me, without killing me."

"You shall soon see that," said I, and changing places, I laid her down, lifted her petticoats and was into her in a moment. She begged me to proceed slowly, and to lengthen out our pleasures as much as possible. We had a most glorious and truly delicious fuck; my lovely and charming mistress giving me most extatic pleasure by the exquisite pressures of the internal folds of her delicious and lascivious cunt.

We lay enraptured for long after we had spent, and then resumed our sitting position, and arranged every thing in order, as the time for the return of my sisters from their hour of recreation was close at hand.

Our conversation naturally turned upon how we should arrange for our next meeting. Miss Evelyn insisted that we must not think of meeting more than once in three or four days, as otherwise we might raise suspicions fatal to our meeting at all. However reasonable this was, I raised an outcry against such a tantalizing delay, and begged hard for a shorter period between our intervals.

"It cannot be my darling boy, remember discovery would separate us for ever. By prudence, we may long continue these delicious meetings." I suddenly suggested that as I slept alone in the little room, which, when the spare room was unoccupied, was far away from every one, she might steal along at night, when all were asleep, and thus I could enjoy the whole of her exquisite charms, without hindrance. She did not reply, but I could see her eye sparkled, and her cheek flushed as if already in imagination she was revelling untrammelled in all the luxury of voluptuousness such a plan opened out. However, she did not at once accept, but kissing me fondly, called me her dear and ingenious boy, and said she would think over my suggestion. We resumed our lessons on my sisters' return. Miss Evelyn was again four days before she gave me another opportunity of an amorous meeting. It was only my purposed insubordination that obtained me this interview. We again indulged in all the luxuries of carnal enjoyment, as far as could be done, incommoded as we both were by dress and locality. Reverting more strongly than ever to my plan of meeting in my lonely room, I begged so hard that at last she promised to come the night of the following day. I was obliged to put up with this, although I would fain have had her come that very night, but as her passions were evidently gaining stronger possession of her, and she was becoming more loving, and more voluptuous than ever, I felt certain she would not disappoint me on the next night. The delicious idea of revelling in charms I had so often furtively gazed on, kept me away from my sisters next day. Under a plea of headache I went early to bed, and took up some oil, to oil the hinges and lock of the door, to be prepared for my loved mistress. I lay long awake, and was almost in despair of her coming, when I heard the clock strike twelve. All at once I became aware she was at my bedside. She had entered the room with so gentle a step that though on the watch for her, I did not hear her even when she opened the door, shut, and locked it. She had come in her dark-grey cloak, and when at my bedside this was dropped on the floor, she stood in nothing but a very fine and thin chemise. She flung herself in my arms, as I rose to embrace her, and we instantly sank closely clasped in each other's arms. I was far too sharply set to practise any preliminaries. I turned her on her back, and was into her in a moment, with one vigorous thrust, which almost took away her breath, and gave her intense delight. I was too quick for her, however, as I spent in two or three

shoves into that delight-giving cunt. But as this hardly allayed the fires of my too ardent desires, the convulsive
internal movements of her unsatisfied orbit quickly restored
my scarcely reduced member to a renewed vigour. Miss
Evelyn being greatly excited by the unsatisfying nature of my
first bout, was extremely warm, and throwing her arms and
legs around my body, we again rushed headlong into all the
fury of fucking, and as my previous spendings had somewhat
reduced the power of immediate discharge, I was able to suit
my movements exactly to those of my most active companion,
and we sank together in all the voluptuousness of satisfied
desires, lying long locked in each other's arms, before we
were again in a state to renew our combats in love's delicious
domain. We spent the interval in whispered vows and fond
endearments and embracings of each other's naked charms,
both of us admiringly passing our hands over every part of our
bodies.

Miss Evelyn at last concentrated all her attention on my
well-developed member, which she most endearingly embraced and fondled tenderly, very quickly putting him into an
ungovernable state of erection. I was lying on my back, and
she partially raised herself to kiss my formidable weapon; so
gently putting her upon me, I told her it was her turn to do
the work. She laughed, but at once mounted upon me, and
bringing her delicious cunt right over my prick, and guiding
it to the entrance of love's grotto, she gently sank down upon
it and engulphed it until the two hairs pressed against each
other. A few slow up and down movements followed,
when becoming too libidinous for such temporizing delays,
she sank on my belly, and began to show most wonderful
activity of loins and bottom. I seconded her to the utmost, and
finding she was so excited, I slipped my hand round behind
and introduced my middle finger in the rosy and very tight
orifice of her glorious backside. I continued to move in and
out in unison with her up and down heavings. It seemed to

spur her on to more vigorous actions, and in the midst of short gaspings and suppressed sighs, she sank almost senseless on my bosom, I, too, had quickened my action, and shot into her gaping womb a torrent of boiling sperm.

We lay entranced in the raptures of satiated desire for a long time. At last she came to her senses, and fondly kissing me, turned off, and we lay side by side closely embraced.

"Oh! my beloved Charlie, what exquisite delight you have given me; you are the most delicious and loving creature that ever could be created. You kill me with pleasure, but what was that you were doing to my bottom? What put such an idea into your head?"

"I don't know," I replied. "I put my arm round to feel the beautiful globes of your bottom, and found in grasping one that my finger was against a hole, all wet with our previous encounters, and pressing it, found that my finger slipped in; you gave it such a delicious pressure when in that the idea entered into my head that, as it resembled the delicious pressure your enchanting other orifice gives my shaft when embracing you, this orifice would like a similar movement to that which my shaft exercised in your quim. So I did so, and it seemed to add to your excitement, if I may judge by the extraordinary convulsive pressures you gave my finger when you died away in all the agony of our final rapture. Tell me, my beloved Miss Evelyn, did it add to your pleasure as much as I fancied?"

"Well, my darling Charlie, I must own it did, very much to my surprise; it seemed to make the final pleasure almost too exciting to bear, and I can only account it a happy accident leading to an increase to pleasure I already thought beyond the power of nature to surpass. Naughty boy, I feel your great instrument at full stretch again, but you must moderate yourself, my darling, we have done enough for to-night. No, no, no! I am not going to let him in again."

Passing her hand down, she turned away its head from

the charming entrance of her cunt, and began handling and feeling it in apparent admiration of its length, thickness, and stiffness. Her gentle touch did anything but allay the passion that was rising to fever heat; so sucking one of her bubbies, while I pressed her to me with one arm under her, and embracing her on the other side, I passed my hand between our moist and warm bodies, reached her charming clitoris, already stiff with the excitement of handling my prick. My titillations soon decided her passions, and gently prompting her with the arm under her body, I turned her once more on the top of me. She murmured an objection, but offered no resistance; on the contrary, she herself guided my throbbing and eager prick into the voluptuous sheath that was longing to engulph it. Our movements this time were less hurried and more voluptuous. For some time she kept her body upright, rising and falling from her knees. I put my finger to her clitoris, and added to the extatic pleasure she was so salaciously enjoying. She soon found she must come to more rapid and vigorous movements, and lying down on my belly embraced and kissed me. Toying with our tongues I put an arm round her waist, and held her tight, while her glorious buttocks and most supple loins kept up the most delicious thrust and pressures on my thoroughly engulphed weapon. I again stimulated her to the highest pitch of excited desires by introducing my finger behind, and we both came to the grand crisis in a tumultuous state of enraptured agony, unable to do ought, but from moment to moment convulsively throb in and on our engulphed members. We must have lain thus languidly, and deliciously enjoying all the raptures of the most complete and voluptuous gratification of our passions, for fully thirty minutes before we recovered complete consciousness. Miss Evelyn was first to remember where she was. She sprang up, embraced me tenderly, and said she must leave me at once, she was afraid she had already stayed imprudently long. In fact, it was near five o'clock in the morning. I rose from the bed to fling my arms round her lovely body, to fondle and embrace her exquisite bubbies. With difficulty she tore herself from my arms. I accompanied her to the door, and with a mutual and loving kiss we parted. I to return and rapidly sink into the sweetest slumber after such a delicious night of most voluptuous fucking.

She came again three times in the next six nights; each time we renewed our mutual joys, with ever increasing voluptuous indulgencies. On coming to me for the fifth time, she said—

"Dear Charlie, I have only come to kiss you, and say I cannot stop."

"Cannot stop!" I cried, "and why not, beloved Miss Evelyn?"

"I am not well, but cannot explain more."

I had sprung out of bed, and clasped her in my arms, then passing a hand down to her beauteous and well-covered mons Veneris, I found that she was tied up there in cloth. I immediately remembered how my loved Mrs. Benson had been exactly in the same way. I then also remarked the peculiar odour of breath, but pretending ignorance, I begged to know what had happened to my darling little grotto.

"I cannot tell you more, my dear boy, but it will keep me away from you for four or five nights."

"But why should that be the case; cannot you let me enter that delicious cave of delight only once?"

"No, no, impossible! my dear Charlie, absolutely impossible! It would do me very great harm, and you too. Let us be quiet in that way, and I shall be the sooner well again to come and embrace you as before."

"Oh! but darling, how can I support five nights' absence, I shall go mad with desire and burst—feel how he grows, and is longing for his loved companion."

Her soft and gentle hand caressed it. I thought to succeed by a *coup de main,* but she was too quick for me.

"No, Charles, I am serious, and you must not try to force me, or I shall never come near you again."

I saw she was in earnest, and flung myself on the bed in a pet.

"Come, my darling Charlie, be reasonable, and I will do my best to give you some satisfaction. Lay yourself on your back —so. I will kneel on the floor at right angles to you, because you must not attempt to touch me down there. That is a dear boy."

So taking my prick in her soft hand, she gently moved it up and down; then, suddenly stopping, took it into her mouth, sucking as much as she could get in, and titillating the knob with her tongue, while one hand frigged at the root of my prick and the other gently handled my two crisped-up cods. She prolonged the pleasure by occasional pauses, and at last, on finding the electric-like sensations coming, she hastened her movement, and I poured a torrent of sperm into her mouth. She continued her delicious sucking until not a drop more was left for her to swallow. This was the first time she ever gamahuched me, but it was not the last by scores of times. Ever after we improved upon the model, and added other endearments. When not under her courses, we mutually gamahuched each other, and she was the first to repeat upon me, with the intensest gratification, the delicious introduction of a finger behind while gamahuching me. At present, when she had thus taken the edge off my carnal appetite, she lovingly embraced me, and left me to my lovely slumbers. Of course, the four days' grace, saving two more passing visits "to keep me cool," as she said, turned all to the advantage of my sisters, whom I fucked and frigged to their utmost gratification and delight.

I thus passed about four months, Miss Evelyn becoming a perfect adept in love's delicious mysteries; but, although I had attempted to enjoy the orifice of the lower temple of Venus, my member was too large, and gave too much pain, to completely succeed, so that I became the faithful worshipper at the more legitimate altar of love. My sisters were gradually developing their forms. Mary particularly so. The hair on her quim had increased to a most charming curling profusion. Her hips spread out, and her bottom, hard and prominent, promised to be very large. Eliza, too, began to show increased bubbies, and an enlarged and mossy mons Veneris.

We were approaching summer, and near the full of the moon, Mary had complained of feeling very low spirited, and very much inclined to cry. I tried to comfort her, and thought success would best attend my efforts if I fucked her. So enticing her down into the garden, we entered the summer house, and I at once proceeded to action. She was rather unwilling, she could not say why, but had an instinctive reluctance. She yielded, however, to my entreaties, and I fucked her without apparently exciting her in the usual way. I consequently withdrew as soon as I had run the first course, and at once discovered what ailed poor Mary. My member was covered with blood. For the first time her courses had come upon her. She was greatly alarmed, but I told her I had heard it was quite natural to young women when they reached a certain age, that she had better tell mamma at once, who would instruct her what to do. I carefully wiped my reddened member, and then retired to my room to purify myself. That very night, on Miss Evelyn coming to me, I found she was exactly in the same state. She gave me my usual relief with her soft hand and caressing lips, and then left me for five nights, as at that time.

I now found myself reduced to my dear little sister Eliza. Up to this time I had never actually fucked her, and her maidenhead was still intact. She was now approaching fourteen, and the down on her charming little cunt was becoming more decided; her bubbies too, under the erotic excitement of my *attouchements* and gamahuching, had assumed a decided prominence. My finger had somewhat rendered the opening of her little pinky slit more easy of access. So I resolved to complete her carnal education and fuck her thoroughly. The opportunity was perfect; both Miss Evelyn and Mary retired to their rooms to lie down at our usual hour's recreation, Eliza and I at once hied to the summer house, and locked ourselves in. I immediately laid her down on the long couch, and gamahuched her until she spent in my mouth, and then continued until she was again almost mad with desire. I then told her I should initiate her into a new mystery, more delicious than any she had yet experienced, but that the first initiation was always painful.

"Oh! what is it, my dear Charlie, everything you do is so nice, I know I shall like it—what is it?"

"Then you must know, dear Eliza, that this little cunt of yours is made for the express purpose of having a prick put into it; only, as mine is so large, and you are still so small and so young, I was afraid it would give you too much pain to do it sooner; but now, I think, I may get it in, if I do it gently."

"Oh, Charlie, dear, put it in at once, I have often felt I should like it so; but, as you never attempted to do it, I thought it was a mere fancy of mine. Have you ever put it inside Mary's quim?"

"Often; nay, always, my darling."

"Does she like it?"

"She adores it."

"Then put it into me directly, Charlie."

I wanted nothing better, and told her that in order to thoroughly enjoy it, she must strip. In a minute she dropped off everything, while I took off my trousers—coat and waistcoat having been already laid aside. I had brought a towel to lay on the couch below her bottom, to prevent any telltale stains. Laying her down on her back, with her bottom close to the end, her legs gathered up, and her two feet resting on the sofa, with her knees falling outwards (in the very best position for my intended operation), I put a pillow on the floor, on which I knelt, thus bringing my cock a little above her quim to give me a good purchase. I then first gamahuched her well again, until she spent and cried out—

"Oh, put it in, my dear Charlie, I do feel to want it so!"

She was already well moistened by her previous discharges, and by my licking the lips of her cunt, and covering them with saliva, with which I also, at the same time, wetted my prick itself. I then made the point approach the charming pouting and longing lips of her sweet little cunt, and rubbing it first up and down between the lips, proceeded to insert its knob between them. Thanks to the precautions taken, and the excitement I had raised by my previous caresses with tongue and prick, the immediate entrance was effected with greater ease than might have been expected. No sooner was it in about an inch beyond the knob than the passion of excitement I had raised so stimulated the natural lubricity of Eliza's nature that she heaved up her buttocks energetically, letting her knees drop quite down sideways, thus favouring to the utmost my forward thrust made at the moment, so that my prick was sheathed in an instant more than half his length, and but for the obstacle of her maidenhead, which he then met with, would have been entirely engulphed. As it was, it gave her a very sharp pang of pain, which made her shrink back, and utter an—

"Oh! Charlie!"

"Do not fear, I will be gentle, keep still a moment and then you will find the pain pass away, and great pleasure follow."

So we lay still for a time, until I felt those involuntary internal pressures, the true precursors and infallible indicators of rising desires; so commencing a slow and continuous in and out movement, I shortly produced such an excess of pleasure in her delicious orbit, that her movements became almost furious, and nature alone prompted her to second me

with as much art as if she had already been long instructed
in the delicious movements so calculated to add to the libidinous delights of true enjoyment.

But Eliza was a rare example of a truly salacious and
voluptuous nature, and proved herself in that way far in
advance of Mary; although she was of a very warm temperament, Eliza's passions were far more excitable, and in the
end she became one of the most voluptuous fuckers possible, abandoning herself to all the wildest raptures that the
most erotic nature could suggest. Of this, hereafter; at present I had worked her up to the utmost pitch of excited
desire; she was in the very act of discharging, and as I
withdrew for a final thrust, she heaved up her buttocks in an
agony of pleasure, I felt it was now or never, and striking
home with all my force, I burst with irresistible strength
through every obstacle, and tore my way inwards, until
sheathed to my very cods. Poor Eliza! at the very moment
she thought herself in the seventh heaven of delight, she
experienced the most excruciating agony. She gave a piercing
cry and fainted away; her arms fell senseless from my body—
her legs would have also fallen, but twining my arms round
them, I continued for several successive thrusts to penetrate
fully and easily into every recess, for I myself was wound up
to a fearful state of excitement. I died away in an excess of
joy, sending a torrent of balmy sperm to soften and mitigate
the pain of her terribly torn quim. Finding that Eliza could
not regain consciousness, I rose somewhat in alarm, and was
horrified to see the quantity of blood that followed my withdrawal. It was fortunate my forethought of the towel, as it
had not only saved the sofa, but helped to stanch her swollen
and bleeding quim, and to wipe the blood from her thighs
and bottom. I had effected all this before the dear girl showed
the least symptoms of animation. She first sighed, then shivered, and at last opened her eyes, and looked confusedly at
me, and asked—

"What has happened to me, Charlie?"

Then observing how she was lying naked, she recovered her complete consciousness of all the circumstances of the case.

"Oh! Charlie, now I know; I thought you had killed me; Charlie, oh! it was so frightfully painful. How could you hurt me so, and just as I thought it was the most heavenly pleasure I had ever experienced in all my life."

"My darling, it is all over now, and it will never hurt again, and we shall both of us have greater pleasure than ever, but not just now; it has been greater pain to you than I thought it would be, and for the present we must not attempt any more." I helped her to rise, but she felt very faint, and I had great difficulty in getting her dressed. She was shocked to see the bloody state of the towel. I told her to put my handkerchief between her thighs, and partly up her slit, to prevent any marks of blood staining her shift. I then laid her down on the sofa, while I ran to get some water from the fountain in the garden. I took a glass and the towel with me. I returned with the water, which greatly refreshed Eliza. I begged her to lie still as long as she could stay. However, when she attempted to walk, she found herself very much incommoded with the smarting pain. I was terribly afraid lest this would be observed when we got to the house, so I suggested she should purposely fall down when in sight of any one, and say she could not move because she had hurt her knee by the fall.

This stratagem succeeded admirably. We were seen approaching by Miss Evelyn, my mother, and Mary. Dear Eliza acted her part admirably, was seen to fall heavily, and screamed. They all rushed out, we lifted her carefully on her legs, and supported her to the house, she complaining of the pain in the knee and ankle. My mother insisted on her going to bed at once, and having embrocations and hot towels applied. Eliza let them do as they liked, and eventually was left to quiet repose, which soon relieved the painful sensations she had undergone. Next day she complained of great stiffness, and walked lame, but thought the hot applications had prevented the swelling, so thus happily passed off all observations of suspicion of the real circumstances of the case. It was not until the third day after that I attempted to make an entrance. Of course, I excited her first to the utmost by a long continued gamahuching. She then let me, but with fear and trembling, introduce my bursting member into the delicate folds of her cunt. As I was very gentle in my movements, the pain was scarcely felt, and when once well sheathed, and the first thrusts given slowly and luxuriously, the whole lubricity of her nature was soon awakened, and by the time I was ready to spend she was as ready to second me, and we died away in a mutual flood of delighted extasy. She held me close, and would not let me withdraw.

"No, Charlie, it took some trouble to get it in, let it stop where it is so deliciously engulphed," and at once anticipating her natural desires, she began the most exquisite pressures upon me, which very shortly brought us both up to the point of demanding more active measures. However, I rather restrained her, and told her we must retard our movements to increase our pleasures, because mere quick repetitions would only exhaust her, without yielding the true extasies of enjoyment. I, therefore, taught her the pleasures of the slow movements, and I worked her up to spending point, without giving way myself. The dear little creature clung to me with the most close and endearing embraces, as if she should force a complete amalgamation of our two bodies, and died away in the sweetest bliss of contented desire, with such a heavenly expression of extasy on her face as made me devour it with kisses. I had great difficulty in restraining myself from precipitately following her example; her delicious movements at the moment of spending, and the close pressures on my prick, were so exciting that resisting them was quite a triumph of control. I succeeded, and lay quite quiet, embalmed in the delicious suction of those exquisite folds of her charming little cunt, which exercised the most delightful pressures as well as suction on my enraptured prick. I left it entirely to her to lie as we were as long as she pleased, or to again begin the dear delightful friction that should once more make us dash on passion's furious course, to end as usual in the ever delicious extasies of the final crisis.

This last bout had been a double one for my sister; she all but swooned away with the rapture my spending in unison with her produced. She declared it was a death of the most delicious extasy, which it was perfectly impossible to describe. She clung to me, kissing me in the most endearing manner, and telling me how happy I had at last made her by completing the insertion of my prick in her cunt. It was worth the suffering of twenty times as much agony to arrive at so exquisite a result as every fuck I now gave her conferred upon her. We adjourned to the flower garden, that we might be seen playing together, and not excite suspicion by our constant disappearance, now that we were only two together. Of course, Mary knew what we were at and probably guessed that I had completed the initiation of Eliza. She smiled, and gave me a significant pressure of the hand, when we met again in the school-room to resume our lessons. For two days more I enjoyed Eliza all to myself; at each new fuck she became more and more perfect in conferring as well as receiving pleasure.

On the third day, Miss Evelyn whispered, "to-night," as she gave me a stolen pressure of the hand. She came, and we indulged in every whim of our fancy. I had further the delicious pleasure of gazing on all her naked beauties, as it was daylight before we parted; I had gamahuched her twice, and fucked her five times. She gave me credit for a long fast, and allowed so much indulgence on that account, but told me I must in future be more moderate, for her sake, if not for my own. She allowed three nights to pass before again coming to me. I cannot say I regretted it, because now that Eliza was initiated, as well as Mary, we indulged in the most delightful orgies of fucking and gamahuching at the same time. At first we used to fuck with one laid on her back to be fucked, while the other backed on her knees over the face of the one being fucked, and was gamahuched by her, while I introduced my finger into the rosy orifice of the bottom before me. But we found the most voluptuous way was for one to lie down on her back, and the other on hands and knees over her. She thus brought her mouth over the cunt of the one lying down, and presented her bottom to me, who knelt behind her. The one below guided my prick into the cunt above her face; she had thus all the satisfaction of seeing our action, while with one hand she tickled my cods, and the other felt my bottom-hole, and inserted a finger. Meanwhile, she was gamahuched and bottom-frigged at the same time by the one I was fucking, and we used all three to die away in agonies of enraptured delight, to recommence with a change of places between the two girls. Sometimes I tried to introduce my prick into the rosy little orifice of Mary's backside, but, although the finger-frigging gave her much additional pleasure while her cunt was operated upon by my virile member, she as yet could not support the insertion of my large prick. I had not even attempted little Lizzie, but one day, when Miss Evelyn and Mary were again under menstruation, and I had dear Lizzie all to myself, she was seized with such an irresistible desire to ease herself, that she had only time to get behind a bush and squat down. I remained waiting for her, when she called to me, to ask if I had any paper. I advanced to give her some. She was in a half-standing position, with her clothes held up to her waist. While giving the paper, my eyes accidentally fell upon what she had voided. I was struck with its extraordinary thickness. I made no observation at the time, but it raised an idea that preoccupied me much. I had often thought over the pleasure that fucking Mrs. Benson's bum-hole had given me, hence I had tried to initiate both Miss Evelyn and Mary in that delightful route of pleasure, but, as before stated, had been unable to succeed with them from the great developement of my weapon. Thinking that if they could not bear the insertion, there could be no possibility of success with my younger and less developed sister, I had never attempted with Lizzie more than the insertion of one finger. It is true, with her it seemed to produce more excitement than either upon Miss Evelyn or Mary. The sight of the extraordinary dimensions of the matter she had voided now suggested the idea that if her apparently very small and rosy-lipped bottom-hole could allow so large a mass to come out, with gentle efforts my scarcely larger machine might be inserted. I determined to try the initiation into that route of delight the very next day. Remembering that dear Mrs. Benson always made it a rule that she should be first well fucked and gamahuched, and the prick well moistened, I began by exciting dear Lizzie to the utmost. I first fucked her, and made her spend twice to my once; then gamahuched her until she implored me to shove my prick into her. I had managed to introduce my two forefingers at once into her bottom, and had frigged her while sucking her cunt, without apparently giving any pain; on the contrary, from her movements I fancied she felt greater excitement. I took care to enlarge, as much as possible, or rather to stretch her bottom-hole as open as I could with my two fingers. It was at the moment of her greatest excitement, when she was pressing me to fuck her at once, that I said—

"My dearest sister, there is still another mystery of sensual voluptuousness that you have as yet not experienced or been initiated into, and I am about to instruct you in it."

"Oh, what is it? dear Charlie; but do anything you like, and as quick as possible."

"Well, then dear, it is this sweet little orifice in your bottom that I am going to introduce my prick into. It may give you some little pain the first time, but by gentleness of movement, and halting from time to time when it hurts too much, we shall get him completely inserted, and then it will be an immense pleasure to both of us."

"Dear, dear Charlie, do as you like, your darling prick can only give me the greatest delight; I am dying to have him into me, I don't care where, as long as I get the dear creature into me. I suppose I must be on my hands and knees."

Upon which she turned with great agility, and presented the two hard and already promising globes of her charming backside. I lost no time in first thrusting my prick up to the hilt in her cunt, to moisten it. It made her shudder again with excess of lust, and she exercised such a pressure upon it that I had some difficulty in withdrawing it. It was so snug and nice therein that it was a great temptation to run a course in her cunt at once, but having the other object in view, and knowing that I wanted all its stiffness to succeed, I did summon up courage enough to withdraw; then applying the very plenteous saliva in my mouth that gamahuching her had stimulated, I added it to the already moistened prick, and applying some to her bum-hole, and introducing a well-wetted finger, I put the knob of my formidable prick to the small and smiling orifice that lay before me. The disproportion struck me as so great that I dreaded success would be much too painful for her, but remembering the dimensions of what had come out of it, I boldly proceeded with the operation. I got in over the knob without making her flinch, but, as I proceeded to push gently forward, and had got in about two inches, she cried—

"Stop a little, Charlie, it feels so queer—I can't bear it in further."

I stopped where I was, but slipping a hand under her, I applied my finger to her clitoris, holding her bottom tight against me with the other hand round her waist, so as not to lose ground. My agile finger soon worked her passions up, and I felt her bottom give convulsive twitches on my prick. I allowed her to become still more excited, and then gently pushing forward found I was slowly, and almost imperceptibly, gaining ground. My prick was then inserted about two-thirds of its length, when, thrusting rather too sharply, she again cried out, and, but for the arm that held her fast round the waist, would have unseated me.

"Oh, Charlie, dear, do stop; it seems to choke me, and makes me feel so queer, that I thought I was going to faint."

"I shall lie quite still, now, dear Lizzie. It is quite in"—this was a little bit of deception to calm her fears—"and when the pain of insertion passes, which will be the case in a minute, we shall have nothing but pleasure."

So I kept my prick just where he was, but redoubled my frigging her clitoris, and very soon brought her up to spending point, resolved that I would not attempt complete insertion until I felt she was in the raptures of sensual discharge. This quickly came upon her, and it was the delicious movement of her own buttocks that sheathed my prick to the hilt without an effort on my part, and so far from giving her pain, made her positively scream with the intense voluptuousness of her sensation in spending. She could not speak for many minutes, but continued the exquisite pressures of the sphincter muscle on my enraptured prick. But for my determination not to give way, and rather to wait for another bout that would completely initiate dear Lizzie in all the luxury and abandon of this delicious mode, I must have at once vigorously finished my own course. My restraint was well rewarded. The first words my beloved sister uttered were those of almost delirious joy at the extraordinary delight I had given her. Never, never, had any fuck so enraptured her. She turned up her lovely face to me, and tears of sensuality and voluptuousness filled her eyes.

I had hardly begun my titillations on her still excited clitoris, which, by the way, had lately considerably developed itself, when she was as eager for another bout as I was. I held sufficient restraint on myself to practice every salacious movement, that I might give Lizzie such exquisite pleasure as should induce her on future occasions to grant me the use of her charming bottom-hole whenever I should desire. I worked her up to the utmost pitch of the most salacious excitement, and at the moment when she spent, in an agony of shrieking extasy, I poured a perfect flood of spunk right up into her entrails, and we both sank forward, but without unseating me, quite overpowered by the intensity of our delight. When we came to our senses I rose from off her. On withdrawing my prick I found a few traces of blood, but of no moment. I wiped my prick on my handkerchief, and also wiped between the cheeks of dear Lizzie's bottom, for fear any tell-tale marks should be made on her linen. I then helped her up, and she threw her arms round my neck, and sweetly kissing me, thanked me for a new lesson in love, which had overwhelmed her with delight.

Thus ended the first lesson that Lizzie ever received by that route of pleasure, and I may incidentally state that she was peculiarly constituted for giving and receiving the most exquisite pleasure in that way. She afterwards developed into a magnificent woman, with one of the naturally largest and finest backsides I almost ever met with; and she came to love backward fucking to the utmost extent. In after-days, when married, she told me that her husband was a *muff*, who had no idea of enjoying a woman but in one way. She had often deceived him, and slipped it into her bottom-hole without his ever having any suspicion of the sort of pleasure he had given her.

Three months passed with the rapidity of a dream, while we indulged in these scenes of delicious lubricity and voluptuousness, without ever attracting any observation within the house and, more curious, without Miss Evelyn either discover-

ing or suspecting anything between my sisters and myself—
thanks to my natural powers and the unfailing resources of
youth. Both she and my sisters thought they each gave me as
much as I could get through, and, therefore, neither ever
imagined I could seek carnal delights in other arms. So it was
but now there happened one or two events which had a considerable effect on the after-tenour of our loves.

A neighbour, a very nice good-looking man, about thirty-
five years of age, a gentleman farmer, very well off, had for
some time past always waited for us at the church door on
Sundays, apparently for a chat with mamma, Miss Evelyn, and
us. He treated and evidently considered us as mere children,
nor did he appear to fix particular attention to any one.

One Monday my mother received a note from him, to beg
she would grant him a short interview on the following day,
as he wished for her advice on a subject of much interest to
him. Mamma's reply begged him to come at eleven o'clock,
when she would be happy to see him.

He came, and was particularly neatly dressed. My mother
had been very agitated all the morning, and looked flushed
and nervous as the hour drew near; I really believe the old
lady fancied it was for an idle avowal to herself that he was
coming. Be that however as it may, the object of his visit
turned out to be a proposal to Miss Evelyn, with an offer of
marriage. He was ready to make such settlements upon her as
could not but be satisfactory. He told my mother that before
speaking to Miss Evelyn, whom he had loved from her first
appearance in the parish, and whose quiet, modest character
had daily made a deeper impression, he thought it only his
duty to first break the subject to her, and to ask her permission for an interview with Miss Evelyn, and next, if he was
acceptable to her, for leave to visit at our house, while courting
his wished-for wife. He further stated that he had never ventured to hint the state of his feelings to Miss Evelyn, and
prayed my mother to be the kind intermediary in opening the

subject to her, and to beg as a favour that she would grant him an interview to state his case in person on the following day, so that he might learn his fate from her own lips. My mother, although probably inwardly a little disappointed, had the interest of Miss Evelyn too much at heart not to take up the matter warmly, and urged, with all the volubility elderly ladies can so well exercise, whenever the marriage of a younger friend is in question, all the benefit that would accrue to her from so advantageous a proposal. Miss Evelyn was really taken quite by surprise, and stammered out some vague expressions of wishing for time to consider.

"Stuff and nonsense, my dear, remember your dependent position, and the advantages this match holds out to you. You must not think or talk of delay. He will be here to-morrow, and I hope his lover eloquence will soon decide the question in his favour."

Poor Miss Evelyn burst into tears and said it was so sudden, and she was so ill-prepared to take any decision. She would, however, think over it very seriously and in the morning be better able to give an answer. My mother seeing that she was much agitated by what she had told her, very kindly said—

"Give the children a holiday this afternoon, and I advise you to keep your own room, and write to your widowed mother, to tell her of the offer, and to ask her advice how you should act."

We thus had many hours to ourselves; I had heard all that had passed, and felt a sad pressure at my heart, when I began to realise the fact that the proposal of Mr. Vincent would, if accepted, lead to our separation, and deprive me of my loved Miss Evelyn. The idea made me very sad, and I showed no alacrity in taking advantage of our extra hours of recreation with my sisters, until Mary began to rally me about my melancholy, and asked what I meant by it. I at once said—

"Don't you see, if Miss Evelyn marries Mr. Vincent we shall get another governess, and can we ever expect to get one who is so kind and excellent a teacher, and who troubles us so little at our *games*."

"Ah! that is very true, and we should be horribly annoyed if we were watched and interrupted. However, more reason that we should make the most of the present moment, so come along, Charlie, and let us have some real good fucking. We have plenty of time, mamma is not very well. No one will come near us, and there is nothing to hinder our having a jolly time of it, all three stark naked together, so come along."

Her words had already changed the current of my ideas; before she ceased speaking my prick responded, which her quick eye immediately observed, and patting it with her hand, she said—

"Ah! my dear little dummy, I am glad to see you are of my opinion, so come along."

Away we went, and a most glorious afternoon of orgies we spent.

Miss Evelyn came to me at night and threw herself into my arms, in an agony of sobs and tears, and pressing me to her throbbing bosom, she sobbed out—

"Oh! my dear Charlie, I love you so dearly, you have become as necessary to me as life itself. I cannot bear the thought of parting from you, my loved one. You, whom I have initiated into all the delights of mutual love. Oh! the thought of parting is bitter, and breaks my heart. Oh! love me, my own darling boy, and press me to your heart."

I did more, for, as I have before stated, a woman's tears have a never failing effect on the erective nerves of my machine. It was but the commencement of a night of most luxurious enjoyment. Miss Evelyn put no restraint either on herself or me, but indulged in every act of lubricity and voluptuousness that her salacious passions could suggest, as if she already felt that these delicious nights of *abandon* and voluptuousness were drawing to a close. In fact, when eventually she left me in the morning, and I thought over all she had said, it became evident to me that she had already made up her mind to accept the very advantageous offer made to her. The instinctive intelligence of woman had at once shown to her that such an opportunity was not to be lost for the sake of a mere boy, whom circumstances must naturally soon remove far away from her. At the same time, doubtless, the idea that I was all her own making, for she never had any suspicion of my previous initiation, held a charm over her, to say nothing of the powerful weapon she had so unexpectedly found by her side, and which had so great an influence over her passions. We spent a most luxurious night, and hardly closed our eyes, notwithstanding my afternoon's debauch; such is the power and resources of nature, in a well-constituted youth of fifteen and upwards, that Miss Evelyn had rather to force our embraces, than to stimulate by any artificial excitement my ever ready prick. I won from her a promise to come next night, and let me know what fate was in store for us.

Next day Mr. Vincent was true to his appointment, mamma received him with Miss Evelyn by her side, and after the usual compliments, rose and apologised for leaving them, as she had household duties to attend to. Miss Evelyn informed me afterwards that Mr. Vincent, on my mother leaving the room, rose from his seat, and approaching her, said, in the most frank gentlemanly manner—

"You are aware, my dear Miss Evelyn, of the object of my visit, and I augur from your kind condescension in giving me this interview that my suit is not disagreeable to you."

Then taking her passive hand, and pressing it to his heart, he continued—

"I have loved you, Miss Evelyn, from the first moment of my seeing you. I feel that my future happiness hangs on your lips, for without your love, my life would now be a blank. I am here to-day to offer you my hand and fortune. If I have not yet your heart, I seek to be allowed to cultivate your society, that I may try to win it."

Then seeing that she was greatly agitated, he begged her to be seated (for she had risen when he approached and took her hand), he led her to a sofa, and seated himself by her side. He pressed for an answer. She said—

"You must be fully aware, Mr. Vincent, that your generous offer has taken me greatly by surprise. I feel most grateful to you for it, but must implore you to allow me to pause, until at least I have heard from my mother, to whom I will communicate the noble offer you have made to me, a poor governess, who cannot but feel grateful to you for condescending to think of her in such a way."

"Ah! say not so, my dear Miss Evelyn, and believe me, it is no sudden impulse that has driven me to your feet, but ardent love, and real admiration of your great beauty and admirable conduct ever since you entered this family."

The dear creature smiled through her tears upon me when she recounted those terms of affection that Mr. Vincent poured out to her.

To be brief—before they parted he won from her that his frequent meetings at church, and elsewhere, had gained him something more than esteem, but hopeless of ever becoming his wife, she had done her utmost to suppress warmer feelings. Oh! woman, thy name is deception! So she sent him away the happiest man in existence. He rode over every day afterwards, and was with Miss Evelyn from four to five; indeed, he was often the cause of our having half an hour's longer recreation. He also frequently dined with us. Miss Evelyn's mother naturally jumped at the offer, and most delightedly gave her consent.

When Mr. Vincent heard of this, be became very urgent in claiming an early day for making him the *happiest of men*. Miss Evelyn wanted a delay of six weeks, but this raised such an outcry on his part, seconded by my mother, that at last she was driven from six weeks to a month, and then to a fortnight from that date; so all became extremely busy in getting ready marriage dresses, &c. The marriage was to take place from our house, and my mother insisted that she should provide the marriage breakfast. Mrs. Evelyn was invited to our house for a week at the time of the marriage, to keep my mother company. My two sisters and a young sister of Mr. Vincent's were to be the bridesmaids, and a young man, courting Miss Vincent, to be bridegroom's man. So all was thus arranged, and eventually came off most happily. When Mrs. Evelyn arrived she occupied the spare room, where charming Mrs. Benson had so deliciously initiated me in all the pleasures of sensuality and passion.

To return to the day when Mr. Vincent had his first interview, and declared his love and admiration, and ended with the offer of marriage. Before going away, he rang for mamma, thanked her for all her kindness to him, informed her how happy Miss Evelyn had made him in granting permission to prosecute his suit for her hand, &c. Then begging the favour of a chaste kiss, he left all radiant with hope.

The interview had natually been very trying for Miss Evelyn, and she was so evidently nervously agitated that my mother begged her to go to her room, and lie down to repose herself, as after so much agitation she must be quite unfit for any school work, and that she herself would hear our lessons that morning and give us an afternoon's holiday in honour of the happy event that had occurred.

We thus, my sisters and I, were thrown again into another prolonged opportunity of fully enjoying ourselves, but, notwithstanding the wonderfully regenerative power that nature had gifted me with, I felt that if I wanted to enjoy again my dear Miss Evelyn, who had promised to be with me that night, I must not only restrain myself from such excess as we had indulged in the previous day, but also manage to get some sleep, of which I had scarcely tasted the night before, so I contented myself with first gamahuching and then fucking each sister; afterwards again gamahuching them, and making them each spend five times, so as to satisfy them without exhausting myself, and then finishing off with a delicious fuck in Lizzie's bottom-hole, while each gamahuched the other. This quite satisfied them, and they allowed me to steal up to my room to sleep, Mary promising to call me in time for tea. I slept the sleep of the just for some three hours, and came to tea perfectly ready for anything that could happen that night. It was well it was so, for now that there could not be any long lapse of time before we must part, Miss Evelyn became a very glutton for pleasure, and every art and position was made use of to stimulate and lengthen out our joys. She came every night, even up to the very night before the marriage, although in the last three nights before the event came off, her mother, Mrs. Evelyn, slept in the spare bedroom with which my room communicated. Nevertheless, we met and carried on our amorous sports with bated breath and suppressed sighs.

We had of late often tried in our moments of greatest excitement to introduce my prick into her delicious tight little bottom-hole. Once, by a sudden manœuvre, I managed to get in at the moment she was spending, and actually made an entrance as far as about two inches beyond the nut, and I think I should have fully succeeded at that time if my own excitement had not made me spend too soon. This oiled the way, and my prick, having already fucked several times, becoming too limp, the squeeze of her bottom actually forced him out, as if she were voiding herself naturally. I fancied that, at the moment, but for my too excited passion, she would have rather I had completely initiated her. However, the night preceding her marriage, I at last succeeded. We had fucked in every varied way. She was on her knees, with her head on the pillow, and I on my knees, behind her; this was a favourite way of hers, as she declared I got further in, nay, seemed to touch her heart and fill her whole body; besides the frigging her clitoris and the action of my finger in her bottom-hole added

greatly to the raptures this position gave her. She had been already well fucked, and we had mutually gamahuched each
other, so her whole system was in a most excited and well-
moistened state. Taking care to put two fingers at once into
her bottom-hole, I worked them so as to stretch it as much
as possible, while exciting her with my prick in her cunt, and
a finger on her clitoris. Just as she was going into the raptures
of spending I dropped from my mouth a quantity of saliva
onto her bottom-hole, and as she was pushing her buttocks
back to me I suddenly withdrew my prick, and with one
vigorous thrust housed him half his length in her delicious
bum-hole. She almost cried out aloud at the suddenness of the
attack, and would have flinched away but for the grasp of
both my hands upon her hips; a more vigorous shove sent
me up to the hilt against her beautiful buttocks. She whispered—

"For heaven's sake, dear Charles, do stop a moment, I can't
bear it, and must cry out if you do not be quiet for a time at
least."

As I was safely fixed, it exactly suited me to remain still, for
had I gone on, a push or two would have made me spend.
Now fairly engulphed, I wished not only to fully enjoy it
myself but, if possible, make her enjoy it too. So remaining
quite still, as far as regarded my prick, I stole one hand down
to her clitoris, and began to excite that; the other I ran up to
her bubbies, and played with the nipples, a thing which I
had found out excited her almost as much as playing with her
clitoris. Her passions were soon reawakened, and the involuntary twistings of her loins and pressures of her sphincter
convinced me that in a very short time I should work her up
to the utmost; and so it was, and immensely she enjoyed both
her own spend and mine when she felt my hot spunk shooting
up into her very entrails. We sunk gently on our sides after
this bout, but without unsheathing me; and here embracing,
kissing and tonguing each other when she turned her head,

and sometimes sucking the nearest nipple to me, we soon once more were in a state to renew our delicious combat; and a second course was run in the delightful callipygian recesses of Venus's second temple of lubricity. This was our last bout, for, alas, it was getting the hour when the house would be all astir. My lovely mistress embraced me most tenderly, and acknowledged that I had at last taught her a new pleasure. She wept as she tore herself from my arms, and I wept too when she left me, as I thought I had now lost her for ever as a mistress, and what a charming one she had been to me!

Morning came, and with it bridesmaids, bridegroom, and man. To church we all went, my sisters perfectly enchanted with the idea of being bridesmaids, and beautifully arrayed in new dresses. They were also still more delighted with some handsome jewelry presented by Mr. Vincent. In their eyes he became the handsomest and finest man they had ever seen. The breakfast went off as usual, and when the bride, who had changed her bridal dress for a neat travelling one, came down, pretty near all were in tears on taking leave of her. She pressed me tenderly to her bosom, and whispered—

"Courage, Charlie, dear."

It was almost too much for me, but I managed to restrain any extreme demonstration of my grief. The carriage door was shut, and off they rattled to spend the honeymoon at Leamington. The friends assembled remained until the evening, and after the sensations of the day, and the fatigues of the previous night, I was glad to get to bed. I cried myself to sleep, thinking that another at that moment was revelling in all the delights of amorous enjoyment of those charms that had been so long in my sole possession.

Thus ended one of the most delightful episodes of my life, and although I, at some rare intervals, from time to time found an opportunity of enjoying my loved mistress, they were flying fucks, very delicious, but very unsatisfactory.

This was the first great incident that had an effect of chang-

ing the tenour of our existence for some time, but I will reserve the details of our after-adventures for a second part of
these reminiscences of Early Experiences.

END OF VOL. I.

Volume II
The Romance of Lust

◆(C◆(C◆(C◆(C◆(C◆(C◆(C◆(C◆(C◆(C◆(C◆(C◆(C◆(C◆(C◆(C◆(C◆(C◆(C◆(C◆(C

T he house was scarcely itself even the day after the marriage. Mrs. Evelyn was still with us, and did not leave until the following day. She and my mother spent most of the day in the summer house, so that our pastimes therein were interrupted. Mary complained of severe headache, which, in fact, was the premonitory symptom of her courses, which declared themselves violently in the evening. I had arranged with my sisters to steal up to their room when all were asleep, as now that we had lost our governess they had it all to themselves. I went, of course, but found only Eliza capable of entering into our sensual enjoyments. I made her come to me in Miss Evelyn's bed, and while fucking her, was thinking all the time of my darling governess; and even when I was fucking her I could only remember the complete insertion of my prick into Miss Evelyn's bum-hole the very night before her marriage, and wondered whether or not her husband had discovered her loss of maidenhead. And yet, I fancied woman's natural cunning would easily deceive him, as millions before him have been deceived. Coupling Mary's attack and Miss Evelyn's choice of the marriage day on the full moon, I could not help imagining that she intended to help her deception by the advent of her menstruation. It will be seen hereafter how far I was correct in my conjecture. I passed a delicious night in the arms of my charming Lizzie, and only stole away just in time not to be observed by the early-rising servants. Mrs. Evelyn departed the next day. My mother, feeling poorly, desired Lizzie to sleep with her, so perforce I had to pass a very quiet night, but which the agitation and excessive venery of the last week rendered very acceptable.

Another week passed without anything particular beyond Mary being able to join Lizzie and me in our orgies. The doctor had recommended my mother to go for a few weeks to the seaside, and she resolved that we should all go for six weeks before engaging a new governess. So we left town for a charming little retired village on the west Welsh coast. It was but a small place, with one street, and some straggling houses here and there, but with a beautiful stretch of sand ending in abrupt rocks. Our lodgings were but small; a sitting-room and bedroom above a shop, and two rooms over that. I slept in the small back room off the sitting-room, my mother had the front upper room, and my two sisters were in the room beside her, with only a thin partition between them, so we found ourselves obliged to seek for some outside place to enjoy the erotic pleasures that had now become necessary to us. Very few visitors ever came near the retired little village. In our explorations we found that at the far end of the sands there were some nice retired spots behind the rocks, which soon became the scenes of our sensual enjoyments. The place was more than a mile from the village, and we could see if any one was coming towards us for the whole distance; but still as we might forget how fast time flies, we prudently established either one or the other of my sisters as a sentinel to give us warning if any one was approaching. So I took them in turn, laid them down, had a mutual gamahuche, and then a fuck; after which the previous watcher took the place of the one just fucked, and the same process was followed in her case. We had done this for three days, and

were congratulating ourselves upon having found out so safe
a place to indulge all our propensities in. We always spent
the mornings with mamma, who kept us so far to our lessons,
but after our midday meal, which mamma also made her
dinner hour, she retired for a siesta, and we went out for a
long walk and something better. I have said we fully enjoyed
the first three days without any apparent chance of discovery.
On the fourth, while Lizzie was on the watch in front, and
Mary and I after a delicious gamahuche had just died away
in all the extasies of a prolonged fuck up to the moment of
discharge, and I was saying to her—

"Did not that feel delicious, and was it not up to the hilt?"

"I should think so, with such a rammer as that up her
cunt," said a strange voice close to us.

You may easily suppose how we startled with surprise.

"Oh, don't do that, I did not mean to spoil sport," said the
same voice.

It was a very gentlemanly man, with a soft quiet voice,
and charming amiable expression of countenance, who stood
smiling upon us close to our side, with his breeches open,
and his standing pego in his hand. So great was our surprise
that we never thought of the state we were in. Mary lay
with legs spread out, and belly exposed, and cunt gaping
open; and I with my breeches down, and my great big cock
pendent, it is true, but hardly diminished in thickness. The
stranger said again—

"I am not here to spoil sport, on the contrary, to aid you
in every way. I accidentally observed you two days ago. I
am here, a stranger, like yourselves. I know you to be brother
and sisters, and admire you all the more for being above the
usual prejudices of that relationship. But you must be
aware that as I know all about you, the best way is to let
me be a participator in your sport; and then you not only
shut my mouth, but it will be the means of vastly adding to
all your pleasures, as well as giving me the most intense

satisfaction. Now, for instance, your elder sister there, who was about to replace the younger on the watch, will be all the more satisfied, if I first fuck her. Don't be alarmed, my dear," said he, as he observed a sudden move of Mary, who all at once recollected how exposed her whole person was. "I shall do nothing without your full consent, but I am quite sure your brother, who takes you each in turn, will rather be pleased than otherwise, to see you in my arms, or I much mistake his character."

I could not help, internally, thinking how exactly be had hit off my very thought, for I had just been calculating, in my own mind, how much better it would be for us to make him a participator with us, rather than an enemy by a refusal. So I at once averred that as it had turned out, it was likely to add greatly to all our pleasure, and I begged Mary to let him have his way. The natural reluctance of woman to appear too easy of access made her simulate a refusal, but as she still lay on her back, I leant over her, and opening her legs, begged him to kneel between and help himself. He gallantly, on kneeling, first stooped forward, and gave a good lick-up of all her cunt's spunk-covered lips, and then proceeded to gamahuche her, which quickly made her as anxious for his prick as he was to fuck her. As soon as they were fairly at it, I whistled, and beckoned to Lizzie to come up. You may easily imagine her surprise to see Mary in the arms of a strange man; but as the sight had had its usual effect on my sensitive organ, and as it was standing, almost ready to burst, I made her kneel opposite to them, and introduced my prick into her cunt from behind, so that we could both see the delicious fuck going on before us. It redoubled our excitement, and all four of us spent together in cries of rapture. After this bout we sat down to make further acquaintance, which, you may suppose, was not difficult, after such an introduction. Our new friend gave us some hints very useful for future proceedings, meanwhile he was feeling young Lizzie's cunt with one hand, and my prick with the other, very nicely and gently frigging it. He brought me to full stand very quickly, and then made me lie on my back, while he proceeded to admire and praise the extraordinary developement which he declared was the greatest for one of my age he had ever met with, and his experience was very extensive. When it was at full stand, he stooped forward, and in the most delicious manner sucked my prick. It was more exciting than when either of my sisters, Miss Evelyn, or Mrs. Benson had gamahuched me. He also inserted a finger in my bottom-hole, and eventually made me spend in his mouth, which he greedily swallowed, nor did he cease sucking until every drop was drawn out of me. This had, of course, excited him, and he said—

"Now, I must have the young one in her turn."

Lizzie, nothing loath, lay down on the grass at once, I conducted his prick into her cunt, and frigged his bottom-hole, while their bout lasted. His prick was one of the middlings, not very long, nor very thick, but of a uniform size throughout, without any large projection of the nut, like mine. He advised us to stop for that day, and to walk towards the village with him, and then when in full sight, but far beyond hearing, we could sit down and concert measures for future pleasures of the most delicious lubricity.

"I see," he said, "that we shall just hit it. I shall greatly add to your pleasures, and you to mine; you have something yet to learn, and I am the very person to instruct you in even higher delights than any of you have yet enjoyed."

We followed him as desired, and, seated on a sand hillock, we held a long conversation, and arranged everything for future indulgencies. We agreed to meet at the rocks next day at our usual hour, he undertaking to be there ahead of us, to see that no lurking stranger should have hidden himself as he had done that day. He would think over the matter in the meantime, and contrive some way of meeting where we could be fully at ease, and strip ourselves naked, so as to enjoy a complete orgie of the most salacious lubricity. He showed us where he was lodged, a small inn a little way out of the village with its front to the road, and behind the stables there was attached to it a small cottage, consisting of a bedroom above, with a dressing-room, or small bedroom if necessary, over the passage; the door opened upon the coast, and there was no other communication with the inn than by going round past the stable yard to the front door. The servant of the inn came round in the morning, and laid his modest breakfast of tea, eggs and toast, and when he was done, cleared away and made his bed, &c. He took his dinner in the inn parlour at the hour the landlord and family dined. Nothing overlooked his windows, and he was sufficiently away from the village not to be easily observed, still less so from the inn; so that on approaching his lodgings from the sands he was almost as safe from observation as if he had lived in a lonely house far distant from any other. I am thus particular in describing his lodgings, as the advantages of the situation afterwards induced us to turn them to profitable use. Our friend's name was MacCallum, James MacCallum, an offshoot of the great Scotch clan of that name, then in about his thirtieth year, fond of sporting, particularly fishing. His room was surrounded with the necessary implements, and he much frequented Wales from its advantage of possessing so many good trout streams. He it was who gave me a taste for the piscatory art, and I afterwards accompanied him on many a fishing excursion, which often led to new and singular erotic adventures, of which I may, perhaps, hereafter recount a few. His ordinary residence was London, and our present acquaintance led to some most intimate relations of true erotic extravagance, of which more anon.

Meanwhile we met at the rocks on the next day, a Saturday. We found Mr. MacCallum at his post, and all being secure, proceeded to action. It was Mary's turn to take the first watch. Our friend constituted himself master of the ceremonies. He desired me to take off my breeches, and Lizzie to take off her gown and ease her corset, for as yet she wore no stays; then telling me to lie down on my back, he made Lizzie kneel at my head, with her bottom to me, and then to press back so as to bring her charming little cunt over my mouth, her under-petticoat and chemise being well canted over her shoulders. I thus had complete command of her clitoris with my tongue, and she could sink her buttocks quite down on my face, so that I could shove my tongue well up her cunt, and lick up all her spendings when she discharged; and at the same time, while embracing the charming plump hard buttocks with one hand, the other was left free to frig her bum-hole, and stimulate her passions up to the utmost. I have already told you how naturally she had taken to posterior pleasures. While thus engaged, Mr. MacCallum proceeded to gamahuche my prick in the most delicious manner, for he had an art in this delightful accomplishment that far exceeded that of the many by whom I have been gamahuched —of course, he added the *postillon,* as the French say, by frigging my bottom-hole at the same time. He made me most voluptuously discharge in his mouth at the very instant dear Lizzie was pouring into mine her delicious spendings. We lay enraptured for some time before we could stir. Then rising, I wished to return the compliment Mr. M. had paid my prick, by sucking his. But this he declined, saying—

"I shall teach you all a new pleasure before we part, and my powers are not quite so active as your youth enables you to be, so for the moment we will indulge in close observation and sweet caresses of our members until by gentle titillations I get you two more prepared for the amorous contest—"

He gamahuched Lizzie while handling my prick, and a very short period elapsed before he had us both in such a state of excitement that we were ready for anything he chose to direct. This time he also required me to lie down on my back, but he placed Lizzie on the top of me, and guided my prick himself into her delicious tight little notch. When fully inserted, which was completely accomplished before she quite lay down upon me, he desired us to go slowly to work. For a short time, with his face close to my cods, he watched the in and out movement of my prick, inserting a finger into both Lizzie's bottom and mine. Then rising, he said—

"Stop a little, my dears, but don't withdraw. I am about to give your sister a lesson in the double action of most delicious pleasure."

Then spitting on his prick, and applying a quantity of saliva to the rosy orifice of her bottom, he proceeded to insert his prick—little thinking how fond she was of taking pleasure in this route, and how often she had already enjoyed it. He took every precaution not to hurt her, and to be as gentle as possible, telling her to push out her bottom, and to strain as if she wanted to void something, which he told her would facilitate his entrance, and give her less pain. You may imagine how secretly pleased Lizzie was; she did all he desired—and with great gentleness he succeeded in sheathing his prick up to the close junction of his belly against her buttocks.

"Capital, my dear, you have borne it admirably. I see you will make an apt scholar; now you will have nothing but the most extatic raptures from the action of two pricks at once. Now, Charles, it is for you to work, and for your most charming sister to continue only the exquisite pressures she is already at this moment so rapturously conferring on our excited members."

We thus commenced the first lesson we ever had in the double fuck. Dear Lizzie was almost mad with the agonising sensations of rapturous pleasure the double thrusting produced upon her erotic nerves. I, too, felt the rubbing of Mr.

M.'s prick so closely upon mine, for the slight membrane dividing the bottom passage from the vagina, by the powerful stretching of the two members between which it was sandwiched, became so thin a division that it really appeared as if there was nothing between our pricks. Such extatic excitement brought matters to a speedy conclusion. Lizzie screamed so loudly with her excess of pleasure that it somewhat alarmed Mary, who came running up to see what was the matter. Her surprise was great at the sight she beheld, but we were far too deliciously wrapt in the lap of most salacious luxury and lubricity to be sensible to any interruption. As for Lizzie she was in convulsions of extasy, which ended in quite a hysteric attack which rather alarmed us, and made us withdraw from the exquisite sheaths in which we had been engulphed with such rapture. It was some time before dear Lizzie recovered her senses, and then she burst into tears, declaring she had never before known what pleasure meant, and she had been in the seventh heaven of delight, that she could wish for no better death than to die in such agony of pleasure. She then threw herself into Mr. M.'s arms, and kissing him with the utmost fervour, said—

"Oh, you dear man, how I love you for teaching me such a delicious way of loving; you shall have me whenever and wherever you please. I shall love you as much as I do my darling brother Charlie."

She then turned to me and warmly embraced me too. Then, putting on her gown, she proceeded to take up the watch, while Mary remained to be likewise initiated in the luxury of the double fuck. She somewhat dreaded the experiment, but having witnessed the extasies of pleasure it had thrown Lizzie into, she was not unwilling to try if it could be accomplished with Mr. MacCallum's somewhat less massive member. He put us through the same preliminary manœuvres of backing Mary on her knees over my mouth, and while he sucked my prick, he feasted his eyes at the same time on

Mary's really finely developed buttocks, giving him promise of great after-pleasure. He even begged me to leave her bottom-hole to his finger so that he frigged the bum-hole of the sister while he sucked the prick of the brother, a combination which afforded him the most racy delight. Mary was greatly excited, and spent most copiously in my mouth, while I quickly followed suit in the mouth of Mr. M., who did not allow a drop to be wasted. When we had reposed ourselves sufficiently, his lascivious touches and caresses and praises of our parts soon sufficiently re-excited us to let him see if we might again proceed to action. As before, I lay down on my back, and Mary, straddling across me, had my prick guided into her longing cunt by the hand of Mr. M. When I was fairly engulphed in her hot and throbbing cunt, she began her exquisite *casse-noisette* pressures, which talent she possessed in the greatest perfection; then bending down to me I clasped her in my arms, and glued my lips to hers in a loving kiss and tongue embrace. Her bottom presented itself in all its beauty to our worthy master of the ceremonies, who, delighted with its more fully blown beauties than that of the younger sister, paid first due homage to it by fondly kissing it, and thrusting his tongue up the rosy orifice, titillating her excessively, then wetting his prick he applied it to the tender rosebud-like dimple at first without success, Mary telling him she did not think he could possibly succeed.

"Patience and perseverance, my dear girl," said he, "will enable me to get into a mouse; we must try another way; it is that great huge monster of a prick in your cunt that is so blocking up the route as to close almost entirely the way to the more secret temple of salacious delights. Withdraw for a moment."

I did so; upon which he plunged in an instant up to the hilt in her cunt and gave a few shoves to excite her and throw her off her guard, for he told us afterwards, the first difficulty was all owing to Mary's involuntary opposition, by squeezing in her bottom-hole, instead of pushing it out. When he thought he had sufficiently excited her, and made her suppose he was going to continue regularly fucking her, he suddenly withdrew the two fingers he had in her bum-hole, by a jerk substituted his prick, and before Mary was aware, had sheathed it more than halfway into her bottom. She gave a half scream, but his hold of her hips, and my close embrace of her waist, for I all along knew what he was at, prevented her from flinching and throwing him out, which was her first impulse. He said—

"I will keep still, and any unpleasant feeling will go off in a moment."

He stopped for two or three minutes, which I occupied in first rubbing the end of my prick on Mary's clitoris, which was a well-developed one, and when by her nervous movements I found her passions were being roused, I slipped it into her tightened cunt without much difficulty. Mr. M. took the opportunity of finding me penetrating to glide in on his point of attack up to his utmost limit. Mary gasped again, and declared it was choking her. However, by a little more patience, and then by very gentle movements, we gradually worked her up to the utmost state of excitement, and she, as well as both of us, went off in a delirium of enraptured felicity. She lay panting and throbbing between us for nearly a quarter of an hour.

I was already in a state for renewed efforts, but Mr. M. rose, and withdrew his reeking prick from the tight recess in which it had enjoyed such extasies, and told us we must be content with that day's work, expressly as he had a plan in his head for the next day, that would require us to have all our erotic powers at command. Then, as before, we approached the village, so as to be seen, but not overheard, so that our going away to more distant places should create no suspicion. Mr. M. then informed us that we could come to his cottage the next afternoon, instead of the rocks; we should be able to undress ourselves in the buff, and have a perfect orgie of salacious delights. We heartily approved of this plan, and after an amusing conversation, we parted to meet the next day on the sands, but in the contrary directions to the rocks, for the purpose of afterwards approaching his cottage from the least observable site.

After dinner the next day we started at our usual hour apparently for our ordinary promenade, but after leaving the village, and allowing most of the people to be safely stowed away in church for the afternoon service, we turned on our steps and made for Mr. M.'s door. He saw us coming, and was ready to admit us, without knocking. We immediately adjourned to the bedroom upstairs, and lost no time in all of us stripping stark naked. After some preliminary admiration of the two girls, whose forms were certainly cast in beauty's mould, we lay down in bed. I and Lizzie mutually gama- huched each other, with the usual accompaniments in the charming orifices of our bottoms. Mr. MacCallum and Mary, for he had taken a great fancy to her and her splendid bottom, followed our example, After we had a happy and most delicious spend, and then mutual embraces and kisses, we put the girls into all conceivable poses, until we were once more ready to go on with something more serious than gamahuching. Mr. M., as usual, acted as master of the ceremonies, and ordered Mary to lie down on her back, then Lizzie reversed upon her, so that she could gamahuche Mary's cunt, and tickle her bum-hole, while Mary was to frig Lizzie's clitoris with one hand, and play with my cods with the other, Mr. M. himself guided my prick into the delicious bottom-hole of Lizzie, and when we were all fixed, and he had frigged my bum-hole with two fingers, he said—

"Now I am going to initiate you, Charlie, into the delight of being alike operator and receiver."

So saying, he moistened his tool and spit in' my bum-hole, and proceeded very gently to introduce his prick therein. I have described his cock as not very thick at the point, consequently the first part introduced itself very easily, but when the pillar pushed its way in, and began to stretch the parts, it produced a curious sickening feeling, very like as if I had received a kick on the bottom; so I was obliged to ask him to halt a little. He was too experienced in the art not to fully understand my feelings, and knew well it would go off in a minute or two, if I was left quiet. So pausing until I told him he might now try to get in further, he drew back a little and applying more spittle to the shaft, gently and firmly, and slowly guided his prick up to the hilt, or as far as his belly and my buttocks would allow. Again pausing a little, until feeling by the throbbing of my prick, which produced the same pressure on my bum-hole, that I was warming to the work, he began slow movements of thrusts in and out, which, together with the hot and voluptuous pressures and movements of my own little partner excited both by Mary's finger and my prick, began to fire my passions, and we soon grew very fierce in our movements. Nothing I could ever have imagined equalled the extraordinary and delicious extasy that the double action produced upon my erotic nerves. I gasped, I shuddered with the agony of intense pleasure, and at the moment when the grand and rapturous finale approached, I actually brayed exactly like a donkey, which, in after cooler moments, amused all of us. The action of pleasure had come upon all at once, and we sank in an inert mass on those below us. How poor Mary endured it astonished us, but the scene had so excited her that she said it never occurred to her, and she felt nothing. We eventually rose, and after a necessary purification, partook of wine and cake, which Mr. MacCallum, with great foresight, had provided. After that he would not allow us to fuck for some time; and we had a regular romp all about the room, which we enjoyed very much, and nothing was heard but slaps on our bottoms, and the wildest rollicking laughter—until our two cocks, by their stiff-standing, showed that we were again ready to enter on new combats. This time Lizzie lay down, Mary gamahuched her. Mr. M. got into her bum-hole, and I proceeded to attempt to do the same to him, but all to no purpose. I was too heavy hung for his bottom-hole, a very small one for a man. He had every wish to accommodate me, but do what I would, I could not overcome the physical difficulties. So reversing our positions, I lay on my back, Mary straddled over me, my prick was put into her cunt, and stooping down, and presenting her anus, M. succeeded more easily than the day before in getting into her bum-hole. Lizzie standing up with a leg on each side of Mary's and my body, brought her quim up to M.'s mouth, and he luxuriously gamahuched her, while his finger acted *postillon* in her bottom. The erotic storm raged with great fury for a long time, and then, growing more fast and furious, brought us all standing in extasies of the most salacious enjoyment, for us to sink once more into the annihilation of satiated desire. We lay long wrapped in close embrace. Recovering our senses in long-drawn sighs, we again refreshed ourselves with wine and cake, and as our passions were not so quickly reawakened as those of our more exciteable companions, we proceeded to gamahuche them, without their exercising a like skill upon our pricks. We then had another romp, and replacing Mary below and Lizzie above, I, this time, fucked her cunt, at her request, as she said it must not be altogether neglected. M., as previously, took me behind, and as there was a greater facility, so there was greater enjoyment, and as our previous exertions had taken off the sharper appetite, we were enabled to draw out our pleasure to a much greater length, until at last we died away in all the agony of such a glorious conjunction of parts. We had one more delicious general fuck before we parted. Lizzie was again fucked by me, and buggered by Mr. M., which she declared she preferred to any other combination, my prick so deliciously gorging her tight little cunt, and making M.'s prick, from the pressure of my larger weapon in the cunt, feel as tight in her bottom as my prick did, when nothing but Mary's finger was in her cunt. We ran our course with even greater luxury and lasciviousness than before. Lizzie actually was hysterical with the force of her enjoyment, and we all sank sideways off poor Mary, and lay long locked in each other's arms. This, for that day, ended our most delightful orgie. We purified ourselves, and then dressed. We parted with many sweet embraces, and promises of renewing the delightful scenes we had just gone through, and, in fact, we often and often repeated them, varying from time to time with a visit to the rocks, lest we should draw observation upon us by constantly going to the cottage.

Our six weeks came to an end so rapidly that we could hardly believe the time had already passed. Mamma one morning informed us we were to leave on the day after the next. You may suppose our disappointment, but there was no help for it. We met that day at the rocks, we were melancholy at the thought of parting with our charming friend, whom we now really loved. We were not near so fiery as usual, but resolved to have one thorough good orgie the next day at the cottage, as a farewell benefit to us all. We met, as agreed on, and put in force every art to augment our pleasures, and every contrivance to excite anew our powers to the utmost. Both M. and I must have spent six to seven times, but the girls being more easily excited in their finer organs of coition, went off in extasies some nine or ten times; until fairly exhausted, we had, from want of power, to give up the game, dress and part. We hoped to meet again. The girls wept at parting with our delightful friend, to whom we owed so many delicious orgies. We exchanged addresses, and he promised to come on a fishing excursion to our neighbourhood, where he hoped we should find means of renewing the lascivious sports we had already so much enjoyed. We tore ourselves away from him at last. It will be seen in the sequel, that unforeseen events carried me to London, or rather away from home, before we could meet again; and it was in London, at his own chambers, where we again renewed our charming intercourse, and practised every art of venery.

We returned home, and mamma again advertised for a governess, and stated that she required one of not less than thirty years of age, and with much experience in teaching. Numerous responses were made to the advertisement; but one lady desired to see mamma and her pupils before accepting the place, at the same time forwarding very satisfactory testimonials. Mamma was rather struck with the style of letter, and the unusual demand of previous acquaintance before entering into final arrangements. So she wrote to Miss Frankland, begging her to come and spend three days with us, and if her visit should prove as agreeable to both as her letter had done to mamma, she had no doubt matters might be arranged to their mutual satisfaction. Accordingly, at the expected hour, Miss Frankland arrived. She was, to our then thinking, an elderly lady, rather above thirty years of age than under, of tall and commanding figure, somewhat large, but no superfluous fat, broad shouldered, and wide hipped, with bosoms well separated, but not too prominent. Her hair was coal black, and her eyes equally so, but with the most determined expression, rendered more so by very thick eyebrows, which met in the middle. She showed also a well marked downy moustache, and the small curly hairs below her head, at the back of her neck, literally lost themselves beneath her high-necked dress. She always wore long sleeves, and never showed bare arms. I afterwards found the reason of this was that her arms were so black with thick hair that she was ashamed to let them be seen, although, in reality, beautifully formed and plump. Her mouth was large; it showed animal passion, but at the same time determined firmness of character. You could not call her handsome, but there was altogether an appearance of face, expression, and person that might well be styled a fine woman. As for us, at the period of first seeing her, we only marked the determined character of her countenance, and at once dreaded her becoming our governess, as we felt we should not only have one who would master us, but who would also be severe in every way. Youth is often a better physiognomist than it is credited with. It will be seen in the sequel whether we had judged correctly or not. Suffice it to say that her three days' visit ended in her being perfectly satisfied with the offered position, and mamma being equally satisfied with her. We did not know at the time, but afterwards found out, that she had made it a *sine qua non* that she should have carte blanche as to the use of the rod. She had observed to mamma that she thought we had been too leniently treated by our late governess, and it would be necessary to exert severe discipline, which, in her own experience, she had always found most efficacious. My mother, who had during the last two months found us rather headstrong and wilful, quite chimed in with her idea, and gave every authority to do quite as she liked, either with her girls or her son.

Terms being so arranged, Miss Frankland required a week to make all her arrangements before definitely taking up her new residence. My mother, thinking we should be well kept in on the arrival of Miss Frankland, left us in uninterrupted liberty until then, you may be sure we improved the occasion, and did our best to make up for the loss of our inestimable and amiable friend, Mr. MacCallum. Not only did we make use of the summer house by day, but every night I stole up to my loved sisters' room, where we tried to emulate the luxurious scenes of lubricity we had lately been so deliciously indulging in at the seaside in Wales. Of course, the week passed far too quickly, and on the appointed day my mother drove into the town to bring Miss Frankland home, on the arrival of the coach. My two sisters accompanied her, as something or other was always wanted for the girls; and as Miss Frankland and her luggage would quite fill the carriage on their return, I was left by myself at home, a most fortunate circumstance, as it turned out.

I was somewhat annoyed at being left alone. But how true it is that "man proposes and God disposes." Had I gone with them I should have missed a most delicious and unexpected treat. I had strolled to the summer house in a sort of despair at the lost opportunity of again fucking my sisters before the arrival of the dreaded governess. I was listlessly gazing out of the window when I suddenly became aware of a lady waving her hand to me from a gig coming down the road which our summer house commanded. In an instant I recognised Mrs. Vincent. To run down the hillock, unbolt the private door, and welcome her to our house, was the work of a moment. I begged her to get out and walk to the house through the grounds, her servant could drive round to the stables and wait there. She did so at once. I never said a word of all being absent until I had her safe in the summer house. Without a word I seized her round the waist, and pressing her back on the couch, quickly unbuttoned my trousers, and pulling up her petticoats, was pushing my stiff prick against her belly before she was almost aware of my intentions.

"My dear Charlie," she cried, "what are you at? We shall be discovered, and it will be my ruin."

"Oh, no, my ever loved Mrs. Vincent; they are all away to town, and we have nothing to fear."

She loved me too well to make further resistance; on the contrary, seconding me with all her accustomed art, we both quickly sunk in all the voluptuous raptures of satisfied desire. I would not quit my position, but kissing her rapturously, I shoved my tongue into her mouth, and stopped her remonstrances. The excitement of meeting her after a two months' separation stimulated my passions to the utmost, and with hardly bated breath I began a fresh career, but with more moderation and greater pains to make her a perfect participant in the raptures I myself was receiving. She thoroughly enjoyed it, and being relieved from any fear of surprise, after my informing her of the absence of all the family, she gave way to all the force of her ardent amorous propensities, enjoyed our delicious fuck thoroughly, and spent at the same time as myself with screams of satiated passion. After this I withdrew. She kissed me most tenderly, and said I was as bad and wild a boy as ever, that she loved me too tenderly ever to refuse me anything I desired, and begged me to sit by her side and talk of old times.

"No," I said, "on the contrary, tell me all about yourself; I have not seen you since your marriage day, and I want to know how the after-part went off. I was in dread lest our embracings should have left traces that would make your husband suspect you were not all he had anticipated."

"You are a strange boy, my dear Charlie, and more of a man in every way than many ten years older than yourself. Who would have thought such ideas would have been running through so young a head. Well, my darling boy, I was somewhat uneasy on that very point myself, and, indeed, had fixed the marriage day when I expected I should be unwell on the very night, but in that I was disappointed; nothing came, and I was driven to act in the best way I could. I kept my legs close together. I got my hand down to that part of my person, and kept squeezing my affair as close as possible. I pressed hard with my fingers on his weapon as he forced an entrance, and all at once gave way with a scream of apparent pain, as he gave an extra thrust, and let him penetrate at once. An inexperienced husband takes much on credit and imagination, I quite satisfied him that he was the first possessor of my person; but, oh! my beloved Charlie, I found I was really ready in the family-way, and you, my dear fellow, are the father of the baby now within my womb."

"What? I! I! the father of your baby? Oh, dear, darling Mrs. Vincent; oh, say that again."

"It is indeed true, my dear Charlie; and the knowledge that I first possessed you, and you me, reconciles me to giving my husband a child that is not his."

"My child! my child!" I cried, and I danced round in a paroxysm of delight at the idea of being a father. It seemed at once to elevate me to manhood, and puffed me up with pride. I rushed upon dear Mrs. V., embraced her most warmly, and pushing her back on the sofa, said—

"I must see how the little angel looks in his cell."

I turned up her petticoats, and exposed all her beauteous belly, already by its swelling showing there was more there than ever went into her mouth. Her cunt too had become more prominent. I stooped, kissed her lovely quim, gave it a good suck, then gamahuched her till she cried out for my prick to fuck her, and a most exquisite and rapturous fuck we had. The thought that I was baptising my own babe with my sperm stimulated my lubricity, and we ran a course of the most libidinous delights until we dissolved away in the most voluptuous death-like exhaustion of satisfied desires.

"Charlie, my darling, you must get up; remember you may injure the dear little creature by too great an excess, so pray rise."

I rose at once, but only to embrace her most tenderly. She complained of feeling somewhat faint, and said we must now go to the house to get some wine. We put ourselves in order, and all radiant at the thoughts of paternity, I strutted along as proud as a peacock, and thinking no small beer of myself. I hardly knew whether I stood on my head or my heels, and was quite extravagant in my conduct. Dear Mrs. V. was obliged seriously to caution me before I could come to a proper reserved behaviour in presence of the servants. She rested about half an hour, and was about to order the gig up to the door, but I implored her to send it round to the road below the summer house, as I should all the longer have the pleasure of being with her. She smiled, and again gave me a pat on the cheek, as much as to say, "I understand you, you rogue," but did as I suggested. So we proceeded through the grounds, and were at the summer house some time before the gig could be harnessed and come round to the road below. I did not wait for that, but embracing darling Mrs. V., wanted to push her down on the sofa.

"No, no, dear Charlie, that will tumble my dress too much, and we shall have no time to put it in order; stop, I will kneel on the low couch, and you will stand behind, I can guide you from below, and you know I always thought you got further in and gave me more pleasure that way than any other."

She knelt down, and I canted her clothes right over her shoulders, and exhibited her fine buttocks, which, now she was in the family-way, had widened out, and were fatter and rounder than ever. First gluttonously kissing them, I brought my prick right against them. Mrs. Vincent projected her hand behind, seized and guided him into her glowing and longing cunt, and he plunged at one bound up to the hilt.

"Gently, Charlie dear," she cried, "remember our dear baby is there, and you must not be too violent."

This at once reduced me to moderation. I had a hand on each hip, and as I slowly glided in, I pressed her splended buttocks backwards to meet me. I kept my body upright so as to enjoy the lovely sight of the movement of her bottom.

"Put your arm round and feel my clitoris, Charlie, dear."

I did so for a minute, and then whispered—

"It is such delight to gaze on your splendid bum in action, so pray apply your own finger to your clitoris, and let me enjoy the lovely sight."

"Very well, darling."

And I could feel her frigging away most furiously. This enabled me to introduce first one and then two fingers into her most delicious bottom-hole. When I found she was in the greatest state of excitement, I suddenly shifted my prick, and substituted it for my fingers. In her surprise and excitement, she had no time to resist, and I glided in, not too rapidly, quite up as far as I could go. She flinched a little, and called me a bad fellow, but I held her hips too tight to allow of her unseating me, even if she had wished. I begged she would let me go on, for I had never forgotten the delight of doing it this way the night before her marriage. She made no reply, but I could feel redoubled action with her finger on her clitoris; and the muscular twitchings of her loins and sphincter soon convinced me that nothing would please her better than finishing our course where I was—and most delicious it proved. We should have died away in loud cries of agonised delight but for the necessity of prudence, for doubtless the gig was then awaiting but a few yards off. My darling mistress seemed unwilling to let me withdraw; she held my prick in such close and firm embrace, throbbing on it from moment to moment, and so exciting him that she shortly felt he was again stiffening inside of her. She rose on her legs, and by that action unsheathed me. Then, turning round, she threw her arms about my neck, and most tenderly embraced me, thanking me for having given her such exquisite proofs of love.

"But I must go, my dear Charlie, and I hope we shall have occasionally some other delicious opportunity of enjoying such raptures again. Say everything kind to your mother and the girls, and tell them I shall come ever again shortly and see them all."

I saw her into her gig, and watched her until a turn in the road hid her from my sight. I returned to the summer house, and kissed the spot she had last pressed with her lovely body. My soul was filled with love of her, and pride that I was man enough to put a babe into her belly. I strutted about the room, and if any one could have seen me I should doubtless have appeared ridiculous. Mamma, our new governess, and the girls returned to tea. I told them of Mrs. Vincent's visit, and her regret at finding them absent, also of her promise to drive over again on an early day. My mother hoped I had been attentive to her. I said I had, as well as I could, and had got some wine and biscuits, as she complained of not feeling very well, she thought the jolting road had tired her.

It may well be supposed that after the impression our new governess had made upon us, we were very attentive for some time. Indeed, her system of teaching was really excellent, far superior, in that respect, to our former governess. She had a method of interesting you in what she was teaching, and for quite two months we paid such great attention, and made such really extraordinary progress, that she could not help praising us highly to mamma while we were in the room. This was bad policy, because, with the natural thoughtlessness of youth, we fancied ourselves so clever that we became less attentive. This was patiently borne with for some time, probably in consequence of our previous good behaviour. But at last Lizzie was somewhat impudent when blamed rather harshly by Miss Frankland.

"Oh! it has come to that, has it? We shall see."

She continued our lessons until four o'clock as usual, and then desired Lizzie to remain where she was; she dismissed Mary and me, locked the door on poor Lizzie, and went away, doubtless for a rod. She soon returned, and locking herself in, most severely whipped poor Lizzie's bottom. She sent her out when it was finished, and Lizzie joined us, weeping bitterly from the pain she was suffering. We laid her on the couch, and turned her petticoats over her head to cool her bottom, which she declared felt as if burning hot coals were spread over it. I kissed the dear red buttocks that were all covered with weals and looked like raw beef, but no blood had been drawn. We fanned her with our handkerchiefs, which she said was a delightful relief. In a very few minutes she began to wriggle her bottom in a state of excitement, and cried out—

"Dear Charlie, do shove your prick into my cunt, it has begun to long for a fuck."

I wanted nothing but this to instantly act, for the sight of her bare bum had already made my cock stand as stiff as iron. She raised herself on her hands and knees, presenting the back entrance to her cunt, and telling me it was there she must have it instantly. I plunged up to the hilt in a moment, for she was as juicy and moist as if she had spent, which it is more than probable was the case. Very few powerful thrusts on my part, seconded by energetic action on hers, and she spent again with a scream of delight, and with a pressure on my cock that almost hurt it. She hardly paused a moment before she cried out—

"Shove on, dear Charlie, push it in further if you can, I am burning with desire."

She wriggled her backside in every way in the most lascivious and delicious manner, and when she felt the crisis approaching, by the increased swelling and hardness of my prick as well as the peculiar electric effect at the moment, she met my flood of sperm with so copious a discharge that it literally spurted out and deluged my cods and thighs. She held me tight, and would not allow me to withdraw until I had myself spent four times and she seven at least. We then rose, her nerves calmed by the repeated doses of hot boiling sperm shot into her interior. She declared that never in all her fucking had she felt such insatiable desire, or more ravishing delight in satisfying it, that she would undergo a dozen such floggings to have the same rapturous enjoyment.

"I am sure," she said, "it was all the effect of the rod, I never felt anything like it before."

Mary all this time had been but a spectator, and a pleased one to see the erotic fury of her sister and my powerful efforts to allay it. It is true we had both had a delicious fuck during the time poor Lizzie was catching it on her backside, and I had just gamahuched her deliciously afterwards as Lizzie came in in such pain.

Miss Frankland had retired to her room, and looked still flushed and somewhat wild looking when she joined us after the usual hour's recreation. As may well be supposed, we were all as attentive as possible. There was one circumstance that evidently pleased Miss Frankland immensely. When Lizzie, in her turn, went up to repeat her lesson, she suddenly threw her arms round Miss Frankland's neck, and with tears running over her cheeks, sobbed out—

"Dear Miss Frankland, pray forgive me, and let me kiss you, for I love you dearly."

There was a bright sparkle of delight in Miss Frankland's eyes. She clasped Lizzie round the waist, and drew her to her lips in a long sweet kiss of love, which seemed as if it would never end. We observed Miss Frankland's colour rise. She at last put Lizzie away, and said she was a dear amiable girl, whom she could not help loving.

"Go to your seat, you are too agitated, my dear, to say your lesson just now; so send Mary up."

Lizzie came back to her seat, but I could not help fancying I saw a complete expression of erotic desire on her countenance. When afterwards we were alone together, she told us that when the governess kissed her, she felt Miss F.'s tongue glide into her mouth, and "tip her the velvet" in a most delicious and exciting manner, and she believed that if they had been alone they must have given each other mutual embraces of a warmer description. This led me to think that Miss Frankland was herself rendered lecherous by the action of even wielding the rod. Lizzie during the whole of the next week did nothing but rave of the excessive excitement that her whipping had put her into, and the extreme felicity she felt in having her salacious lechery satisfied. We were not able to meet every day, for frequently Miss Frankland accompanied us, and joined in the youthful sports we then gave way to. Lizzie continuing to harp on the extraordinary enjoyment the whipping had procured her, after it was over, fired the imagination of Mary, until she was wound up to a pitch of actually longing to be whipped. In such a case it was easy to incur the penalty; she had but wilfully to neglect her studies, and she was sure to get it. This she accordingly did, and it resulted as before. When released, she rushed to the summer house, and without any preliminaries, called upon me to fuck her directly; and a very similar scene followed to that which had occurred when dear Lizzie was whipped. Mary did not, however, give way to the uncontrollable desire to throw herself into Miss Frankland's arms as Lizzie had done. Miss F., as usual, retired to her room after the punishment was over, and was late in coming down, with the same flushed face and excited eye. I became convinced that she herself was salaciously excited by the act, and I began to fancy that with such passions, if I could but excite her in any way, it might be worth my while. When once these lecherous ideas were raised in my imagination, desire soon painted her with every charm of beauty, and I became excessively lewd and anxious to possess her. The more I looked at and scanned the really beauteous proportions of her finely developed form, the more my determination to have her took root, and grew strong within me.

About this time Miss Frankland, who had become a great favourite with mamma, obtained permission to take possession of the spare bedroom, with an understanding that she was to cede it to any visitor who might come. Of course, this circumstance made my desire to get into her good graces doubly strong, inasmuch as the opportunity of sleeping with her afterwards could be so easily effected. I determined to watch her when retiring to bed, and try to get a view of her naked form. For this purpose I removed the stopping of moistened bread I had put in the hole I made to see Mr. Benson fucking his wife. I lay awake, until she came to bed. I saw her undress, but only caught sight of her naked bubbies, over her chemise. As I have said, they were not large, but widely separated, with a fine flat neck up to the throat. I mean that she showed no collar bone, which is a great beauty in woman. She had evidently been quite naked, and had used the bidet, but the extent of the slit in the door did not allow me to command the part of the room where she had used it. I remedied this defect next day, and the following night was rewarded with a most glorious sight. You may well suppose that I did not let sleep overcome me, but was at my post as soon as ever I heard her enter her room. I was on my knees in a moment, at my peep-hole, and saw her deliberately undress to her chemise. She then arranged all her magnificent head of hair, brushing it out as far and further than her arms would extend; and after well brushing and combing it, she plaited and rolled it up, in a great big rouleau behind, then washing her hands, she drew out the bidet, poured water into it, and then divested herself of her shift. She was standing in front of the dressing-table, with two candles shining on her, so that when she lifted her shift over her head; I had a well-lighted full view of her wonderfully covered belly. She was all over hair; it was as black as coal, and shone as if polished in all its beautiful curls. I am now an old man, but never have I seen the equal to that dear woman in a hairy belly. It was quite up to her navel, and several inches down the inside of her thighs, be-sides running thickly in the chinks of her bottom, and with two bunches where the beautiful back dimple is usually situated, as thick, and even thicker than ordinary women have in on their mounts. In addition to this, there was a beautiful little line of curls that ran up her belly, as far as between her bubbies, to say nothing of the very hairy thighs, legs, and arms. I never saw a more deliciously hairy woman, and she was all that such excessive growth of hair denoted—passionate and lecherous to a degree, when once she had confidence in her companion, to let her feelings have vent. Of course, I am now describing my after-experience; at the moment I was only dazzled by the extraordinary richness and quantity of that exquisite ornament—hair—not only in splendid quantity on the head, but in a profusion such as I had never then and have not since witnessed. I was struck dumb with astonishment and admiration. She laved her hairy cunt, and all the adjacent parts, then wiped herself dry, put on her night-gown, extinguished her light, and, of course, got into bed. So did I but only to toss and tumble, and at last, in troubled sleep, to dream of that most gloriously covered cunt, and to imagine myself revelling therein. So great was my excitement that I had the first wet dream I ever experienced. It is needless to say, it was under the dreaming idea that I was enjoying to the utmost that wonder cunt.

I was quite exhausted by morning with such a restless night, and was not only very *distrait,* but was really so fatigued that I could not attend to my lessons. Of course Miss Frankland noticed this, and being unaware of the cause, attributed it to wilful idleness and bravado of her authority. She spoke very gravely and seriously to me, and told me if I did not improve my conduct by next day it would be her painful duty to punish me with severity.

"I expect to see you exhibit very different conduct tomorrow, otherwise you will drive me to do that which I would much rather not."

It rained hard that afternoon, and we had to amuse ourselves within doors. On retiring for the night, I determined to watch again for Miss Frankland, but my want of rest the previous night overpowered me, and I fell fast asleep until far in the night. I rose and crept to my peep-hole, but all was dark. I could hear Miss Frankland breathing heavily. The thought at once struck me that I might safely steal up to my sisters' room, as they were now alone, since Miss F. had the previous night removed to the spare bedroom, where she was now fast asleep. So softly opening my door, and leaving it ajar, I crept along the passage, gained my sisters' room, and gently awakening them, jumped in between them, to their great joy and satisfaction. We immediately began with a

gamahuche, I taking Mary's cunt, while Lizzie crossed her
legs over her head, and was gamahuched by Mary, whose
finger was at the same time acting *postillon* to her charming
bottom-hole, while I had the exquisite prospect before me of
their operations. As soon as ever Mary spent I made Lizzie lie
down on her back, with her head towards the bottom of the
bed, Mary knelt over her in the opposite direction, presenting
her very full backside, which was daily developing larger
proportions. I plunged into her cunt, plugging her little rosy
bum-hole at the same time with my middle finger, while Lizzie
did as much for me, at the same time rubbing Mary's clitoris
with the fleshy end of the thumb, while Mary, at the same
time she herself was fucked and frigged in two places, was
employed in gamahuching Lizzie, and frigging her bottom-
hole with two fingers, Lizzie declaring that one finger felt as
nothing. We lengthened out our delicious proceedings until excess of excitement compelled us to give way to all the
fury of our feelings, and we managed to spend all together
with such rapturous and lascivious delight as rendered us
quite powerless for some time. We then had a delicious
cuddle, the girls having each one hand on my prick and the
other on my buttocks. When we had once more worked ourselves up to fucking heat, we reversed the previous position,
and I fucked Lizzie. Mary was gamahuched and bottom-
fingered by Lizzie, while she employed herself with Lizzie's
clitoris and my bum-hole. Lizzie was far hotter and more
salacious than any of us, and spent copiously on my delighted prick, which enjoyed excessively the warm bath of
glutinous liquid that was poured down upon it. I gave a few
slow-drawn thrusts in and out, to moisten well its whole shaft,
and removing my two fingers from her delicious bottom-hole,
and wetting it with my saliva, I withdrew my prick from the
reeking sheath of her cunt, and to her great delight slowly
housed it in her longing and exquisitely delicious bottom-hole,
keeping it quiet there for some time, so as not to spend before

Lizzie was ready. I enjoyed the delicious throbbing of her body, which at last becoming too exciting, I stooped over her, passed a hand under her belly, replaced Mary's fingers, rubbing her clitoris while Mary frigged her cunt with two fingers thrust into it. We thus quickly brought matters to an end, and died off in all the extasies of satiated lust. As daylight was beginning to dawn, I tore myself from their loving embraces, gained my room in safety, and slept the sleep of the just until late in the morning.

My orgie with my sisters had so far satisfied my animal passions that I rather began to dread the severity I knew Miss Frankland would use if I came under her hand. This made me so far attentive next day as to satisfy her; and as it was a fine afternoon she came out to walk in the garden, while we innocently amused ourselves. That evening I kept awake, and again enjoyed the superb display of Miss Frankland's wonderfully hairy cunt, all the lower part of her body was as black as a chimney sweeper's. The sight awakened every lustful feeling within me. I felt I must possess her, and determined to brave the severest infliction she could give me with the rod. I somehow, instinctively, arrived at the conclusion that this extraordinary profusion of hair could only grow where nature had implanted the hottest animal passions, and had but to greatly excite them to turn their lust to my advantage. I determined that to-morrow I should bring things to a crisis, and that I might be equal to every effort I went to my bed, and did not attempt to steal up to my sisters' room. Next day nothing could be made of me in the morning; Miss Frankland sternly warned me that if such conduct was pursued after dinner nothing should save my skin from a severe scourging. However, my mind was made up, and I went in "for the whole hog," as our vulgar Yankee cousins say. I was more idle and insubordinate than ever. Miss F. looked thunder; at four o'clock she ordered me to stay, and the girls to go. She then locked the door, took out from the desk a formidable rod, and told me to approach her. I did so—really half in fear, for she could look dreadfully fierce and determined, in which case I came up to her side.

"Now, Charles," she said, "your conduct, for two or three days past, has been such as I cannot put up with. Your mother has given me full power to punish any of you severely, if I think you deserve it; you are getting to be of an age that I hoped you would have so acted as to give me no cause of offence, but I am sorry to see my hopes are disappointed. I am now about to punish you, submit to it quietly, or it will be all the worse for you. Unbutton and put down your trousers."

I felt I must submit, but when brought to this point I really so much dreaded her that there was not the slightest erection in poor cockey.

While I was undoing my trousers, I observed that Miss Frankland had quite lifted up her outer frock, and had sat down, evidently intending to flog me across her knee. Both being ready, she told me to put the footstool by her side and kneel upon it, then desiring me to bend forward over her knees she put one hand over my body to hold me down; then uncovering my bottom, and taking the rod, which was by her side, she raised her arm and gave me a fearful cut, which made me not only flinch, but cry out most lustily. Blow followed blow, causing at first great agony, that made me cry again in good earnest; then the very continuance of the blows seemed to deaden the parts until I hardly felt them. This was succeeded by a titillation and lascivious excitement which speedily brought my prick out in the fullest vigour. I then began to push it against Miss Frankland's thigh, and to wriggle myself nearly off her knees. Seemingly to prevent this, she passed her left arm quite round my body, bringing her hand under my belly, and, apparently by accident, against my prick, which she grasped, and I could feel her hand pass both up and down it as if she was measuring its length and thickness, continuing all the time to shower down blow after blow on my devoted backside. As she held a firm grasp on my prick, I pretended to be evading the blows, while in reality I was thrusting it in and out of her hand with the utmost energy and excitement, which speedily brought on the delightful crisis, and with a cry of rapture I gave down a copious discharge into her hand, and sank almost senseless on her lap. I pretended complete loss of consciousness, which she believing, she gently felt, and even frigged a little, my prick, pressing me the while close to her body, and then I felt a shudder run through her whole frame. I have no doubt she was in a paroxysm of lust, and had spent. I gave her time to recover a little, and then pretending to come to my senses, but in a confused state of ideas, said—

"Oh, what has happened? I have been in heaven!"

Then raising myself, and apparently only just recognising Miss Frankland, I threw my arms round her neck, and exclaimed—

"Dear Miss Frankland, do flog me again if it will produce again such extasies as I never before experienced."

Her face was flushed, her eye shone with all the fire of libidinous passion. My prick had hardly lost its stiffness when I spent, and was now projecting out firmer than ever.

"Why, Charles, I thought you a mere boy, while you are quite a man with such a thing as this."

"Oh!" I cried, "do continue to hold it, you give me such pleasure!"

"Has anyone else ever held it in this way?"

"No, I never felt anything like it before."

"But don't you know what this is meant to do?"

"Oh, yes, it is what I piddle from."

She laughed, and asked if it was often in its present state of stiffness.

"Every morning when I awake it is so, and it hurts me very much until I piddle."

"And has no one ever taught you any other use of it?"

"No, what use can it be of?"

"You dear innocent boy, if I could trust you, I would teach you a secret that this dear thing would greatly enjoy. But can I trust you?"

"Oh, certainly, dear Miss Frankland, I know what you mean now, to repeat the delicious sensations you gave me a few minutes ago. Oh, do, do! do it again, it was far too nice for me ever to tell anybody, as long as you will do it for me."

"Well, Charles, I will trust you. Do you know that women are differently formed from you?"

"Yes, I used to sleep in mamma's room, and I have often been surprised to see that she piddled from a long hole, and had not got a doodle like I have to piddle from."

"My dear innocent Charlie, that long hole was made to take in this dear fellow here that is throbbing almost to bursting in my hand, and if you promise me faithfully never to tell any one, I will teach you how it is done."

You may be sure my protestations of secrecy were most earnest.

"Look here then, my dear boy, and see what I have got between my legs."

She laid herself back on the long chair, drew up her petticoats, and exhibited to my charmed gaze the wondrous wealth of hair she possessed. Opening her legs, I saw the wide-spread rosy lips showing themselves in beautiful contrast to the coal-black hair that grew in the greatest profusion all round the lower lips, and extended also some five or six inches down the side of each thigh. But what at the moment most astonished me, and drew all my attention, was to see a deep red clitoris standing out from the upper part of her cunt quite stiff, and as long and as thick as the middle finger of a man. I very nearly betrayed myself at the sight, but, fortunately, was able to keep up the character of apparent ignorance I had hitherto shown, and said—

"You, also, have got a little doodle to piddle with?"

She laughed, and said—

"It is very different from yours. Give me yours here, that I may kiss it."

She fondled it for a second or two, and then could not resist the impulse to take it into her mouth and suck it.

"Oh, what pleasure! I shall die!"

"Not yet, dear boy; kneel down there, and I shall instruct you in the real secret of pleasure."

But, before she could do anything, I threw my head down, crying out—

"I must give this pretty little fellow a taste of the pleasure you have just given mine."

And in an instant I had the delicious thing up to the root in my mouth, sucking furiously at it. Her twistings, and up and down action of her loins, showed how rapturously I was exciting her, in fact, I brought on the crisis, when she pressed my head down hard upon it, and closed her thighs on each side of my head, as she poured over my chin and breast a perfect torrent of sperm. A minute after she seized my arms, and drew me up on her belly, then slipping her hand down between us, she seized my prick and guided him, nothing loath, into her burning hot and foaming cunt. She placed her hands on my buttocks, and pressing me right up to the hilt, began a movement which she told me how to second, that in a very short time brought down an exquisite spend from me. The idea that she was giving me the first lesson in love, and of being the first possessor of my person, seemed to excite her lust to the utmost, and she immediately followed my discharge with another, so copious that it spurted all over my thighs. Her force of pressure on my prick in her agonies of enjoyment was so great as nearly to hurt me. I never knew any one but her with such strength of pressure of cunt on the prick. She has often actually brought tears into my eyes, so powerful was her grip that it made me really feel as if in a vice. She lay back

with closed eyes and panting bosom in a rapturous trance of
lascivious lubricity, her throbbing cunt holding me tightly
pressed between its palpitating folds in the most delicious
imprisonment, and from time to time grasping my prick with a
pressure that very shortly restored it to its fullest vigour and
stiffness. She was as hot as fire and responded immediately to
the renewed life she found stirring within me. She gave way
to her salacious lust with, if anything, a more passionate excess than the first time. My superb weapon seemed to stir up
within her a force of lubricity that nothing could seem to
satisfy. Her hands clutched my buttocks convulsively, and
seemed to wish to force my whole body into her wildly excited cunt. With such vigour was the action carried on that
the grand crisis soon arrived, most rapturous to both, and almost maddening to Miss Frankland. The heavings of her
body and gaspings for breath were quite hysterical, while,
with one of those real vice-like pressures, I felt as if she were
nipping my prick in two. It was not a mere throbbing pressure, but a long continued convulsive squeeze, as if her cunt
had been seized like the jaws of the mouth with lock-jaw, and
could not open. It was nearly ten minutes before she recovered
her senses. She seized my head between her hands, kissed me
most lovingly, declared I was the dearest creature that ever
lived, that she had never before had any one who had so
satisfied her, and filled her with inexpressible rapture, &c. This
fondling had again brought up my prick to full stand. Miss
Frankland said—

"Dear Charlie, we must be prudent, as the time is drawing
near for your sisters' return."

But there was no stopping, the exquisite pleasure of her
splendid interior cunt pressures was irresistible. My movements
speedily determined matters in my favour. Miss Frankland's
temperament was far too warm not to quickly set her passions
to the highest fucking heat; and again we had a most exquisite fuck, lengthened out more luxuriously by the more

urgent fires of desire having been moderated by the three previous discharges. With more *abandon* we both sank in the death-like extasies of the delicious melting away in all the luxury of contented and voluptuous discharges. Miss Frankland lay for some short time luxuriously closing in my delighted prick, but raising her body, she said—

"Charles, we must cease for the present."

And, pushing me away, I was forced to withdraw; but her dear cunt seemed as reluctant as myself, and held my prick so tight that I had to pull hard to draw it out, and, at last, he left with a noise like drawing a cork from a well-corked bottle. Before I rose, or she could hinder me, I threw myself down and glued my lips to her reeking cunt, and greedily licked up the foaming sperm that had surged out of her well-gorged quim. She with difficulty drew away her body, but as I rose she clasped me to her bosom and kissed me most fervently, and licked her own sperm off my richly covered lips. Begging me to button up, and putting herself to rights, she desired me to sit down by her side. She wiped my mouth with her handkerchief, arranged my disordered neck-tie, collar, and hair. We then embraced most tenderly, and she thanked me for the immense gratification I had given her; she praised my parts as being of extraordinary development and more satisfying than any she had yet had any experience of. This was the second time she referred to other experiences. I took no notice of this all the time, as if I was supposed to be too ignorant or innocent to think any harm of it, but I determined in some excess of passion to get her to give me a recital of some of her previous experiences.

Before my sisters came in, she said—

"I shall try and arrange some means for our meeting unobserved to-morrow. Meanwhile, you must sit as if you had been severely punished, and I shall assert that you had done everything to resist my authority, for which I had punished you further by not allowing you to leave the school-room."

I said not a word to Miss F. about the ease of meeting by merely opening the door of communication between our rooms. I was afraid to make her suspicious of a former use of it. But I determined, when she came to bed, to rap at the door and beg her to open it, and I had no doubt she would be as delighted as myself to find with what facility she could indulge to the utmost every libidinous passion which her lascivious nature could suggest. My sisters returned, and appeared disappointed that I had not been able to join them, as they had anticipated a glorious fuck or two each, after the whipping had excited me as it did them. They told me afterwards they had been obliged to content themselves with a double mutual gamahuche, but it did not make up for my absence.

While they were all engaged after tea, I slipped up to Miss Frankland's room to see that the key was in the lock of the door between our two rooms. I opened it, oiled the hinges, and locked it again from her side. I also, with a view to sometimes slipping up to my sisters' room, oiled my own and their doors, hinges, and locks, as now that the ice was broken with Miss Frankland, it would be necessary to be doubly careful not to exite suspicion of my visits to my sisters. Having finished everything to my satisfaction, I joined them in the drawing-room, and while my sisters were playing duets on the piano to mamma, I challenged Miss Frankland to a game of chess. She, of course, was a far superior player to me, but our legs meeting under the chess table, her little charming foot sought mine, rested on it, and pressed it from time to time. This distraction of her ideas enabled me to win two games successively. My mother sent the girls to bed, and told me to follow their example, but as I did not wish to lie long waiting for Miss Frankland's appearance in her bedroom, I pleaded for relaxation in the hour of retiring, to enable Miss Frankland to regain her chance of beating me, at the same time pressing her foot as a sign to her to second my request. She took the hint, though she had no idea of the object. Mamma came near us to look over our game. This induced Miss Frankland to play with more caution and thought, and she won three games in succession, making her the final winner. Mamma now said I must go to bed, as it was very late for me. She still treated me as a child. I, however, had gained my object in obtaining nearly two hours' delay in going to bed, so that I had not long to wait before I heard Miss Frankland enter her room. I determined to let her finish her toilet before I called her attention to me. I watched through my peep-hole, and could now calmly and leisurely see all the beauties of her well-developed form, and the rich wealth of hair she possessed. She went through all her ablutions as usual. I observed she also used a syringe to thoroughly purify the inside of her glorious cunt. When she had dried herself, and was about to pull on her chemise, I rapped on the door of communication, and in a loud whisper called her attention to me.

"Are you there, Charlie?"

"Yes, pray unlock the door and open it, that I may come to you."

She actually had not yet discovered that the door, locked and bolted on her side, communicated with my bedroom, but her delight at the discovery was greater than her surprise. I flew into her arms, and was hugged to her bosom, and covered with kisses. But as my prick was in a bursting state of erection, I drew her to the bed, upon which we both threw ourselves, she on her back, and I above, and in an instant I was engulphed up to the cods in her glorious and glowing cunt, and we ran an eager course of rapturous thrustings, until nature could stand no more, and we sank in all the delights of a most delicious mutual spend. I lay soaking in bliss for some time, and after fondling each other, Miss Frankland said—,

"Get up, dear Charlie, and let us get into bed."

For we had been in too great haste to do otherwise than tumble on the top to it. My charming bed-fellow also rose for a necessary purpose, which I had interrupted when I knocked at the door. She sat down on the *pot de chambre,* and a mighty rush of water followed. I cried—

"Oh, do let me see you piddle from your beautiful fanny."

I still kept up my character of innocence, and used none but infantine words in reference to our organs of generation.

She laughed, but pulled up her shift, and raised her thighs above the pot, so advancing the light, I had the delicious sight of her wide-stretched cunt, pouring out a stream of piddle with great force. Her position brought out all the beauties of the vast wide-spread mass of black curly hair that thickly covered all the lower part of her magnificent quim, ran down each thigh, up between her buttocks, and opening out on her back, had two bunches just below the two beautiful dimples that were so charmingly developed below her waist. There was as much hair there as most women have on their mons Veneris. Her whole body had fine straight silky hair on it, very thick on the shoulders, arms and legs, with a beautiful creamy skin showing below. She was the hairiest woman I ever saw, which, doubtless, arose from or was the cause of her extra-ordinary lustful and luxurious temperament. The sight I was indulging in brought out my pego in full bloom; as we both rose she saw it sticking out under my shirt.

"Off with all that, and let me gaze on your charming young perfections."

I did as she desired, begged her to do the same, and there she stood, in all the glory of her superb form. We encircled each other's naked bodies, and then turned each other round to gaze on all the exciting charms displayed to each other.

"Come, my darling boy, and let me kiss and fondle you all over."

She laid me on my back, reversed herself above me, and taking my prick in her mouth, after first feeling it most gently, and praising its large proportions, again declaring it was the finest she had ever seen, she began to gamahuche me with a skill such as I had never before experienced, and gave me the most exquisite and most luxurious delight. For my part, seeing her wonderful clitoris, stiff standing out of the bright red lips of her luscious cunt, I took it bodily into my mouth, sucked it, and rolled my tongue about it, to the evident delight of my salacious companion. Her buttocks rose and fell, and the lips of her cunt immediately before my eyes opened, or closely pressed the lips together, showing the delicious nature of her enjoyment. I felt her put her hand to my bottom and insert her finger, and begin frigging me there. I let her see how it pleased me. She stopped a moment, to beg me to do the same to her, anticipating my earnest desire to do so. I lost no time in following her example. The parts adjacent were well lubricated by our previous indulgence, and first inserting two fingers into her deliciously juicy cunt to moisten them, I slipped one of them into her charming bottom-hole, and finding great ease of space, slipped the second in as well. My other hand and arm embraced and caressed her magnificent backside, which rose and fell on my face with unwearied speed, as my finger frigged her bottom-hole in unision with her movements, and my mouth more closely sucked her stiffly excited clitoris.

Her whole body became convulsed with erotic movements, showing what force of lubricity our mutual embracings were most rapturously exciting. I, too, grew wild with desire, and was equally energetic in my movements, and would have thrust my prick down her throat but for her hand, which grasped the lower part of the shaft. The rapturous crisis came at last and laid us prostrate with soul-killing extasies. We each retained the dear object of our mutual caresses within our lips and our fingers remained within the delightful recesses that had so much contributed to the excessive raptures we had enjoyed. We lay for some time in this sweet languid enjoyment. Miss Frankland then rose from off me, saying—

"My darling boy, we must now get into bed."

We did so, quite naked as we were, closely embracing, and covering each other with kisses and caresses, murmuring soft terms of endearment, and in whispered accents told of the extatic joys each had given the other. Our hands wandered over every charm. Miss Frankland had an art of gently passing her fingers over my prick that had the instant effect of raising him into the fullest vigour. It was the most exquisite method of feeling my cock I ever experienced. She seemed scarcely to touch it, but drew her fingers along its length, from foot to head, with a delicacy of touch I have never found equalled by any other woman. The effect was magical, and invariable, no matter how many times I might have fucked her before. With her hot temperament, and excessive lubricity, it was almost a necessary art. She was one of those libidinous natures that could well employ several men at once. At my happy age, she found ready to her hand one who could respond to her every desire in every way, so happily does nature second youth and health that she never found me wanting, when called on. There was no excess of lubricity we did not afterwards practise. We satisfied our passions in every way in which they could be indulged, nor did we hesitate at any thing which imagination could fancy would stimulate them. She was surprised at my aptitude, and rejoiced and congratulated herself on having found so powerful and charming a satisfier of her libidinous nature. How delighted she was to think she was the first to cull the sweets of my innocence, and how happy to find so apt a scholar, who in one sweet lesson became a master of the art. The more I gained experience of the charming sex, the more I appreciated the wisdom of the counsels of my really first and ever loved mistress, dear, charming, lovely Mrs. Benson. How truly she had foretold that all who might hereafter think that they were giving me the first lesson in love would doubly, trebly, a hundred fold enjoy the sweet intercourse from such self-deception. Here was my fiery Miss Frankland, who had had considerable experience in the amatory world, pluming herself upon instructing an innocent youth in all the mysteries of the passions for the first time. It evidently added immensely to her excitement. Indeed, in our after-conversation, she avowed that as it was the first time she had ever taken the maidenhead of a youth, so it had been the greatest degree of excitement she had ever experienced. I might fancy her delight at finding combined with such a satisfaction a wonderfully well-hung youth, and who proved so apt, and so equal to every luxurious whim that the most erotic lust could suggest. But I digress. At present, her magic touch had brought me up to bursting point, she threw a leg over me, and raising her body, said she would help herself this time. Guiding my prick to the wanton lips that were longing for him, she sank slowly down on the stiff pole on which she was so delightedly impaling herself, until our hairs were crushed beneath her weight, and nothing more could be engulphed. She again rose, until the edge of the nut showed itself at the mouth of her cunt, and then as slowly sheathed it again. She continued this exquisite movement for some time, to our delicious mutual enjoyment, then falling down on my belly, and telling me to pass my arm round her bottom and finger her as before, she glued herself to my lips, our tongues interlaced, and shot in and out of our luxurious mouths; our movement grew fast and furious, until we again sank in all the luxury of the last grand crisis. It was the very act of voluptuous rapture, and we lay lost to every sense but that of erotic extasy and satisfied lust. When we recovered our senses, she lay down by my side, cuddling me most closely, and toying and prattling, until she thought we had paused long enough. She slid her hand down to my prick, and very quickly, by her delicious and delicate handling of it, renewed its full vigour. Throwing her right leg over me, while lying on her back, she heaved up her body into a position half turned to my belly, I lying on my side; she then bid me embrace her other thigh between mine, then guiding cockey to the entrance, she gave a push backwards, to meet my forward thrust, when it was instantly sheathed to the hilt.

"Now, my darling boy, in this way we can lengthen out our pleasures as long as we please; you can make me spend oftener than yourself, which will satisfy my very lustful nature, and not overexhaust your young powers."

Giving one or two delicious side wriggles to her bottom, and nestling her backside close to my belly, she told me to pass my left arm under her waist that I might embrace her left bubby and finger its nipple, a proceeding which she told me was as exciting as playing with her clitoris—then turning her head, our tongues interlaced; she put my right hand down to her stiff-projecting clitoris, which I continued to frig just as I might have done to a boy's cock. Keeping up a slow in and out movement with my prick, excited by so many points of lascivious friction, she spent most copiously before I was prepared to join her. Her head sank back in the extasy of her discharge, drawing away from me, and leaving my mouth free. I instantly dropped it upon her other firm and elastic bubby, at which I sucked away, pushing my prick as far as possible into her cunt, and leaving it there, without movement, to enjoy the rapture-giving pressures of her delicious cunt, slowly passing my hand up and down her still sufficiently indured clitoris. She lay for some time in the luxurious enjoyment of the position, then once more sucking my lips, she thanked me over and over again for the pleasure I had given her, heightened as it was by knowing that it had not exhausted me. I began to move slowly in and out, keeping up my movements at the other points of excitement. She was ready on the instant to second me, and as she meant this time that we should spend together she left nothing to desire. Her movements were of the most exciting and stimulating description, and we were not long before the extatic moment arrived, and we sank in the lap of luxury, pouring forth streams of extatic bliss. We lay close locked in the most delicious embrace, only conscious of unutterable joy. It was some time before we could venture to break this exquisite trance of enjoyment. It was followed by the sweetest toyings and prattlings, until again my delighted prick, stimulated by the internal pressures of the luxurious sheath in which it had remained engulphed, again awoke her scarce-slumbering passions to dash on pleasure's heavenly course. Again she spent before me with, if anything, increased rapture, and, after a pause, renewing her lascivious movements in response to my own, we sank in a perfect death-like swoon of thoroughly satiated lust, and gradually and imperceptibly fell into the deepest slumber for many hours, locked as we were in each other's arms. Her wonderfully retentive power of cunt held my happy prick a willing prisoner through our long sleep. I awoke first, to find it standing stiff within the charmed circle which even in her sleep was deliciously grasping it with its nervous folds. I passed my hand down to her clitoris, and began fucking her. She heaved her bottom up and down, and murmured some incoherent words, being evidently still under the influence of sleep, and probably dreaming of some former events, for in her half expressed murmurings, I could make out something—

"Henry—my only—ever loved one—meet again—oh! how ineffable—how exquisitely delicious. Do push it in—more faster —beloved of my soul."

She clasped me with a hug, as if she would make but one body of us both, and spent with a scream of agonized delight, pouring down and spurting out a perfect torrent of boiling spunk all over my cods and thighs.

"Dearest, beloved Henry, it is too much," she uttered, and fainted away.

I lay quite still, and determined not to speak until she should come to herself. It was evident her dreams had brought back some former loved and happy man and no doubt the fact of my being in possession, in full fuck, had made her believe in the reality of her sleeping thoughts. She was quite a quarter of an hour before recovering her senses; daylight had broken, and she looked round in a sort of alarm, and exclaimed—

"Where am I?"

Then her eye catching my face—

"Oh! my darling Charlie, it is you! I have been dreaming of being far away, and, I suppose, the fact of your dear weapon throbbing within me made me think of former events. Well, the dream had its pleasures, if only in a dream."

"It was no dream, my dear Miss Frankland, or at least, only partially so, as far as regarded your loved Henry—for that was the name you applied to me, and most deliciously did you embrace me under the idea, and die away in an excess of pleasure I quite envied; but you alarmed me by really fainting afterwards. I am so pleased to have turned a mere vision of the night into extatic reality, and I am not at all jealous of your former lover, because had you not had any, you would, probably, never have loved me. Oh, no! I should never be jealous of you my dear mistress. I would even like to see you in all the extasies of passion, in the arms of another, provided that I should share in your delights."

She listened in an astonishment, acknowledged that she had imagined herself in the arms of one she had greatly loved, and had thought the whole affair was a dream, and was not conscious of its absolute reality as to her being fucked.

"Well, I must have mine now, feel how it is bursting for relief."

"Yes, yes, the dear fellow, push him away, my Charlie, and you will see, I shall enjoy the real Charlie quite as much as the dreamt-of Henry—of whom I shall some day speak to you. You are worthy of him and of me—and I fear I shall love you as I do him, far too dearly."

Then lending herself to the work we were at, she did, indeed, exert all her lascivious power, and we enjoyed such a fuck as seldom falls to mortals here below. We lay prostrate and panting with satisfied lust, until prompted by the urgency of natural wants we were both obliged to rise and relieve ourselves. My darling mistress then used her bidet and told me to lave my parts in the basin, as it was not only cool and refreshing, but also reinvigorating. After which as it was now broad daylight, she allowed me to pose her, and turn her in every position, that I might admire and handle every part of her superb form. Her bottom was larger and harder than any I had yet seen, and, indeed, excepting one, of which, dear reader you will presently hear something, it was about the finest in form and size of any I ever met with. Of course, this handling was not effected without producing erotic excitement in both parties. Miss Frankland had occupied herself as much with me as I had done with her, and her beautifully large clitoris was showing its head in full stand out from among the vast mass of bushy curls surrounding it. I proposed we should have a mutual suck on the floor, with her bottom to the light, that I might have a full view of all her glorious parts. She humoured my fancy, and pulling a couple of pillows off the bed to prop up my head, she stepped across my body, and kneeling down, took my prick in her mouth, and brought her splendid backside and lascivious cunt down to my face. I first glued my lips to the open cunt, thrust my chin in, and then my tongue, as far as I could reach, licking the luscious moisture which our previous handlings had excited; it was as sweet and delicious as cream. This stimulated her very much, and she closed the sides of her cunt upon my tongue so closely as to give it a good squeeze. I never saw a woman but her, who had such a wonderful power in that way. My nose actually felt it was reciprocating the pressures of the cunt, so I changed the venue, and slipped my tongue into her bottom-hole, evidently to her excessive delight. But things were approaching a crisis, and she cried to me to take her clitoris in my mouth, and substitute fingers in both the other orifices. This I quickly did, while she sucked and postillioned me, handling the root of my prick, and my buttocks with the delicious gentle titillations in which she had such skill, until, in an excess of joy, we both poured a tribute of sperm into each other's mouths, and both greedily swallowed it. After this we got into bed again, to have one loving cuddle before parting. Of course, it ended in raising such a storm of desire as a fuck could only allay—she said—

"My loved Charlie, this must really be the last."

I told her it had so excited me to see her splendid bum before my eyes when we were on the floor that I should like to kneel behind and put it in that way. I really meant into her cunt, but she thought I meant her bottom-hole, and said—

"Well, you are a strange boy, what on earth made you think you could put that great big thing of yours into my bottom-hole; but, to tell you the truth, after being well fucked, I rather like it that way, so you shall try, but you must be gentle in getting in."

I said, "I did not know I could do it that way with my prick, I meant to put it into your cunt from behind, but now, from what you say, I should like to try what the other is like."

You see, I was keeping up my apparent ignorance. She turned on her face, and keeping her head on the pillow, drew up her knees to her belly and exposed to the greatest advantage her glorious backside. I knelt behind, but previous to beginning, I glued my lips to the delicious orifice, and shoved my tongue in as far as I could, and deliciously excited her. Then approaching my stiff-standing prick, and thrusting it into her cunt up to the roots two or three times, so as thoroughly to lubricate it, I withdrew and placed it before the smaller temple of lust; then, by a gentle uniform pressure, I gradually and almost imperceptibly glided in to the utmost extent. She pushed her bottom out, and, I could feel, was straining as if to void something, which is the real method to accelerate the entrance of a prick in that enchanting channel with the least difficulty and pain. We then com-

menced a slow movement—she wanted me to stoop forward
and place my arm round her body, and frig her clitoris, but
I begged her to do it herself, and allow me the luxury of looking on the delightful wriggling of her superb backside, and
also the sight of my own prick surging in and then withdrawing. She humoured me, and we had a most exquisite fuck. Her
bottom-hole had hardly so tight a pressure as she could
exercise with her cunt, but, nevertheless, it held me in very
firmly, and had a peculiar heat which was most exciting. We
both died off together, she so completely overcome with
extatic delight that her body sank flat on the bed, drawing
me with her, without unsheathing my weapon. We lay for a
short period, she convulsively shuddering from time to time
with the intense degree of excitement this delicious route had
produced upon her. At last she begged me to rise and relieve
her. As we must now separate, I rose. She assisted me in my
ablutions, put on my night-shirt, conducted me to my bed,
fondly kissed and thanked me for the exquisite night of every
species of delight I had conferred upon her, promising a
repetition the following night. She left me and locked the
door of communication, but previously unlocked mine, in case
I should oversleep myself.

Thus ended the first delightful night I ever passed with
that most charming and deliciously lascivious woman—the
first of many scores that followed, but in none of which were
her raptures more intense, if as much. She ever after dwelt
on the night when she had been the happy means of initiating
me into all love's mysteries, for she never knew of my previous
experiences, and always plumed and prided herself on being
my first instructress.

The next day I was somewhat somnolent, of which you
may be sure Miss Frankland took no notice. She retired to
her own room when we went for our recreation. My sisters
scolded me for not coming to them the previous night, but I
told them that Miss F. had continued to move about her

room for so long a time that I had fallen fast asleep, and even
then had not had enough, as they might have observed how
sleepy I had been all day. However, to satisfy them, I gamahuched them both, and fucked them both while each was
giving the other a second gamahuche, so that then each spent
three times to my twice. I thus kept in my forces for the
renewed delights I anticipated at night. I went to bed early
and slept soundly at once, having no anxiety about keeping
awake, feeling certain that Miss F. would awaken me as soon
as she was ready to take me to her arms. She came, and we
passed another most delicious night of every salacious and
libidinous enjoyment. A third night followed, which differed only in the lascivious proposition of Miss Frankland
to deflower my bottom-hole with her wonderfully prominent
and elongated clitoris, little dreaming that there, too, she had
been anticipated by our loved and charming friend Mac-
Callum. She had, however, all the imaginary pleasure of first
possession. As you may well suppose, I did not attempt in any
way to enlighten her ignorance thereon. We had gamahuched
each other, I had fucked her twice in the cunt and once in
her bottom-hole, when the fancy seized her to bugger me
with her clitoris. Of course, I made no objection; on the
contrary, sucking it up to a proper stiffness, I placed myself
on my hands and knees in the most favourable position to
satisfy her erotic fancy. She first slipped her tongue into my
bottom-hole, then spit upon her clitoris, and then anointed
my aperture with the delicious slime of her well-fucked cunt,
and then with the utmost ease pushed the dear thing up to
its utmost limits. I humoured her in every way, wriggling my
bottom sideways, which she declared was a vast improvement on her back and forward movements. She passed her
arm round my belly, and with that exquisitely delightful
touch on my prick for which she was so distinguished, she
excited me to the utmost, making my *sphincter ani* respond
to the throbbings of my exquisitely delighted prick, and

equally exciting her lascivious passions with the idea of first possession of that narrow abode of voluptuousness. She could feel by the electric excitement of my prick how near I was to spending, and quickening the action of hand and clitoris, we both died away together in all the raptures that such an extra exciting conjunction could produce.

Several nights thus passed in the indulgence of every form of the most lascivious enjoyment. We used to amuse our moments of relaxation in trying who could suggest any new position or varied manner of effecting the delicious junction of our bodies. On one occasion, recurring to the state of excitement her flogging had thrown me into, I asked her, as if I did not know the fact very well already, if the application of the rod on the bottom of a woman, or the mere act of being flogged, at all excited her sex. She told me both acted with great force on her erotic nerves. She thought, from experience, that being whipped caused the greatest excitement and produced the greatest longing to be fucked.

"Then," said I, "do you think it had erotically excited my sisters?"

"Certainly, especially your sister Eliza. I do not know whether you noticed her sudden impulse to embrace and kiss me after her return to school work the day I flogged her; that was a stray erotic impulse, and had we been alone, I could not have avoided responding to it in a way that would have delighted her, and initiated her into some of the delicious mysteries of venery. Nay, I think, but for my happy discovery of your great and delightful merits, I should have sought for and found an opportunity of being alone with that dear girl, for you must know we can lasciviously embrace our own sex with immense mutual pleasure, and although not equal to that which this noble fellow"—(taking hold of my prick)— "inspires, is not without its merit, and even as a little variety from time to time is very enticing."

"Then, I suppose, you still have some hankerings after the virgin charms of dear Lizzie?"

"I have, and what is more, I believe both Mary's and her passions have already developed themselves. I have sometimes fancied I heard suppressed sighs and gentle movements going on in their beds, and I shrewdly suspect they were practising masturbation on each other. I did not interfere, and after what has passed between you and me, I will tell you that I had a little plan in my head to let them proceed to such lengths that when I chose to make the discovery they would be at my mercy. I then could initiate them in every lascivious and voluptuous delight that woman can have with woman. The happy discovery of your excellences, and the the perfect facility my change of room has given for meeting without the slightest chance of discovery, has for the present driven that idea out of my head. I am, however, indebted to it for the change of room, as I asked for it solely to leave the two girls the utmost liberty to indulge in their voluptuous mutual enjoyments, certain that it would increase and give them every desire for the further instruction I could impart to them."

"I suppose you would have fucked them with this dear stiff little thing?" said I.

"Oh, yes, you darling, but you have so excited me talking about it, that you must fuck me directly."

We indulged in a most exciting fuck, and when recovered from the confusion of ideas the delightful crisis always produces, we resumed our conversation on the interesting subject of my sisters. I observed that she had not lately flogged them again.

"All your fault; I am now so satisfied with you that I no longer seek for relief to pent-up desires in that way."

"Tell me, dear Miss Frankland, did flogging my sisters excite you much?"

"It did, even to spending; but the fear of proceeding further with them at that time rendered me ferocious. The very severity I used was as it were in revenge for stopping short of other salacious embraces, but if once I had gone so far

as to make them partakers of my lubricity, I should never
have flogged them again so severely, but only to such a
gentle extent as would raise their passions to an uncomfortable pitch, rendering them slaves to my burning lust. Even
now I have, from time to time, a desire to do so, especially
with dear Eliza, as I think she had far more of venereal lust
in her nature than Mary. You would not object, dear
Charlie?"

"Not in the least, if you will only give me the voluptuous
satisfaction of hearing all the details from your lips afterwards; it would stimulate us both to additional raptures, and
spur our desires to renewed combats."

"I don't think it wants much to do that; your glorious prick
is as hard as iron."

"It was the lascivious idea of your enjoying Lizzie that
made it get up, but I must fuck you again or it will burst."

"I, too, my dear boy, am inflamed at the idea; put it in
behind this time; I have a great letch in that way at this
moment."

I did as I was directed, and so great was the agony of
delight when we died away that she sank on the bed dragging me after her, and we lay almost insensible, soaking in
bliss for quite half an hour. We did not again renew our conversation that night, but I determined to push her forward
to carry out her idea, and also to give Lizzie a hint to second
her wishes in every way, without giving her any idea of what
had passed between Lizzie and me, and being equally reserved as to my nightly connection with Miss Frankland.

The following night we passed again in all the amatory
delights we could imagine. After our deep midnight sleep,
which always took place locked in each other's arms, and
poor cockey held firm as if in a vice, I awoke her first, and
found my prick stiff-standing in her cunt, which was involuntarily pressing it in the delicious interior folds. I began
moving gently, until she was so excited as to quite wake up,

when she joined me in all the raptures of a delicious and voluptuous fresh morning fuck. We then rose to satisfy natural wants, and cool our excited nerves by a copious ablution. As we were returning to bed, I observed that Miss Frankland took something out of her wardrobe wrapped up in a handkerchief, and placed it under her pillow with a certain air of mystery. I said nothing. After purifying ourselves we always indulged in a voluptuous gamahuche; after which Miss Frankland generally asked, as a favour, that I should finish off *in culo*. I loved her delicious bottom-hole too dearly ever to refuse. She placed herself as usual on her knees, thighs well drawn up, and head down, so as to make the most of her glorious backside. After I had followed the usual preamble of thrusting in and out of her luscious and juicy cunt so as to lubricate my prick well, I then introduced it, always with the slow and gradual pressure, until it was sheathed to the hilt, when we generally paused some minutes to reciprocate mutual throbs and pressures. In this lascivious pause I saw her hand steal under the pillow, and draw out the handkerchief and put it under her belly. I shortly found a considerable substance entering her cunt, and making my quarters still more tight and narrow. I began to move, and found the substance in the other entrance keeping time to my movements. I had a tight hold of her projecting clitoris, which I had frigged up to a stiff-standing point. I slipped my hand down and found she was dildoing herself with what proved to be a very handsome dildo, in not very formidable proportions.

"That's right, my darling," I cried, "why did you not do it openly, you ought to know that my greatest wish is for you to enjoy these salacious meetings in every possible voluptuous manner; frig on then, my beloved, and be sure that if it adds to your delight it adds to mine."

"Thank you, my darling Charlie, shove away, I am in the

seventh heaven of delight in having as good as two pricks working in me at once."

She would have explained more, but her words were cut short by the extasies the double fuck produced, and she spent copiously before me, on finding which I held back, and was rewarded by making her spend eventually with the utmost excess of delight twice to my once. By this time it was broad daylight, and too late in the morning to enter into any conversation on the new partner in our amatory combats, which was reserved for the next meeting.

This did not occur so soon as we expected, for that day Miss Frankland's flowers declared themselves. It was a fortunate thing for me that she had them at the period of the new moon, and as Mary had them at the full, it enabled me to dedicate a night or two to my beloved sisters, who considered I had been neglecting them of late. I said I had not felt very well, and that I began to think that our excessive fucking was becoming too much for me; that they must remember I was one to two, and I felt if I continued to over-exert myself I should break down and fail altogether.

"That would never do, dear Charlie, and it is very true you do twice our work and more, because we don't pour down such a torrent as you do when we spend; you must take care of yourself, we will not be so exacting in future, but cool ourselves first by a mutual gamahuche between Lizzie and me."

I thus arranged a certain amount of cessation of fucking in that quarter that I might dedicate the more to the far more exciting powers of the delicious and salacious Miss Frankland.

I had always remained in my own bed until I heard her heavy breathing, denoting that she slept, before I dared to leave my own room to go to my sisters. The desire of racking me off, as dear charming Mrs. Benson used to call it, might have seized her, and my absence would have discovered all.

However, she had, no doubt, considered that it would be all to her advantage that I should be left perfectly quiet to recruit my system, after the heavy drain on my amatory resources which she had kept up for the previous fortnight. She never sought in any way to excite me until a day and a night after the cessation of her menses. She told me it was much better to have done with it entirely at once, rather than by erotic excitement keep up the discharge for a week or more.

"And it is not, my dear Charlie, from any want of randy lust on my part, for, especially at first, there is an extreme desire to be well laboured by the biggest prick one could find in existence; the natural irritation of the parts seem to be increased by the way in which the sensual system is affected in that quarter. Former experience has taught me that it is much better to bear this, than by seeking for erotic excitement to keep up the natural discharge for twice as long as it would otherwise endure. Besides which, there would have been a danger of affecting your dear health. Sometimes conjunctions, at such a period, produce a urethral irritation very prejudicial to a man, and such as might deprive me of the delight of your embraces for some weeks. So you see, my own beloved boy, that in every way it is prudent to avoid any amorous excitement at such a period, however hard nature may press for venereal relief. Some women hazard all this, and for a momentary gratification, run risks perfectly unwarrantable, not only for themselves, but above all for their lovers. I, too, my darling, have had my day of imprudence, and knowing the result, I should be both cruel and stupidly insensate to let you run the risk of what already occurred."

As she recounted those sage counsels, I could not but remember my loved Mrs. Benson, whose advice had been of such service to me, and here was another loved mistress instructing me in further matters connected with the sex. It certainly was a stroke of great good fortune for me to have met at so early an age two such admirable women, not only most amorous and lascivious, but instructing me in the real knowledge of their sex, and the world, at the very time that they were indulging my every lascivious desire, as well as their own. Mistresses of their art, no mystery in love's catalogue of excitements, and of means of gratifying the same, was unknown to them. But they knew, too, how to inculcate wisdom for future conduct. I owe every amatory success of my after-life to the admirable teachings of these two charming and estimable women.

The next night, after we had sacrificed sufficiently often to Venus to enable us more calmly to resume the delightful discussion on the various ways of pampering and exciting the passions, I turned the conversation on flogging; for to take you, dear reader, into my confidence, I was seized with an uncontrollable letch to flog the superb bottom of my loved mistress. I had often seen it palpitating under the vigorous attacks of my stiff-standing pego, while belabouring either of the delicious entrances to the temples of lust. I had often given her glorious bottom good sound slaps of the hand, but I longed to apply to it in earnest a good birch rod, see it flush to a raw meat hue, and then to shove my prick with the utmost force into either or both of the delicious orifices. I thought the best way of arriving at this desired object was to recur to her own description of a less severe flogging exciting the passions with pain; and as she had also admitted that it excited her equally to be flogger or flogee, I proposed that she should exercise a gentle discipline on my bottom, to try its efficacy. She jumped at the idea, but there was no rod in her room, perforce the ceremony was put off until the next night. On that occasion, she advised me first to indulge in every excess of lubricity, and when nature should begin to flag, then the real efficacy of the rod would be experienced. She aided me with the utmost skill in every act of most voluptuous and luxurious venery, and we mutually poured down six tributes to our blessed Mother Venus, with very little cessation, for we both wished to feel somewhat exhausted, before trying the effects of the birching system. We lay quiet for a short time, and then dear Miss Frankland began exciting me, but only in an ordinary way. My prick had already been too well satiated with the previous encounters to respond at once to the calls made on it.

"Ah," said she, in her sweetest way, "I see we want the rod here. Prepare yourself, sir, and take care to make no resistance, or it will be the worse for your bottom."

Following her cue, I began to implore pity, to promise I would behave better in short time, etc., etc. But she was inexorable, and ordered me to lie across her knees. Then, taking me round the waist, she gave a smart cut or two, really sharp, that made me for the moment wince.

"Take care, sir, you are resisting, and you know your punishment will be severe, if you so continue."

"Forgive me, mistress dear, and I will never do so again."

"We shall see."

Cut three, sharp, though not so severe. I did not flinch.

"Ah! that is something like a good boy, now we shall have no difficulty."

She began a series of less and less severe blows, until it ended in a gentle irritable titillation which very shortly began to show its effects by the stiffness of my pego—fiercely shoving against the naked thigh of my loved castigator, who, passing a hand round my body, laid hold of it, delighted to find how efficacious her proceedings had been. Pretending to be quite exhausted, she sank back on the bed, and said she could do no more. I sprang upon her, and we had two more *coups* without withdrawing, with the greatest excess of voluptuousness. It was now my turn, and as she let me slip out of her delicious cunt, I took that up as a cause of dissatisfaction.

"What! you naughty girl," I cried, "is that the way you treat your master, bundling him out of his room in that manner; here, give me the rod, I must make your bottom pay for your ill conduct—here, kneel on this footstool, and lay your body over my thighs, no resistance, or it will be the worse for you."

"Oh! pray, sir, do forgive me this time," and she knelt at my side, and pretended to cry. I forced her down, and she presented her glorious backside, in all its splendour of rotundity and size, before my delighted gaze. I seized her round the waist, and first gloated my sight with all the full and lascivious charms, not only displayed, but in my power, and I armed with a splendid rod. I gave her two or three sharp cuts, which made her beauteous buttocks wriggle, but called forth no remonstrances; but as I continued, in all the rage of lust the exercise excited, to flog away most severely, she begged me to be somewhat more gentle. But I flogged on with increased vigour, until she began to writhe under the severity of the punishment I was inflicting. She struggled fiercely, at last, to be free, but she was completely in my power, and I did not spare her until I saw that, changing from severe pain, her feelings were turning to a storm of lechery and lust. She became frantic with excitement, and screamed out—

"Cease, darling Charlie, and fuck me directly. I am dying for it."

I threw down the rod, jumped on the bed, and drew up her loins, so that she was placed in a kneeling position; she herself seized my bursting prick, and carried it to the lips of her cunt, where he instantly engulphed himself to the hilt. Her movements became lascivious beyond expression, and were urged with a vigour, which brought down in a very short time a torrent of sperm from both of us. We were too much excited to stop short, and almost without a pause, a second course was run still more voluptuously. She was not even then satisfied, but making me lie on my back, she reversed herself upon me, and we commenced a mutual gamahuche. I succeeded in making her spend again, and she was able to bring my pego up to a standing point.

"Now, Charlie, dear, we must finish off behind."

So getting again on her hands and knees, she guided my willing prick to the narrower abode of felicity. After first steeping it for a moment in the moisture of her foaming and reeking cunt, I thrust it into her bottom-hole. I seized hold of her clitoris, she had her dildo all ready, and working it herself with one hand, we ran a last course of most lustful and lecherous enjoyment, which ended in such killing raptures that we both sank all but insensible on the bed. Exhausted as we were by the wild excesses we had indulged in, we fell, without moving or regaining our senses, into a deep and profound slumber, until almost too late in the morning, so that I had to regain my room the moment we awoke, without attempting any further amorous toyings. Thus ended my first experiences as a flogger. The sensation was so new, and the temptation to lay on with a vengeance was so great, that I had gone beyond all reasonable bounds in inflicting such a severe punishment on the glorious bum of my beloved Miss Frankland. I must, however, do her the justice to say that she comprehended and excused the feelings under which I acted, only begging me, on any future occasion not to let them carry me away so far as they had done on this. We several times renewed this bum flogging, but with more moderate inflictions—sufficient to highly excite without actually punishing the patient, whichever of us it might be.

We often after this made flogging the theme of our discussions, and I gradually led on to the idea she had expressed of Lizzie's evidently amorous disposition. She still affirmed that such was her conviction. I then suggested that it would be worth her while to try and gratify it, as well for Lizzie's sake as for the satisfaction of her own letch in that way.

"I suppose you could easily find a pretext if you desired to do so?"

"Yes, easily enough, the idea excites me, and I shall indulge it."

I do not remember what the pretext was, but Lizzie was kept in next afternoon at four o'clock—Mary and I proceeded to the summer house. I knew we should not be interrupted by Lizzie, and that I need not hold in for her satisfaction. So I gave Mary all the benefit of our being alone, and we had four most exquisite and refined indulgencies in every attitude admitted of by the legitimate entrance to love's temple. For, as yet, I had never been able to gain an entrance to the narrower orifice, which was too small for my formidable weapon to penetrate. It is odd how easily Lizzie accommodated me in her delicious bottom-hole, while Mary, older and more womanly in form, was as yet unable to make room for me in that strait path of bliss. When night came I was all curiosity to know how my dear mistress had carried on matters with Lizzie. She told me that Lizzie had been somewhat nervous at first, but she had spoken kindly to her, told her how her amiable and loving conduct after her first whipping had won her affection; that she did not mean to be so severe as on the former occasion, but that discipline must be kept up.

"So come, my dear girl, drop off your frock, as I shall mine, that the bundle of clothes may be out of the way, as well as to avoid their being creased."

Seeing that Lizzie still trembled a little after she had dropped her gown, she took her in her arms, and kissing her lovingly, desired her not to be afraid—she would not punish her much.

"Lift up all your things, my dear, and let me see if any marks of the former punishment remain."

Lizzie had a very prominent and very promising bottom. Miss Frankland felt it all over, and admired loudly its form and firmness, declaring it was quite beautiful to look at, and how womanly it was growing.

"Turn round, and let me see if you are as womanly in front. Upon my word, a well-formed mount with a charming mossy covering."

Her hand wandering over her form excited Lizzie, whose face flushed and eyes glistened with rising desires. Miss Frankland herself became moved, but proceeded at once to lay her across her lap, and began with gentle switches, just sufficiently sharp to attract the blood in that direction, which, of course, acted with double force on all the already excited erotic organs, and Lizzie began to wriggle her bum in all the lasciviousness of lust under the excited gaze of Miss Frankland, who, seeing how matters were going on in her favour, increased the force of her blows, but only sufficiently to still more lecherously excite her patient—until, driven to an excess of lust, she cried out—

"Oh, my loved Miss Frankland, I am dying with pleasure, do embrace and caress me."

Miss Frankland lifted her up, and drew her to her bosom and lips, and, while sucking her tongue, slipped her hand down and found Lizzie's quim wet with her flowing spunk, and her little clitoris stiff with the erotic passion that was consuming her. She frigged her until she spent again, while their tongues were in each other's mouth. As Lizzie spent, Miss F. shoved a finger up her cunt, which, of course, met with no resistance, but as Lizzie possessed in perfection the art of nipping, she was sufficiently tight to leave a doubt of anything but finger-fucking.

"Ah, you little puss, you have been playing with this before now, tell me the truth?"

"I will tell you everything, if you will only play with me again. Ever since you flogged Mary and myself, we have both been so often burning down there, and have found out that feeling it, and pushing fingers in, was so nice, although at first we often hurt ourselves. But you do it so much better than Mary—oh, do, do it again, dear Miss Frankland!"

"I shall do it much better, my darling, with what I have got down there—look here!"

And, lifting up her petticoat and chemise, she exposed, to the absolute astonishment of Lizzie, her extraordinary mass of hair, and her fiery red clitoris glowing and sticking out of its black mass of curls.

"How beautiful!" cried Lizzie. "I declare, you have got a doodle, for which I have been so longing; I must kiss it."

Stooping down, she took it in her mouth, and sucked it.

"Stop, dear Lizzie, we shall both enjoy it."

Taking the cushion from the chair, she lay down on her back on the floor, telling Lizzie to turn her face the other way, and to kneel down across her body, so that both their mouths could adapt themselves to each other's quim.

Lizzie told me afterwards that she took care to show no previous knowledge, but to let Miss Frankland apparently initiate her into all the ceremonies of gamahuching.

Miss Frankland glued her lips to dear Lizzie's charming quim, while Lizzie took her extraordinary clitoris into her mouth. After a few ardent caresses Miss Frankland pushed a finger up Lizzie's bottom-hole, then paused an instant to tell Lizzie not only to follow her example in that respect, but to use her other hand in her quim while sucking her clitoris. Then, both adapting themselves as prescribed, they gamahuched on, until both could no longer move from the excessive raptures produced by their profuse discharge. After this first bout Lizzie became curious to see all the wonderful hair-covered organ and limbs of Miss Frankland, who gratified her to the utmost extent of her wishes. Nor did she leave this inspection entirely to Lizzie, but reciprocated it. Undoing her dress above, she uncovered the charming budding beauties of Lizzie's bubbies, and began sucking the nipples. Their mutual caresses and handlings very quickly refired these hot and lecherous women. After a little renewed gamahuching, until both were wild with excitement, Miss Frankland proposed to put her clitoris into Lizzie's quim; told her to kneel down, and kneeling behind her, she sheathed it with ease in the hot and juicy folds of Lizzie's beautiful cunt. Passing her hand under Lizzie's belly, she frigged her clitoris until again nature gave down her delicious tribute, and they sank in all the voluptuous languor that follows. A third time they renewed their salacious and lascivious raptures, then resumed their dresses so as to be ready to receive us. Miss Frankland begged Lizzie to keep her counsel and not reveal, even to Mary, what had passed. But Lizzie urged Miss F. to admit Mary into the new mysteries she had just herself been taught, and said she could assure her that Mary had a far more beautiful body than hers, and would like it quite as well as she did.

"Well, my dear, I shall think of it, and find an occasion to flog her, as I have done you."

"Oh, that will be jolly!" cried Lizzie. "She will like it just as much as I do; it is so nice, you must flog me every day, dear Miss Frankland. I loved you from the first, I adore you now."

They embraced most lovingly, but our return put an end for the present to any further conversation.

These details were accompanied and interrupted by two or three delicious and most voluptuous fucks, without once withdrawing my burning prick from her equally heated and throbbing cunt—for her description of these proceedings was most exciting. When she had finished, I withdrew, that we might gamahuche each other, and lick up all the delicious spunk in which her juicy cunt abounded. We then renewed our combats, sacrificing to holy Mother Venus in both orifices. Then we slept as only easy-conscienced people like ourselves could sleep; and, like giants refreshed by slumber, renewed our devotions on every altar before separating in the morning.

Two days later Mary was initiated by Miss Frankland in a like manner to Lizzie, while Lizzie and I made the most of our

time in the summer house. Excited by her naïve description
of her scene with Miss Frankland, we indulged in every
salacious device that we could cram into the hour's absence,
which, by the way, we lengthened out by more than a quarter
of an hour, for which Miss Frankland thanked me at night.
Her scene with Mary had been one of even greater lubricity,
in consequence of Mary at once lending herself to everything,
and acknowledging that she knew from Lizzie what she had
to expect. Besides, Mary's more developed form and something
about her greatly excited Miss F., and she was quite amorous
upon her. She had done so much in the way of spending, that
after I had gamahuched and fucked her two entrances three
times, she required the stimulus of the rod to bring her up
to the highest point of lascivious lubricity. And, to tell the
truth, I afterwards required and received it myself. Thus our
voluptuous passions acted one on the other, and we passed an
exhausting night in every excess and refinement of venery, in
which Miss Frankland's dildoes, for she had two, of different
sizes, played no small part in both our persons.

Now that the ice was broken, I easily persuaded Miss F.
to have occasionally first one and then the other of my sisters
to sleep with her, alleging that an occasional early night's rest
would recruit my powers, and that when she dismissed her
bedfellow in the morning, I could finish her off in force; she
could thus initiate them in mutual floggings, and in the use
of dildo. Of course, I need not say that my ultimate object
was to succeed in our making it a general orgie. In this
indeed it ended, but not exactly as I had intended. That
mattered not, as long as the desired object was attained. I
had the delightful opportunity, too, of watching through my
peep-hole many of the delicious scenes of lubricity enacted,
and when driven to the fiercest excess of passion, I used to
withdraw, steal up to the unoccupied sister, and vent my
raging lust in every indulgence with her.

This had been carried on for about a fortnight, one or

other of the girls sleeping every other night with Miss Frankland. Lizzie, it appeared, had often professed to long to see a real cock, and had managed to worm out of Miss F. that she had enjoyment of mine. The little hussey importuned Miss F. to let her see me fucking her, saying that she could easily hide behind the curtains, and I would never know. Miss F., whose passions were at the utmost tension of desire, consented, and placing Lizzie where she could see without being seen, opened my door, but found an empty bed. She at first suspected that I had gone to one of the female servants, but thought she would make sure and see if Mary was not the object. So she stole softly upstairs, and found us in the act of enjoying a double gamahuche, which as it was early morning light, she could see without difficulty. She had the kindness to let us enjoy it to the end, and then dragging me off, said—

"Oh! Charles! this is dreadful! Why could you not be content with me?—have I ever refused you? Do you know this would be the ruin of all of us if ever it should become known? You are too young to know the dreadful consequences of discovery."

Here she burst out in a torrent of tears—it was evident from real fear of the sad results that might ensue, and not from any feeling of jealousy. I threw myself into her arms, and as she had herself acknowledged our intimacy, I had less difficulty in alluding to it. I caressed and fondled her, and told her there was no fear of discovery—less now than ever—as we would be all interested alike in keeping our secret; she would cover my intimacy with my sisters, and they would cover my intimacy with her. All at once she said—

"How long has this been going on?—tell me truly."

I had long prepared myself for such a question, and at once replied that after the description of the libidinous scenes that had taken place between her and them, and her exquisite account of their young charms, I got so lecherous upon

them that I had sought Mary out while she was engaged with
Lizzie, and Lizzie when Mary was with her; they were both
too much delighted to refuse me anything, and we had now
enjoyed each other about a dozen times. I had previously
told my sisters to support any story I might recount to Miss
F. Lizzie had stolen up after she found Miss Frankland had
passed through my room, and now both confirmed the tale
told. We surrounded Miss Frankland, caressing her in every
way. My pego got terribly excited. Drawing up my night-
shirt, I said—

"Let this dear fellow make peace between us, and become
equally dear to all. I know, my loved mistress, that my
sisters are longing to see him exercised on your glorious person, and buried in your delicious hairy cunt, so let me offer
up sacrifice to its juicy charms. Lizzie has just said you
sought me for the purpose—see, the dear clitoris is raising
its head—let Mary lie down under you to suck your clitoris,
and see my prick close above her eyes in vigorous action filling your exquisite cunt. You can gamahuche her and Lizzie
can look on behind, witness the glorious sight, and act postillion to my bottom-hole."

"Well, my beloved children, the die is cast, it is no use
crying after spilt milk, so let us make the best of it. I never
could resist the eloquent look of this loved and long thick
thing, that was made for giving poor woman all she could
crave for."

So arranging our relative positions as I had prescribed, we
ran a course of the most luxurious and salacious enjoyment
imaginable. Lizzie, who had taken possession of one of the
dildoes, manipulated herself, while watching every voluptuous
movement of our bodies, and we all managed to spend most
rapturously together. We could not affort to do more at that
moment, as time was creeping on, and the household would
soon be astir. Miss Frankland regained with me my room, her
own door being locked, and kissing me tenderly, said I was a

bad boy, but she supposed it must eventually have come to this, so it was well it was sooner than later.

Thus passed our first general orgie, which was the precursor of many much more luxuriously and salaciously libidinous, and which I shall more minutely describe as events progress.

Miss Frankland would not allow us to have a general orgie the next night. She was now aware of our summer house doings—only of late begun, as she supposed—for my story had been too plausibly off-hand not to deceive her, especially as she had felt convinced by all that occurred on our first fucking that she had had the delightful pleasure of taking my maidenhead. She was quite satisfied on that head. But she now suspected that what I had just begun I should be too glad to repeat. She accompanied us to the garden in our recreation hour, so that nothing erotic took place. We sat down all together after a little running about, and Miss F. opened to us a rule of conduct we must in future pursue. She said—

"However delightful it would be for you all, as well as for myself, to meet every night, it would in the first instance become a dangerous habit, dangerous because of engendering carelessness in the necessary precautions against discovery; and next, and above all, because it would be the destruction of our loved and darling Charlie, who could not possibly long continue such excessive venery as three loved objects at once would constantly require of him."

Seeing my inclination to interrupt her, and declare that I felt quite equal to it, she stopped me, and told us I was too young to know what such excessive indulgence would lead to; that we must trust to her experience and be guided by her, and we should all find the advantage of it. Three times a week was the utmost she could allow, when we should be all together. The other nights she would take care that I committed no excess. Such were the sage counsels of this admirable woman, and such in future became the programme of our proceedings. I rebelled and kicked against what I thought at the time too great a restriction, but I eventually became convinced that greater pleasure followed the enforced delays. Of course I slept with Miss Frankland on what might be called our off nights, but she soon established a custom of restraining my spendings to twice a night, allowing me to excite and make her spend as often as I pleased. I was difficult to manage at first, but eventually settled down in great regularity to the rules she dictated, and, indeed, enforced. I soon found out the wisdom of her proceeding, for often afterwards my lagging efforts required the spur of the rod to be applied in earnest for the completion of our orgies.

The second night after the discovery of my intercourse with my sisters was the first of meeting all four together, in Miss Frankland's room. We had been sent, as usual, early to bed, and Miss F. had privately recommended us to go quietly to sleep as soon as possible, and not to be under any anxiety, as she herself would go for the girls, after all the household had retired. As for me, it was the plan I had always adopted, as it enabled me to reap the greater amount of enjoyment, and its longer continuance, by the rest I had previously secured. Winter had passed away, and summer came round again. It was a lovely, warm, moonlight night. As soon as we were all assembled, stripping to the buff was the order of the night; then followed charming embraces and mutual posings, so as each should admire the beauties of all. Hands wandered everywhere over every charm, chiefly concentrating on the wonderful and finely developed form of the fascinating Frankland, whose richness of coal-black hair was so deliciously exciting. It soon became necessary to calm the first effervescence of our passions, which we always did by a general gamahuche. Miss Frankland, who had taken an extraordinary letch for Mary, paired off with her, while Lizzie and I accommodated each other. Miss Frankland, who had provided herself with a store of dildoes, furnished us all with one, differing in size, according to the intention of their application. As Mary's bottom-hole as yet could only accommodate a moderate size, Miss F. kept the smallest for her particular use, the others were indiscriminately used. Thus armed, we proceeded to enter on all the voluptuous excesses of gamahuching in every form, lengthening out our pleasures as much and as long as possible, that we might pass the whole night in the most libidinous raptures. When the extatic moment overtook us, our mouths had to cease their operations to give vent to the expressions of the rapturous nature of our feelings. We lay panting for some time before being able to rise and resume our mutual caresses. Now that we had taken off the edge of our lustful appetite, we prepared more calmly for further and more voluptuous combinations. The upper coverings of the bed were entirely removed, so that it presented nearly a square field of combat for love's encounters, admirably adapted for its purpose. We held a council as to our next movements, and finally decided to begin as follows: Mary to lie down on her back, Lizzie reversed above her, Miss Frankland was to indulge in her letch for Lizzie, which was that of fucking her bottom-hole with her extraordinary clitoris, while I was to fuck Miss Frankland's cunt, and postillion her smaller orifice with two fingers, Lizzy was to postillion Mary with her finger, while gamahuching her, Mary to apply the smaller dildo to my bottom-hole, and frig Lizzie's cunt with a larger one. It was also agreed we should run two courses in this voluptuous group, varying only in the substitution of my prick in Miss Frankland's bottom-hole, instead of her cunt, in which was to be placed one of the dildoes. We were none of us to press matters to a speedy termination, but to make the most of the exquisite conjunction of our parts. We enjoyed a most salacious and voluptuous fuck, and so managed matters as all should spend together in perfect raptures of lubricity and lust. Notwithstanding the pleasure of the final discharge, we managed, as previously agreed, to hold our mutual positions, our parts palpitating with repeated throbbings on or in the delicious quarters with which they were conjoined. These soon reawakened our passions, which we as yet had done but little to calm, and when sufficiently heated, the slight change agreed upon was effected, and I plunged up to the hilt in the glorious and hairy bottom-hole of the divine Frankland, who gave almost a scream of delight as she felt my huge pego rushing up into her burning entrails. We had to pause some minutes to allow her excitement to subside to a certain extent, or she would have discharged after two or three thrusts of my potent weapon. We then proceeded more leisurely, and after drawing out our enjoyment in the most salacious and voluptuous manner, the extatic moment seized us all together, with such an excess of wild enjoyment that with screams of almost agonised delight, we poured into or upon each other whole torrents of hot boiling sperm, and sank almost insensible into a confused heap of naked forms. We were a long time in recovering our senses. Then disentangling ourselves, we rose and laved our parts in cold water, not only to purify ourselves, but as a stimulant to further exertions in all the wildest excesses of lubricity that any of us could fancy. But we always managed so as to make Miss F. think that she was the author of any new salacious idea or suggestion. In fact she nearly was so in every case, for her experience in every letch, and its gratification in every form of libidinous refinement, was great and we owed to her many new and delicious combinations in our salacious orgies. After partaking of wine and cake, which Miss F. had taken care to secure, we indulged in some delicious romping and pulling about of the rich curls and hairy coverings of nearly all Miss Frankland's superb form. The girls above all admired the magnitude, hardness, and beauty of her truly magnificent buttocks, and what with one now and then sucking her bubbies, and at other times toying with her already standing clitoris, we soon brought her to such a state of excitement that, seizing hold of Mary, she got her on the table and gamahuched her, while Lizzie, creeping under, sucked her clitoris, and I pushed my prick from behind into her cunt. We brought on a delicious spend, and the glorious creature died away in excess of pleasure along with Mary, while I had not yet arrived at the climax. So I contented myself with making my prick throb to her delicious squeezings, until the fatigue of the position required us to break up the pose. She was so far calmed that she could now propose and discuss after-proceedings, and what our next form of enjoyment should be. As Mary had had an extra spend with Miss Frankland, Lizzie was now placed on her knees, with her head well down. I thrust my prick into her longing cunt. Miss Frankland standing up, strode across Lizzie's body in front of me, here I introduced first a smaller dildo up her bottomhole and then a larger one up her cunt, both up to the cod pieces. She then pushed forward her belly and put her stiffstanding clitoris into my mouth, and placed her two hands on my head. I then passed one hand under her open legs, and seizing both dildoes in one hand, proceeded to work them up and down both holes at once, in unison with my suction of her clitoris, and my fucking movements in Lizzie's cunt, who at the same time was frigging her own clitoris with her fingers. Mary, armed with two dildoes, applied one to my bottom-hole, while she fucked herself with the other. In this way we ran a most exciting and delicious course. Miss F., in the extatic moments, seemed as if she would have pressed my head into her belly. She was so charmed with the voluptuous delights this pose had given that she cried out we must not change until another course was run. Lizzie said she must change from front to back, and begged Mary to hand her a dildo with which she might frig herself. The women were ready directly, but my pego was longer in answering the call, so Miss Frankland told Mary to apply the birch rod skilfully.

This she did with great art, working the dildo, which was still in her cunt while so occupied. The effect was almost electrical, and my glorious rampant prick filled dear Lizzie's delicious and longing bottom-hole to her utmost delight. Miss F. begged Mary to give her a gentle stimulus with the rod. Nothing could better have pleased Mary, for she afterwards admitted she had long had the greatest letch to flog that glorious and immense backside. With such stimulants as these this course proved one of the most salacious and voluptuous we had yet had, and the extatic ending was accompanied with screams of delight, as we died away in the deathlike swoon of rapturous and satiated desires. We again rose to purify and refresh ourselves, and for some time after lay closely embraced on the bed. As Mary had not yet had my prick in her cunt, Miss F. proposed that I should fuck her, that Lizzie should kneel close behind us, she could fuck Lizzie's bottom-hole with her clitoris, and work one dildo up my bottom, while she worked a second in her own. No sooner said that done. Lizzie's head was shoved almost below Mary's belly, so as to bring Miss F. close enough to me to operate as she desired, and we ran another delicious course with such extreme pleasure that all sank sideways down on the bed and dropped into a sound slumber. We did not awaken until so late that we only had time to lave ourselves in cold water, finish off with a general gamahuche, and then regain our separate rooms. On this last occasion Miss Frankland said she must gamahuche me, as she delighted to break her fast on cream. The joke amused the two girls amazingly.

It was about this time Mrs. Vincent gave birth to a fine boy. I have not spoken of her since our first interview after her marriage in the summer house, when all had gone into the town to bring out Miss Frankland. We had only had two stolen interviews since that time, which I have not mentioned, because they were too hasty, and with too little comfort to have been thoroughly enjoyed; then she became too heavy with child to afford me any further opportunity. Mamma wrote a congratulating letter to Mr. Vincent, wishing him joy of the advent of a son and heir, little dreaming that her own son was the father thereof. This brought a visit from Mr. Vincent to beg that mamma would kindly become godmother to the little fellow. My mother at once assented, and asked who the godfathers were. He said an uncle, from whom they had expectations, had consented to be one, but he was at a loss to know whom to ask as second.

"Why not ask Charlie, he was always very fond of your wife as his governess, and he, too, has an uncle from whom we hope some day to receive something handsome."

"That is a very good idea of yours, Mrs. Roberts, and if you will kindly send for Charles I shall put it to him, and if he consents, it saves me all further trouble."

I was sent for, and, you may be sure, accepted immediately, thanking Mr. Vincent for the honour he did me, and hoping that Mrs. Vincent would be equally agreeable that I should be godfather, although so young.

"Leave that to me, my dear wife is so much attached to me that my wish is her law, so do not make yourself uneasy on that head."

It may well be supposed I was not at all uneasy, but quite certain that it was the very thing Mrs. V. would have proposed if she had not been withheld by prudence. We heard afterwards from Mr. V. that she had simulated objections on account of my youth, but the very first moment she could say a word to me in private it was to tell me what delight it had given her that her husband should have fulfilled in the matter the very wish nearest and dearest to her heart.

The ceremony eventually came off as had been proposed, but it was at very rare intervals that I could find an opportunity of renewing our old combats in the field of Venus. Meanwhile I had no reason to regret this as far as indulgence of my erotic passions went, because, for nearly two years, that is until I had passed my eighteenth birthday, I continued to enjoy uninterrupted bliss in the arms of the luxurious and fascinating Miss Frankland, or in orgies with her and my sisters, which culminated in every excess of venery capable of being enjoyed by three women and one youth. In fact, we all indulged rather too freely, if I may judge from the fact that, at least to Miss Frankland and myself, the rod had almost become a necessity, and occasionally even my sisters admitted it gave them a fillip. Under the able tutorship of Miss Frankland we became the most perfect adepts in every voluptuous indulgence of lubricity. But I must also give her the credit of never neglecting our education. Indeed, I may say it gained by the intimate union of our bodies. For that estimable woman impressed upon us that to keep her friendship and confidence we must do justice to her teaching. I have already said her system of instruction was very superior to anything we had previously known, and now that she had won our unbounded love and affection, there was nothing we were not ready to do in school to second her efforts for our mutual improvement. She had very superior attainments—spoke French and German like a native, had sufficient knowledge of Latin and Greek to ground me well in them, and her knowledge of music was very superior. I have hardly ever heard anyone with a more charming touch on the piano. In the two years that followed our first orgie we made really astonishing progress. We all spoke French very fairly, had a pretty good knowledge of German, especially Mary, who really spoke it well; as for myself I was well up in French, fairly so in German, and with a very good ground work of Latin and Greek.

It was about this time that an event happened which completely changed the order of my life. My mother had hinted that I had some expectations from an uncle. These were very vague. He was my father's brother, but they had never agreed, and we were almost strangers to each other. He died, and one day we were all surprised, not to say delighted, to hear from his executor, a Mr. Nixon, a rich merchant in London, that my uncle had left my mother four hundred pounds a year as long as she did not marry again, but at her death the said annuity was to be divided between my two sisters, independent of any coverture. The residue and bulk of the property was settled on me, under trust to Mr. Nixon until I was of age, with a request that I should be brought up to the law and entered as a barrister in the Inner Temple. Further, a sum of five hundred pounds was allowed for a new outfit, in every way becoming to all of us. Mr. Nixon announced that in a fortnight he would take the opportunity of being in our neighbourhood to come over and make the necessary arrangements consequent upon the altered state of affairs. He added that the residue of the property would yield about one thousand pounds a year, and that, therefore, my education must be looked to more closely than it probably had been. Here was, indeed, a change. My father had left the house and grounds, and something like six hundred pounds a year in the funds, entirely to my mother as long as she remained a widow, or until her death. Afterwards one hundred and fifty pounds per annum to each of my sisters, and the house and residue to me—a moderate income requiring other efforts to make it comfortable to one's upbringing. Here I was now the heir eventually to something like fifteen hundred pounds a year, two country houses, and a very fair house besides attached to my uncle's house. You may easily imagine the joy of the whole family when from somewhat pinched economy, we found ourselves in easy circumstances, with at once quite double our previous income. We indulged in somewhat wild dreams of what all this might produce; but mamma brought us to our senses by informing us that until I was of age Mr. Nixon would entirely control our destinies, and that it was more than probable he would insist upon sending me to a public school. This news dashed all our hopes to pieces with a vengeance, because it was precisely on our greater freedom that we had been counting, and now there was every probability our delightful intercourse and delicious orgies would come to an abrupt termination. We exchanged sad and crestfallen looks on hearing this from mamma, and met in a very disconsolate humour that night in Miss Frankland's room; but that charming and estimable woman cheered us up with the hope that if a temporary separation did occur, it would only lead to our safer and more perfect reunion hereafter.

"And, to tell you the truth," she said, "my dear Charlie, we have been of late too much for you, and your health and constitution will benefit by a forced inactivity, for I have observed some symptoms about you lately that prove we three have taxed you too hard. I have no doubt I shall be retained as governess to your sisters, and leave me alone to keep them to a point that will not disappoint you when we meet again, which must always occur at intervals of not longer than six months."

To our loving minds six months seemed an age. At the same time Miss F.'s remarks had, to a certain extent, reassured us, and although we could not enter into our orgie with the usual fury and letch, nevertheless we managed to pass a night sufficiently rapturous in the enjoyment of our libidinous passions, which many would have thought excessive.

In due course Mr. Nixon made his appearance. He was a pleasant-looking elderly gentleman, and a complete man of the world. Finding that I had been educated entirely at home under governesses, he fancied I must be a milk-and-watery ignorant youth, and had already hinted as much to mamma— who, having told me, put me on my mettle. Mr. Nixon sent for me into the parlour alone, and began an agreeable conversation apparently leading to nothing, probably with a view not to render me nervous and timid, gradually turning the conversation upon educational subjects. He was agreeably surprised to find the progress I had made, not only in historical and geographical subjects, but in languages, and above all was surprised at my knowledge of Latin and Greek. He was particular in asking if some clergyman had not lent his aid to the governess. After dinner, during which he paid great attention to Miss Frankland, he warmly complimented her on her system of teaching and its extraordinary success. At the same time he observed that, as his dear old friend had desired that his nephew should become a barrister, it would be necessary he should be sent to some clergyman taking a few boys, and then to King's College, London, before entering a barrister's chambers. Miss Frankland at once admitted the justice of the remark, and hoped that Charles would not shame her teaching.

"Quite the contrary, I assure you, Miss Frankland. I have been struck with the admirable ground work you have established, and especially the advantages you have given him of the knowledge of modern languages. I am so much pleased that I intend to beg of Mrs. Roberts to keep you as the able governess of the girls until they are so much older as to require a little knowledge of the world which a metropolitan ladies' school is sure to impart."

All this was said with a certain deference of manner to Miss Frankland, that I felt certain the old gentleman was greatly struck with her person, as well as her system of teaching. But of this it is probable my readers will learn more hereafter.

My mother, hearing of the intention of sending me to some clergyman, immediately suggested that her own brother-in-law, the Rev. Mr. Brownlow, rector of Leeds, in Kent, a retired village close to the castle of that name, would be a suitable person. He was a gentleman who had taken honours at Cambridge, and was in the habit of receiving one, two or even three young gentlemen, but never more, to prepare them for the universities. At that moment she knew by a letter from her sister that he had a vacancy. His name, she

said, stood high as an instructor, as Mr. Nixon would find
on inquiry; and as Charles had never been away from home,
it would be a great satisfaction to her to know that he was
under the care of her own sister. Mr. Nixon said he perfectly agreed to her suggestion, provided, as to which he had
no doubt, his inquiries justified his sending me there. He left
us with a promise of an early decision, and, indeed, before
the week had passed we received his full concurrence to my
mother's suggestion. So my aunt was written to, and it being
the period of the holidays, Mr. and Mrs. Brownlow were
asked to come over and spend a week, and then I could return
with them to Kent. We had not seen aunt or uncle since we
were little children, and only remembered her as a very
tall immense person. The distance had prevented personal
intercourse, and we only knew of them by interchanges of
hams, Canterbury brawn, and oysters at Christmas time. As
they replied by return of post, saying they would be with us
in two or three days following their letter, you may be sure
Miss Frankland and all of us made the most of what was to
be the last of our mutual orgies for the time. No restrictions
were put upon us, and every night was dedicated to the god
of lust and voluptuousness.

At last the fatal day arrived. My mother and the two girls
went into the town to fetch uncle and aunt out, leaving Miss
Frankland and me to our studies. You may well suppose it
was the prosody of love and not that of grammar that occupied us. There was a tenderness of manner, and a loving
kindness and fondling, which I had not before observed in
Miss Frankland, and which I should have thought alien to
her character. Embracing me tenderly, and pressing me lovingly to her bosom, she burst into a flood of tears, and
sobbed as if her heart would break as her head sank on my
shoulder. I tried to comfort her in the best way I could, and
as my kind reader knows, a woman's tears always had a most
potent effect on my prick, I placed it in her hand, she hys-

terically laughed amidst her crying, but instantly sank her
head down to the loved object, embraced, sucked, and frigged
it until I poured a flood of boiling sperm into her mouth,
which she greedily swallowed, and continued sucking until
not a drop was left. Then rising once more to caress and
embrace me, she said—

"Yes, my own beloved boy, that was indeed a means to
stop my tears, I not only adore it, but have come to love you,
my darling, more than I ever loved anything in my life—you
are my own scholar, bodily and mentally. I shall miss you
greatly, and I bitterly regret our parting; but we shall meet
again, although never with such freedom and ease as we
have done. You will spend your holidays at home, and we
shall make the most of them. I can feel the dear object already
to be made the most of again, and so it shall, dear fellow,
so come to its own nest."

These last fond words were addressed to my prick, which,
already rampant again, was claiming attention. We went at
it, hammer and tongs. Recruited at luncheon, we renewed the
raptures of lubricity as that estimable woman alone knew how
to indulge them. We were the less reasonable, as it had been
decided by us the night before that I was to find out the
habits of the coming couple before I should venture on
leaving my room to slip up to theirs, and thus I had a night of
relaxation before me.

At five o'clock the carriage drove up, and uncle and aunt
were welcomed to our house. My uncle was a tall, portly,
unctuous-looking clergyman, quite a gentleman in his manners, and with a very agreeable voice. My aunt, who was
some fifteen years my uncle's junior, was very tall for her
sex, a fine portly figure, broad shouldered, large bubbies well
apart, a small waist for her size, immense hips and evidently
buttocks to more than match. She was very stout, but stood
firm upon her pins, and walked with great elasticity of step,
showing there was a good deal in her, or rather she could

take a good deal out of anybody. She had a profusion of fair hair, with thick eyebrows, that promised abundance elsewhere. Her eyes were of a deep blue that could look very far into you. She had a very pleasing expression, a small mouth, and very white teeth. Her complexion was exceedingly fair, her arms immense, but beautifully formed, hands and feet small, fat and plump. She looked thirty-five, but was nearly forty, and was altogether a most desirable woman to look at, on a large scale. She embraced me tenderly, which I did not fail to return, and complimented me and the whole family on our late good fortune. The first introduction was altogether most agreeable, and I already began to imagine I might not be so badly off after all.

We were allowed to sit up rather later than usual, and as my aunt was fatigued with her day and night's journey, they were glad to follow our example almost immediately. I had only just time to get undressed, when I heard them enter the room which Miss Frankland had vacated the previous day. This had previously been arranged, and she now slept in my sisters' room, as formerly, until we should depart. I quickly blew out my light, for fear they should observe it shining through the chinks I had made. Kneeling down, I began to watch the proceedings. The first thing my aunt did was to squat on the pot just opposite my peep-hole, and as she held up her dress well, I could see that she had a most prominent mons Veneris, thickly covered with very fair ringlets. Her power of piss was something wonderful, it was like a cataract in force and quantity, and at once made my mutinous prick stand at the mighty rush of waters that could be so plainly heard. As she rose, and before she dropped her dress, I saw her splendid proportions of limb, the like of which had never before met my eyes. Alas! it was but a passing glimpse. However, I determined to watch on, hoping to see a further display in the course of undressing. She took off all her upper clothes, until nothing but her stays and chemise

remained. I could now mark the real grandeur of her proportions. The stays kept in the waist, and allowed the
splendour of her hips and buttocks to stand out in all their
glory. Never in my life have I seen a finer backside than
my aunt had got. I am now speaking from a vast amount of
after-inspection and adoration, but in its covered magnificence
in which I at this moment viewed it, it appeared the finest
backside I have ever met with, and was in fact the one I
alluded to some time back, when I observed that Miss Frankland's was the finest but one I ever saw. It is true, her
stoutness added greatly to its prominence, but though stout,
even very stout, it was not a stoutness you could call fat.
For in after-intimacy, which became of the very closest and
most voluptuous nature, I was never able to pinch her in
any muscular part. She had the hardest, as well as the biggest,
backside I ever met with. I am quite sure that when she
was standing upright, a child might have stood on the
immense projections of her buttocks. Her thighs were positively monstrous in their mighty proportions, as hard as
iron, exquisitely moulded, and of a fairness and smoothness
that rivalled ivory, which, in another respect, they much
resembled, namely, in feeling cold to the touch. Her legs were
worthy of the glorious frame they supported, and finished off
with a pair of charming, clean-run ankles, and very small feet
for her size. As her chemise was short sleeved, the grand
magnificence and beauty of form of her splendid arms
and neck, where the bubbies came out in all their perfection
and brilliancy of skin, were fully displayed. As may be supposed, not a bone was to be traced in her upper neck, but all
was dazzling in colour and flesh, which is such a beauty in
woman. When a woman shows her gaunt collar bones, it is
a proof of bad breeding, and a common nature. Aunt's truly
grand bubbies rose magnificently over her bodice, which I
thought at the time was their support, but this glorious
woman required nothing of the sort, for when perfectly

stripped, her bubbies stood out firm and projecting in all
their grandeur, and they were of the largest, worthy of all
her other fully developed charms. Her belly alone was somewhat too prominent, when standing up, but as she never had
had children, it did not at all hang flabbily, and ended in one
of the most prominent and largely developed montis Veneris
I have ever met with, profusely covered with the fairest of
curls, which did not prevent her lovely creamy skin from
shining through them. She was well provided with hair on
that part, but after the extraordinary hairy covering that
Miss Frankland possessed, and with which I had so often
toyed, all other women appeared as nothing in that way.
My aunt, after donning a night-robe, sat down to her toilet,
and proceeded to let down her massive bunch of tresses.
Here, she was, indeed, richly gifted, her hair was all her
own, in the utmost profusion, and, tall as she was, fell much
below her buttocks, and was so thick that she could let it
spread over both back and front, and completely cover
her nakedness. Titian must have had such another magnificent head of hair for one of his models, for it exactly resembled, except in being somewhat of a fairer hue, his
celebrated Magdalen, in the Pitti Palace, at Florence, where
she is represented covered only with the rich profusion of her
ringlets. Such was my aunt, and often and often afterwards has she indulged all my fancies, by showing herself
off in every voluptuous attitude with this, the greatest ornament of woman, flowing in the utmost profusion over her
glorious and mighty charms. Meanwhile, the doctor had
undressed, but it may well be supposed perfectly unnoticed
by me. I had better game in view. He, too, had donned a
robe de chambre, and sat down by his wife to have a chat
over the occurrences of the day. Of course, their conversation
very naturally turned upon myself. They began by congratulating themselves that the good fortune of the family was
partly reflected on them by the circumstances of my being

put under the doctor's care. The lady remarked how doubly fortunate it was, as the little scandal that had happened had, for some time, prevented their having any pupils at all. The doctor said—

"Never mind that, my love, this little fellow will soon be the decoy duck for others; he seems a nice, gentle lad, but I shall seek to have some talk with him to-morrow, and see what he is made of; boys, under women's instructions, are generally mere milk-sops."

"I don't think you will find it so in this case," added my aunt. "I am not a bad judge of character, and I feel certain that Miss Frankland is too stern and firm of purpose not to have bent any boy's will to her bidding; I fear, on the contrary, she has, if anything, been too severe with him, for my sister told me that she had full power to wield the rod, but, after one or two severe bouts, she completely mastered them, and that their progress was really very great, and most satisfactory, as Mr. Nixon, Charles's guardian, who had examined him, had reported most favourably thereon. But he appears to be insignificant, and undersized, thin as a whipping post, pale, and somewhat sickly-looking, he appears much younger than he is, and seems hardly fitted for what you and I would delight in. Eh! dear doctor?"

I did not understand at this time what her allusion meant, but it was followed by the doctor stooping forwards, kissing her, and, I have no doubt, tongueing her too. He first thrust a hand below her beauteous bubbies, and then pulling up her chemise, began foraging between her legs. She put down her hair brush; and laid hold of his cock, but quickly said—

"Don't excite me, my dear, you see this poor fellow can do nothing without a rod, and we have none here, so be quiet and go to bed, that is a good boy."

Obeying her, he rose, threw off his robe, put on a nightcap, and tumbled into bed, and was sound asleep before his magnificent spouse had finished her toilet. When it was concluded, she took off her stays, and drew her chemise over her head, I doubt if it could have fallen over her enormous buttocks. She then walked across the room in my direction, stark naked as nature made her, and strikingly magnificent in the firmness of her tread, and the glorious uprightness of her truly superb grandeur of form. I was positively awestruck. I could imagine her to be Juno in all her glory before Jupiter, and well he might be tempted to stray to the forbidden path of love, if Juno had such a backside as the enormous and glorious one my aunt possessed. She again squatted down, naked as she was, and poured out another torrent into the pot. I felt overpowered at the sight, and staggered back to my bed, and for the first time in my life felt constrained to rack off by self-pollution the excess of lust the gazing on such superhuman beauties had engendered. I could hardly refrain from shouting out to relieve my till then suppressed excitement, especially when nature gave way, and there spurted forth a jet of sperm, actually from the bed against the door towards which I had pointed my prick while wildly frigging it, and in imagination shoving it into aunt—anywhere; for if ever the saying that "there was plenty of good fucking about all these parts" was applicable to any one, it was supremely so in my glorious aunt's case. Any one might shove his prick against any part of her body, and spend at once from excess of lust, at her very beauty and splendour of form and exquisite colour and fineness of skin. Never, never have I met her equal. Her power of fuck, too, was on a par with the immensity of size, and of a quality to please the most fastidious, or the most lustful. Such were the first experiences that I had of my aunt's person, and as my narrative extends, the reader will become more intimate with her person and proceedings. I sank to sleep, to dream of possessing her in every way, rivalling Jupiter with Juno, and Mars with Venus, mere visions of the night, but which were in after-days converted into sweet realisations of the most voluptuous and rapturous nature.

The next day, at our hour of recreation, Miss Frankland walked out with us, and seeking a retired part of the grounds, while the girls amused themselves, I recounted to Miss F. all I had seen and heard. She at once came to the conclusion that I was destined to fall into the arms of my aunt.

"I am so far pleased, my dear Charlie, that it will be into those of an extraordinary fine woman; you must, after your present experiences with me, have had some one to go to, and certainly you could not have a finer. There will, evidently, be every facility, for I read those hints, which have puzzled you, as intimating any thing but reserve once you are admitted into the inner arcana of their lives, or I am much mistaken. There is one point I must strongly caution you about, and your general prudence and great good sense will make you appreciate its importance. Your aunt is evidently much experienced in erotic pleasures. If at once she found in you the extraordinary adept you are, she would never cease tormenting you until she discovered who had been your instructress. Now it must be evident to you that if she thought you and I were intimate in that way, she might draw evil inferences with regard to your sisters, or if not going so far as to think we had equally corrupted them, it is probable enough she might seek to remove me from their society. So you see, my darling boy, though it may be very difficult to do, you must, for all our sakes, determine to appear quite innocent and ignorant of every thing connected with indulgence in amorous passions. You must not let yourself appear excited, but leave her to take all the initiatory steps, and I much mistake if she will not be extremely ready to do so, but all the more so if she finds you apparently innocent. However much you now know of love's proceedings, you must keep a guarded check upon your feelings, so as not to let your knowledge become apparent in the smallest degree. She will, eventually, be twice as well pleased if she fancies she has had your first fruits. Before you leave I shall give you some short hints as to how to conduct yourself."

All this time I was getting rampageous, so begging her to stoop forward upon a stump, I tilted up her petticoats and fucked her from behind, frigging her delicious clitoris, and making her spend at the same time as myself. It was a hasty fly, but very sweet nevertheless, for we were both conscious that it was necessary to make the most of the short time I had yet to remain at home. I mentioned my aunt's remark about having no rod at hand, and it was agreed that Miss Frankland should put one on an upper shelf of her wardrobe, and accidently leave the key in the door. As this wardrobe remained in the room uncle and aunt were sleeping in, woman's curiosity was sure to induce an examination of it. This answered a double purpose, for Miss F. so arranged things that some excellent books full of little bits of paper inserted here and there, at highly moral or religious passages, led both uncle and aunt to have a very high idea of her moral character—for these were works that apparently could only be for her own private reading.

The rod was placed, and the bait laid next day. Meanwhile, that afternoon, the doctor called me aside, and put me through a conversational sort of examination. I was studiously modest, but being very fairly grounded by the admirable system of teaching pursued by Miss Frankland, I not only satisfied him, but he took occasion to compliment Miss Frankland very highly for the admirable groundwork she had laid. I fancied also, as he continued in conversation with her, that he grew more kindly and unctuous, as if the spirit of lust was infusing itself in his veins, as he continued to converse with and gaze on that most engaging and lust-creating creature.

That night I watched, as before, their preparations for sleep, and heard their conversation. This time the doctor was profuse in his praise of me, but aunt thought I was timid and lifeless; there seemed no spirit about me, as there ought to be, she added, at his age, but this education by females makes girls of boys. I thought to myself, I guess, I shall very soon undeceive you on that point, my dear aunt. The doctor went quietly to bed; aunt stripped and used the bidet, giving me a most exciting and voluptuous view of all her full-blown charms. No sooner was her light out, and she in bed, than I slipped out and crept up to my sisters' room, where three randy cunts were impatiently awaiting my advent with an equally randy and inflamed pego. We indulged in every complicated combination of lust and lubricity, and never ceased until daylight forced my unwilling retreat. Before leaving, as the rod was to be put in the wardrobe, and the key left in the door, it was arranged that the next night the girls, and Miss F., too, if she could, were to endeavour to sleep soundly before I came. For if our stratagem succeeded, I should remain to see the result which would probably occupy more than an hour or two, and I would awaken them by applying Moses's rod to their water courses as doubtless I would be in a rampageous state, if our expectations of the doctor's and aunt's tendencies that way were realised.

I kept myself awake until aunt and uncle came to bed, and then I immediately placed myself *en vedette*. At first no notice was taken of the key being in the lock. Aunt continued her operations, and uncle became somewhat more tentative than usual, when aunt, finding by placing her hand on his prick that it was mere useless desire, rose and scolded him. He grew more emboldened, and followed her up, wishing to feel her splendid cunt. It so happened she had drawn back as far as the wardrobe itself, until the key actually hurt her back.

"Ah what have we here?" she cried, and then turning round, said that as the key had been left in the lock, there could be no harm in looking in. Her husband became as curious as she. Of course, the first things they saw were the prearranged books. They were seized upon with avidity probably with the expectation of finding something smutty, but to their surprise, and especially that of the doctor, it was quite the reverse.

"Well, I should never have thought this; do you know, my dear, I had begun to suspect that, under a demure exterior, there was lurking an enormous deal of animal passion in that Miss Frankland, but if so, these works prove that it is under complete regulation. More's the pity, for she is made for the real enjoyment of the passions."

"Oh you have been speculating in that quarter, have you, you old lecher?"

"Well, my dear, you know we have both liberty to stray now and then, and you, yourself, have not a little availed yourself on our mutual understanding."

"Now, doctor, you are too bad; do I not quite overlook all your weakness for the younger members of your own sex, and do I not lend myself to your fantasies in that way, when chance deprives you of any opportunity of pederasty?"

"Well, well, my love, I was not upbraiding you, you are too dear and too kind to me to permit of any thing beyond a joking allusion; but what have we here? A birch rod! by all that is holy."

Reaching up to the high shelf, he drew down the rod. At first they suspected Miss Frankland operating on herself, but the perfectly untouched state of the rod proved that it was there in reserve only, and had not yet been used.

"What a lucky chance," cried my aunt. "I shall now be able to birch you into something like a fit state to fuck me—and you shall birch me afterwards, if it will only produce a second fuck, back or front, whichever you like."

"You are an angel, my darling wife, and I shall try to content both orifices; it is an abominable shame that with such a gloriously made magnificent woman as God has given me in your noble form, I should ever require any other stimulant than a glance at your exquisitely exciting proportions; but I suppose it is age that weakens our sensibilities."

"You are right, my dear John, for I, who used to think your dear old cock was enough for me, find I require the excitement of younger ones to give me the real excess of pleasure my constitution demands; it would be a shame if I did not humour all your little caprices, when you so readily throw opportunities in my way. I only wish this nephew of mine had been more worthy of us, we should have made him a glorious *bonne bouche* between us, equally to his satisfaction as to ours."

"Well, my dear, the air of Kent, and more manly treatment, may yet develope his somewhat stinted growth, and under your tuition, he may yet prove not so bad an object as you seem to think, at all events, he may serve as a *pisaller*, until a better turns up; but you must proceed with caution, for he seems as modest as a maid."

"My dear John, your modest ones always make the best, when once broken in. I only wish his physique had been more to my liking, but we shall see, we shall see; meanwhile let us both strip to the buff, and proceed to make the most of this happy discovery of the rod—the very thing we most wanted and wished for."

Aunt rapidly twisted up her magnificent tresses, and as rapidly stripped to the skin; the doctor likewise. I assure you he was a well-made, muscular, portly, handsome man, with a large well-filled pair of cods. His pego still hung down his head, but had a certain amount of size, doubtless stimulated by the exciting nature of their conversation and reminiscences. His skin and his cock were beautifully white, and the ball of his prick of a tempting scarlet. I felt at the moment that, if I dared, I would have bolted into the room, and sucked it into such a stiffness as would have instantly satisfied the insatiable cunt of my glorious aunt. This was a delight to be left for a future day, when I allowed the doctor all the credit and pleasure of persuading me to do that which

I was burning with desire to do. But I digress. No sooner were both fully prepared than my aunt, in a stern voice, ordered the doctor to approach.

"Come here, sir, I must whip you, you have not done your duty as you ought lately, and you are a very naughty boy."

The doctor, putting on the air of a schoolboy, begged to be excused this time, but his inexorable mistress was not to be moved, and seizing him by the arm, pulled him over her broad and massive thighs, and with one arm round his waist, seized his cock in her hand, and began whacking away at his backside in such real earnest and, apparently, with all the force of her powerful arm, that I began to think the doctor must cry out in earnest. But he took it all without a murmur, only wriggling his fat and smooth buttocks about in a way that rather inferred satisfaction than suffering. Presently my aunt, who, doubtless, knew by the grip of his prick that matters had arrived at the point her own passions had most at heart, lifted him up, and said—

"Now I must put you in pickle, but as your great red buttocks are too large to be pickled, I shall pickle your prick instead. So come here, sir, and let me put this rampant fellow into my pickle tub, where, I promise, the salt brine will soon bring down his pride."

I suppose this was the sort of childish yet lascivious talk which pleased them both, for uncle, who had risen, and who now presented a much finer weapon than I had given him credit for, pretended to fear this further punishment, and begged and entreated to be let off—he had been punished enough, &c., &c. Aunt, however, leading him by the prick to the bed, threw herself on the edge, and lying back, drew up her enormous thighs almost to her belly, and showed to my gloating gaze her tremendous salmon-coloured gash, all covered with spunk, for the operation had made her spend profusely. I never saw so large a cunt, nor such an extensive triangle as lay on the side of each lip between it and the commencement of the buttocks, beautifully covered with the fairest curls.

"There, sir, is your place of punishment, stoop and kiss it before I imprison your indecent cock within it."

The doctor, nothing loath, stooped and gamahuched her so well that her mighty backside wriggled beneath his head, and made every thing in the room jingle; her hand pressed his head until I thought it would have been pushed in altogether. At last, she spent with a shout of delight. He hastily gobbled it all up, and rising, without more ado, thrust his stiff-standing weapon up to the hilt, I might almost say cods and all, in her longing and magnificent cunt. Here, he soaked for some minutes, and I could see by the convulsive movements of her backside how much aunt was enjoying it. They soon became bent on more active movements, for throwing her splendid legs over his back, she began an up and down movement, much more active than I could in any way have given her credit for. They went at it in real earnest for a longer time than I expected, but when the mighty crisis came, it was with an energy, and passionate struggles worthy of the strength and substance of the two love wrestlers. I could see her cunt all foam again around the roots of the increased size of uncle's very respectable prick, and then they lay in apparent apathy for full twenty minutes, but one could see by the convulsive throbs of their whole bodies what delicious transports of rapture they were enjoying. Uncle was the first to rise, but only to stoop and to greedily lick up all the foaming spunk which the wide-spread entrance to her glorious cunt exhibited. This being done, she, too, rose, and throwing her arms round the doctor's neck, drew his mouth to hers, and seemed to suck his slimy lips, and gain for herself as much as she could of the delicious spunk the doctor had been revelling in. This lasted some minutes. Then my aunt turned him down on the bed, and took a long suck at his prick, now hanging limp, but still of a goodly thickness. Then she thanked him for the great satisfaction he had given her, and declared it was almost as good as the first days of their union. Then after toying and cuddling on the bed for a time, she said they must now proceed to a little further castigation, on her bottom this time, as he had promised to give her a double dose.

"Yes, my love, but you know you promised I should take my choice of which temple I should make my sacrifice at."

"My own John, you know, that after being once well fucked, the hinder hole is my preference, that is understood."

They accordingly rose, and uncle, furnishing himself with the rod, desired aunt to kneel on the edge of the bed, and present her magnificent backside projecting out fair for his birching. This she immediately did, and being directly before my eyes, I had a full front view of her gloriously large wide-open cunt, and all the pinky brown *aureola* around her charming bottom-hole, over which the little fair ringlets showed in great beauty. I need not say that my own John Thomas was in all the pride and panoply of prickdom, and ready to burst with excitement. My uncle took the rod in hand as soon as aunt was in position, and placing himself on one side, while his left hand passed under her belly to frig her clitoris, he had his right hand free to inflict any amount of whipping. And, I must say, neither one nor the other spared the rod; they laid it on right soundly, but drew forth no word or sign of complaint. My aunt soon began to wriggle her stupendous backside, in a way to show how very exciting the birching was to her. Her exquisitely creamy white skin began to see the scarlet of the blood rushing to the surface under the infliction received. The redder it became, so did the evident palpitating movement of her two resplendent orbs increase, until uncle, too, showed how the glorious sight was stimulating his less easily excited system, by the stiffening and uprising of his pego. Aunt's hand slipped down to it, and being well acquainted with its habits, pronounced it to be as equally ready as herself. Turning her body length-ways, but still on her knees, the doctor scrambled up behind her, and first stooping, licked up the foam on her cunt, for she had already spent once; and then, rolling his tongue about the beautiful indentation leading to her delicious bot-tom-hole, he thrust it in as far as he could there. Then rising on his knees, he first plunged his jolly good prick into her cunt for two or three shoves, and then drawing it out well lubricated, presented its point to her exquisite bottom-hole, and plunged it up to the hilt at a single thrust. Aunt gave a cry and shudder of delight as she felt it penetrate to her very entrails. The doctor, satisfied for the moment, lay soaking in the exquisite pressure that aunt's *sphincter ani* was applying to his happy prick. He looked down upon her glorious but-tocks, handling them with evident pleasure. I saw aunt's hand steal down to her cunt, and could observe that she was actively frigging her clitoris. She shortly cried out to uncle not to be so idle, but to commence the delicious movements she expected from him.

He did—they did; and such a scene of excitement it was to see so magnificent a woman with such a mighty backside in all the agonies of enjoyment that I could hold out no longer, but seizing my bursting prick in my hand, two or three rapid movements up and down, and tight graspings of the shaft, brought on the extatic rapture of so lascivious a spend that I actually fainted and fell heavily on the floor. It was fortunate that aunt and uncle were so hotly engaged that an earthquake might have shook the house without their being conscious of it. So as I only fell from my knees it never disturbed one moment of their pleasure. I must have been some minutes without consciousness, for when I came to my senses, and was able to resume my inspection, I found their crisis was past, but that uncle still lay soaking in the narrow cell he so delightfully occupied. He was gazing with evident pleasure on the still palpitating buttocks of the divine backside immediately below him. Neither was in any hurry, but they dwelt for a considerable space of time in this repose of lubricity. At last, his cock, reduced in bulk, slipped out of its close quarters. Then, rising, and helping aunt out of bed, they warmly embraced each other, kissed and tongued, and aunt thanked him for a most rapturous fuck. Aunt then sat down on her bidet, and uncle used the wash basin. After purifying themselves, and aunt showing all the extraordinary fine development of her glorious form, they put on their night-dresses, blew out the lights, and tumbled into bed. I immediately hastened to gain my sisters' room, with my cock standing stiffer than ever. I entered gently—they were all asleep. My two sisters lay reversed, with their heads between each pair of thighs; they had evidently fallen asleep after a mutual gamahuche in the very attitude in which they had spent. Miss Frankland had apparently waited for me, but feeling drowsy, had thrust her very fine hairy backside right out of bed, ready to attract my attention the moment I should come. So gently approaching, and bringing the light to bear on the beautiful sight, I spit upon and lubricated the end of my prick, and very gently introduced him into her ever delicious cunt. I managed to fully engulph it before applying my finger to her bottom-hole, and my other hand to her clitoris. She had already in her sleep involuntarily squeezed me with her usual force. Then, suddenly applying all my energies, I began an active movement, which instantly awoke her. She was as ready for the sport as I was, and in a very few minutes we ran a most rapturous course of intense delight, and spent with an energy which proved the strength of the excitement I had been under. As I was standing by the bedside, and she lying on it with her fine bottom projecting beyond the edge, it was not a position to remain long in; besides, I was still dressed. So, withdrawing, I undressed myself. My sisters had slept through all this, so first preparing everything for an excessive orgie, by getting out dildoes and birch rods, we awoke the two darlings, who, rising, stripped to the buff. The three dear creatures were all curiosity to know what had kept me so long—more than two hours and a half, and what had been done.

I recounted all the proceedings, except in so far as they had talked of initiating me, for neither Miss Frankland nor I wished my sisters to be acquainted with that matter. They laughed heartily, and little Lizzie said she must act aunt, first flog me and be fucked; then be flogged by me, and have my darling prick up her bottom-hole to follow. We laughed and humoured her, and that scene came off with considerable *éclat*. Miss Frankland fucking Mary, for whom she had a great letch, in the cunt first, and in the bottom, after my example on Lizzie, in the second place. Lizzie and I then laved our parts and prepared for fresh encounters, and we then began a more regular course of the most lascivious lubricity, in which dildoes and rods played conspicuous parts, both becoming necessary under the excessive indulgencies of these last few nights. I stole to my room long after daylight, and slept soundly for an hour or two. You may be sure our lessons were of the lightest in these few days that were left us, and I was allowed to doze off during school hours.

Miss Frankland again walked with me alone in the garden, to give me, as she thought, last lessons in the way I should act with aunt, who she now felt more certain than ever would very soon attack and carry my person when she reached home and had the place and time all to herself. I listened with apparently great attention; as the reader knows, I was already an adept in the art she wished to indoctrinate—thanks to the admirable advice of my ever charming real first instructress, the lovely Mrs. Benson. But I could not help thinking how completely these two admirable women had the same wisdom and knowledge of the world with which they were so anxious that I, too, should become conversant.

The next night the doctor and aunt went quietly to bed,

the doctor declaring that his previous night's doings would prevent any more that night. So I only had one more gaze at all aunt's magnificent beauties, which had a never failing effect on my excitable weapon, and which she sent away when her light was put out in a perfectly fit state for the work that awaited him in my sisters' room. I came upon them sooner than expected, and found the three rolled into one body, two gamahuching each other, and Miss Frankland's clitoris in Mary's bum-hole. For a wonder they did not hear me as I gently opened the door, and I patiently waited till the lascivious crisis brought down a delicious spend from them all. When clapping my hands applaudingly, I cried—

"Bravo! bravo! encore!"

I was so far glad, for to confess the truth the pace was telling, and I began to require more and more of the rod. However, we had but this and the next night at our disposal, and the knowledge that we must soon cease our delicious orgies nerved us all to increased efforts.

Again our passions raged furiously, and broke out in spurts of foaming sperm. Every desire our lascivious lubricity could suggest was carried out to increase our pleasures or renew our exhausted resources, until time warned us again to separate.

The next day there was no school time—it was spent in packing and preparing for departure. My poor mother took it much to heart—she was a most affectionate creature, as innocent as a babe. I often wondered where we three got all the natural wantonness of our characters, for mamma had nothing of it. I suppose it must have come from our grandparents, as aunt had it in the fullest degree, and was almost the equal of the adorable Miss Frankland, who only excelled her in having Greek blood in her veins, which, doubtless, accounted for the extreme heat of her lubricity. Some day I will recount the chief events of her romantic story, which she herself, in after-time, fully related to me. The day was a sad one for us all, even sadder than the next, the actual day of departure. As often happens, the anticipation of evils is greater than the reality when they come.

That night my aunt and the doctor had another whipping bout, but this time she only succeeded in getting a single course out of the doctor. As before when all was over, I slipped away to pass the last delicious night with the dear creatures with whom I had now carried on the most rapturous orgies for more than two years past. My sisters were rapidly developing into remarkably handsome fine young women, especially Mary, who, having the advantage of a year and a half over Lizzie, was naturally more filled out and formed, although Lizzie promised in the end to be, and in fact became, the finest woman, and had also by far the hotter temperament of the two. We passed the night in orgies the most refined, interspersed with tears of regret at our parting, and soft endearments leading to perfect furies of lubricity, until I was nearly fainting with exhaustion. We tore ourselves asunder with difficulty, and the three angelic creatures held their door open, and with streaming eyes watched my receding form; twice, on looking back, I could not help returning again and again to throw myself into their arms for a last loving embrace; but like all things human it came to an end, and I reached my bed and sobbed myself to sleep.

It is needless to dwell on our parting next day. My mother accompanied us to the town where we were to take a coach. It drove up. My poor mother could hardly utter her blessing and farewell, and I saw the tears coursing down her venerable cheeks as she waved her handkerchief before the coach turned the corner that shut us from her view. Of course my heart was full, whose could be otherwise when quitting home for the first time. My aunt put her arm round my waist, and laid my head on her ample bosom, and comforted me as well as she could; but a full heart must vent itself. Fortunately, we had the inside all to ourselves. My aunt was very tender, and so was the doctor. I soon sobbed myself to sleep; even in the bitter grief of the moment I had some slight comfort in the idea of pressing those glorious orbs. My aunt frequently kissed me, and I returned it with full pouting lips, which I fancied rather pleased her. I slept until the coach stopped for supper, ate heartily, and, as may be supposed after my late week of hard work, soon again slept like a top.

I did not awake until it was broad daylight, and, like all heavy sleepers, was awake and sensible of what was going on before opening my eyes. I became conscious that a hand was gently pressing and apparently taking the size of my standing pego, which the pressure of water on my bladder had occasioned to be in an erection of the hardest. I lay quite still, continuing to breathe heavily, but unable to prevent sundry throbbings of my pego, occasioned by the soft hand of my aunt, who was gently following its form from the outside of my trousers. It appeared she had only just commenced her manipulations, not having previously observed the bulging out of its large dimensions under my trousers. She pressed her knee against that of the doctor opposite, who I presume, was dozing off, and in a whisper I heard her draw his attention to my extraordinary development.

"Feel it, my dear, but very gently, so as not to waken him, it is the largest prick I have ever felt, and altogether beats the late Captain of Grenadiers you used to be so jealous of."

The doctor did feel, and I think aunt would have unbuttoned my trousers, had not the coach suddenly pulled up at the inn we were to breakfast at. So perforce they shook me up. I acted the suddenly awakened sleeper very well. As soon as we were out of the coach, I whispered to the doctor—

"If you please, uncle, I want to piddle very bad."

"Come here, my dear boy."

And taking me behind some wagons in the innyard, where we would not be seen, he said—

"Here, we can both piss down this grating."

And, forsooth, to encourage me, pulled out his own standing pego. I saw what he wanted, and out with my own in all its length and strength.

"Good heavens, Charles, what an immense cock you have got—does it often stand like that?"

"Yes, uncle, every morning it hurts me so until I piddle—it gets worse and worse, and bigger and bigger—it was not half so big a year ago. I don't know what to do to cure myself of this hardness, which is very painful."

"Ah, well, I must speak to your aunt, perhaps she can help you. Have you ever spoken to anybody else about it?"

"Oh, dear no! I should have been quite ashamed; but when I saw you also had the same hardness, I was very glad to ask your advice, dear uncle."

"Quite right. Always consult me about that part of your body, whatever you may feel."

We breakfasted, and I could see, on regaining the coach, that uncle and aunt had a satisfactory exchange of words on the subject. We got to the Rectory in Kent in time for dinner, at which I was the object of great and devoted attention of both, especially of my aunt.

Our previous long journey made an early retreat to bed a necessity for all of us. They both conducted me with much *empressement* to my bedroom, a very comfortable one, having a communication at one end with a corridor, and, on the right-hand side entering, another door communicating with my uncle's dressing- and bath-room, and these opening into their bedroom, which had a similar dressing-room on the other side fitted up with wardrobes for female gear, and dedicated to my aunt's sole use. I was left to a quiet night's rest, which I most thoroughly enjoyed, and slept profoundly until late in the morning. I was awakened by my uncle drawing all the clothes off me. Of course, I was rampant, as usual. He gazed for a moment or two without speaking at my enormous cock at full stand. He then said it was nine o'clock, and breakfast was ready, that he had not liked to disturb me sooner, as I was in so sound a slumber, but now it was time for me to get up.

"I see," he added, "that your doodle, as you call it, has got the hardness you spoke of yesterday."

Then he laid hold of it, and gently squeezed it—it filled his grasp. He evidently enjoyed the pleasure of handling it, but contented himself with saying that my aunt must see to giving me some remedy the next day, when she should come and inspect it in the morning, so as to see how hard it was, and how it hurt me.

I replied that it would be very kind of aunt, but what would she think of my showing my doodle to her; mamma had told me, when I slept in her room, always to piddle in a corner, and never let anyone see it.

He laughed at my apparent simplicity, and said—

"Your mamma was quite right as to people in general, but it is quite a different thing with your aunt, whose close relationship authorises her doing what she can to relieve her dear nephew, in whom we both take such an interest; besides, I suppose your mamma never saw it in this size and hardness?"

He was gently handling it all the time of our conversation.

"Oh, no! mamma never saw it but at night, when it was quite shrunk up, and that is nearly a year ago, when I used to sleep in her room; it is since then it has grown so large and hurts so much, and throbs so violently as it is doing now in your hand. It makes me feel so queer, dear uncle, and I shall be so much obliged to dear auntie if she will but give me a remedy to relieve the pain I suffer."

He laughed again, and said—

"I shall speak to your aunt, and we shall see—we shall see; but get up now, we shall find your aunt waiting for us. So make haste and dress; come down stairs, you will find us in the dining-room."

He left me, and I could hear him laughing to himself, as he walked along the corridor, doubtless at my apparent innocent simplicity. I saw at once that I should be called upon to show myself a man next day; but I already felt the advantage of the advice both my admirable mistresses had given me, as to making all new conquests believe that they had my first fruits. I determined to adhere to the game I was playing, and I foresaw that the pleasure of supporting such a thing would greatly enhance the delight aunt would naturally take in being fucked by my really monstrous cock. I was soon down to breakfast, and was most warmly embraced by my gloriously beautiful aunt, who, in a graceful dishabille, looked more charming than ever. She hugged me for more than a minute in her arms, and devoured me with kisses. I have no doubt the doctor had recounted our interview, and by the sparkle of her eye, and the flush on her face, as she so closely embraced me, she showed that already her passions were excited, and she was longing for the hour in which she could indulge them. However, all that day, they were kept under restraint. The doctor had some parish business to attend to, and aunt leaving me for an hour after breakfast, while she attended to some necessary household affairs, afterwards took me all over the house and grounds, and then we had a walk through the village. The house was one of those snug rectory houses situated in their own grounds which abound in England, but few have so glorious a prospect as was seen from the front of the house. Leeds, in Kent, is situated on the ridge of hills running east and west, and commanding views over the rich and beautiful weald of Kent. The rectory faced the south, and the ground falling rapidly beyond the garden left a splendid landscape in full view. Although close to the village and the church, both were planted out by a thick belt of evergreen trees, which extended to north and east, sheltering the house and grounds from every adverse wind. The house itself was very commodious, but unassuming. The south front had a large projecting half-circle, with three windows in it and a window on each side of the half-circle; this formed the drawing-room below and my uncle's bedroom, and two dressing-rooms above. To the right, looking at the house, there was a wing with an open-arched passage leading to a greenhouse and vinery, while above ran a suite of three rooms, each with one good-sized window overlooking the garden. These were the three rooms kept for the same number of young gentlemen who might be taken in for preparation for the University—a number the doctor never exceeded. Of these rooms I was at present the only occupant. They were built so as to be shut off from all the rest of the house by a door on the landing, leading into the corridor, from which a door communicated with the doctor's dressing-room, and with each of the three rooms. At the end was a water-closet for general use. I have already mentioned the first of these rooms had a second door of communication with the doctor's dressing-room, and this was appropriated to me. Below these rooms, but looking north, and communicating with the village by a covered way and having a play-ground into which it looked, was the school-room, taking up about half the space of the rooms above. Beyond the covered way to the village was a quiet garden square, into which the doctor's study looked. This study was separated by a passage from the school-room, and had double baize doors both on the house and school-room sides. It was in fact the doctor's sanctum sanctorum, of which more will be told in the sequel. In this manner the school-room part of the house was quite shut off from the rest, and was nowhere overlooked. To return to the habitable part. The west front contained a small library, opening from the drawing-room, and beyond a comfortable dining-room, communicating with the kitchen and offices, which overlooked the courtyard of the entrace to the house, above these were the domestics' bedrooms, &c. The entrance was from the north into a handsome entrance-hall, with a good broad staircase leading to the upper landing, which, turning westward, led to three extra bedrooms above the library and dining-room. It was thus a very convenient house and well-adapted for a clergyman adding scholastic duties to his other ministrations. I forgot to say that the first bedroom, in the west wing, had a door of communication with my aunt's dressing-room, which I afterwards found had often served for amorous propensities by making it the bedroom of some favoured lover. The grounds were charmingly laid out with a profusion of flowers. There was a perfectly shaded walk in the east shrubbery leading from the greenhouse down to a most charming summer house overlooking the very finest prospect, and perfectly secure from all observation. It was furnished very appropriately for amorous purposes, the couches being low, broad, and with patent spring-cushions. In the sequel it was the scene of many a bout of lubricity. My aunt took me through all that I have described. When we arrived at the summer house, I could see that it was with difficulty she restrained her great desire to possess me; I would most willingly have rushed into her longing arms, and fucked her to her heart's content, but prudence withheld. I had undertaken to act a part, and must go through with it. No doubt aunt was withheld by a similar motive. She and the doctor had resolved that nothing to alarm my modesty— heaven save the mark!—was to be attempted till the next morning. So with a deep sigh she led me away from the summer house into the village, where we met the doctor, and returned to luncheon. After luncheon the doctor took me for a walk again through the picturesque village along the ridge of hills, to enjoy the beautiful views of Leeds Castle, the doctor giving me very many interesting historical details connected with it. After a most pleasant and lengthened walk we returned in time to dress for dinner. I found that one of the rules of the house was that no matter, whether alone or with com-

pany the doctor invariably insisted on regular evening costume at dinner-time. This has many advantages. In the first
place it gives at least half an hour's occupation, an object in
itself worth something to persons living in the country, and
then it gives a *cachet* or rather *chic* to your dinner party,
however small it may be, and is in itself a certain amount of
restraint on excessive exuberance of spirits, and thus may be
considered as a disciplinary element of education tending to
keep up that reserve and self-restraint characteristic of
Englishmen.

Beyond a marked attention to me in every way, our dinner
and evening passed without anything worthy of record. I
was evidently high in their favour, probably for the reason
that both began to have great hopes that I would serve their
purpose in every way. We retired early to rest, and I thus obtained three nights of uninterrupted rest, recruiting me after
all the excesses I had indulged in before quitting home. It
was so far fortunate, that I was thus ready to satisfy the
strong passions of my aunt, who was insatiable when once her
lust was let loose. I awoke earlier than on the previous morning, and shortly afterwards, hearing a movement in the doctor's dressing-room, I feigned sleep. It was as I expected, the
doctor coming to me in company with my aunt. They approached my bedside. I had laid myself on my back purposely
to allow the thin summer-covering to be lifted up and bulged
out by my stiff-standing pego. I heard the doctor whisper to
aunt, to draw her attention to it. She gently slipped her hand
under the clothes, and grasped it in her soft fat fingers, upon
which it throbbed so violently that I thought it politic to
waken at once. My aunt was not at all put out, but held it
still in her hand with a gentle pressure. She said—

"My dear nephew, your uncle has brought me to see if I
cannot relieve the extreme hardness and pain you feel in this
immense thing of yours. Let me see it."

She now threw off the coverlet, and brought to light my
large prick in all the glory of the stiffest stand.

"My word! what a monster!" she cried.

Her eyes sparkled, and her face flushed as the sight met her full gaze. The doctor approached, and also handled it with evident delight.

"My dear, will you be able to put it into your natural warm bath? It is so very large!"

"Oh! I have not the slightest doubt but that I shall be able to soothe and deliver it of all pain—poor fellow, how it throbs! Does it hurt much, dear Charles?"

"Oh, yes; your hand seems to make it even harder than before, but, at the same time makes me feel so very queer, as if I were going to faint. Do relieve me, dear auntie, the doctor says you can if you like."

"I will do so, certainly, my dear boy; but the method is a great secret, known only to your uncle and myself; and you must assure me you will never mention it to any one, or tell how I cured you. It is only my strong affection for you that makes me anxious to do anything I can to relieve you. Do you promise to be discreet?"

"My dear aunt, you may be sure I shall be too much obliged to you ever to think of revealing your great kindness. Do, pray, do it at once; I feel so queer, and I am bursting with pain."

"Well, then, make room for me beside you, and I shall lie down; the doctor will cover us up, and I shall soon reduce the stiffness."

She got into bed, lay down on her back, pulled the sheet over us, laying bare her splendid belly, and, at the same time, opening her magnificent limbs and desiring me to get upon her, telling me she had a sheath in her body, which, when my hard doodle was put within, would soon relieve it of its stiffness. I got awkwardly upon her. She seized my standing prick, and placing its knob between the already very moist lips, told me to push it in as far as it would go. It glided into its delicious sheath up to the cod piece in a moment.

"Oh, heavens!" I cried, "how nice! Dear, dear, auntie, what shall I do now, I feel as if I were going to die."

My apparent innocence seemed to add to her pleasure. She threw the sheet that covered us on one side, and with arms and legs clasped round my body, begged me to move my bottom up and down, so as to make my doodle go in and out. I followed her directions, and she seconded me with rare art, squeezing my instrument with wonderful pressures as I withdrew and she retired, to meet again the up and down shock with the most lascivious delight. I felt the hand of the doctor embracing my testicles and gently pressing them. I became aware that the crisis was approaching, and shoved home with a cry of rapture, but remembering my part, I exclaimed—

"Oh, I am dying, dear aunt; oh! oh! stop! stop! I—can't—can't—bear it." I sank away, but could hear aunt murmuring—

"Dear, darling, delicious boy, I never had such a glorious prick in me, or a better fuck before. I fear the dear child has fainted from the excess of pleasure, and the newness of the sensation, but his glorious prick still throbs deliciously within me—only feel its root, doctor, how stiff it is."

I felt the doctor grasping it, making it throb violently as he did so.

"The dear boy is as stiff as ever. You will get another fuck out of him the moment he comes to himself. I am glad of that, for it is delightful to see you at it, especially with so splendid a prick operating upon you—it is the greatest treat you have ever given me in that way."

"I don't wonder at that, my dear, for I never met with such a fine prick in my life before, and little thought my nephew could have had such a splendid one in his trousers when we first saw him. Oh, I am lewder than ever, and am spen—spen—spending. Oh!—oh!"

And she poured down another copious hot flow on my enraptured prick. I let her revel in the extasies of her second lascivious discharge until I found that her libidinous passions were again excited and longing for more active operations. I pretended not to know where I was, and began a faltering—

"Oh, where am I? What has happened? I have been in paradise!"

Lifting up my head, I apparently recognised aunt in surprise—

"Oh, dear; how came I here? Oh, remember, auntie, you promised to relieve my hardness, and it seemed so nice, but I feel it is harder than ever; you will try and relieve me again, won't you, dear auntie?"

"Certainly, my dear nephew, you must do as you did at first, move in and out, and I shall second you; and perhaps we shall succeed this time better than before."

Of course, I was less *gauche*, and she more energetic. I felt the doctor insert a moistened finger up my fundament, and move it in unison with our thrusts. Aunt cried out to me to go on faster and faster, and we soon came to the grand crisis, dying away together in sobs and sighs of delighted enjoyment. I again sank on her noble panting bosom, really overcome with the rapture-giving delights of that most delicious cunt. On lifting my love-humid eyes to the face of my aunt, she seized my head in both hands, and drew my lips to her in a long, long kiss of satisfied lust, and thrust her tongue into my mouth, which I immediately sucked. She then begged me to give her mine. After tongueing together for a minute or two she asked if my doodle was in less pain, and if its hardness was reduced.

"A little, dear auntie, but I feel it is getting hard again—you must try once more, if you please—oh! it is so nice!"

And my prick throbbed up and stiffened to prove the truth of my words. But the doctor here interrupted us by saying that he must have his own stiffness reduced, at the same time presenting his really fine prick at full stand before our faces.

"You must get up, my dear boy, and your aunt will allay your new hardness in another way, in which she will be able to relieve both our hardnesses together."

Reluctantly I rose, withdrawing my reeking prick at more than half stand. Looking down as I rose on the truly large and magnificent foaming gash from which I had just withdrawn, I cried—

"Oh, dear aunt, what a wonderful sight it is; I must kiss it for the efforts it has made to relieve me."

I threw my head down upon it, kissed it, licked its wide open lips all foaming with fuck as they were, thrusting my tongue in as far as it would go. This evidently gave aunt great delight. But the doctor drew me off, told me to lie down on my back, and made aunt straddle over me. She took hold of my now completely standing prick, bent it back, and directing it aright, sank upon it until her ample bush of hair lay crushed on mine. She rose up and down two or three times in a slow delicious movement, and then bending forward, glued her lips to mine while I threw my arms round her glorious body.

I could feel the doctor getting up between my legs on his knees, and then felt his prick was rubbing against the lips of the cunt fully distended round my large pego, doubtless for the purpose of lubricating it before thrusting it into aunt's magnificent backside. I felt the rubbing of his prick against mine through the thin partition, as he glided slowly up into her entrails. We then began our joint movements, but aunt beat us both, and spent twice before joining in our final finish, which was ushered in by loud cries of delight from all three as the death-like extasy seized us, and we sank in that half unconscious state of supreme bliss. It was some time before any of us spoke a word. The doctor rose first, and without drawing his prick from the delicious orifice in which it had been engulphed, showed by the way it hung down its pendant head, that aunt had at all events allayed its stiffness. He desired aunt to rise also, but I felt by her throbbing cunt, and the pressure she put on my prick, as she rose from it, so that it came out with a loud flop, that she would fain once more have done me the service of allaying any stiffness that might re-arise. However, it was much limper than before, although still of a goodly thickness. When she got on her legs, she stooped forward, kissed it, took it in her mouth, and most lovingly sucked it, saying how delighted she would be to relieve me whenever it was troublesome. They begged me to get up and dress, and we should meet at breakfast. They then withdrew, to complete their own toilets. I lay for some minutes in the dreamy delight of thinking over the delicious event that had just taken place, and amused at the last remark of my aunt, which seemed to infer that she thought I was innocent of the real meaning of the performances that had just taken place. I determined to act as if it were so.

We met at breakfast, aunt kissed me most lovingly. I thanked her for her great kindness in relieving me from pain in so delicious a manner, and told her I could not help loving her more than I had ever loved any one before, and said I hoped she would kindly relieve me every morning, for I always suffered at that time from the painful hardness, though I should never be sorry for that, as long as she would so kindly allay it. I put my hands quite in a childish way on each cheek, and held up my mouth for a kiss, which was given to me in the lewdest way. She called me her dear boy, and told me that she would always help me as she had done that morning, as long as she found I was discreet, and never told how she did so. You may be sure that my promises were most earnestly reiterated. So we kissed again, and sat down to an excellent breakfast with sharpened appetites from our early exercise, and did full justice to the viands set before us. The doctor gave me a book of history, and desired me to read for a couple of hours, and said that at luncheon we would talk over the subject of my reading. I studied attentively for the time prescribed, and then aunt came to ask me to walk in the grounds with her. Insensibly or not, she led me to the summer house, and sat down on a low ottoman. I sat down beside her. She drew me to her, kissed me, and clasped me to her bosom, murmuring terms of endearment, and pressing me to her glorious bubbies. Of course, my unruly member fired up at once. To prevent her imagining it was lasciviousness that prompted me, I said—

"Oh, my dear aunt, I do so want to piddle, my doodle at once gets as hard as wood if I at all restrain the inclination to do so, just feel how stiff it has become; will you let me go and piddle?"

"My dear boy, I will go with you, and unbutton your trousers for you."

We went among the trees. Her busy fingers undid my trousers, and helped to bring forward my lordly cock in its glory. Fortunately, I did want to piddle, and aunt held it up as I did so, her eyes sparkling with lust as she handled it, and her face flushed with her excited passions. She remarked what an astonishing size it was, gently rubbing it up and down. Of course, it became more rampant than ever. Throwing my arms round her stooping neck, I asked her if she could not again relieve the excessive hardness and pain it was in.

"To be sure, my dear boy. Come here again into the summer house, where we cannot be observed."

We entered. She put a cushion on the floor for my knees, threw herself on her back, and lifted all her petticoats well over her belly, exposing her very hairy cunt, and its splendid pinky gash, already moist from her excitement. I threw myself on my knees, and stooping down, said—

"I must kiss the dear reliever of my pains."

I kissed and tongued, until my aunt begged me to raise my body, and come upon her, that she might quickly put me out of pain. I rose, and slipped my stiff member up to the hilt in her longing cunt almost taking away her breath by the suddenness and completeness of the insertion. Her legs and arms were round me in a moment, and at it we went hammer and tongs, until we quickly spent with cries of delight, and sank in momentary oblivion, soon to recover our full sensations, and dash again on passion's furious course, this time aunt pouring down her hot boiling discharge before me, and again when she felt the torrent of my sperm shooting up to the top of her womb. Our final crisis was even more extatic than the first time, and we lay longer in the soft languor of the after-sensations. The excessively voluptuous nature of her inward pressures soon re-illuminated all my libidinous desires, and refired my prick with renewed force. We soaked for a short time, each indulging in the delicious inward throbbings, until our lust could stand no longer such mere preliminary work, and stimilated anew, we rushed with freshened passions into the fray. The fiery nature of my lustful aunt paid down two tributes to Priapus to my one. This time our sensations were so extatic in spending that we really lost all consciousness, and lay for long locked in the closest embrace. I could feel that we were both becoming re-excited, but my aunt begged me to rise, saying that was enough for the present, the stiffness was allayed, and my weight was too much for her to endure longer. I rose, but again buried my face in the wide gash of that glorious cunt, and before rising completely, I licked up the delicious foam, and even ventured to give, as it were, an accidental lick to her little knob of a clitoris, for she was not much distinguished in that way; she shivered with excitement, when I touched it, and even pressed my head down upon it, when she felt the pleasure pressure.

"My dear boy, what exquisite delight you give me! Continue for a little to keep moving your tongue on that hard projection."

I did so. Her splendid backside wriggled below in the fullest enjoyment. She rapidly came to the extatic ending, nearly thrusting my whole face into her vast orbit, and spurting out a very torrent of sperm, all over my face and neck. She seized me by the shoulders to draw me up, that she might kiss me. My prick had regained its full vigour, and could not fail to slip in of itself into that most lascivious and gaping cunt when it reached the entrance. My aunt started at such an unexpected result, but was too much gratified to hesitate for an instant. Throwing legs and arms around me, her supple loins were in immediate action. I myself was equally in a state of wild lubricity, so that our course was even more rapid than at first, and we both spent and sank together in the delicious after-languor as soon as the extatic joy of the first rush of the exquisite discharge was over. My aunt, who could not but be most highly gratified, still kept up the appearance of relieving me, she desired me to rise, and said we must go, as luncheon time was at hand.

"But, my darling nephew, you must yourself endeavour to keep down your hardness, and not allow it to become stiff so often—you will injure me with your violence."

"Oh, my darling aunt, you give me relief with such exquisite pleasure that my doodle seems to harden only for the purpose of your relieving it—see how it is again bulging out of my trousers," for she had buttoned it up. She put her hand upon it, and squeezed it, but said, with a deep sigh—

"Come along, come along, or I do not know what might happen."

She drew me away, but by the manner in which she squeezed my arm, I could feel she was herself still greatly excited. Her prudence alone enabled her to resist further indulgence, as she seemed to think I was still unaware of the real nature of our proceedings. We found the doctor waiting for us at the luncheon table. He guessed by the flushed face of my aunt the nature of our late employment, and asked if I had been again troubled with my unnatural hardness.

"Yes, poor fellow," said my aunt, "it appears that whenever he wants to piddle, and cannot do so at once, it troubles him in that way, and I have had some difficulty in allaying it. I succeeded at last, but I have told my dear nephew that he must endeavour himself to restrain it in the daytime, as it is not always in my power to relieve him."

"Quite right, my love; my dear Charles, you must endeavour to follow the wishes of your of aunt."

Of course I promised, and with such a look of innocence that I could see they exchanged smiles at it. We sat down to luncheon. Afterwards the doctor, seating himself by my side, began a conversation on the historical subject I had been studying. Our conversation became really very interesting. The doctor was a man of great erudition, and of varied knowledge, and had a manner, special to himself, of making almost any subject most interesting. Hours flew by, and it was only when aunt entered about five o'clock, to take a cup of tea, as was her wont, that we were aware how time had flown. The doctor praised my knowledge of history, and the pertinency of the questions I had put to him, in a manner highly flattering to me, and I could see that I had risen much in his estimation, quite apart from any erotic influences. He proposed a constitutional walk before dinner, and much interested me by his instructive conversation during it. Our dinner was most agreeable. In the drawing-room aunt, a most admirable performer on the piano, enchanted us with her skill and taste. The doctor challenged me to a game at chess. He was, of course, far superior to me, but he praised my style of play, saying I should become a great proficient with time and practice. We retired, as usual, about half-past ten, the doctor seeing me to my room, and promising to bring aunt in the morning to see if I was still troubled with that painful hardness. I thanked him warmly, but with much simplicity, as if quite unaware of the real nature of the application of the remedy. He left me to my repose. The quiet nights of sound sleep made my day efforts pass off without any exhaustion, and I felt my erotic powers increasing in force.

I slept soundly, and so long that I was only awakened by the caressing hand of my aunt on my stiff-standing pego. She had gently lifted off all the coverings, and I lay quite exposed to eye and touch.

"Oh, my darling aunt! how kind of you to come this early to relieve that troublesome thing."

I held out my arms. She stooped down to kiss me. I clasped her to my bosom. Our lips met, and our tongues darted fiery lust into our bodies. She threw herself down by my side, I was onto her in a moment. The doctor took hold of my pego, and guided it into the delicious orbit of his wife. Dear aunt begged me to do as I did yesterday, if I wanted relief. Our action became fast and furious. Her legs and arms wound round me in loving pressures. Her active backside wriggled in delight. The doctor had introduced first one finger, and then two, into my fundament, and added greatly to the fury of my lust, so that I spent in an agony of pleasure, as quickly as the fiery lust of my aunt produced her hot and plentiful discharge. I sank on her charming bosom, panting with the force and fury of our coition, but like all very fast fucking, my virile member hardly flinched from his first vigour, and a very few of aunt's exquisitely delicious internal pressures sufficed to bring him up to the fullest stiffness. We were about to plunge again with renewed ardour into all love's wildest excitement, but the doctor insisted upon our first changing places, that he, too, might have his hardness allayed. Our change of position was instantly accomplished, and dear aunt, after impaling herself on my upright member, sank on my bosom and was clasped in my longing arms. The doctor scrambled up behind her, and lost no time in sheathing himself in her fine and beautiful bottom-hole, and then we ran a double course of delight, dear aunt taking the lead as usual, and deluging us with her hot and delicious discharges before we were ready to pour into her a double dose of delight, which again made her spend with fury and cries of rapturous enjoyment, in which we both joined, and then sank in love's exquisite inanimation. On recovering ourselves the doctor withdrew, but I was already as stiff as before. Aunt began a most effective and delicious movement above me, which soon brought on another grand finale, and we died away in mutual delight. I could feel that the doctor was gently handling my cods, both during and after our last combat. When, by our mutual throbbings, he saw that we were about to become fit to enter on another career, he begged his wife to rise from off me. But the idea of losing her and her extra pressures made my prick immediately resume an erect position, so that when she rose from off it, it was shown in a completely standing state.

"What! again, Charles?" said the doctor. "Your member is sadly unruly. My dear, you must again try to allay it, but put yourself this time on your knees, and we shall see if that position be better adapted for the purpose of relieving this immense object."

He was gently and admiringly handling it all the time. His wife was quite aware of his object, and, indeed, so was I. Our last bout had helped to restiffen his prick, and although not yet quite rampant, it was evident that when my bottom was in full view, and so placed as to be got at with facility, it would be quite as stiff as necessary. When his wife had knelt down, and by lowering her head had exposed all the wondrous grandeur of the most superb backside that ever met my eyes, my prick bounded with joy. The doctor still grasping it, and feeling it throb so wildly, saw that his game was sure. He pointed out all the beauty of aunt's second orbit of love, and told me it was in that he had allayed his own hardness, and as the other orifice had not succeeded in quieting me, he recommended my entering within the narrow path of extasy. I professed no surprise, but seemed to take it quite as a matter of course in the simplest innocence of manner. Uncle continued to handle my tool as I mounted on my knees behind aunt. Guiding the almost bursting weapon into the delicious cunt in the first place, to be lubricated there, and then telling me to withdraw it, he directed it to the smaller orifice, and desired me to push gently and smoothly in. It glided in slowly up to the meeting of my belly against the enormous buttocks of that sublime backside. There I paused for a minute or two within the throbbing sheath. Aunt had pushed her bottom well out, and by the action of apparently voiding, had faciliated the entrance. She winced once or twice, but on the whole, as she told me afterwards, took in my enormous tool with less difficulty than she expected. After a few slow movements, during with I caressed and devoured with admiration the glorious orbs beneath my dearest gaze, uncle desired me to lean forward and embrace my aunt's splendid bosom. As soon as I did this, and began slowly to thrust in and out of the delicious sheath in which I was so rapturously engulphed, I felt uncle's hands wandering over my buttocks, followed by the introduction of two fingers into my anus. My throbbings on them showed how much he pleased me. He asked if it added to the pleasure I was enjoying.

"Oh, yes, dear uncle, immensely."

"Then," said he, "as I, too, am suffering from hardness, I shall try to allay it in your bottom, as you are doing in my wife's; don't be afraid, if I hurt you I shall stop."

"Do just as you like, dear uncle, both you and aunt are so kind as to do all you can to relieve my pain, and I should be very ungrateful if I did not do all in my power to relieve you."

"You are a darling boy, and I shall love you dearly."

He knelt behind me, and spitting on his cock, presented it at my bum-hole, and pressing gently forward, soon sheathed it to the utmost depth. He did not hurt me at all, as I was too much used to be dildoed there to have felt any difficulty of approach, but I deemed it politic to beg him to be gentle from time to time, as if it were a virgin vale he was entering. He fancied as much, and that was just as good. When once he was fully within, after a few throbs, which were felt most deliciously on his delighted prick, we proceeded to more ac-

tive work. Aunt, in the meantime, by more pressure on my
prick, and by frigging her own clitoris, which I was quite
aware she was doing, had spent profusely; and, as the case
with all the mucous membranes of the body which sympathise
with the cunt's discharge, her bottom-hole became quite
moist and deliciously heated. The doctor and I then went
at it with fiery force, and soon gave down nature's tribute, and
mutually poured a flood of sperm up the entrails we were
respectively belabouring.

We lay for some time after in all the luxury of soaking in
the delicious apertures. I fell to nothing, and reluctantly withdrew. I had again become rampant, and keeping myself
more erect, with a hand on either immense hip, I devoured
with greedy eyes all the glories beneath my gaze. Fired by
such a truly magnificent sight as these huge buttocks were,
when in an entire state of wriggle, I again spent with cries of
agonised delight, and in all the extasy of fully satiated lust,
sank almost insensible on the broad and beautiful back of my
aunt, who herself had spent several times, squealing like a
rabbit, and eventually falling flat on her belly overcome with
exhausted lust, drawing me with her still held a willing prisoner in her glorious and exquisite bottom-hole. We lay entranced for some time, until the doctor, who, during our last
bout, had purified himself, told us we must now get up. With
difficulty I tore myself from out of that delicious sheath, and
rose with my cock at last pendant. The doctor congratulated
me on the success of the last move. His wife lay still panting
with all the delight of satisfied desire, and we had to help her
up. She threw herself into my arms, and hugged me close to
her heaving bosom, kissed me tenderly, and hoped she had
relieved me of all pain. I was her own darling boy, and she
would always be truly happy in relieving me of that incon-
venience whenever it troubled me. I was internally amused
at their continuing to keep up this idea, but I humoured them,
and appeared the most innocent simpleton, notwithstanding

all that had occurred. The day passed much as the previous one. After two hours' reading, aunt again proposed a walk, which, of course, ended at the summer house, where again a pressure of water brought on the painful hardness, which aunt succeeded in allaying after four most exquisite bouts of love, varied by a throroughly good double gamahuche between the last two acts. Aunt must have spent at least ten times, and appeared thoroughly contented, but continued to attribute it to her gratification at having relieved me of my painful hardness. Again I passed hours in instructive conversation with my learned uncle and after a similar evening to the last, retired at our usual hour.

Next morning I was awakened by uncle alone, who told me that my aunt was somewhat poorly, and could not come.

"I am sorry it is so, for this little fellow is as hard as usual."

"Oh, I am so sorry dear aunt is poorly, both on her account and my own. What shall I do, dear uncle? It is so hard and painful."

"Well, my dear boy, I must try to allay it myself. I love you too dearly to leave you in this state. I am not so good at allaying this painful attack as your aunt, but as you know you were successfully relieved in her bottom, and I in yours, yesterday, we shall try to-day if I can accommodate this huge fellow, of which I have some doubts. Take off your night-shirt as I do mine, it will be more commodious."

In an instant we were both stark naked. We threw ourselves into one another's arms and lovingly kissed each other. Our tongues met in a delicious sucking—our hands took each a prick, and we had a most exciting and loving embrace. The doctor then took my prick in his mouth, sucked it a little, and well lubricated it with his saliva, spitting on the lower part of the shaft and rubbing it round with his finger. He then knelt, and presenting a really beautifully rounded bottom of the fairest hue, he pushed it out, showing a light brown corrugated bum-hole, most tempting to look at. He desired me to

wet it with my saliva. I stooped and applied my mouth and
tongue to the appetising morsel, and thrust my tongue in as
far as it would go—to his evident delight, leaving it well moistened. I then brought my prick to the entrance; he shoved his
backside well out, and acted as if he desired to void himself.
A firm but slow pressure quickly engulphed the knob.
The doctor desired me to rest a moment, and drop some
spittle on the shaft. Again it was firmly pushed forward,
and gradually it won its way up, the belly against the buttocks,
without much flinching on the doctor's part. After resting a
while, he desired me to bend forward and feel his cock while
I should move backwards and forwards in the sheath until I
was relieved. I had a most delicious fuck. The doctor's
bottom-hole was quite hot internally. His pressures with the
sphincter were exquisitely delicious, and he had acquired the
charming side wriggle so exquisite in quim fucking. Of course
this was an old letch of his, which his position as school-
master had given him so many opportunities of indulging in,
and the still greater pleasure of initiating others in it. At this
very moment he was delighted with his delusion about me in
that respect. Of course I never undeceived him, and he had
all the extra delight of the idea. My younger and hotter
passions had made me spend before he could; so after indulging me in a delicious soak after the extasy of the discharge, he
drew my attention to the rigidity of his own member, which,
he said, I must now allow him to allay in turn.

"Of course, my dear uncle, I am too sensible of your great
kindness in relieving me to hesitate about giving you the same
relief."

I now withdrew. He rose for a mutual loving embrace, and
then I stooped, and taking his fine milk-white prick with its
lovely vermilion knob into my mouth, most deliciously sucked
it, making my tongue tickle the entrance to the urethra, to
his infinite delight. He murmured out soft terms of endearment; then getting exceedingly lewd, he begged me to kneel

down as he had done. He then kissed and gamahuched my bottom-hole, making my prick stand and throb again with delight. Then spitting on his prick he quickly sheathed it in my glowing backside. After pausing to enjoy the exquisite pleasure of complete insertion, he stooped, and passing a hand round my belly laid hold of my stiff-standing prick with one hand, while he gently pressed the ballocks with the other. We then proceeded to active measures. He soon made me spend, which I did with loud cries of delight, giving him the most exquisite pleasure by the pressures the act of spending made me exercise on his pleased prick. He soon resumed his thrusts, and eventually we both spent together in the most extatic joy. I sank forward on the bed, dragging the doctor with me still imbedded in the rapture-giving aperture of my backside. We lay long in all the enchantment of delight. At last he withdrew completely reduced, but was surprised to see me still in a rampant state. When I got up he took my prick in his hand, praised its noble proportions, and again stooping, took it in his mouth, frigging the lower shaft with one hand; he then introduced two fingers into my bottom-hole, continued his suction and movement on my prick in unison with the working of his fingers up my bum-hole, and in this manner quickly produced a delicious discharge in his mouth. I had placed my hands mechanically on his head, and I nearly choked him as I thrust my prick halfway down his throat as I spent. He greedily swallowed every drop, and then rising, embraced me lovingly, telling me I had given him the greatest treat in the world, and he loved me dearly. After this he invited me into his dressing-room, and we both entered the bath together and mutually laved each other. Then dressing we joined aunt at breakfast. She had not the least air *d'une malade*, but with a sly smile hoped the doctor had proved as efficient as herself.

"Oh, yes, my dear aunt, and I am so much obliged to both of you for your solicitude to relieve the pain I suffer in the morning, but it seems to me that it more frequently and more severely attacks me than ever. I only hope I shall not tire out your kindness by such frequent appeals to your aid."

"Oh, my darling nephew, do not imagine anything of the sort. We are but too happy to be of any service to you."

This was accompanied with a knowing smile cast at each other, caused by my apparent uncommon simplicity, but which they were evidently glad to see. We sat down and enjoyed a capital breakfast.

The day passed quite as the two preceding ones. Aunt asked me to walk with her, and as before ended by leading me to the summer house, where, after relieving my distress symptoms, as she called them, three times, and finding that the relief was still inefficacious, she proposed to try if by adopting my uncle's position she could not be more successful. So kneeling on the low ottoman, and throwing her clothes over her back, she exposed all the glories of that most splendid backside, and dazzled my sight with its huge magnificence and ivory-like surface, perfectly milk-white, the pureness of which was equally perceptible through the rich light curly hair that spread bush-like between her legs, and wandering beautifully upwards between the cheeks of the enormous orbs, stole round the charming corrugated aperture that I was about to penetrate, the rosy circle of which appeared all too small to admit my very large virile member. I threw myself on my knees, and first licking out the wide open lips of her wonderously fine cunt, and taking care to pay my respects to the small knob of her indurated clitoris, I transferred all my attention to the smaller and most charming orifice. After kissing it most lovingly, I thrust my tongue in as far as it would go, and rolled it about to her infinite delight, while with my left hand below I kept pressing and frigging at her excited clitoris. She wriggled her glorious backside in all the agonies of the delicious excitement until she spent most profusely, actually hurting my tongue with the tightness of the squeeze her sphincter muscle gave as she poured down her plentiful discharge over my chin and neck. In her grand excitement, and wild with the fury of her lust, she cried out—

"Oh! fuck me, my darling, and shove your glorious prick into my bottom-hole. Oh! fuck—fuck—fuck me directly!"

Inwardly delighted at this natural outbreak of her passions, naming matters by their more appropriate terms, I replied by acts, without any words at the moment. It may well be imagined I was myself in the most rampant fury of desire. So bringing my raging prick up to her magnificently large cunt, all foaming as it was with her recent discharge, I plunged with a furious bound up to the codpiece at once. She met my forward lunge with a backward push and a cry of delighted satisfaction. I moved a few times in and out, so that my prick was white with the foam of her delicious cunt. Then suddenly withdrawing, I presented it at the entrance of the more secret temple of Venus, and more gently pushed it home, she helping me with outthrust buttocks and outward straining of the entrance, so that I most charmingly glided slowly into the glowing furnace that was awaiting with such lascivious desire to engulph and devour my longed-for prick. For, as I have before observed, my dear aunt was gluttonous of a bottom-fuck, after being so fucked in cunt as I had already served her. It was so deliciously tight and hot that I lay in the exquisite rapture of complete insertion for some minutes. I had seen my aunt's arm move in a manner to convince me she was frigging her own clitoris, in fact, the movement of her hand frigging herself was felt by my codpiece. I let her continue, until finding by the involuntary wriggling of her bottom that she was about again to spend, I aided her with my prick, and had hardly made many moves before she poured down another tribute of lust, with a squeal of delight, and with such pressure on my prick as nearly drove him at once to a similar discharge. I did my best, and succeeded in not following suit. My aunt was insatiable, and I was glad to let her spend as

often as possible, and I so managed matters that she spent
again before joining me in the final crisis, which seized us together, and we died away in joyous cries of thoroughly,
though but momentarily, satisfied desire. I sank on that
magnificent back, as the languor that follows the extatic moment overtook me, but it was only for a short time. The exquisite internal pressures that my amorous and glorious aunt
was exercising on my delighted prick were too exciting not
to rapidly produce a reaction; nonetheless rapidly that it
was in such a delicious retreat as the pleasure-giving aperture
of that gloriously exciting backside. I was lying down on her
broad back, so passing one hand round to her large but firm
bubby, I took its nipple between my fingers. The other hand
sought the knob of her still stiff clitoris. I excited both while
making a very gentle move with my hardly fully standing
prick. I felt at once how this gratified her, indeed, she often
afterwards assured me that such frigging, with the movement
of the softened prick gently working within her, was most
exciting, and almost better than when it was in full force. I
soon made her spend again. Another of her delights was to
have a stiff prick shove away into her the instant after she
had spent, when she herself was at the moment incapable of
action on her part. She in after-days proved that her greatest
pleasure was to have a fresh-standing prick near, to take the
place of one that had made her spend, and had spent itself,
and have it thrust into her with all the vigour and lust the
sight of the previous fucking had inspired and fired it with.
At this moment, as I had not spent, it was the exact counter-
part her libidinous imagination could have desired. I fucked
and frigged on until we both gave down in cries of joy our
united tribute to Venus. We both sank this time down on the
couch in utter forgetfulness of all but the extatic bliss with
which we were overcome. We long lay soaking in all the delightful sensations my adorable aunt's convulsive clutchings of
my prick with her delicious close pressures excited. At last she

begged me to withdraw, although she could feel me now re-stiffening under the delights of that exquisite interior. I would fain have recommenced.

"You must not, my dear boy, it is more than nature can support, and I must consider your youth; you have delighted me even beyond previous delights—rise then my love, and let me embrace, thank, and love you as I shall always do."

I rose, and we threw ourselves into each other's arms, lovingly kissing and tongueing each other. Aunt then buttoned me up, first kissing and taking a mouthful of my prick for a moment between her lips, and then putting him away, calling it "my pretty doodle." I seized the expression, and said—

"Dear aunt, you called it my prick just now, and begged me to fuck you, and to shove it well into your cunt. Are these the real names for my doodle and your Fanny, and what does "fuck" mean, my darling aunt? Do tell me, dear auntie? and teach me the language I ought to use when you are so kindly relieving me of the pains of my now so frequent hardness. I don't know whether you have observed it, dear auntie, but I never enter this summer house with you, but it becomes pain-fully hard at once; to be sure you give me such exquisite pleasure in relieving me that I could wish to have constant hardnesses as long as you were near to calm them. Is this natural, dear aunt, or a disease? Pray tell me, and teach me all the endearing terms you so lavish upon me while I am reduc-ing my hardnesses."

My apparent simplicity evidently pleased her. She prob-ably thought, too, that as I must sooner or later really thoroughly understand the nature of our intercourse, it would be much better she should, as it were, make a confidant of me, and attach me more securely to herself. She begged me to be seated and she fully explained everything to me. Of course I was even better acquainted than herself with all she com-municated, but I confirmed the idea she evidently entertained of her being my first instructress by various naïve remarks on all she was telling me. Of course I proved an apt scholar, and by my close-put questions brought out all her own knowledge, and left nothing for me to learn. At the end, I said—

"Do all women have such a delightful sheath—cunt I mean —between their legs as you have, dear aunt?"

"Yes, my darling; but you must never stray to others; you will find none so fond of you, or I may add, without vanity, so capable of satisfying this dear fellow; but come, I see it will be dangerous to allow him to stay here longer."

She rose, but I quickly unbuttoned and produced my prick in an almost grander state than ever. I begged of her to let me have one more "fuck" now that I knew what it all really meant. I put it into her hand. Her own previous descriptive lesson had aroused her lasciviousness. She fondly grasped it, and stooping down, kissed it, saying she could not resist its eloquent look. Throwing herself back on the couch, with her clothes up, her feet on the edge, and her legs apart, her glorious cunt lay open in its moist magnificence. I threw myself on my knees and gamahuched her until she spent: and now, knowing her greatest letch, I instantly brought my bursting prick up to her foaming cunt, plunged in and began a furious movement, accompanying it with all the most endearing bawdy phrases she had just, as she thought, taught me.

"Oh, my most gloriously cunted aunt, do I fuck you? Wriggle your arse faster—that's it! Do you feel my prick up to the hilt in your delicious cunt? Oh! what pleasure you do give me!"

She replied as broadly. Passing her hand down she pressed my cods, and asked if thus squeezing my ballocks added to my pleasure.

"Oh, yes, my love, your cunt, your arse, your bubbies, are all delicious. Oh, I never before knew there could be such additional pleasure to our fucking as using these endearing words produce."

We were both so excited by the bawdy terms we so profusely used that we went off in the utmost excess of extasy, and died away thoroughly satiated with our libidinous and most lasciviously delicious fuck. It was time to finish. So sliding off her, I again buried my face in her delicious gaping and foaming cunt, my mouth, lips, nose, and cheeks were covered with sperm; she drew me to her lips and licked it all off. Then repairing our disordered dress we returned to the house, and found the doctor impatiently awaiting us. Our flushed and excited faces at once showed that we had been indulging in the greatest excess. He joked aunt upon her skill in allaying such frequent attacks as I now appeared subject to.

Aunt informed him that she had inadvertently in her lust made use of expressions which had betrayed so much to me that she had found it necessary to leave me nothing more to learn, and I was now fully aware of the true nature of our connection; after luncheon he himself might further enlighten me, for she was certain that complete confidence would be the best policy to pursue; it must come about, sooner or later, and it was far better it should come from him than that I should learn it elsewhere. He said she was quite right, and that he would further instruct me after luncheon, so we set to work on the viands before us, to which I did ample justice.

I was thus, as they supposed, newly initiated in the mysteries of the coition of the sexes. I shall reserve further details of our more intimate and expansive experiences for the third volume of this true Romance of Lust, and still of Early Experiences.

END OF VOL. II.

Volume III
The Romance of Lust

*A*fter the luncheon, which closed the last volume, a churchwarden occupied uncle for about an hour. When he had left off, uncle proposed a walk in the garden. I could see at once what this was meant to lead to, as he almost immediately turned in the direction of the summer house. When we got there he sat down on the couch, and begged me to sit beside him. He opened the subject at once by saying—

"My dear Charlie, I am very much pleased that your aunt has opened your eyes to the real nature of our actions with you, which your simple innocence had imagined to be a mere kindly relief to the overgorged vessels of your virile member. Accident might have made you acquainted with this through some less interested channel, and you might have innocently betrayed your future position. I believe you to possess a large fund of good sense and discretion, and the advice I shall give you as to the conduct to pursue in future will not only be received with confidence as meant for your future good, but listened to attentively and acted upon. The world, my dear boy, and by that I mean Society in general, condemns the practices we have lately been indulging in with you. Their narrow prejudices ignore the fact that nature alone prompts to these delightful acts, and that the great God of nature gifted us with the powers necessary for their performance. But, as the world has chosen to brand them with its censure, men of prudence, like myself, whilst apparently conforming outwardly to such stupid prejudices, know how in secret to fully enjoy them. I am blessed in your darling aunt with a wife who fully understands and humours my desires. She is rarely splendid in the glorious beauties of her body, and in temperament hot as the most erotic of our sex could desire. Even in your ignorance you must have felt the wonderful power of conferring carnal extatic pleasure she possesses, and have heard how, in the energy of her passion, she allowed her lust to betray her into the use of grossly bawdy terms, but which, as they have enlightened you when best prepared to receive such knowledge, is rather fortunate than otherwise. I speak thus frankly to you, my dear boy, because I have found you of a rare facility in giving and receiving erotic pleasures, and of a temperament worthy of the descent from the same stock as your aunt. You are worthy of each other, and formed to enjoy to the utmost each other's carnal delights, and I bless my happy star that has brought you both under my own roof. Henceforth there must be no secrets between us. It was at my earnest wish that your aunt relieved you; and, of course I had my own object in view. In the first place I require some extra excitement to be able myself to indulge in these delightful combats in love's domain. You and your aunt's copulations were to me more exciting than you can imagine. You will have observed, too, what is the real quarter to which, when excited, I pay my devoirs. Glorious as is the backside of your incomparable aunt, your young charms, virgin in that respect, excited me still more. I began by gentle touches, and then tried the insertion of my finger, when I saw you were far too busy operating within the orbit of your lustful and lusty aunt to observe or even feel what I was doing. I found a facility about your bottom as perfect for enjoyment as your truly magnificent prick or cock was fitted for operating in its way. It was then I suggested to your aunt to mount upon you, and afterwards made you aware that your aunt possessed another aperture which could equally well allay what you then looked upon as a source of pain. My object was to lead you to the same point. Your innocent docility lent itself with easy simplicity to all my desires. I saw that you entered readily into your aunt's glorious bum-hole, and allowed me to work with two fingers in your own. Finding that it rather gave you pleasure than otherwise, I proposed to abate my own stiffness in your bottom. Your affectionate docility enabled me to obtain unfailing extasy. Your after-fucking of me, while I was in my wife's bottom, conferred the utmost erotic bliss upon me, as you have experienced when operating and being operated upon. These—these are the moments of a felicity your stupid prejudiced worldlings know nothing of; and these are the pleasures which, now that we have initiated you into all their secret mysteries, we will enjoy to the utmost. To the true votaries of these love orgies grossness of language is a stimulant to passion. Fuck—frig—bugger—cunt—prick—ballocks—bubbies—arse-hole—are all sacred words only to be pronounced when in the exercise of love's mysteries. At all other times a guarded decency of word, act, and gesture is imperative, as enhancing the delight of an unbridled vocabulary in the voluptuary of raging lust. I shall from time to time inculcate sage precepts on this point—enough for the present. Let us now indulge in mutual embraces."

So ending, he took me in his arms and glued his lips to mine. Our tongues met. Both our hands wandered, his on my prick, which immediately responded to the touch, my hand was placed on his prick, but which was only at half-cock. I rapidly unbuttoned, and brought it forth, then stooping I took it in my mouth, and sucked it and fingered the root with my hand. Then passing my other hand below, I sought to penetrate with my finger into the interior of his fundament. He rose to a standing position to enable me to enter his anus more easily. His prick quickly standing fiercely showed how much I excited him. I ceased not until he was in an agony of pleasure—forcing my head down on his prick until it entered almost completely into my mouth, and shooting his sperm right down my throat. I continued to suck and frig him until I produced somewhat of a restiffening of his prick. He begged me to rise, that he might take mine in his mouth, desiring me at the same time to take off my trousers and lie down on the couch. I did so. He knelt at my side, and first handling and examining it with loudly expressed admiration of my noble weapon, he took its head in his mouth, and then with his hand on its lower shaft, and finger up my fundament, brought on a similar crisis as that I had produced on himself. He just as greedily swallowed all. I had allowed my hand to fall down by the side of the couch, where it encountered his prick, which had resumed its pristine vigour.

"Come my dear uncle," said I, "and let us put it into its favourite corner."

I rose, and kneeling, turned my backside full in his face. He stooped, caressed, kissed, and tongued the rosy orifice. With the plentiful saliva with which the operation of sucking my prick had filled his mouth, he moistened my bum-hole and his own prick, and then easily glided up to the hilt within my delighted backside. Resting for a while in all the extasies of insertion, which I heightened by my internal pressures, he seized my prick which had stood again at once at the pleasing sensation occasioned by the introduction of his prick in my bottom. Thus frigging my prick and fucking my arse, with occasional pauses to lengthen out our pleasures, he at last brought matters to a most exquisite termination, and died away in cries of joy as we poured forth a mutual torrent of sperm. Uncle continued soaking in all the blissful after-sensations, which I did everything in my power to enhance by the delight-giving pressures of my sphincter muscle. When he withdrew and rose to his legs, he helped me up, and drew me to his bosom, and we had a long kiss of gratified desire, tongueing each other the while, and handling our ballocks with mutual gratification. My uncle was profuse in his praises of my docility and aptitude, declaring that his pederastic enjoyment of my person excelled all he had ever experienced in his long practice of the habit, and my delicious sideways wriggle was superior to the very fine bum-fucking his adorable wife had the art of giving him: then there was the further excitement of handling the very finest prick he had ever met with.

"It is no flattery to you, my dear Charles," he said, "but mere justice to its superb dimensions and admirable power."

Here he stopped, and sucked anew its reeking head, getting a few more drops out. We then purified ourselves—a basin with water was kept in a small cupboard purposely for such occasion, for I afterwards learned the place had been the scene of innumerable contests of the same kind with aunt and other boys. Having readjusted our disordered habiliments, we left the grounds, and took a long quiet walk in the fields; the good doctor inculcating admirable advice to me, whom he considered an innocent tyro in love's ways. Nevertheless, all he taught me only strengthened my high opinion of the wisdom of dear Mrs. Benson, and the adorable Frankland, whose opinion of what was likely to happen to me at the rectory had been so quickly realised. We returned in time to dress for dinner. The evening passed as the previous ones. I was conducted to my room, and left alone to recruit my forces by a quiet night's rest. I may here incidentally mention that it was a rule of uncle and aunt, very rarely departed from, to send their favourites to their lonely couches as a means of restoring their powers, and reinvigorating them for daylight encounters—both the dear creatures loving to have the fullest daylight on all the charms of their participants in pleasure, at the same time yielding an equally undisguised inspection of their own. This was their principle reason, but they also considered it advisable as a restorative, and a useful precaution not to overstrain the energies of the youths they both so much enjoyed. My late experiences at home had already taught me the advantage and utility of a quiet night's rest after frequent contests in the fields of Venus and Juno.

I slept on this occasion with a deep and continuous slumber, until I was awakened by my uncle, who came to summon me to the arms of his wife, who, in the splendour of her full-blown charms awaited me in her own bed, naked as the day she was born. Her arms outstretched, she invited me to the full enjoyment of her glorious person. The doctor drew my night-shirt over my head, and in a moment I was locked in the close embrace of that superb creature. We were both too hot to wait for further preliminaries, but went at it in furious haste, and rapidly paid our first tribute to the god of love. The doctor had acted postillion to both of us, with a finger up each anus. The exquisite pressures of my aunt's cunt reinvigorated me almost without a pause, and we proceeded at once to run a second course. Uncle got three fingers into her divine bottom-hole, as her legs were thrown over my waist, and her immense buttocks well thrown up enabled him to have full play between the cheeks of her backside. This double operation made the dear lascivious creature spend again in a very few movements, and giving her hardly time to finish her discharge, I fucked on with double force, and with prick as hard as wood, as fast I could work. This furious onset, which was the most exciting thing she knew of, rapidly caused a third discharge. To prevent my own prick from spending too quickly, I held somewhat back; then again we went at it fast and furious, and the dear lustful creature, with cries of joy, spent again with me, and fainted from excess of pleasure; but her glorious cunt continued to throb on my delighted prick, as if it would nip it off by the roots. I never met with so lusciously large a cunt, or one with a greater power of pressure. She could quite hold even an exhausted prick a complete prisoner in these most delicious and velvety folds. Great as was the power of Miss Frankland's cunt in that way, aunt beat her. I may here mention an occurrence that took place some time after this period. It was during a rare opportunity from an accidental absence of the doctor, when I was sleeping with my gloriously beautiful aunt. I had fucked her to her heart's content before we slept, and again on waking, in full daylight, after which we rose to relieve our natural wants. I laid myself down on the floor, that I might completely see my dear aunt piddle from her splendid cunt. It was a glorious sight, which instantly fired my passions and was at once followed by a fuck on the floor, my aunt's enormous backside being quite cushion enough, and we enjoyed the novelty of the thing amazingly. She was loud in her praises of my indefatigable prick, which, with its vigour and superb dimensions, was beyond all she had ever seen or felt, and just fitted her large and luscious cunt, which had never before been so well filled. This remark reminded me of a desire I had long had to have a thorough investigation of that immense and splendid object. I expressed a wish to that effect.

"My darling boy, anything you like, you could not have a better opportunity, my legs point to the window, so you have the fullest sight—look, feel, frig, fuck, or bugger, all is at your free disposition—only give me a pillow from the bed, as the floor is too hard for me to continue so long as you are likely to be."

I jumped up and gave her two pillows. Then laying her limbs wide open, with knees bent, the magnificence of that luscious cunt lay in all its grandeur before me. I have before described what a large, but splendidly proportioned woman

she was—small feet, and clear-run ankles, large, but admirably turned calves, very small knees, above which rose the
very finest and fleshiest of thighs, worthy supporters of what
I have already described as the largest and finest backside
my eyes ever lighted on. Immense hips, and wonderfully and
naturally small waist, above which were her superb, large,
fine, and firm bubbies that stood out when naked, as hard
and firm as those of the youngest of women; a charming
neck, and well-posed head with most pleasing and beautiful
features crowned the whole. Her arms were superb, and
equal in proportion to her other grand and splendid limbs.
The flesh was of the most delicious creamy white, without a
spot or a blemish. The hair of the head, plentiful in the
extreme, and so long and thick that when undone it fell all
around her and below her superb buttocks, so that she
could shake it out all round, and completely hide her nakedness. Often and often has she allowed me to pose her in
every way, and shake it out all over her, and well she might,
for no matter how often I might have fucked her previously,
it was sure to produce at least three more encounters, one of
which was always in her backside, a most favourite way with
her and which she declared was by far the most pleasurable
provided the other aperture had been previously well fucked.
With such a taste, of course, her greatest pleasure was to
have two pricks in her at once, the *ne plus ultra* of erotic
satisfaction. To return to the inspection I was about to
describe, which was really the first at my full disposition, for
although I had often gamahuched, felt and seen the beautiful object, it was when my passions were excited, and when
the gratification of lust alone prompted me, a state of mind
opposed to close observation of natural beauties. Now, repeated tributes to the god of lust had cooled my ardour for
the moment, and left me to the perfect enjoyment of the
sight before me, with the temper to inspect its full-blown
beauties in the minutest way. I have said before that my

aunt had one of the broadest, most prominent, and most beautiful mounts of Venus that I ever saw. It was thickly covered with beautiful silky fair curls, which did not hinder you from seeing her exquisite skin below. The sweep round, to pass between her thighs, was bold and graceful. In the middle was a well defined semi-circular depression, from whence the large, thick and beautifully pouting lips of her cunt commenced, which in her present position lay partially open. You could just see where the clitoris lay snug. I have already observed that this was not largely developed, nor were the inner labia of her cunt at all projecting, indeed, they were not visible, unless her legs, with bent knees, were stretched apart, as at present. On each side of these luscious pouting lips, and the long immense pinky gash, was a triangle of considerable space, such, in fact, as is only to be seen in a woman of the splendidly large proportions of my aunt; this was covered as much as her mount with fair silky curls, which ran down to her beautiful corrugated and rosy bottom-hole. Nothing could be finer or more beautiful than the sight, as she thus lay fully exposing every part in the broadest daylight. After handling and admiring all, I laid the lips well back and apart, and there they kept open. Nothing could be more charming than the interior of that most enchanting cunt, of an exquisite salmon-pink in colour, nothing was out of order. The clitoris, which bulged out in excitement from my touches of all the parts around, lay first in the upper partition of the pouting lips; then became below, slightly open, a charming entrance to the urethra, larger than usual, to allow the mighty rush of waters to pour from it when piddling; below this was the opening of the vagina, which I parted with my fingers, and could see even to the corrugated sides of that exquisite pleasure-giving sheath; then followed some sinuosity of pinky flesh, whose duty it was to stretch to allow the largest prick to penetrate. Half-an-inch beyond was the rosy orifice of her bottom. Such was the exquisite scene before my delighted eyes. I proceeded with my internal examination. Thrusting in three fingers of each hand, I forced open by literal pressure the lips, until I could see to a depth of four or five inches. It was a most beautiful sight. The sheath appeared to have ribs running round it about half-an-inch apart, and I could see they were the means of causing the exquisite pressures her cunt could so extatically exercise. Indeed, excited by my *attouchements*, I could see them contracting and relaxing. It was, doubtless, these ribs that seemed to exercise a sort of peristaltic motion on the prick, when reposing at full stand in that glorious cunt. I was able so widely to open this splendid vagina that I thought I would try to get my hand altogether in. Projecting my fingers forward, with the first and fourth drawn under the middle ones and the thumb between, I pushed them forward, and as the whole cunt was reeking with my last discharge, and was well lubricated, I glided on; there was a little difficulty at the knuckles, but I exerted a slight, gentle pressure, and in all went. Aunt winced a little, and asked what I was doing. I told her.

"It is all in, my darling?"

"Yes, Auntie."

She closed upon it, and squeezed it quite hard.

"Oh, how nice!" she exclaimed, "push it further in."

I advanced, and could feel the end of her womb, which appeared like three points to fingers and the thumb drawn together, and looked at endways is something like what it felt—of course, without the nails. Aunt asked me if I could double my fist where it was. I had no difficulty, as the part yielded to the greater bulk. Aunt cried out—

"My darling boy, that is delicious; push it further in."

I did so, and began working within her, backwards and forwards. She wriggled her splendid backside in extasy, and before I had made a dozen movements, poured down upon my hand and arm a torrent of almost boiling liquid, and went off with a cry of enjoyment. Her arms and legs relaxed, and she lay quite still in the utmost after-enjoyment, but with a pressure on my arm and fist quite wonderful. Knowing how she liked the movement to be continued at such a moment, I worked in and out slowly. She soon recovered, and again seconded my movements, and again went off in all the fury of lust, accompanied with shouts of excitement, urging faster movements, and again went off in all the fury of her most libidinous nature, and spent most profusely. All this had now brought me into as furious a state as herself. I wanted to withdraw and substitute my prick, not only from the state of excitement I was in, but also to experience the effects of such a well-stretched cunt upon my lesser-sized weapon. But so tight did my aunt hold my imprisoned hand that I could not withdraw. I begged her to let it go, as I wanted to fuck her instantly, but she prayed me to give her one more of such exquisite manœuvres, it was a joy beyond anything she had ever before experienced, so she begged her darling boy to join. On I went as she desired, and a more exciting picture of furious lust never met my sight. I helped her final discharge by thrusting two fingers in her bum-hole. Never shall I forget the grip she gave my arm and fingers when she spent. It was positively painful, and showed the enormous force of passionate lust. She went off in such a fury of excitement that I thought she had fainted outright. But her pressures continued all the time. It was long before she recovered her senses, and my arm was aching, and my prick bursting. At last she exclaimed—

"Oh! where am I? I have been in paradise."

"Dear aunt," I cried, "do let me out. I am bursting to fuck you, and I can't get my arm out, if you don't relax your grip of my wrist."

"I can't help it, my dear boy, it is involuntary, put your other hand on my mount, and pull steadily, but not with a jerk."

I did so, and really it required considerable force to withdraw it, notwithstanding I had previously unclenched my hand. I jumped immediately upon her, and at one bound plunged into that vast cavity, up to the cods. It immediately closed upon me, and tight as she usually held me, she really appeared to do so this time tighter than ever, so wonderfully gifted was that longest, highest, and most luscious cunt I ever fucked. You may easily imagine the rapid ending of such raging lust. I spent with cries more like the braying of a donkey than any other sound, and then lay like one dead on that glorious belly, with head reposing between the firm and splendid bubbies, aunt clasping me to her bosom, panting with all it had just granted. We lay long in extatic trance of the delicious after-sensations. Our mutual internal throbbings gradually re-excited all our passions. With renewed ardour I quickly made my lascivious and libidinous aunt spend again on my delighted prick, which kept ramming at her during the swoon-like pause which spending produced; she had taught me this was exquisite delight to her. She soon resumed the full swing of her lust, but suddenly stopping, said—

"Charlie, my darling, withdraw, and shove it in behind."

She quickly turned round, with great agility, prompted by the excess of her desires. I was behind her in an instant, and as my prick was reeking with the fuck she had just so plentifully bedewed it with, and the divine lower orifice had also received its tricklings, I had no difficulty in pushing firmly but not too forcibly right up to the meeting of her stupendous buttocks and my belly. She sighed deeply with delight, when she felt me fully imbedded, and began the delicious side wriggle, while I remained for some minutes quiet, that I might enjoy the superb beauty of those mighty orbs, in all their play of passion. Aunt grew furious with lust. Her hand was actively frigging both clitoris and cunt. She called out to me to shove on; two or three thrusts on my part, and the dear, lecherous creature again poured down her nature. I paused to restrain my own discharge, but made my prick throb within its most exquisite sheath, which never ceased responding most deliciously. It was but for a minute or two, when my own fierce passion drove me to very energetic action. My delighted aunt seconded my movements, fast and furious grew our sport, until, with cries of the wildest lust, we both spent deliciously together. I sank on her glorious bottom and back, and by embracing her superb bubbies with both hands, until her exquisite pressures again renewed my forces, and drove me on to another delightful career, in which again the hot lust of my aunt drew down from her several discharges to my one. At last we sank both together, in all the joys of fully satiated desire. Again I lay for some time on that broad and beauteous back, until aunt said I must withdraw, as she had great natural want. I instantly withdrew, out he came with a loud plop, followed immediately by a tremendous succession of farts. Aunt professed to be quite horrified, but I only burst into a loud fit of laughter and told the dear creature to fart, piss, or shit, whenever she felt inclined, I should only love her the better. She said she must at once do the latter, and was running off to the water closet as soon as she could hurry on some clothes. But I drew out the chamber, and begged her to sit down there at once. It would give me pleasure and excite me as well. She was too hard pressed to hesitate, so sitting down, she had a "hell of a let-fly" as a military friend of mine used to say. I stooped over her back, caressed her bubbies and when she turned up her delighted face, our lips were glued together in a loving kiss, while my nose sniffed the really delicious odour that came from her. When she had done, she begged me to hand her a towel to wipe herself.

"No, no, my darling aunt, nothing of the sort; stoop down forward on to your knees, and I will lick the delicious orifice clean with my tongue."

She laughed, kissed me, and told me I was a darling boy,

just after her own heart, but hardly expected I had already acquired the tastes of my uncle, the rector, whose letch lay in that practice. She let herself down on her knees as her sublime arse raised itself from the pot, and stooping her head low down, presented her immense buttocks before me, with the chink between well stretched open. I move the pot on one side, threw myself on hands and knees, and eagerly kissing the exquisite orifice, greedily licked it clean, and thrusting my tongue well within, rolled it about, to the great delight of dear aunt, whose passions were instantly aroused, and her divine backside began to wriggle. I shoved my thumb up her cunt, and frigged until she spent. Meanwhile my own unruly member had become distended to his full size, and was throbbing with desire. So raising my body erect, I brought him again to the rosy orifice I had just been tongueing, and to my aunt's infinite delight, again housed him as far as he could go, and again began active operations, which I continued until aunt's lasciviousness again made her spend. I paused a little after this, or otherwise I should have gone off myself. Stooping over the glorious bottom, I replaced her hand with my own, and began frigging her clitoris, till her passions, again excited, made her begin extatic movements, in which I joined until the grand crisis seized us both together, ushered in with cries of joy. We spent, and sank down sideways on the floor in quite a death swoon of extatic and satisfied lust. Here we lay quite exhausted for some time. At last aunt let me out, and begged me to rise.

"I must purify you, my darling boy, as you did me."

And seizing my limp prick in her mouth she sucked it clean, until she began to feel symptoms of the resurrection of the flesh. She hastily rose, and said—

"No, Charlie, you have done far too much to-night. I must see you to your bed, that you may get at least a couple of hours sleep."

She took up my night-shirt, threw it over me, led me to my bedroom, tenderly embraced me, and thanked me for such a night of pleasure as she had never in all her life enjoyed the equal. Then locking me in, she retired to her own bed. It may well be supposed that after such exertions, I slept the sleep of the just for many hours. My aunt had frequently come to look at me, but seeing me in so sound a slumber, would not have me disturbed—a politic proceeding, as it resulted in a fuller indulgence in the summer house that day than would have happened if my powers had not been restored by refreshing sleep.

This kind of life had been going on for nearly three weeks. The doctor became less easy to move. One morning I had fucked my aunt twice; the doctor's prick at the end of the second had stiffened to about half stand. I took it into my mouth, which, with handling his ballocks and postillioning his bottom-hole, brought him up to the—full standard. He proposed to bugger aunt while I did the same kind office to himself. A caprice seized me, and I proposed, on the contrary, that we should both fuck aunt's capacious cunt at once. Aunt, for form's sake, cried out against it, but the idea tickled the fancy of my uncle, who would not only enjoy all the beauties of my aunt's glorious backside in motion, but could postillion her as well. So I lay down on my back, aunt mounted me, and presented her splendid bum to the attack of her excited husband. He first thrust his prick up to the hilt in her lucious and well-bedewed cunt; when well lubricated, he withdrew, to allow me to make my place in full possession, then bringing his stiff-standing prick against the root of mine, pressing it well down, he gently shoved forward, and gradually sheathed himself within the well-stretched and capacious orbit of my aunt, who winced a little in pretended pain, but who, by the grip she immediately gave to the double fuck within her, showed how much gratified she was. After a pause of enjoyment, I gave the signal for exact joint movements, both pulling out gently, and sliding slowly in again. Two or three thrusts, aided by the doctor's finger in her bottom-hole, sufficed to make dear leacherous aunt spend profusely. We increased our speed, but still not fast, which quickly re-awakened all aunt's lust. Before we ourselves were ready, the dear lascivious creature again poured down her nature, boiling hot, on our delighted pricks. This produced such excitement upon us that we could no longer restrain our own desire to come to the extatic conclusion. Our movements became more rapid. We each felt the electric-like sensation of the approaching crisis. Aunt doubly felt the influence of our increasing speed and hardness, and was as ready as ourselves to pour down the tribute to the goddess of love or lust, holy Mother Venus. The novelty, the pressure, and the excess of pleasure declared itself in the loud cries of the last crisis, as we all died away in the enrapturing sensations produced by the intense satisfaction our desires had experienced. We lay long wrapped in the after-extasy; aunt's delicious internal movements began again. The doctor's prick had shrunk to a merry piece of inanimate dough, and he withdrew, begging us at the same time to change our position, and let him enjoy seeing me attack my aunt in rear. This inflamed me at once. Aunt rolled from off me. I took my place behind, and we ran a most delicious course, rendered much more excitable to me by the introduction of uncle's two fingers up my fundament, which kept time with my action in the delicious aperture of my aunt's most superb and glorious backside, the movements of which beneath my delighted gaze had not been the least stimulating part of the enjoyment. The crisis was most extatic, and I sank exhausted on her broad buttocks and beautiful back, to clasp her lovingly in my arms and sob out bawdy terms of the warmest endearment. The doctor, who had very much enjoyed the sight, but who pointed out the sadly downcast state of his prick, which had been in no wise excited by the scene, said to his wife—

"My darling, we must have recourse to the grand remedy, I will also initiate dear Charlie into a new mystery of love, of which he can have no idea."

I guessed at once what he meant, but professing extreme ignorance, I begged him to tell me what it was. Aunt rose and said—

"My darling, your uncle requires his blood to be excited by flogging his buttocks with a birch rod."

"How odd," said I, "I never felt anything but the severest pain when I was flogged, and I took precious good care not to deserve it again. How then can it excite?"

"You shall see, my dear."

She opened her wardrobe and produced a formidable rod of fine fresh-cut birch twigs. The doctor begged me to lie down on my back—he got over me, and we commenced sucking each other's pricks. Mine stood at once, as the doctor, in addition to sucking, thrust a couple of fingers up my bottom-hole, and frigged away as fast as he sucked. The doctor's buttocks were left at the mercy of aunt, who flogged away at them with no gentle hand. I spent before the doctor could quite get his prick to standing point, but the copious torrent I poured into his mouth, and his after-suction on my prick, in addition to the red raw state of his buttocks, at last brought him up to full stand. He wanted to put it into me when ready, but aunt said that as flogger she had herself become greatly excited, and must have it herself.

"While this dear prick," throwing herself on it, and sucking it, "shall fuck me at the same time."

I was quite ready, and she straddled across me, and guided my now longing prick into her luscious cunt. She soon stopped, and we tongued each other while the doctor was mounting to the assault on her delicious bottom-hole. As soon as he was housed, we began another charming course, in which aunt, as usual, spent frequently before our less lecherous natures were ready to join in one general and exquisite discharge. We went off in furies of delighted lust, and then

sank exhausted in the delicious after-sensation. We long lay
in the sweet inanition and luxury of satiated lust. At last we
disconnected ourselves, rose, and laved each other with cold
water, more as a restorative than as a purification. Aunt and
I had two bouts after—one in front and one behind. The
doctor would not allow a fresh application of the birch, as
he said it would only produce so great an exhaustion as
would require days to restore. I retired after this, but ever
afterwards the doctor was regularly birched before he could
even copulate once. Sometimes he required to flog my aunt's
glorious bum to excite his fading powers, declaring that it
was almost as exciting as being flogged. He even gave it me
gently, although I hardly ever required it, but I professed
my surprise at its efficiency.

The holidays were at an end, but I was as yet the only
boarder. There were, however, some twenty or thirty youths
from the neighbourhood, who were day scholars at the doctor's school. Among these the doctor had his pick in the
flogging way, but he never allowed them to know anything
of our other proceedings, or to imagine that the birching
which took place was otherwise than as a punishment for
faults or inattention. However, I was generally the chosen
companion of these whippings, in which I acted as horse,
or holder of the boy to be flogged. Of course I took good
care to expose as much as possible their lovely cocks, as
well as their plump bottoms, and as this excited me as well
as the doctor, it often ended, after the culprit was dismissed,
in my flogging the doctor, followed by a mutual rack off in
each other's bottoms.

There was one fine, plump, girlish-looking youth, named
Dale, who was here for the first half. He had not as yet
been brought up for punishment, although the doctor had
confided to me the letch he had taken to flog his fine fat
bottom. One day, Master Dale brought a sealed note from
his widowed mother, who lived about a mile from the village,

in a charming cottage ornée. The doctor read the note. By chance I was looking at him, and saw a smile of joy light up his features.

"Come here, Master Dale," said he in a mild and gentle voice, "your mother tells me that you have behaved in a most shameful manner to your pretty young cousin, who is residing with your mamma."

Master Dale blushed scarlet, for he was not aware until now that any one had been a witness to the scene that had taken place between him and his pretty cousin.

This was what had passed. The cousin, a lovely girl of fifteen, was in a secluded spot in the garden, near an arbour, the preceding afternoon. She was bending down, tying up a flower close to the ground, which made her stoop to such a degree that she could only reach it with ease by having her legs wide apart. Her back was towards the walk by which young Dale was advancing. As he approached unheard by her, he could not fail to see peeping out between the stretched open expanse of snowy drawers the inner part of her well-rounded globes of dimpled ivory. Her shift had somehow worked upwards, and revealed all the charms of her delicate young bum and plump white thighs. The sight inflamed the youth beyond measure. He crept up noiselessly quite close to her, and, stooping down until his head was below the level of her raised petticoat, he feasted his eyes for some time with the lovely prospect before him, her little virgin rosebud slit, its pink and pouting lips, plump little mount already delicately shaded with a curly foliage that promised soon to be much more dense, together with the swell of her lovely young thighs and calves. All this was quite unsuspected by the object of his admiration, who was absorbed in her garden operations. At length, however, the excited youth could not resist the temptation of applying his soft warm hand to the parts he was admiring, which made Miss scream

slightly—she thinking it was some insect up her petticoats—
exclaiming—

"Oh, dear! oh, dear!"

But turning her head round, she discovered the delinquent.

"Forgive me, Ellen dear, but really you exposed so very
pretty a sight while stooping that upon my word I could not
help it."

Now girls are curious as well as boys, perhaps more so;
and if the truth must be told, Miss had for some time past
longed for an opportunity to become better acquainted with
things in general, and, therefore, thought here was a chance
not to be thrown away. So, after some little show of resistance
on her part, for decency's sake, it was agreed between them
that he should have a good look at *hers*, if he would afterwards show her *his*. Miss Ellen had never seen a male "diddle,"
as she and her young playfellows called it, not even that of a
boy, and she was all excitement and expectation to feel with
her own hand the "funny thing," for so a communicative ser-
vant-maid had described it, who at the same time had fully
explained the theory of its use, which made Miss long to
obtain some practical knowledge also. So to the arbour they
both adjourned. Miss Ellen first lay back upon the seat, while
the young rogue unfastened her drawers, and pulling them
down, feasted his eyes with a full view of her virgin charms as
long as he pleased, for Miss Ellen was a lecherous little maid,
who really felt a precocious pleasure in being thus exposed to
the close observation and admiration of one of the opposite
sex, although for form's sake she covered her blushing face
with her delicate little hands. He touched *it*, pressed *it*,
rubbed *it* with his finger. Her thighs trembled and opened.
Taught by nature, he imprinted a burning kiss on the lovely
little quim before him. She sighed, and mechanically put her
hand on his head and pressed it closer to her naked skin.
Guided by his feelings, he indulged in movements of his lips
and pressures which speedily excited the amorous little maid

to such an extent as to make her give down with a deep and trembling sigh the first tribute of her virgin cunt. Feeling the warm liquid oozing from the pouting orifice on his closely pressed lips, he could not help tasting it with his tongue. This reawakened very quickly the sensibilities of the lecherous little thing, and awoke her to the desire to practise a like pleasure with his cock. So reminding him of his promise, she made him stand up before her, while she undid his trousers with her fairy fingers, all trembling with excitement, and drew out his stiff affair, which already gave promise of a very respectable future, now swollen to a size it had never before known. Delighted at the sight of so bewitching a plaything, she made him lie down as she had done, and kneeling beside him, with cheeks glowing with excitement, she closely examined every part of the rampant little member. Strange to say, no hand, hardly even its owner's, had as yet invaded its virgin precincts, and it had not yet had its ruby head fully uncovered, although he was upwards of fifteen. The delight caused by the touch of her warm hand pressing and encircling his stiffened cock was most exquisite. She was not long, however, before she became curious to see what could possibly be underneath the skin that covered its rounded head. In her toying she sought to draw the skin back over the head, a slight cry of pain from him caused her to stop. But when, be she young or be she old, is a woman's curiosity to be baulked. She had managed to draw it back a short way, and now it suddenly occurred to her that by the help of a little moisture her object might be accomplished without hurting the dear fellow. By an impulse of passion she stooped and took the rosy head into her delicious little mouth, closing her coral lips around it, and lubricating it with her tongue, to the intense gratification of the youth, who involunarily wriggled his body about voluptuously, and could not help raising it up to her mouth. This movement, combined with the pressure of the lips, perfectly succeeded, without further pain, in completely unhooding the

charming little cock she was so deliciously embracing in the
soft folds of her lips. She lifted up her head to see the result.
The tight foreskin had closed below the nut, and left the now
fiery red head bursting with excitement, and visibly throbbing
with intensity of passion. Her joy and delight at this full
revelation of the "funny thing," as she continued to call it,
now knew no bounds. She drove him nearly frantic with her
ardent caresses—she again drew the covering over the vermillion head, and still finding that it did not easily return
again, she thrust her head down upon it, and with lips, mouth,
and tongue began again her attempt to unhood it. Poor Dale
was brought up to the wildest state of excitement, his hands
involuntarily pressed down her head, his body rose to meet
it, and at that ravishing instant the grand crisis seized him,
and, with a cry of delight, he shot forth his first tribute to
Venus within the delicious mouth in which he was enclosed.
The extatic gush poured down the throat of the dear girl,
and she gulped it all down by the mere effort to avoid choking. Poor Dale's hands fell down insensibly from her head,
which she instantly withdrew, and gazed on the youth. To
her great surprise she beheld the so lately rampant weapon
drooping its head and withdrawing within its shell, while
some few drops of a milky white creamy like liquid were
slowly oozing from the small orifice off its head. While she
gazed it reduced itself to a mere shadow of its former state,
and the foreskin slowly covered again the so lately fiery and
bursting head. She was lost in wonder, and was about to express her surprise at the strangeness of the whole affair, but
they now became aware that footsteps were approaching.
Fortunately for them, as they thought, the noise of the gravel
underfoot was distinguishable at such a distance that they had
time to arrange their clothes, and when Dale's mother appeared at the arbour, she found them, on entering, quietly
seated and talking together; and thanks to the youth's discharge in his cousin's sweet mouth, without any tell-tale flush-

ings of his face. Little did they suspect she had already seen all.

This then was Master Dale's misconduct, and this it was that had been fully and minutely detailed in the note sent by this mother to the doctor, with a request that he should punish him well in whatever way he should think proper. The note further begged to know the terms for his becoming a boarder with the doctor, as she could no longer have him residing in her house with her orphan niece, whose guardian she was. You may easily imagine the double delight of the doctor. Another boarder, a point of some consequence to him after a previous scandal which, although hushed up, had deprived him of house pupils; and now with two, he foresaw a quick return to his full number; and then his delight at having to flog young Dale, and the erotic pleasure of drawing from him the exciting description of their young loves and voluptuous actions.

"Now Master Dale," said the doctor, "you and I have an account to settle, follow me."

And without a word further he led him into his private room, where, as was generally understood in the school, he birched the worst offenders. Arrived in the room alone with the young culprit, he locked the door, and taking a large cutting birch rod from a closet, sat down on a sofa. He called the youth to him and told him to unbutton and let down his trousers, and tuck up his shirt well under his waistcoat. This being done, the doctor said—

"Now, Master Dale, we shall see if this birch will cool your itching for feeling your pretty cousin's private parts."

Poor Dale had never yet been punished more severely than by the hand of his mamma, and certainly trembled at the sight of the formidable birch rod threatening his now bare bottom; yet, notwithstanding his fears, the allusion to the pretty private parts of his cousin so fired his imagination that his cock instantly stiffened and stood out, to the infinite delight of the doctor, who augured therefrom a future further felicity. Keeping him standing close beside him, and enjoying the sight of his youthful charms so deliciously exposed immediately before his eyes, he proceeded—

"So, Master Dale, you have, it seems, been gratifying yourself with looking and feeling between the legs and thighs of a pretty young girl of fifteen, your cousin, is she not?"

"Yes, sir," sobbed out the youth.

The doctor's gaze was fixed upon the stiff and rampant member of the youth, watching the throbbings produced by every allusion to the luscious scene of the day before.

"Now, come, tell me all about it," said he, putting his arm round the sobbing boy's waist, and making him stand still closer beside him. "Was she such a very pretty girl?"

Another throb of the rampant member.

"Yes, sir."

"And you saw all her legs, thighs, plump little bottom, rosy pouting little slit"—(*throb—throb—throb*)—"moist with the dew of excitement and amorous play eh?"

The little machine seemed ready to burst at the thought of it.

"And did it have the same effect as I see it now has on *this?* Dear me, how naughty it is."

And here the lecherous doctor took the rampant little cock in his hand and pressed it.

"And what did she do to this, did she touch it so?" squeezing it gently.

"Yes, sir," stammered out the youth, who was getting greatly excited.

"And so?" said the doctor, passing his hand gently and caressingly up and down the stiffened and throbbing little cock.

"Yes, sir."

"And so, too, I'll be bound," pushing back the foreskin off the head, and as quickly replacing it, several times.

"Ye—es. Oh! sir; oh! oh!"

The boy's feelings, as the doctor swiftly frigged his cock, began to be exquisite. The doctor could not resist the temptation of bringing things to a crisis. Clasping the youth tightly with one arm, he continued his toying with the plaything in a quick exciting manner, apparently without reflecting upon what he was about, uttering, at intervals—

"Dear me," and "how naughy it was of you; but how pretty she must have been to tempt you to do so, was it not?"

The lovely youth was now in paradise. In the exquisite sensations of pleasure he felt he was losing all consciousness when the doctor suddenly stopped short and said—

"This is indeed, a pretty piece of business, seducing your young cousin; you must be cured of such doings in future by means of a good flogging with an excellent birch rod, and on this your saucy bottom."

Here he let fall the arm that had clasped the boy's waist, and let his hand wander over the plump, hard, and lovely orbs. The doctor now took up the rod which he had previously dropped to occupy his hand with the charming young prick he had just been so deliciously frigging. Shaking the rod angrily at the now trembling youth, he exclaimed, in a fierce voice—

"Now, you young rascal, down, down on your knees, and beg to be flogged."

The poor boy was forced, trembling, to obey. This over, the doctor commanded the delinquent to lie down across the sofa. Reluctantly he complied, but at last he straddled across it with his snow-white plump backside fully bared to view, and a fair mark to the threatening rod. He looked like a young Adonis displaying his beauties to a satyr. The doctor was greatly excited at the lovely prospect, and gloated his eyes on the beautiful display, and, then and there, there sprang up a determination to fully enjoy the ravishing of these virgin charms before many weeks were over. Lifting the rod on high, he cried out—

"Now, you young villain, I'll teach you to look up young ladies' petticoats again, I warrant."

Clasping him tight round the waist, the rod descended smartly on the lovely hillocks of the boy's charming backside.

"There! there!" cried the doctor at each blow.

"Oh! sir, oh! Do pray forgive me!" screamed the beautiful youth, as he felt the stinging strokes descend on his hitherto virgin posteriors.

"Oh sir. Oh! sir. I'll never do so any more. Oh! sir. I won't indeed. Oh! pray, sir, have mercy."

The doctor, whose erotic passions were fully aroused, was deaf to all his entreaties, and kept on flogging harder and harder, and faster and faster while the poor boy's bottom bounded and tossed upon the sofa; but he was kept in a firm position by the strong arm of the doctor, who, to hold him the faster, had laid hold of the stiff cock still at full stand.

"No, no," said he, "you shall not escape my cuts, I assure you," cutting at the lovely delicate buttocks with all his might.

"Oh! oh! sir; mercy, mercy; I can't bear it."

"You must bear it, you young rascal you shall have no mercy until I have made your bottom bleed for your crime."

The poor youth, from the pain he was suffering, bounded up and down on the sofa as he felt the stinging blows descend upon his bottom. This action caused his standing cock to rub up and down in the doctor's warm hand, who seemed to have accidently laid hold of it. The effect was such that the poor youth hardly knew whether he felt most pleasure or pain, for while his posteriors were of a burning heat, the warmth flew to the opposite part, which was so deliciously clasped in the doctor's caressing hand. He ground his teeth with pleasure and pain, he ceased to cry out, but sobbed and moaned with the excess of indefinable feelings. The doctor never ceased lecturing him, dwelling continually on the beauties of his lovely young cousin and the scene in the arbour. He thought but of her, of her lovely pink little slit so sweetly shaded with soft downy short curls; how she had so charmingly caressed his cock, until he felt a heave and a shudder, another, a sensation as if he was going to expire, a short cry, a catching of his breath. Wildly and vigorously he thrust his member down on the doctor's warm hand, he shut his eyes, he felt not the rod, although the doctor redoubled the strokes with all the force of his arm, and drew blood at every cut. A bound, a convulsive start, and he felt as if his lifeblood were coming from him—out it spurted in large drops on the sofa and on the doctor's hand. The youth had with difficulty shed another tribute to Venus. For a moment or two he felt as if in paradise, but a sharp cut from the rod quickly aroused him. He was soon fully alive again to its tortures.

"Why, you young rascal, what is this you have been doing on my best sofa, eh, sir?" said the doctor.

Another sharp stroke demanded a reply.

"I, sir. Oh! sir; indeed I—that is—indeed, I don't know."

"No lies or evasions here, sir, for they will not avail you. Your bottom shall pay for this nastiness. Why, what is it? What can it be? I never saw the like of this in my life, I declare," and he examined it with his eyeglass, saying more to the same effect.

Poor Master Dale was, we know, quite in the dark as to what it could be, or how it came there.

"Has this ever occurred to you before," asked the doctor.

"Yes, sir, yesterday, when my cousin was caressing it in her mouth," replied the frightened youth, "but I really don't know how it happened, and did not mean any harm."

"Oh, indeed!" said the doctor, "your mother did not mention that, did she see you?"

"No, sir, it happened just as she was coming through the shrubbery, and was all over before she reached the arbour."

"And so your cousin took it into her mouth, why did she do that?"

"She was curious to see what was under the skin of its

head, and finding it would not go back without hurting me, she put it into her mouth to wet it and make it go back easier, which it did for the first time; she pulled it forward again, and again put it into her mouth to push the skin back with her lips, when I felt funny all over, and something came out of me into her mouth."

"Indeed! Well, you must tell me all about that another time. This flogging will be enough for the present, but I shall punish you for your nastiness some other time. Put up your trousers, in a day or two I shall want you in this room to pay for your dirty conduct."

The poor boy retired, sobbing hysterically.

The second day after this the doctor sent for Master Dale, who, in the meantime, had occupied the bedroom next to mine. The doctor was in his private room in his dressing-gown, long and flowing, so that for the moment it concealed the fact that he had nothing but his shirt on below it. He received Master Dale somewhat sternly, saying—

"Now, sir, for your punishment for your last nasty misconduct."

"Oh, sir," said the frightened and trembling youth, "I really could not help it," and he began to cry. "Oh! pray, sir, don't flog me so hard again."

"The more trouble that you give me, the harder will be the flogging. Now take off your jacket and waistcoat."

The youth did so.

"Now come close to me."

The doctor then lowered down Dale's trousers, and raising his shirt, contemplated with great pleasure the pretty belly of the lovely boy, and then turning him round, under pretence of seeing if the weals of the last flogging were still visible, he gazed on his white firm backside and swelling thighs, examining the marks still left from the previous punishment. He then turned him round, and inspected the pretty little cock, which, under the mortal fear he was in, hung down its head in a limp and pitiable state.

"And so this is the little offender," said he, applying his hand to it, and squeezing and pressing it gently. "What a naughty little thing it is!"

The youth could not avoid showing the pleasure these lascivious caresses gave him, and smiled.

"Oh, don't smile, sir, this is no laughing matter. Look at the marks of the mess you made on my sofa," pointing to it. "I can't have my furniture spoiled in this manner, so if your little cock is to be naughty again, I must flog you upon my knees, but first come here; take off these trousers, which hanging about the legs are only in the way—there. Now sit down on my knee, and tell me all about this naughty little thing."

He drew aside his robe, so that the boy's bare bottom came in naked contact with his brawny naked thighs, and the youth could feel the doctor's prick swelling up, although that part was still covered with his shirt. The doctor, taking hold of the youth's now standing prick, asked if it had ever behaved so badly before the scene with his pretty young cousin.

"No sir, never. I never thought of it until I got sight of her bare bottom and other parts by accident."

The doctor continued his toyings, caressing the young balls, and feeling all over the plump and firm backside.

"Why, he is going to be naughty again!" said the doctor, as the youth's prick throbbed under his exciting touches. "I must flog your bottom for all this, for it is very naughty and improper. Why, you seem to take a pleasure in it."

"Oh, sir, I never felt anything so delightful," said Master Dale.

"The more reason I should punish you, but remember, you bad boy, if you are to do that dirty thing again, you must do it on my knee, and not on the sofa."

The doctor then took the birch in hand, and with his arm round the boy's waist, drew him to him, but before laying him across his knee, he slipped the boy's shirt over his head, leaving him stark naked in all the glorious fairness of skin and beauty of form. The doctor's eyes gloated over the charming sight, but becoming too excited to pause longer, he drew up his own shirt, displaying his fine pego at full stretch. He bent the boy's warm body over his brawny thighs, and with his arm pressed his glowing form against his own rampant pego —Dale's young stiffened cock rubbing against the naked thigh he lay on. The doctor now raised the rod, and said—

"Now, sir, for your punishment, I must flog this round, hard, little bottom, till it reddens again."

Whack, whack, went the birch rod, but with much less force than on the previous occasion, but still sufficiently sting-ing to cause the youth to move up and down, rubbing his cock against the doctor's thighs, and causing him such ex-tasies as hardly to allow him to feel the blows. His warm soft flesh, too, rubbing against the doctor's large, stiff tool, soon put them both in a delirium of delight. The doctor then changed his position, and drew the boy more over his belly, so that his great prick could get between the boy's thighs, rub-bing under his balls in the trough between the buttocks, while the boy's cock rubbed against the doctor's belly.

"Now," said the doctor, "I have got you fast, and must teach you not to play such naughty tricks in future."

Whack—whack, again went the rod, causing the most de-licious movements of the boy's backside upon the doctor's excited prick, and not less upon his own, which was rubbing against the doctor's belly, giving fresh pleasure at each repeti-tion of the blow. But neither of them had spent yet. The boy's bottom was now red with a glowing heat, and his cock was in a state of intense excitement, and the doctor's tool was as stiff and randy as possible. The doctor now ceased his flogging, and squeezing the boy tight against his person, said—

"Well, you have not done that naughty thing to-day—the flogging has done you good."

The lovely boy looked up and smiled. He had felt the doc-tor's large prick working away between his thighs, and pressing against the cleft of his buttocks. As the doctor relaxed his hold, the boy turned half round, thus releasing it from its confinement. Looking down, he beheld the large stiff monster imbedded in a forest of dark curly hair, presenting a startling contrast to his own small member, which was as yet hardly fledged with a silky down around it.

"Ah!" said the doctor, who observed the flush of excitement the sight of his superior prick gave the boy, "what a shame it is of you to compel me to flog you in this manner, without my trousers. I must give you a lecture—so sit on my knee, thus," placing him so that his lovely bottom should press against the huge prick. Taking the boy's cock in his hand, he said—

"How stiff it is."

"Yes, sir, I can't help it."

"Well, you must not play such naughty tricks. I can't allow it. You are too young yet."

The doctor worked the skin of the sweet boy's cock up and down.

"Was that the way your pretty cousin played with it?"

"Yes, sir, and then she took it in her mouth."

"And did you like to have it done to you, you bad boy?"

"Oh! yes, sir, it is such pleasure."

"Does it really give you so much pleasure?"

"Yes indeed, it was most delicious."

"Dear me, I must try if it would do so to me, take hold of my cock and rub it up and down, as she did, that I may know how it feels."

The dear boy had already longed to do so, but had been afraid to say so. He now seized with avidity the noble prick, so stiffly standing beside him. He could hardly grasp it in his hand, and worked the skin up and down in the most delicious manner. The doctor was in extasies.

"Oh, you naughty boy, to teach your master such bad things."

"Is it not very nice, sir?" said the charming youth, as the doctor's buttocks responded to every stroke of his hand.

"Well, it is, indeed, very nice, I could not have believed it; but if ever I catch you at it again, you may be sure I shall flog you."

And the doctor responded to every rub upon his prick with another rub upon the boy's cock, until almost at the same moment a most delicious mutual spend was the result of their lascivious toyings.

"Now," said the doctor, "put on your clothes, and remember you must avoid such naughty tricks in future, or your bottom will pay for it."

The doctor made me aware of this, and arranged for a meeting of us three, under the pretence of inattention which I was to simulate and draw young Dale into some fault that would require punishment. It was also arranged that I was to initiate him still more into the secret pleasures of mutual satisfaction, so as to prepare him for still greater gratification to the lecherous doctor, who liked nothing better than "teaching the young idea how to shoot."

Accordingly, after passing a delicious night with my lovely and glorious aunt and the doctor, in which we practised every delightful method of enjoyment, and in which the doctor stimulated himself by recalling and describing the exciting interview with the innocent youth, I left them, and entered young Dale's room. He had insensibly kicked off all the clothes, and lay on his back exposed, with his promising young cock at full stand, throbbing from time to time; and by the involuntary movements of his body, and the smile on his face, he was evidently realising, in his sleep, the scene he had enacted with his pretty young cousin. He was quite charming to look at, his young and throbbing prick was deliciously fair, and you could see the blue veins coursing through it, the top was only partially uncovered, the point of the head showing its vermillion tip in fine contrast to the creamy white and crossed blue veins of the stiffened shaft. His balls were as yet not fully developed, but such as they were, they formed a closely drawn up little bag, crimped and wrinkled, and felt as hard as stones. I gently handled them, which made him heave his bottom in evident extasy. It was all so beautiful and enticing, and I could not resist stooping down, and taking the delicious morsel in my mouth. Pressing the glorious head with my lips, I thrust, to his infinite delight, the foreskin back, his buttocks instinctively rose to meet my voluptuous and lascivious proceeding. He awoke on the instant, but in that dreamy state that made him think he was only realising the previous dream. His hands embraced my head, and pressed it down closer on the delicious prick which already touched the back of my mouth. He cried out in an extasy of delight.

"Oh, my darling Ellen, what a joy you are giving me. Oh! oh! it is greater than I can bear."

I felt by the electric stiffening of his young cock that the crisis was close at hand. I tickled his tightened balls with my hand, and pressed a finger hard against his bottom-hole, but without entering more than the depth of the nail, at the very instant that he poured his young tribute into my longing mouth. I immediately swallowed the greater portion, lubricating the still throbbing shaft with a part. For some minutes he lay on his back, with closed eyes, in all the after-enjoyment, heightened by the continued suction of his still throbbing prick, which I kept up for a short time. At last he opened his eyes. It was broad daylight, and when I lifted my head, his eyes seemed almost to start out of their sockets in a sort of incredulous surprise, at finding it was not his dear young Ellen, but me, his school companion. For a minute or two he was speechless with consternation, until taking hold of his fast receding little cock, I asked if I had not given him quite as much pleasure as his darling Ellen had previously done.

"Is it you? and Ellen! how do you know anything about my cousin?"

"Your cousin, is she? I did not know that, but when I came in, you were dreaming of her, and muttering in your sleep the delight she gave you by sucking your prick; so I thought I would give you the true pleasure of the thing, and thus realise your dream; besides, I, myself, not only love to suck a prick, but also to have my own sucked, and I could neither resist the opportunity, nor fail to be delighted that you should already have practical knowledge of its enjoyment—did I not give you the greatest pleasure?"

"Oh, yes; it was most delicious, and then I thought it was my pretty cousin, even after I awoke, which made it doubly delightful, for I had no idea it would be so nice with another boy."

"Why not? see this charming little fellow is already raising himself up again at the mere thought; look how its head is showing its ruby face, and how it throbs. Ah! I must suck it again—it is so delicious."

I threw myself upon it, and devoured it at once, rapidly moving my head up and down, and titillating the orifice of the urethra with my tongue. I quickly drove him half mad with excitement. My mouth was full of saliva. I slobbered some out on my fingers, and lubricated all about the aperture of his charming backside, and then, as he became still more furious in the upward lunges of his bottom, and downward pressures of his hands on my head, I thrust my middle finger up his fundament, and worked away, frigging it in unison with the movements of my mouth. I drove him half frantic with pleasure, the extasy again seized him, and with a cry of agonised delight, and a convulsive shudder, he poured a still more copious draught of love's essence into my mouth, which, as before, I greedily swallowed. He lay panting in extatic joy for a much longer period than before, with convulsive upward thrusts of his still half-stiffened prick within my mouth, which still continued its pressures and suctions to his infinite delight. At last I rose. He held out his arms. I precipitated myself into them; our lips met in sweet embrace. I thrust my tongue into his mouth, and solicited him to do the same, and we had some delicious tongueing, nature having at once achieved his love education. We were closely entwined in a loving embrace. I had become terribly excited notwithstanding the hard work I had undergone during the night, and my prick stood stiff as iron pressing against his belly. Suddenly the thought occurred to him that he ought to gratify me in like manner as I had done him. He proposed it, and begged me to turn from off him, and lie on my back. I immediately complied, and pulling up my shirt, displayed my immense splitter in all its glory.

"Good heavens!" he cried, "what an enormous cock! Why, it is bigger than the doctor's."

"Oh! you have seen the doctor's, have you?"

He blushed, and acknowledged it. I drew from him an account of their proceedings, which I already knew, but I was at the same time delighted to have surprised the acknowledgment from himself, in his wonder at seeing my large proportions. I made him show me all he had done to the doctor, and the doctor to him; as all this was paving the way for future proceedings with the doctor—in fact, the innocent youth was already playing into our hands. His admiration of and handling my prick was meanwhile exciting me up to the greatest pitch. As I had continued questioning him regarding his proceedings with the doctor, he could only play with my prick in his hands. Now that matters were getting too warm for further discussion, he stooped down, but could only get the head and a small portion of the upper part of the shaft into his mouth. His lips closed beneath the gland in the most exquisite manner. I begged him to grasp the lower part of the shaft with one hand, and to thrust a finger of the other up my bottom-hole, which I had already lubricated by spitting on my fingers and conveying the saliva in the desired direction. He obeyed with the docility of an apt apprentice—and thus working in unison,

quickly brought on the extatic crisis. I seized his head in
my hands, and, at the final discharge thrust it down on my
delighted prick, as I poured out a perfect torrent of sperm,
nearly choking the poor youth with the length of prick I
thrust into his mouth. He was obliged to withdraw for an
instant to take breath, but I was pleased to see that he
instantly resumed his delicious sucking of my prick, which
he continued to do until it gradually shrunk up to very
diminished proportions. I then drew him upon me, and we
had another sweet embrace of lips and tongues, and then,
side by side, we held a long converse on erotic matters. He
told me all the tale of his affair with his cousin, and, although
I was already well acquainted with it, I was glad to draw
all the particulars from himself. I had seen the note his
mother wrote to the doctor. The minuteness and undisguised
description she had therein given struck me as very strange,
and I augured that she herself must be a lewd and lecherous
person, to have done more than merely hint at the affair,
instead of dwelling, doubtless in erotic delight, on such details. So I pumped him as to what sort of woman his mamma
was. His description showed that she was a fine, full grown
woman, old, in his opinion, but in reality in the prime of life,
between thirty-five and forty. He had not scanned her proportions with any erotic thought and did not seem to attach the
idea of the woman to her—only that of the mother. But I drew
out of him that she was broad in the shoulders, full in the
bosom, with a small waist, small feet, and small hands, a very
fine head of hair, and fine eyes—evidently a desirable woman.
Already I had set my imagination in play, and began to hope
I might some day work my way into her favour. It will be
found how well I succeeded, as these true memories will
describe when I arrive at the period of my success with her.
For the present I had advanced the erotic education of the
dear youth considerably, and thus prepared him for further
initiation at the hands of the doctor and his glorious and
magnificent *cara sposa*, who had already determined to en-

joy his first fruits in cunny land. We had a similar enjoyment, carried somewhat further the next morning, in which we practised more fully the frigging of the bottom, and discussed the pleasure it produced. I was gradually leading him on. That morning I purposely arranged that we should be late in entering the school-room. The doctor sternly reprimanded us, and told us we must attend him in his private room after twelve o'clock. Poor Dale turned pale as he heard this, dreading the punishment to come of which his experience was so recent and so severe.

At twelve we, apparently ruefully, entered the doctor's *sanctum sanctorum*. He had preceded us by some few minutes, and had already donned his long dressing-gown, by which I was certain that he had at the same time doffed his pantaloons.

"Now then, boys, you must prepare for your punishment, I cannot allow this evidently wilful inattention. Off with your clothes except your shirts and stockings."

We hesitatingly stripped; poor Harry Dale weeping at the thought of the dreaded punishment. I deemed it prudent also to draw a long face. The doctor spread a towel over his sofa, saying we had such naughty cocks that we were constantly dirtying his sofa. He then desired us to kneel on it with our heads down, and our tails well up. He then rolled up our shirts, and tucked them in above the small of our backs, in doing which he indulged in various lascivious touchings, which excited us as well as himself, and all our three cocks were at full stand. Harry Dale turned his head to gaze at mine, and could not resist putting his hand upon it, and gently pressing its large stiff shaft. Young Dale's smaller, but very beautiful member, which was daily developing itself in a striking manner, also excited me, and I reciprocated his caresses.

"This will never do," said the doctor, "I must flog this evil spirit out of you."

He threw off his dressing-gown to be more at his ease he

said, and taking rod in hand, applied it gently in turns to each of our projecting bottoms. It was not for punishment but for excitement that he operated upon us. He quickly threw our bottoms all in a glow, and our excitement became intense, and we wriggled our bums in evident delight. This was the point the doctor wished to attain, that he might arrive at his desired object, which was the possession of young Dale's bottom-hole.

"Stop, stop, my dear boys, I see you are at your naughty tricks again, but there must be no spending yet; get up. We must all strip to the buff, and I shall show you how they used to flog me when I was at school. Stand up, Charles."

I did so, and the doctor for an instant handled, in evident delight, my huge stiff-standing pego, drawing young Dale's attention to its much larger dimensions than his own.

"Now, lean half forward on the sofa. Dale, put your arms round his waist, and stow away this charming rampant little fellow between the cheeks of Charles' buttocks. Charles, do you spit on your hand, and moisten between the cheeks, and then press with your hand his throbbing young prick against the cleft."

I did as directed. Young Dale felt so deliciously sheathed that he thrust his cock well forward.

"Now," said the doctor, "you are properly horsed, as we used to say, and now, for a little more flogging of these fine hard, rosy mounts," and he lasciviously caressed them before applying the rod.

Whack—whack—whack—fell the strokes, sufficiently sharply to make Master Dale wince and wriggle his bottom to and fro. Quickly the exciting pleasure overcame all pain, and his lust rising, he thrust furiously in the artificial channel he was operating in. I now shortened the grasp of my hand on his shaft, and pressing it somewhat upwards, raising my buttocks at the same time, I directed it so fairly upon the aperture that at the next push it entered fully two inches within; then again favouring his return stroke, he completely sheathed himself up to the meeting of his belly against my buttocks. I gave him a pressure which had an instant effect, and he began to thrust fast and furiously, evidently enjoying it to the utmost. I let him feel the full enjoyment of his new quarters, only telling him to lay hold of my cock and frig me; and then I cried out to the doctor

"Flog him well, sir, he has thrust his cock into my bottom-hole."

This was the very thing the doctor most wished for. So he continued his flogging only to such an extent as to still more inflame the lust of the now lecherously excited boy, who shortly brought on the final crisis and died away in delight as he shot his first tribute within the divine temple of Priapus. At the moment of the crisis coming on, the doctor had ceased his flogging and wetting two fingers gradually introduced them into the bottom-hole of young Dale, and frigged him in unison with his movements into me, so that the extasy was almost more than the poor boy could bear. He lay almost inanimate on my back, but his still throbbing half-standing cock responded to the inward pressures I was exercising upon it. The doctor had ceased his flogging to admit and caress the well-formed posterior of the charming boy. Becoming greatly excited, he drew him off me, and closely embraced him, but professing at the same time to be greatly shocked; his prick, meanwhile, gloriously stiff, pressed hard against young Dale's belly. The doctor then relaxing his hold, young Dale gazed, with pleased enjoyment, on the size and stiffness of the doctor's cock, and, by an impulse of passion, took it in hand, knelt before him, and put it into his mouth, and sucked it lasciviously. The doctor placed his hands on Dale's head, and pressed it down for a minute or two, and then begged the dear youth to rise, as he did not yet wish to spend—thanking him for the exquisite pleasure he had given him.

"Now," said he, "it is your turn to flog, so Charlie, you must be horsed upon me, and Harry Dale shall take a first lesson in the art of flogging upon your posteriors."

The pose was arranged as before. My formidable weapon was placed between the cheeks of the doctor's fine fat backside. His hand pressed my cock as I had done to Dale's. Dale took the rod in hand, and at the very first cut made me wince, for the young rogue laid on with a will. The doctor had applied a good quantity of saliva to the end of my prick, and thrusting out his buttocks, he quickly guided it into the longing orifice, in which I vigorously sheathed myself to the utmost extent. I seized his cock and squeezed it gently, but he begged me not to make him spend, but to enjoy myself to the utmost, crying out, at the same time to young Dale—

"Flog him well, Harry, for he has thrust his great tool up my bottom-hole; it is wonderful how it ever could get in."

Indeed so little could young Dale believe in the possibility of such a thing that he stopped flogging to assure himself of the fact, by both touch and sight. I drew my prick out and in that he might be perfectly satisfied of the truth, and the doctor wriggled his backside to and fro to show what pleasure it gave him. Of course, all this was preliminary to the grand attack he meant afterwards to make on the virgin aperture in young Dale's bottom. After Harry had assured himself of the fact, he pitched into my poor bottom with redoubled vigour, which, though it greatly excited me at the moment, made my poor bum smart for days afterwards. I quickly sent a torrent of sperm far into the entrails of the doctor, to his great delight, but he tenaciously avoided spending lest his powers should fail to overcome the natural obstacle of a virgin bottom-hole, especially in one so young as Dale. Consequently, after retaining me for some few moments in the delightful pressures of the internal folds, he allowed me to withdraw, all reeking with my own sperm. It was now the doctor's turn to be flogged by me, while he was horsed on Harry's loins. As Harry had already found out what pleasure a bottom-hole gave to the plugger of it, and had also seen how the doctor seemed to enjoy, and so easily engulphed, the much larger weapon I possessed, he had no idea there could be any pain accompanying it, and consequently he lent himself entirely to every direction that was given him. He placed himself in the easiest position, stuck his bottom well out, stretching wide the channel between the orbs, and exposing a charming little rosy aperture most tempting to the sight; indeed, the doctor instantly knelt to pay his devotions to it, devouring it with kisses, and thrusting his lecherous tongue within its tight little folds, taking the opportunity to thoroughly lubricate it with his spittle. This preliminary, followed by a little frigging with his middle finger, which produced nothing but pleasurable sensations in the dear youth, completely captivated him. The doctor wisely informed him that the first attack was sure to be somewhat painful, but that if he felt it so, he was not to draw away his body, but simply to complain, and the doctor would instantly remain quiet without withdrawing, and he would then find that the strange sensation would rapidly pass off, and allow a further progress, which would be again arrested if the pain was renewed. In this way he would eventually find that the pleasure would become indescribably delicious, as he had seen how both Charlie and himself had enjoyed it. Poor Dale assured the doctor he might proceed at once, and he would be perfectly docile. So the doctor first asking me to suck his cock a little to moisten it well, put the charming youth in the best position, telling him to strain as if he wished to void himself, then applying his well-lubricated pego to the rosy orifice, by gentle pressure, he succeeded, with hardly a twinge of pain to the dear boy, in housing the head and about two inches of the shaft within the delicious receptacle. Here the pain became so great that young Dale would have withdrawn himself away from the doctor had the latter not taken the precaution to seize him by the two hips, and hold him as if in a vice, but without attempting a further insertion then.

"Keep still, my dear boy, and I will not move, and you will find in a minute or two that the strange sensation will pass away."

Turning his head to me, he said—

"Charlie, gently frig the dear boy."

I immediately did so, which rapidly had the effect of exciting him up to a pitch that made him forget all pain, and he even thrust his bottom further back, and as I had taken the opportunity of the pause to drop some more spittle on the lower shaft, a further gentle pressure forced it in almost up to the hilt. Here, again, young Dale cried out to stop, it was so painful.

The doctor paused again. I continued caressing his now inflamed and stiffened prick. His convulsive twitches, caused by my lascivious caresses, were followed by involuntary wrigglings, which of themselves completed the entire inserttion of the doctor's excited prick. He still continued quiet, allowing the passions of the youth to become still more excited. Then gradually and gently withdrawing, and as gently again thrusting within, he went on until the youth's movements betrayed the raging lust that possessed him-- then the doctor increased his pace. I frigged on fast and furious, and in a few minutes they both died away in wild excess of the most extatic joy. As to Dale, his gaspings and wild cries of delight proved that the final joys were almost too great for him to bear. The doctor had drooped his head upon his chest, and closed his eyes, in all the gratification of having ravished the first fruits of this charming youth's beauteous bottom, and I could see by his momentary convulsive thrusts, and the pressures of his hands on Dale's hips to draw the bottom more completely against his belly, as well as by the broken sighs that heaved his bosom, how exquisitely he was enjoying his triumph. Gradually his cock reduced its dimensions, but even when quite down and soft, it left the tight sheath it was in with a "plop" showing how well and close those delicious folds had embraced it. The doctor would not allow young Dale to rise until he had embraced and kissed the lovely bottom that had just yielded him such intense satisfaction. Then, drawing the youth to his bosom, he embraced him most tenderly, and thanked him for the heroic manner in which he had borne the attack, and told him he would never suffer so much in after-attacks as he had done in this first taking of the virginity of his bottom-hole.

It was thus this dear youth was initiated into our mysteries, and henceforward he became an apt disciple, and by being introduced into our interior circle, added much to the variety and enjoyment of our orgies. For, as may well be supposed, my glorious and most lecherous aunt thoroughly enjoyed the taking of his first tribute in the legitimate temple of holy Mother Venus. I was present on the occasion, which was supposed to be unknown to the doctor. The first coup was on her belly, the sight of which and her truly magnificent cunt wildly excited Dale, and his cock stood stiffer and really bigger than ever. It was quite surprising how rapidly it developed when once he got thoroughly into hardness. He fucked aunt twice, spending as rapidly as she herself, lecherous as she was at all times. I acted postillion to them both. I stopped further combats until I too could enter the field. So aunt mounted upon him, and falling forward lent her divine backside to all my fantasies. Twice we ran a course without changing. Then aunt herself claimed my big prick for the contentment of her randy cunt. We quickly changed positions. I, on my back, received dear aunt's delicious cunt on my stiff-and-hard-as-wood-standing pego. She straddled over me, and sank her luscious orbit down upon me until our two hairs were crushed between us. Here, by rising and falling, she had another delicious discharge before bending down to be embraced by my loving arms. She then presented her most glorious bottom to the wonder and admiration of dear Harry, who had been caressing and kissing it, and at the critical moment had thrust a frigging finger in, and turning his head in front had greatly increased the pleasure of my loved and lecherous aunt by sucking the large nipple of her wondrously fine bubby. When once she was fairly down on my belly, Harry scrambled up behind, and quickly inserted his already fine but still comparatively small prick, which, of course, found ready entrance where my splitter had previously opened and greased the way; but he gave a cry, almost of pain, or at least of surprise, on finding the sudden grip which my aunt, with her wonderful power of pressure, instantly gave him. At it we went, fast and furious, until again the grand crisis overtook my lascivious aunt, who spent deliciously. We boys both paused a second or two to allow her to enjoy her discharge to the utmost; then recommencing with increased vigour and speed, we soon both discharged at one and the same time our freights into the delighted vessels that were conferring such exquisite enjoyment upon us. Aunt, too, did not fail to join us at the extatic moment. We lay for many minutes panting in all the after-sensations of the most exquisite joys humanity can revel in. We kept it up for several hours, aunt sucking young Dale's toothsome prick while I gamahuched and postillioned her to her infinite satisfaction. In this way, and with repeated changes from one receptacle to the other but always both occupied at once, we at last gained a reprieve, and retired to well-deserved repose. The doctor, who had kept out of the way on this our first bout with my glorious aunt, afterwards apparently surprised us together, and, after giving us and receiving a pretty sharp flogging, he joined in all the extasies of our orgies. He especially delighted in being into my bottom while I fucked his wife, and he himself had the double pleasure of having young Dale's fast growing pego into his bottom at the same time. It was some time longer before I succeeded in completely sheathing my huge prick in the delicious bottom-hole of the dear youth, but at last I succeeded to the utmost extent of my wishes, and although I continued to hurt him for some weeks after the first attack, he could at last entertain me with perfect ease, and we were thus enabled to play successively into each other's bottoms, and every one of us enjoyed the exquisite delight of fucking and being fucked at the same time.

As we grew more lasciviously intimate, I often turned the conversation on his mother and cousin. At last I told him, I thought from his description that his mother would be a good fuck, and that if ever I had the opportunity I might cover his attack on his cousin by fucking his mother; only we must lead her to believe that she took my virginity. The idea pleased him. He began to think his mother must be a desir-able woman for me, as I was so largely hung; and then the opportunity that I would give him to enjoy his longing for his cousin was an inducement to second my views to the utmost. Towards the close of the half-year his birthday occurred, and his mother could not do less than have him home for the day. She felt that her niece would be in greater security when Harry begged she would allow him to bring with him the doctor's nephew—myself, to wit—telling her that we had be-come very close friends as well as schoolfellows. I had previously told him I should play the complete innocent, but should take care some time or the other during the day to put myself in such a position that his mother should get a glimpse of my prick, so that if not immediately successful, I might pave the way for future success. His birthday fell on a Saturday. We were only asked to spend the day, with the intention of returning in the evening. Accordingly, on the happy day we made our appearance after breakfast. I have before said that his mother lived in a very pretty cottage ornée, about a mile and a half from the parsonage. We were most kindly received by her. She first lovingly embraced her son, wishing him many happy returns of the day, declaring that he was much improved, &c. She then turned to me, and gracefully and kindly bade me welcome. The niece was a charming girl, just budding into womanhood. She blushed greatly in welcoming her cousin, and bashfully did the same to me. We spent the earlier hours in conversation; the mother having much to ask and to hear from her son, from whom she had never before been separated. I had thus time to scan her well. She was a fine, broad built, well standing up woman, with broad shoulders, and hips that gave promise of good form beneath. Without being beautiful, her face was a well formed oval, with really fine eyes, to which her son's description had hardly done justice. It appeared to me that a good deal of suppressed passion lurked in their expression, and I already began to think she would be a real *bonne bouche* if once we could come to close quarters. After luncheon we strolled in the garden. The leaves had already fallen, but the afternoon was bright and warm for the end of November. I told young Dale to keep close to his mother, and not show any wish to stray away with his cousin—feeling certain that if she became anxious about their movements I should have no chance to play off my little game. All went as I could wish, we threw his mother off her guard, and she then began to show closer attention to me. I acted the ingenuous and innocent youth to perfection, but at the same time, in thinking of her charms, I let my prick get up to half-stand, so as to show its large proportions under my trousers. I very soon perceived that it had struck her notice, and her attention became concentrated upon me. She questioned me a good deal, and especially sought to find out if *peculiar* intimacy existed between her son and me. I played the innocent, and professed that the utmost intimacy existed; but when she tried to find out if it had gone to what she really meant, I gave such an innocent character to our intimacy that she was quite convinced of my thorough ignorance of all erotic tendencies, and she became more endearing in her manner of addressing me.

Harry and I had previously agreed that after I addressed to him some particular frivolous remark, he should seize the first occasion near a shrubbery to go on more ahead, and alarm his mamma by turning round a corner. Our stratagem succeeded. She immediately hastened to follow them. As soon as she had turned the corner I drew out my tool, now at full stand, and placed myself so that when she returned she should see it fully developed, while I would take care not apparently to see her, but be intent upon piddling. To the utmost of my wish it fell out. She had told her son to stop and returned to join me. My eyes being turned downwards did not let her become aware that I was watching for her, but I could see the bottom of her petticoats as she turned the corner, and also that she came to a sudden stop, which must have been at the moment she caught sight of the noble proportions before her. I took care to pass my hand once or twice backwards or forwards while pissing, and then shook my prick deliberately, and exposed the whole length and breadth of it for a minute or two before buttoning it up, during which I could see she stood perfectly still, rooted to where she had first stopped. After I had buttoned up, I stooped down, apparently to tie my shoe, but in fact to give time for it to be supposed I had not seen her previous approach. So when I rose up she was already at my side. There was a flush on her cheek and a fire in her eye that showed the bait was swallowed. My role was to play the perfect innocent, and appear quite unconscious of her having seen me.

She took my arm, and I could feel that her hand trembled. She led me along, hastily at first, until we joined her son and niece. After that she became uncommonly endearing in her manner to me, making such remarks as she thought would show her that I was not so innocent as I looked, if my replies had jumped with her expectations. But I was in reality too experienced not to pay her off in kind, and ended in making her believe that she had a perfect virgin to deal with. We walked on, she was evidently much preoccupied, becoming at times quite silent for a minute or two, and then, gently pressing my arm, she would make some endearingly flattering remark, at which I would look lovingly but innocently up to her face to thank her for her kind opinion. On these occasions her eyes sparkled in a peculiar manner, and her colour went and came. After a while, her hand left my arm and rested on the opposite shoulder, in a half embrace, which became warmer and warmer, her conversation became more affectionate. She was profuse in her congratulations that her son had found so charming a schoolfellow; and here she halted, and turning half in front of me, said that she felt that she could love me as if I were indeed her own dear son; and, stooping slightly, she sought a kiss of maternal affection. I threw my arms round her neck, and our lips met in a long and loving kiss—very warm on her side, but a simple though affectionate kiss on mine.

"Oh!" I said, "how happy I shall be to call you my mamma, and I will love you as if you were it, it is so good of you to allow me to do so. This half-year has been the first time in my life that I ever was separated from my mother—and, although my dear aunt is as kind as possible to me, still I can't call her mamma. My guardian won't allow me to go home for the Christmas holidays, but now I shall have a dear, kind new mamma to make me happy." Here I again raised my lips for an embrace, which was given with even more than the previous warmth. Her arm had fallen to my waist, and she pressed me with energy to her bosom, which I could feel was unexpectedly firm, and even hard. I had great difficulty in keeping my unruly member down, that she might think I took her warm embraces as nothing more than affectionate friendship. I succeeded, however, and this, of course, more

than ever convinced her of my entire ignorance of carnal
desires. As I closely embraced her, and glued my lips to
hers, she became greatly agitated, trembled visibly, sighed
convulsively, and then pushed me from her, and seemed
suddenly to recover herself, seized my arm, and hurried on
after her son. For, as may well be supposed she had purposely loitered behind to allow them to get out of sight,
before she indulged her uncontrollable desire to embrace me.
She spoke not a word until we came in sight of them, apparently sauntering along, innocently enough. But Harry
afterwards told me that having seen how his mother had
halted to gaze at my prick, which he knew beforehand I
meant she should see, he had watched us through the
shrubbery, and afterwards had noticed her warmth of manner to me, and the loitering of her walk. He had turned a
corner some distance ahead of us, and was out of sight
when his mother stopped to embrace me, as described above.
He guessed she would be in no hurry to follow him. So
rapidly advancing with his cousin, he got some way before
us, and choosing a place where he could see us through the
bushes when we did follow, he sat down on a garden seat,
and drew his cousin on his lap, asking her if she did not
regret their hasty separation after their last delicious interview, and telling her his mother had seen them, which was
the cause of his being sent as a boarder to the doctor. She was
much surprised to hear this, as her aunt had never breathed a
word of it to her; and she had been greatly distressed at his
being sent away from home. Of course his hands were not
idle; but first unbuttoning his trousers, he put his cock, now
much increased in size, into her hand. She at once observed
how much larger it had become, and began to caress it. He
meanwhile was busy frigging her little clitoris. He found that
she was already quite moist, and he had hardly frigged her
a minute, when a sigh and an "Oh! how much more pleasure
you give me than my aunt does." She spent profusely, grasp-

ing his prick with painful tenacity. Her breath was taken away for some minutes. When she recovered a little, and was gazing lovingly with half-closed eyes upon him, he at once recurred to her unexpected confession.

"When does my mother do this to you?"

"Ever since you were sent away; your mother took me to sleep with her, as she said, she felt so lonely after you left. For some time she used to embrace me very lovingly, and hold me close pressed to her bosom. As I always went to bed before her, I was generally sound asleep when she joined me. I used at first to wonder how when I awoke in the early morning my chemise was drawn up close to my neck, and your mother's was in the same state, and our two naked bodies closely united by the embracing arms of your mother. I even one morning found that my hand was held by hers against that part which you are now feeling so nicely. She had fallen asleep in this position, but I could feel that she was as moist there as you have just made me. I could not help feeling it was very nice, and gently removing her hand, I began to feel all over her in that part and, do you know Harry, she is all covered with such thick and curly hair there. In groping about, I felt the lips pouting and thick, and on trying I found I could get my fingers in. I pushed on, I got up to the knuckles, when I felt it give such a convulsive pressure upon them, and her body was projected towards me with a heave of her bottom, then drawn back, and pushed forward again, while her arms pressed me closer to her, and she commenced some loving expressions in her sleep. I felt something grow hard against my thumb, it was just what you have been feeling.—'Oh! go on,' she cried."

"I renewed my tickling operations again, and I made her spend," Harry continued. "As she came to her senses, I gamahuched her; I thrust my tongue up her sweet little cunt, and licked up all the delicious spendings. As I rose, with prick erect and standing stiff out of my trousers, she seized it in her mouth, and, with very little sucking, made me spend to excess, and the dear girl swallowed it with all the luxury of the utmost voluptuousness. We had no time for more at that moment, as I caught sight of mamma's dress through the trees. I buttoned up hastily, and we strolled along, as if nothing had happened. It was in our after-walk, when we had allayed mamma's suspicion, that my dear Ellen continued her confessions."

The stiff thing pressing against her thumb was mamma's clitoris, which, by her account, is wonderfully developed. She, knowing from her former experience with me that it was the point of most exquisite enjoyment, turned her finger upon it, and began awkwardly playing with it. It was at this moment that the greater excitement awoke mamma, who finding to her surprise what Ellen was doing, seized her hand, and pressing and rubbing it with more art against her clitoris, continued its action with exclamations of delight, declaring that Ellen was her dear precious loved girl, and then with a positive cry of delight, spent profusely over Ellen's hand. After panting for some time in perfect bliss, she turned and took Ellen in her arms, kissing her most warmly, and thrusting her tongue into Ellen's mouth, and then demanding hers in return. After much embracing, mamma asked her how she came to do what she found her doing when she awoke. Ellen described how she found her hand held against it, and then two naked bodies pressed against each other—that she was surprised at this, and wondered how it came so; that on moving her hand she felt mamma give a throb down there, and a push of her body forward, which made her finger slip easily in, this still more surprised her, as she had tried often if her fingers could get into her own, but it hurt her so much that she had given it up as impossible; and now she had found one where all her fingers, up to the knuckles, slipped in quite easily; the inside movements, and the heavings of her aunt's body, showed that it gave her pleasure. In continuing her movements she had felt a hard body at the upper part pressing against the side of her hand; she withdrew her fingers to feel this strange thing, and in doing so aunt awoke.

"And you know the rest, dear auntie, I was so glad that I had given you so much pleasure."

"Dear, dear girl!" her aunt replied, "I shall love you more dearly than ever; yes, and you, too, shall have the utmost pleasure. I have long wished to initiate you into the secrets of womanhood, but thought you too young to be able to keep secret such intimacy as we may indulge in. Often in your sleep with your lovely naked charms exposed to me, and pressed against my own lascivious person, have I enjoyed you, and even made use of your own hand all unconscious in sleep, to excite me to a still greater pitch; last night I had enjoyed you to the utmost, kissing your lovely budding and hidden charms, and must have unconsciously dropped off to sleep with my hand still pressing yours against my secret charm. But now I must initiate you into the same joys, even in a more exquisite way."

"Upon this she begged me to throw off my chemise, while she did the same. We stood up to do this, and your mother took the opportunity to pose me in every way, admiring and kissing me all over. I did the same to her, and I can assure you, dear Harry, your mother is far better made that I am, both in the bosom and the bottom, and with such firm thighs and legs, and her affair is so well developed and pouting, and with such silky curls all around it. I can feel you passing your fingers through the curls of mine; but though it has more than it had when last you felt and caressed it, it is nothing to dear auntie's. When she had much excited me, and was evidently herself greatly so, she desired me to lie across the bed on my back, and to draw my knees up so as to let my feet rest on the edge. She then placed a footstool in front, and kneeling upon it, after first feeling and caressing me down there, she glued her lips to it, and after sucking a while began to play with her tongue upon what you have been so deliciously rubbing. She licked me most exquisitely, and soon made me die away in extasy of delight. She sucked it for some time after, while I lay in a languid state of joy. When at last she rose, she threw herself on the bed, and our two naked bodies became closely united in the most loving embrace. Her lips were wet with the moisture that had escaped from me, its peculiar aromatic odour *m'enivrait* and I could not help licking the creamy juice from off her lips.

" 'Oh, my beloved aunt,' I cried, 'you have given me the joy of paradise, I must try and do as much for you.'

" 'My darling Ellen, you will make me positively adore you. I now only regret that I had not sooner taken you into my confidence, as I at once perceive I might have done so in perfect safety. Yes, my darling, you shall indeed try, and I shall instruct you as we advance how to obtain the greatest amount of pleasure from our libidinous and lascivious enjoyments, delights that are without risk, and from which we shall have no anxieties as to fatal results, which are the consequence of connection with the opposite sex, who only make use of us for their own sensual enjoyment, and abandon us at the very moment they ought to console and cherish us the most.'

"Dear aunt, again embracing me tenderly, threw herself in the same position I had previously lay in. I knelt on the cushion as she had done. But before proceeding to do as she had done to me, I could not help pausing to gaze with delight on her natural charms. Oh! dear Harry, you cannot imagine the beauty of that part of your mamma. Her stomach is of the purest white, smooth and firm, round and beautiful. Below a crease commences a large plumped out swelling seen through the fair and thick silky curls that so much adorn it, then grandly rounded sinks down between her thighs, and the beautifully pouting lips rise richly tempting through the thickest of hair, that goes far beyond between the large

rounded orbs that project behind. At the upper part of the
lips, where they form a deep indented half-circle, I could
distinguish a stiff projecting object, as long and thicker than
my thumb. I now know that this is the centre of exquisite joy.
Your mother had since taught me to call it her clitoris, and
says that although seldom so strongly developed as in her
case, it exists in every woman and becomes stiff and excited
as the final crisis of joy approaches. I glued my lips around
this charming object, and sucked it, and played with my
tongue around its point. Your mother, in an extasy of delight,
wriggled her bottom below me, and with both hands pressing my head down on the excited point, gave utterance to
the most loving and sensual expressions. She begged me to
pass the flat of my hand under my chin, and introduce my
thumb within the lips below, where I was sucking, and move
it backwards and forwards as much as I could. I did so, and
immediately found that it added greatly to your mother's
delight. Faster and faster grew her movements, until, with a
cry of delight, a firm pressure of my hand against her affair,
and still firmer pressure on my thumb, she suddenly ceased
all movement, her hands relaxed their hold of my head, the
stiffness left her clitoris, and beyond convulsive graspings of
the interior of her affair upon my thumb, she lay for some
time inanimate. At last she recovered her senses, she seized
me under the arms, and drew me upon her belly, her hands
pressed my bottom down close upon her person, until I
found that my affair was nestled in the rich profusion of
curls that so finely adorned hers. She thrust her tongue into
my mouth, and sucked off all the rich creamy substance that
had flowed from her in such abundance. She blessed the
happy chance that had led her to give me her confidence;
told me that for long she had only enjoyed the unsatisfactory
delight of lonely self-gratification, and said that now we
should revel in mutual delight of every sensual indulgence
that woman can have with woman. We lay for some time

enjoying such delicious communings, until compelled to rise by the lateness of the hour. We have since practised every method of enjoyment given to two of the same sex. Your mother has often introduced her stiff excited clitoris within the lips of my affair as far as it would go, but I have always longed, my dear Harry, for you to penetrate still further with that larger and longer thing you have got, although what I have seen to-day of its increased size has made me greatly fear it can never get in."

Thus ended her ingenuous description. Harry, of course, promised that he would never hurt her, that those parts were made to yield, that, doubtless, his mother's large clitoris had hurt her at first, but had given her great pleasure afterwards.

Yes, that was so, and it was that that gave her courage, and if they could only get the opportunity she would allow him to do anything he pleased.

It may well be supposed this account of Ellen's intercourse with her aunt fired my imagination and made me resolve to have her. Indeed, I began to conceive that there would be no occasion for me to make any effort, that all would be done by dear mamma herself. We had returned to the house after this agitated walk. Mamma was evidently greatly preoccupied, but at length she appeared to have come to a final determination, for she told Ellen to go up to her room, and begged us two boys, as she called us, to go out and amuse ourselves for an hour. It was during this interval that Harry narrated his interesting conversation with his cousin. Her lively description had set his imagination on fire, and he now declared his regret that it was not to be he who would enjoy his lasciviously sensual mother. Neither of us had any doubt but that she would now find an opportunity of enjoying me. If we had, our doubts were solved on re-entering the house. Mamma first, for form's sake, kissing her son, and then far more warmly kissing me, informed us that she had written to the doctor that we had been such good boys that she would feel greatly obliged if he would allow her son to remain with her until Monday, and also leave his nephew to keep him company and prevent any of his former misbehaviour which, she was happy to say, he appeared to have forgotten, but still it would be better he should have the safeguard of so intelligent and discreet a friend as she was glad to see he had found in the doctor's nephew. My uncle, without knowing exactly what to make of this note, had consented. Hence her joy in being able to communicate the pleasing intelligence— doubly so to me, as I immediately augured the downfall of my assumed virginity. Dear mamma was all radiant with joy, and conveyed me at once to where she intended I should sleep. I marked that it was in an out of the way room, easy of access, but not likely to be interfered with by passers-by.

"And here, my dear son, for you know in future you are always to call me mamma, I hope you will find yourself comfortable, and that you will not be alarmed because you are in an out of the way part of the house, but in case you should, before I go to bed, I shall come to see that you are comfortably asleep."

Here she kissed and embraced me warmly. I repaid her most affectionately, but apparently in all innocence. She sighed, as I thought with regret, that she could not at that moment go further, and then led me away.

The afternoon, the dinner, and the evening passed away without anything worthy of remark, except that mamma was frequently absent and preoccupied. She sat by me on the sofa while Ellen played to us; her hand sought mine, and frequently squeezed it affectionately. Harry sat by Ellen, which enabled me often to raise my head and pout my lips for a kiss in a boyish way. It was never refused. She dwelt on my mouth sensuously with half-opened lips, but apparently afraid to tip me the velvet of her tongue. She frequently gave a shudder and trembled, and was evidently greatly excited. In

the course of the afternoon, Harry and I had had an opportunity of exchanging ideas. I told him I was certain his
mother would come to me that night, and he might be sure
if she did that she would remain till daylight. I advised him to
watch her, and when he saw her leave her bedroom to come
to me, then he could slip into his cousin's room, and effect his
purpose, but to be sure to retire at the first dawn. I said that
if that time his mother wanted to leave me, I would keep
her another quarter of an hour to enable him to put matters
to rights with his cousin, and regain his own room. I advised
him also to put a towel under his cousin's bottom, as he was
sure to make her bleed, and he must take it away in the
morning to prevent any traces of what he had done being
perceived by his mother, and to tell Ellen to feign deep sleep
on his mother's return, and to appear quite unconscious in the
morning of her aunt having been absent. A little before ten
o'clock mamma thought it time for her children, as she called
us, to go to bed. Her son and niece both kissed her, and I, too,
claimed a kiss of my new mamma. It was taken and returned
in quite a passionate way, her lips seemed loath to leave mine,
and her arms encircled me in a very loving embrace.

"Dear mamma," I said, "I shall love you ever dearly."

"My darling boy, I already love you as if you were indeed
my son."

She sent the others to their bedrooms, but escorted me herself to mine. I could see that she trembled greatly, and was
evidently glad to put down the candlestick. She turned down
the bedclothes for me, hoped I would sleep well, and, with
considerable agitation, again embraced me most passionately.
I could feel that her tongue would fain have thrust itself
between my lips. I had great difficulty in restraining myself,
but somehow I managed to do so. She at last left me, saying
she would give a look in to see that I was comfortable before
she herself went to bed. I told her it was very kind of her,

but that there was no necessity for her doing so, as I always went to sleep like a top the moment I lay down.

"I am glad of that, my dear child, but nevertheless I will look in, lest the strange bed should prevent your sleeping."

And again she hugged me passionately against her firm and well-formed bosom, kissing me with a long, long kiss. Quitting me with a deep sigh, at last she said good night, and shut the door, apparently going away. But I fancied that she stopped short, and that I could hear her gently stealing back, probably in the hope of seeing me undress, and of catching a view of my huge pego. So I determined she should have her curiosity indulged. I hurried off my clothes, and before putting on one of Harry's night-shirts, which had been laid on the bed for me, I took up the chamber pot, and turned fronting the key hole, stark naked, and cock in hand. It was at half-cock, but when I had piddled I made it throb and raise its head, and gave it a rub or two, and a shake very deliberately, so that she might be still more bent on possessing it. I took up the night-shirt, and turning to the light, was very awkward in getting it on, so as to give time for a good sight of my prick at full stand against my belly. I then blew out the light, and tumbled into bed very quickly. I listened attentively, and could hear a deep half-suppressed sigh, and then footsteps stealing quietly away. I lay awake cogitating as to how I should receive her, whether to feign profound sleep, and so let her take all the initiative, or whether to pretend that the novelty of the bed, and thinking over her affectionate kindness to me had kept me awake. I decided upon pretending to be sound asleep, chiefly that I might see how she would carry out her designs, and also as allowing me to play the surprised one.

In little more than half an hour after all had retired to rest I saw the glimmer of light through the key hole. I had studied a pose that would facilitate matters. I lay on my back, the clothes partially thrown off my breast, and the hand next to the side on which she must approach, placed above my head. Of course my cock was at full stand and as I had thrown off the heavy counterpane, it easily lifted up, and bulged out the sheet and light blanket. I closed my eyes, and breathed heavily. The door was gently opened, and she entered. She turned to close it, and I gave a peep through a half-opened eye, and saw that she had only on a loose *robe de chambre,* which was thrown open in turning, so that I could see there was nothing but her shift below. I even caught sight of her beautiful bosom, which at once caused my prick to throb almost to bursting, so that when she came to my side, it stood up most manfully. She paused, evidently intent on the sight. She then held the light towards me, and spoke in an undertone, asking me if I was awake. Of course I only breathed the heavier, and lay with my mouth half open, as if in the very deepest first slumber. She then turned her attention to the bulging-out substance, and ventured to touch it gently; then, growing bolder, she still more gently grasped it from above the clothes, and then turned the light on my face, but I gave not a sign. She then put the candle down, and, taking a chair, sat down close to the bed. Here she again spoke to me in a subdued tone. Finding no cessation of the deep breathing, she gently insinuated her hand below the already favourably turned-down bedclothes, and with great care slipped it down to my prick, which she grasped softly. I could now feel her whole body tremble, her breath came fast and short. She passed her hand gently up from the root to the head, its size evidently greatly exciting her. When she grasped the head, it gave a powerful throb. She eased her hand, and, I felt certain, turned to see if it had disturbed me. But I slept on profoundly. She seemed to gain more confidence, for both hands were now applied, and it was evident she had assumed a kneeling posture, the better to favour her designs. I could feel her pass one hand over the other, until she found the head was still partially above the third grasp. I heard her give an involuntary exclamation of surprise at its size. Her curiosity growing by what it fed on, she now commenced with the utmost caution gently to remove the bed-clothes, that she might see, as well as feel. When this was accomplished, she rose and brought the light, again passed it before my eyes, and then moved it down towards my prick. Being sure she was now far too deeply engaged to turn her eyes towards mine, I half opened them, and beheld her bending close over the great object of attraction. I heard her exclaim half aloud—

"How wonderful! I never could have imagined such a thing, and in such an innocent boy, too. Oh! I must possess—yes—I must possess it."

Here she grasped it more forcibly than before. Then, rising, she put the candle on the pot stand, which she removed to the foot of the bed. Then taking my prick in both hands, she gently rubbed it up and down, and even stooped and fondly kissed the nut. It throbbed more violently than ever at this, and I thought it time to start, and appear to awake. She instantly quitted her hold of it, and stood up, but was too agitated to think of covering me. I opened my eyes in apparent great surprise, but recognising mamma, I said—

"Oh! is that you, dear mamma? I was dreaming such a nice dream about you. Oh, do kiss me," purposely not seeming to know that my person was all naked.

She stooped and kissed me tenderly, saying—

"My dear, darling boy. I came to see if you were comfortable, and found you lying uncovered, and with this extraordinary thing sticking up."

She had seized it with her left hand, as she stooped to kiss me. On the instant, I determined to play off the same game that had succeeded so well with my aunt.

"My dear mamma, I should not have dared to speak to you about *that,* but it does give me much pain, by becoming so hard that it throbs, as you may feel, at the least touch. I don't know what to do; and it makes me feel so queer too, especially at the gentle pressures you have just given it; dear mamma, can you tell me how I can cure it, and I will love you so dearly."

Here she stooped and kissed me very luxuriously, actually thrusting her tongue into my mouth. I sucked it, and told her how sweet it was. But my prick becoming perfectly outrageous, I implored her to tell me what I could do to relieve it. She looked at me long and intently, blushing and turning pale by turns.

"Yes, my dear boy, I could relieve you, but it is a secret that I hardly dare confide in one so young."

"Oh! you may trust me, my dear mamma, you know I am becoming a young man, and men must know how to keep secrets, or they would be despised, besides, so dear and loving a mamma as you are to me would doubly make me keep secret anything you confide to me on those terms."

"I will trust you, my darling boy, but you will at once see by what I shall do, how completely I sacrifice myself to do you good."

Upon this, she threw off her robe, and sprang into bed by my side.

"Oh! how nice of you, dear mamma," said I, as I took her in my arms, and kissed her lovingly. "Feel, mamma, how much harder it is, so tell me at once how I am to relieve it."

"Well, my dear child, we women are made to relieve such stiffnesses as this; we possess a sheath to put it in, and then it gradually softens."

"Oh! where—where—dearest mamma, do tell me?"

She took my hand and put it down on her cunt, already quite wet with the excitement she had been in.

"There, feel that, do you not find an opening?"

"Oh, yes, but how am I to get in there—won't it hurt you?"

"I will show you."

She turned on her back, opened her legs, and desired me

to mount on her belly, with my legs between hers, then guiding my rampant pego, and rubbing its great head up and down the lips to moisten it, she told me to push gently downwards, for it was so large that I would otherwise hurt her. Playing the novice to perfection, I awkwardly but gently soon thrust it in, up to the codpiece. She uttered an "Oh! oh!" when it was fairly hilted; then throwing her legs over my loins, and her arms round my waist, she begged me to move my bottom backwards and forwards, always thrusting it in as far as I could. Three or four pushes finished me off, in the great excitement I was under. She, too, died away with a great convulsive sigh. I took care to cry out—

"Oh! my dear mamma—oh! stop. I am dying—I—I—am dy—dy—ing."

Her convulsive internal pressures were delicious, and quickly roused my prick up again. She also had come to, and had glued her lips to mine—giving her own, and then asking in return for my tongue to suck.

"Oh! what heavenly joys, my dear mamma, you did, indeed, reduce its hardness, but just feel—it has got hard again, you must reduce it once more."

"My beloved boy, I shall always be ready to do so, but it must be the most sacred secret between us, or I should never be able to do it again."

You may well suppose my protestations were of the strongest. At it we went again, and again, and again. Mamma declared that I was a most apt scholar. Four times did I pour into her foaming and fiery cunt torrents of sperm. At last she insisted upon my withdrawing, saying it would injure my health to indulge any more. So I withdrew, and we embraced each other most lovingly. I now expressed a wish to see the wonderful place that had given me the extasies of paradise. She lent herself with admirable grace and ease to my boyish curiosity, and even threw off her shift, making me do the same, that she too might admire the undisguised beauties of my form. There was no pretence in the great admiration I expressed for her really superb form, but I expressed it in a naïve and innocent way, that made her laugh heartily, and confirmed her idea that she was not only the first naked woman I had seen, but that she was the first I ever knew, or who had taught me what sensual pleasure meant, and great was her delight in thinking she had taken my virginity, and been the first to initiate me in love's delightful mysteries. Of course, I did everything I could in order to carry on the deception she was so much pleased with, and I may add this was the last time I ever did so, for daily becoming more of a man, I took *things* by the forelock at once, and rarely failed to succeed. We got up, and she turned herself round in every way for me to see the rare beauties of her person—herself explaining to me where she was well made—bosom, buttocks, belly so white and smooth, without a wrinkle, although she had had a son. She was, indeed, one of those rare cases where nothing remains to tell of such an event. Her bosom, without being so large as aunt's, was gloriously white and firm, with such pink nipples, larger than in a maid, but sticking out hard and inviting a suck. Then her cunt—for she laid herself on her back, opened her legs, and allowed me the closest inspection. I have already alluded to her clitoris, as described by Ellen to Harry; it was charmingly developed, about half the length of Miss Frankland's, and not so thick. As I felt her cunt and introduced my fingers to hold it open, she got excited, and Master Clitoris raised his head, and came out of his corner in full stand. I professed great surprise to find she had a little doodle of her own. I purposely used the boyish expression. I began to play with it.

"Oh!" I said, "I must kiss it."

I did so, and began to suck it. She got dreadfully lewd, and seizing upon my now-again-standing prick, drew me upon her, and introduced once more my master weapon. With greater slowness until the final crisis drew near, we had another delicious fuck. She was a woman of very warm passions, and the long pent-up seclusion she had kept herself in with regard to our sex being once broken, now that the flood-gates were opened, there was no resisting the torrent of her lascivious passions. Twice again did we fuck without withdrawing. Then, after hugging and thanking me for the extasies I threw her into, she rose for a natural purpose, and advised me to do the same, and we would then both lave ourselves with cold water to restore our nerves. She laved me and I her. She then insisted on my lying down on my back, while she admired what she called the masterpiece of Nature. From seeing and feeling, she soon came to sucking. Up he got in a moment. Playing the ignoramus, I asked if it was not possible that we could both enjoy that pleasure at once.

"Oh, yes, my dear boy. I am so delighted to find that this pleases you! Lie on your back, I shall get over you in the reverse way, and while I suck this enormous jewel, whose head I can hardly get into my mouth, you shall do as you like with my notch."

"Is that what you call it, dear mamma?"

"That is one name, and it has many others, but you men generally call it cunt, as we call yours prick, it is just as well you should know their ordinary names, as children only call them Fanny and Doodle."

"Prick and cunt—oh! I shan't forget, so let me have that beautiful cunt to suck."

We had a mutual gamahuche, and both greedily swallowed the double result, and continued our caresses of both parts, until they were again in full vigour, and inspired with a desire for more solid enjoyments.

"My darling boy, you are so apt and excellent a scholar that I must show you there are several ways of allaying the stiffness of this dear fellow, who seems as desirous as ever to have his hardness taken out of him. I shall show you how my husband liked best to enjoy me."

She scrambled up on her knees, and presented her very fine bottom, told me to kneel behind and give her my prick in her hand, which she thrust out backwards between her thighs. I did so. She told me it would appear to get further in this way, and, in fact, it did. After it was all in until thighs and buttocks met, she told me to admire, praise, and handle the splendid cheeks of her bottom, and said that such praise greatly excited her. Of course I did so, admiring not only their size and fairness, but also the beautiful curly silk meshes that ran between the cheeks, covered her beautifully pink bottom-hole, charmingly puckered as it was, and ran up to the flat of her back. After I had so excited her, she begged me to lean forward, and to handle one bubby while I should play with her clitoris with the other hand. I did all this tolerably well, but with somewhat of awkwardness. She said I would soon be perfect. We ran again two courses before she fell forward dragging me down without withdrawing, and then turning on our sides, still intertwined we fell off into a deep slumber, and did not awaken till daylight. Mamma jumped out of bed, unseating me by the act. She was alarmed lest the hour should be late enough for the household to be up. I tried hard to persuade her to reduce once more the hardness which had again seized me as she might see and feel for herself.

"No, my dear boy, we must not be imprudent, my niece may have awakened and grown anxious at my absence, and she may rise to seek me; so good-bye, my darling, go to sleep again."

She embraced me tenderly, but I could not prevail upon her to go further, although she promised to seek an opportunity during the day, and to give me as much as I liked the next night. She left me, and I pondered over the lucky chance that had put so desirable and fine a woman into my arms, and also congratulated myself on the stratagem by which I had fully convinced her that she was my first instructress in the art of love, a circumstance ever dear to the ardent imagination of the darling sex. I easily fell asleep again, wondering how Harry in the meantime had got on with his cousin. My dear mamma would not allow me to be disturbed. She had entered my room once or twice, and found me sleeping soundly.

At last she again entered, just as I had satisfied a natural want for which I had risen. To rush to her, to embrace her tenderly, to fasten the door, and compel her, not much against her will, to come towards the bed, to beg her to lie on her belly on the bedside, to cant her petticoats up, to kneel and gamahuche her cunt from behind until she begged me to rise and fuck her, was but the work of a minute or two. And then my stiff-standing pego, aided by the mouthful of thick saliva occasioned by the gamahuche, was directed at her cunt, and driven home as far as the buttocks or her fine backside would allow. My prick being fairly sheathed, I paused for a moment to handle and praise the beauty of her posterior orbs. Then, stooping, I nibbled at her bubbies with one hand, and frigged her clitoris with the other. Sharp set, with my long rest and refreshing sleep, I rapidly ran a first course, but not quicker than the lascivious nature of dear mamma, who joined me in a copious discharge with the most extatic joy, and the most delicious inward pressures. For she was a perfect and most accomplished actor in the combats of love, and in her own way was worthy of my glorious aunt and my loved Miss Frankland, and as thoroughly accomplished as they in all the abandon of lust and lubricity, although at the moment I had only proved things in an ordinary way. Her exquisite internal suctions almost prevented the slightest relaxation in my delighted pego, and after a minute or two of indulgence in the after joy, I began again almost before dear mamma had recovered her senses, when she tried to tear herself away. But before she knew where she was I had succeeded in again firing her ardent and lascivious

nature, and she became as eager for a second course
as myself. This was naturally longer than the first fiery one.
I raised myself upright on my knees, contemplated with the
utmost delight the uncommon active play of her loins, and
the exquisite side wriggling of her very fine backside. I
loudly praised her delicious manœuvres, and seconded them
to the utmost, until getting more and more excited, fast and
furious grew our movements. I bent down to second her by
frigging her clitoris, and the final crisis seized us both with
its agony of joy, and I sank almost insensible on her back. We
lay for a short time lost to every thing, until mamma, remembering the risk we ran of discovery, begged me to withdraw,
and let her go away. She rose and threw herself into my
arms, glueing her lips to mine with a most loving kiss. Then
stooping, she gave my now pendant prick a most delicious
suck, making her tongue play into and around the mouth of
the urethra. This was so delicious that the delighted member
instantly showed its appreciation of the pleasure by starting
up in full swing. Mamma gave it a pat, and said he was a most
charming and delicious boy, who did not know how to behave himself. Again she kissed me, and tore herself away, but
I could easily see the regret was as great on her side as
mine. She told me her son had been as lazy as I was, and said
that breakfast was waiting for us both. I quickly finished my
toilet and found them all at the breakfast table.

Ellen blushed deeply when she saw me. A glance from
Harry assured me he had succeeded, and that Ellen not only
knew what I had been about, but also that I knew what she
had been doing. Hence her high colour when she saw me. I
smiled, and nodded to her knowingly, and as she had observed the intelligent glance that passed between Harry and
me, it did not tend to put her at her ease.

Mamma, of course, knew nothing of what had passed in
her bed while she was with me, and was all affectionate
attention to the whole party, but with a marked tendency to

pay me more particular attention. Our breakfast was late, so we had to hurry ourselves for church. Mamma drove Ellen in a small pony phæton, while Harry and I took a short cut across the fields.

Harry told me how he had watched his mother and had quietly approached my door, and as the bed was exactly opposite the key hole, had seen and enjoyed her proceedings, especially as he knew that I only pretended sleep.

"By Jove," he said, "what a fine woman mother is! I could not tear myself away, and remained until you both went at it again, stark naked. My mother's beautiful hairy cunt, fine bubbies and backside, nearly drove me mad with desire. I could have violated her if she had been alone. And, then, her energy in fucking was superb. I could hold out no longer, but rushed to dear Ellen's side. She was asleep. I took her in my arms, and awoke her by feeling her delicious young cunt. She opened her eyes, and thinking it was mamma she turned round to repay the compliment, and started on having hold of my pego."

" 'Why! Harry dear, how came you here? We shall be caught by mamma.'

" 'Oh, no, my love, mamma is better engaged, and has slipped away to Charlie's room to get done to her what I am going to do to you.'

"She was too much alarmed to believe me, and I was obliged to bring her to your door. I first peeped, and saw you were still at it. Mamma's legs and arms thrown around you allowed me to see your great big thing rushing in and out, and driving home with immense vigour. I whispered to Ellen to peep. While she did so, stooping, I sat down on the floor and gamahuched her. She spent almost immediately, and was so excited that it quite filled my mouth. I rose on my legs, and bringing my prick against her cunt, made an entrance as far as over the nut, but was myself so excited with all I was doing, and all I had previously seen, that I went off in an agony of delight and with a suppressed cry, which must have been heard by you and mamma if you had not been so busily engaged. Ellen had been so excited and so intent on the to her new scene enacting before her eyes, that she had never ceased gazing on it, and left me to do whatever I pleased, but my cry alarmed her, especially as in my last forward push I had sent her head with some noise against the door. She rose, and so unseated me from the slight hold I had got of her cunt. She turned round to embrace me most excitedly, and whispered that we must go elsewhere. I took her round the waist, and we quickly regained mamma's bed. The light enabled me to find a towel. I told Ellen it was to prevent any moisture betraying our acts. She was far too excited and wishful for the article to make the slightest resistance, or even pretence of refusal. I begged her to throw off her shift, as she had seen both Charlie and mamma were quite naked. She at once complied, being now as eager for the fray as myself. I, too, threw off my night-shirt. For a moment we embraced each other's naked bodies. My cock was as stiff as iron. She lewdly laid hold of it, while I handled her charming young cunt. I helped her onto the bed, she at once lay down on her back, and threw open her legs as she had seen mamma do. I stopped and gave her cunt, all oozing with her own and my spunk, a warm kiss, and with a lick or two on her budding clitoris, I fired her even to greater excess than she had yet been in.

" 'Oh, come to my arms, my dear Harry, and let us do as they were so delightedly doing.'

"She had noted with what rapture mamma was enjoying you, and she had noted, too, what a much larger cock yours was than mine; so she had naturally reasoned that if one so big gave her aunt so much delight, my smaller one could not possibly hurt her, hence her eagerness to have me at once. I did not baulk her, but throwing myself between her wide-spread thighs, I soon brought the point of my prick to the longing lips of her little virgin cunt. I rubbed it up and down in between the pouting and self-opened lips, partly to moisten it, and partly to still more excite her lust. I then gently pressed it forward, and introduced just its head, and drawing it in and out, made her beg me to go further. I did so, slowly, until I found there was an impediment. I knew that I must burst through this and that it would hurt her, so I continued withdrawing and re-entering without going further until she became so voraciously lewd as to throw her legs around my loins and heave her bottom up to meet my thrusts. I seized the fortunate moment and with one downright violent thrust burst through every barrier and buried my prick in her up to the very hilt. The attack and its result was so unexpected by Ellen that when she felt the knife-like thrust of agony she gave a shriek of pain, and made an immediate effort to throw me off. I was too firmly seated for any other result of her struggles than the still more complete rupture of her maidenhead, which my forward thrust had partially effected. I lay for some time quite tranquil, and when her immediate pain wore off I commenced a gentle in and out movement, which, without exactly exciting her, produced a pleasing sensation. I then went on faster and faster until the crisis came upon me, and I shot into her a torrent of boiling sperm that by its balmy nature mollified the previous smarting; so that when I had recovered from the delicious extasies of my first success, and my prick gradually resumed its former vigour, I found by the somewhat increased pressure upon it that her passions were re-awakening. Three times did I fuck her before I withdrew, the last one appeared to give her more pleasure, but still she complained of a smarting pain as I passed over and over the shattered hymen. I advised her to rise and lave herself as a relief, and to wash away the stains of blood from her thighs. The towel was a fortunate thought on your part, but, in fact, I had followed in all my movements the sage counsels you had given me from the

experience you had had in taking the virginities of Mrs.
Vincent and your two sisters, or I should otherwise probably
have bungled the matter, although my experience with your
magnificent aunt had naturally put me up to all the art of
fucking. I had some difficulty in persuading Ellen to let me
put it in again, as she declared she had endured perfect agony
when I broke through her maidenhead. However, I gamahuched her well, got her passions up, moistened the shaft
well, and was very gentle in entering and in my first movements. I spent without making her do so. But the well-greased
sheath now allowing more easy movements, she gave down
her nature with considerable pleasure as I spent the second
time. Still there was fear and restraint—fear lest mamma
might come back—so I thought it advisable to retire to my
own room, being quite certain that now the road is open
her lascivious nature will not be long in enabling her to enjoy
the sport to the utmost. By the way, she could not help
wondering how mamma could take in your immense pego;
why, she said, it was as thick as her wrist and much longer
than her hand, and yet it seemed to slip into mamma with
ease and pleasure, 'while yours, dear Harry, which is not
thicker than my two forefingers, and hardly much longer, has
given me such pain.' I assured her it was only for the first
night, and that if she would bathe it with warm water two
or three times during the day, and put up a little glycerine
as far as where it hurt, which her finger could easily reach,
she would find that to-morrow night there would no longer
be any pain felt, and she would enjoy it as much as she had
seen mamma do. With this advice I left her to her repose,
and gained my own room unobserved."

After this we concerted together as to what we should say
to the doctor, who was sure to question us. Mrs. Dale's
cottage was not in our parish, but she had driven over to
our church, partly to throw off all suspicion from the doctor's
mind, and also to thank him for allowing us to stay with her.

We, therefore, knew that we should have to go to the rectory and stay for luncheon. We agreed that we should not on this occasion take the doctor into our confidence, but that we should tell him we had purposely been very quiet and discreet, so as to throw Harry's mother off her guard. That Ellen slept with her, so that it became doubly necessary to gain her confidence. This being arranged before we reached church, we entered. After service we all adjourned to the rectory. The doctor escorted Mrs. Dale, Harry, Ellen, and I my aunt. Aunt, pressing my arm, asked me if I had had Mrs. D., as she seemed a fine woman worth having.

"Oh, dear no. I have had no opportunity, even if she would have consented. I have been playing the ingenuous youth to help Harry with his cousin. I thought we had somewhat thrown her off her guard, but she was still jealous and watched him closely. Ellen slept with her, which rendered things more difficult for Harry. She has closely examined me as to the sort of intimacy existing between us. I threw such an air of candour and innocence over my replies that she was quite delighted Harry had met with such a companion. I fully expect she will break out in praises of my *modest* and discreet conduct."

Indeed, so it turned out, and Mrs. Dale did it with such an air of candour that aunt was quite convinced nothing as yet had occurred between us. While the ladies discussed the dresses and bonnets of all who had appeared in church, uncle took Harry and me for a walk in the garden until luncheon was ready. Here he began, as aunt had done, to question us as to our proceedings, and the reason for Mrs. D. asking permission for us to stay. The same replies that had satisfied aunt satisfied him that nothing as yet had taken place beyond my gaining the confidence of Mrs. D.

"My dear Charlie," said uncle, "you have only now to manage somehow or other to let her see your great big cock without apparently your being aware of it, and I will warrant, from my knowledge of woman's nature, that she will find a way to have you, only mind you play the innocent, and be very awkward, and let her appear to teach you, which will give double pleasure and prevent any questioning as to how you have gained your instruction, if she thought you instructed."

I smiled inwardly at these sage directions, and thought how completely all persons knowing in the ways of the world gave the same advice. But little did uncle then think that I had acted up to the very letter what he was advising for my future conduct. We re-entered the house on luncheon bell ringing. Mrs. Dale complimented the doctor on the advance her son had made both in manners and instruction, and quite naturally congratulated herself on his finding so very modest and gentlemanly a companion in the doctor's nephew—myself to wit.

Returning home, Ellen begged she might be allowed to walk, doubtless calculating on having Harry for a companion. But mamma, while agreeing to her request, was still sufficiently on her guard to take Harry in the phæton, and leave me to escort Ellen. Here was a chance! Ellen blushed, but took my arm as we left the rectory. Uncle gave me a knowing look, and a glance at Ellen, as we parted, as much as to say, I guess what will happen. We walked away steadily enough until the first hedge hid us. I stopped, and embraced Ellen tenderly, saying how glad I was to be able to congratulate her on the happy chance her aunt had given her, by coming to me for the night. She was a good deal confused at thinking that I should know how she passed the night. I rallied her upon this, told her that no secret existed between Harry and me, and that, in fact, if I had not lent myself to the game, she would not have had the opportunity for the great pleasure she must have had in Harry's arms. I knew she had not had much, but I wished to draw her on, and to make her open out as to her feelings, being determined to make the most of any confidence on her part. She replied that, indeed, she had done nothing but suffer, and would not have allowed Harry to do what he did if she had known the pain it would give her, she had been deceived by seeing how much aunt had seemed to enjoy what was so greatly superior in size to what Harry had. I smiled at her allusion to the size of my pego, and knowing that her curiosity must be creating in her a desire to see it, I told her it was well for her, in the first instance, to have had the smaller weapon to penetrate her, and that now she would never again suffer, even by the introduction of so large a one as mine.

"Oh, but when I think of the immense size of yours, I could never dare to allow you to try, although aunt did seem to enjoy it, when you pushed it in with such force."

"My dear Ellen, it was the size alone that tempted mamma, and if I had not been larger than Harry, I doubt if ever she would have come to me at night."

"But how could she dare to do so?"

"Curiosity to enjoy an unusually large cock, my dear."

"Did you know she was coming?"

"Yes, and no. I saw that her passions were excited, when I had once *accidentally* allowed her to see my large proportions."

"Yes, Harry told me what you were about, but I hardly expected aunt would have dared to come to you—how did it happen?"

"Well, if you will promise *never* to let your aunt know that I have told, I shall tell you. She came and found me *apparently* asleep, first felt me, and seeing I did not awake, carefully uncovered me, looked at, handled and kissed it, upon which, as my cock was nearly bursting, and I could stand it no longer, I awoke, and innocently complained of the stiffness I suffered from in that part, and begged her to tell me if there was any means of relieving it. She told me there was, but it was a great secret she hardly dared trust me with—and even if she could do so, she was afraid of a great long thing like *that*, three of her hands long below the head! but that if I promised secrecy, she would try. Then she lay down and taught me how to put it in, and I know you afterwards enjoyed the sight of our being in full action, quite naked—did you not enjoy it, dear Ellen?"

"Well, dear Charlie, it was very exciting, and made me feel queer all over; but is it really three hands and a head long?"

I was delighted at the question, as it showed me she was ready for what I intended should be done. Curiosity once excited was sure to go to the utmost length, if it had the opportunity. I had purposely been hurrying on to gain a dense copse through which our path lay, and I knew there was a snug glade, where we would be in perfect security. It was the dinner hour of the peasantry, and no one else was likely to come that way. Just as we entered the copse, she had put her last question. I told her I would show her, if she would step a few yards beyond the foot path. She objected, for form's sake saying—

"What would Harry say?"

"There is no occasion for him to know anything about it, but even if he did, has he not himself shown you mamma and me in full enjoyment of her sweet charms; but, unless you tell him you may be sure I never shall, it will not take a minute, and as we have already walked very fast, we have plenty of time, and our absence will not be observed."

With professed reluctance she allowed me to lead her where I wished. Having arrived at the favourable spot, I sat down on a gentle slope, and begged her to sit down beside me. As you may well suppose, my prick was rampant, and almost bursting open my trousers, so that as soon as I unbuttoned, out it flew in all its splendour. She gave a half scream of surprise as she gazed upon its large proportions, and declared it looked larger than when she had seen it with aunt. Her face flushed, and her eyes sparkled as she gazed, but she seemed half frightened to touch it. I took her hand and placed it on it. She immediately grasped it convulsively, but sighed deeply. I had lain back on the grass that it might stand out boldly before her and I told her to try if it was not three hands and a head long. She immediately passed one hand over the other from the root, and said it was really monstrous, and she wondered how aunt could have got it into her.

"Oh, my darling, I hope some day you will find that you can take it all in with the utmost delight, but I should not think of trying until you have had some more practice with Harry."

Meanwhile she was handling it with great excitement, and while saying she was sure I could never succeed with her, she was evidently longing to be able to take it in. I saw I must work her up more—so I said—

"Dear Ellen, you know what pleasure it gave you and Harry to play with each other with your mouths, it is now your turn to let me see your dear little thing—and then you must lie over me reversed, so that we may enjoy ourselves with tongues and mouths."

She let me at once pull up her petticoats, but said she feared that even for that she was still too sore from Harry's work last night. I asked if she had bathed it in warm water and put glycerine up.

"Oh, yes."

At first it smarted, but before going to church, she had done it three times, and no longer felt any pain, but still was afraid of my finger going up. I was introducing it at the moment. It passed in its full length without hurting her.

"Now, pull up your petticoats well, and lie down on me, while I do the same with this charming little cunt; my tongue can only give it the utmost pleasure."

She herself was now so much excited that she was ready

enough to comply with my desires. She got upon me, her petticoats well canted over her back. She glued her lips to my prick, and sucked and frigged it with an energy that proved how highly her passions were fired. Her cunt was already in a foam of spendings, which I first licked up. Then sucking her tiny clitoris, stiffly projecting slightly out, I thrust my middle finger up her cunt, and by the wriggling of her backside, saw how much she enjoyed it. Introducing a second finger to moisten it, I withdrew both, and, turning my hand sideways, made each finger enter a separate aperture. She was already nearly in the grand crisis; it came upon her before I was ready. She poured a greater discharge into my mouth than I thought the young thing could have spent. It took her breath away, and she released her suction of my prick for a minute. But on my begging her to continue sucking, she did so with increased energy, and I poured out a torrent of sperm that shot down her throat and nearly choked her, but the dear girl never let go for all that, and sucked away until not only was there not a drop left, but by her delicious titillations she had brought my prick up to its utmost vigour again. I, too, had reawakened her passions. She wanted to renew the sport in this way again, but I begged her to allow me to rub the head of my prick up and down between the well-moistened lips of her cunt, and then to spend with the point, or at most the head, within it. She asked if she could trust me to stop if it hurt her.

"Of course, my darling," I said, "nothing shall be done, or rather everything shall cease the moment you tell me to stop."

Half afraid, yet wishing to try, she changed her position to a kneeling one. I canted her petticoats well over her back, and first kissing and handling her hard and plump buttocks, which promised a future perfection, I stooped and again licked her charming pouting cunt with all its budding fair young curls. Then applying my surcharged mouthful of saliva to my already well-moistened prick, I lubricated it completely from point to root, and then applied it to the half-opened lips. Rubbing it up and down here, and over the clitoris, I excited her to the greatest pitch.

"Oh! Charlie dear," she cried, "try if its head will go in now, and I will try to bear it."

I was only too glad of the permission, and very rapidly got it in over the nut, but it was very tight. I drew it half out again, and then, on repeating this five or six times, found I was imperceptibly gaining ground.

"Oh! dear Charles, it is delicious! Try on, gently."

I did so, and had got rather more than half way in when she went off in an agony of delight, deliciously pouring her warm liquid over my enchanted prick, giving, at the same time, such a push backwards, which, meeting a firm, though gentle forward movement on my part, joined with the natural relaxation following her discharge, drove me up to the hilt in the very tightest little cunt it has ever been my good fortune to sheath myself in. I seemed to fill every cranny, and to have stretched every part to its utmost distention. My aunt with her great cunt had a power of pressure that seemed almost to nip off your prick, Miss Frankland, too, was great in that way. But this was more like a very well made first-rate kid glove, two sizes too small for your fingers, yet giving way without bursting, and fitting every irregularity of the nail or finger; just so her little cunt fitted my prick exactly like a glove, and it was truly most extatic. A gentle withdrawing, and then as gentle resheathing, so excited me that I shot a torrent of sperm up into her very womb. She gave quite a cry of extasy, and I could feel the tight sheath exercising a running movement along the whole length of my prick, and still more tightly closing all round it—if that were possible. It was so exquisitely delicious that both of us were almost instantly in readiness for another course.

She asked if I was all in.

"Oh, yes, my dear, do you think you could have taken any more?"

"Oh, no, it appears to fill me to bursting, and to be up to my very heart. I could not have supported more, but could hardly belive I had it all, as I did not think it possible, and was afraid there was more to come."

"Did it give you any pleasure?"

"Oh, yes; and does so still—push on, dear Charlie, and don't spare me, it is heavenly."

She wriggled and heaved her backside. I seized her by each hip and favoured her side movements by, as it were, drawing her off and on; faster and faster we moved, until at last the crisis seized us both together. Her head sank with a deep sigh, or rather cry of extasy. She would have fallen forward on her belly, but that my grip of her hips held her bottom close up to my belly, with my prick thrust into the innermost end of her cunt, until I felt the three points of the opening of her womb, like the nailless ends of three fingers grasping, as it were, the very point of my prick, and opening themselves to receive the whole discharge of my sperm within its innermost recesses. Nothing could be more delicious, and as I held her fast, I was myself in a state of perfect extasy. At last addressing some endearing expressions, and getting no reply, I found that the dear girl had quite fainted away, and was insensible in every respect except in the continued convulsive throbs of her delicious tight cunt. However, finding that she did not recover her senses, I gently withdrew my still stiff prick. Very little sperm followed the withdrawal. I wiped her cunt dry with my handkerchief, and was glad to see there was no blood stains. I laid her gently down on her back, ran to a little stream, and taking two handfuls of water, came back, threw some on the still throbbing cunt, and sprinkled her face with the drops that still adhered to my palms. This had the desired effect; she opened her eyes, raised herself on her bottom, and threw her arms round my neck as I knelt by her side. Telling me I had made her taste of the joys of heaven, she kissed me, and then burst into a hysterical flood of tears. I comforted her as best I could and asked why she wept.

"I don't know, dear Charles, but the last time made me feel both sick and faint just after you had given me such extasy as I never dreamt was possible. I believe I then fainted, and even now, I don't know why but I feel quite hysterical."

I kissed her tenderly, begged her to rise and come to the spring, where she could drink and said if she sat down on her feet I would bathe and cool her dear little cunt, which would probably put all to rights. She did so, and was quickly quite restored to herself again. She said she supposed it was my enormous size.

"But it did not hurt me, dear Charles, it only gave me too much pleasure; but you will do it to me another time whenever we have any opportunity, will you not, dear Charlie?"

I assured her I should always be too glad to do so, but that we must neither let her aunt nor Harry know of our proceedings. This being arranged, and she having quite recovered from the pallor her fainting fit had caused, we resumed our course homeward, and so hurried on that Harry, who had come to meet us found us getting over the stile of the last field, and was even disappointed that we had got so far, for we were now in sight of the cottage. He had hoped to find us much further back, and that I might have favoured his having a go at his cousin before reaching home. Ellen squeezed my arm. I said it was just as well as it was, for any imprudence might have awakened his mother's suspicions, and prevented a night of pleasure, which would be far better than any uncomfortable field affair.

When we arrived at home, mamma thought that Ellen

looked fatigued, and advised her to go and lie down on her bed, and take an hour's siesta. She told us boys we had better do the same, as she had some private matters to attend to. Harry and I saw immediately what was meant, and we betook ourselves to our respective rooms, I to expect mamma, who did not fail to come, and Harry to watch her, and then made the most of the opportunity with his cousin. I quickly undressed, and when mamma came I found she had divested herself of stays and undergarments; so when she undid her gown, and let fall her shift, she stood in all the naked glory of her beautiful form. I flew to embrace her most lovingly. Both our hands wandered and being both in full heat, we were at it in a moment fast and furious. I drove on, admirably seconded by dear mamma, and we quickly both gave down at the same instant a most delicious libation on the altar of Venus, and then died away in all the after-enjoyment. We lay for nearly a quarter of an hour soaking in the delicious bliss of satisfied desire. Mamma, on coming to her senses, kissed me most tenderly, and declared she had never believed it possible that she could have had such exquisite delight.

"But then, my dear Charles, I never dreamt that any man, let alone a boy like you, could be so magnificently hung. Oh, it is also such joy to me to think I have first taught you the real joys of coition, and tasted the first sweets of that most glorious weapon. My dear Charlie, I must contemplate its beauties in this full light; withdraw the dear fellow and turn on your back."

I did so. She rose, and turning in the reverse position, brought her lovely foaming cunt right down on my mouth. I sucked up all the delicious foam oozing from the aperture. Then drawing into my mouth her half-stiffened clitoris, which was then pendant like a little boy's cock, I soon sucked it into its utmost rigidity, frigging her rich pouting cunt with two fingers, the while. She, on her part, was not idle, first playing with my prick, covering and uncovering its head, which soon made it stand up in all of its glory. She was profuse and loud in its praises. Then getting too excited for mere admiration, she took it in her mouth and sucked it, and manipulated it with one hand, fingering my codpiece with the other. I then found her fingers were feeling and tickling my bottom-hole. She took her mouth from off my prick, and paused a moment; then again applied her finger to my fundament, and made it gently penetrate as far as it would go. The previous pause had evidently been for the purpose of moistening her finger with her saliva that it might slip in easily. I was delighted to find that she had come to this, but pretending ignorance, I stopped my proceedings to ask her what she was doing to my bottom, which could give me such exquisite delight.

"It is my finger, my dear Charles, my late husband was always delighted with my doing this, and used also to add greatly to my pleasure by doing the same to me."

"Shall I do so to you, dear mamma?"

"Oh, yes, my darling boy; moisten your finger first and then do it in my bottom-hole, as you have been doing it in my cunt."

"But I think I can do both at the same time, they are so close together."

"You are a delightful darling; do so, and it will be double pleasure to me."

So I immediately commenced to postillion her to her and my extreme gratification. We soon spent with the utmost delight, and both swallowed all we could get, continuing our suctions until the passions of both were again excited. I now declared I must fuck her again in the kneeling position, in which she had before given me such exquisite pleasure. As she drew a little higher up, I flung my arms round her fine backside, and glued my lips to her bottom-hole, and thrust my tongue in and out.

"Oh, Charles, dear, what are you doing? Oh! how delightful."

And she wriggled her backside over my mouth in a most voluptuous and lascivious way.

"Oh, rise my darling, and fuck me; you have made me so very lewd."

I drew myself up on my knees behind her, and was into her with wild ferocity that made her cry out with joy as she felt the mighty instrument rush within her. I stooped and frigged her clitoris at her desire, but wishing to contemplate the glorious movement of her backside I begged her to frig herself that I might be able to do so. Seizing hold of her lips, I drew her splendid bottom off and on my stiff and glowing prick with such immense delight to her that she went off and spent profusely, the hot stream bathing my delighted prick. But having already fucked Ellen so shortly before, and having spent twice at the present time, I remained for a while quiet, with mamma's exquisite cunt deliciously throbbing round it to the infinite enjoyment of my cock. I stooped and nibbled with my fingers at one of her nipples. I played with and frigged her very fine clitoris, which was soon in stiff-standing excitement again. Being cool myself, I soon worked her up into the wildest state of excitement by my frigging and the throbbings of my prick, aided with occasional long slowly drawn-out movements, and then as slowly regaining ground until within the last three inches, when it was thrust vigourously forward, and kept there for her convulsive pressures on it. I kept this up until she was almost wild with lust, and cried out for more vigorous movements. I did not immediately comply, but continued my exciting proceedings until she bit the pillow in the madness of her lust. Then I drove on fast and furious, amid cries of delight and extasy on her part, until the grand crisis overtook us both at the same instant in a perfect fury and agony of delight. I had previously left the frigging to herself, and had seized her lips and enjoyed the glorious sight of the furious contortions of her bottom under the excessive lubricity of her wildly excited lasciviousness. She died away in such excess of extasy that she would have fallen on her belly but for the grip I had upon her hips, and the pressure with which I drew back her glorious bottom against my belly. I threw back my head in the agony of delight, and brayed like a donkey as I had done once before when fucking the luscious Frankland, and felt the three pointed entrance to her womb close upon and nibble at the point of my prick so delightfully, just as dear Ellen's had done in the wood. As I came to my senses I spoke to dear mamma, and found that she too had fainted away, and was quite insensible to everything but the convulsive inner movements of her delicious cunt. I withdrew and laid her gently down on her side, bringing a tumbler of water, a sponge, and towel, I opened her splendid thighs, sponged and bathed her cunt, which showed but little of the torrent of sperm I had just poured into it. I then sprinkled her face, and she came to with a deep sigh. Her first utterance was to bless me for the joy I had given her, which was in fact too much, and then she burst into tears and became quite hysterical. I thought it odd that I should have produced the same effect upon her more accustomed and more developed organs as I had done on dear Ellen. I comforted her in my boyish way, and asked how it was that the effect should have been different from anything she had previously experienced with me.

"Ah! my dear boy," she said, with a deep sigh, "you have caused me such extreme sensations that I fear you must have got me with child, you seemed to penetrate my very womb, and to excite me far beyond anything I ever previously remember."

"My loved mamma, can I possibly get a child?"

"Get a child, indeed!" she replied. "Yes, a dozen, with such a great monster of a cock, that so excites us poor women."

I embraced her most tenderly, and said I was so happy to think I should be the father of a child of hers.

"Alas! my dear boy, it may be joy to you, but what a sorrow it will be to me if such should be the case; think how I should lose position in the world if it should be known, and even if by going abroad I could hide my shame from the public, still what shifts and contrivances I should be put to to ensure secrecy; but never mind, my darling, I would run twice such risk to enjoy your person, and secure your affection; you must ever cherish and love me, my Charlie, for I risk good name and fame for you; but now I must be gone, or we shall be sought for; try and sleep a little, my dear boy, for I am sure you need it after your exertions, and remember you must gain strength to renew them this night."

She kissed me lovingly, rose, put on her things and left me to repose. But I could not help thinking of what she had said about fearing that that peculiar fuck in which she had fainted portended fructification. If so, I thought dear Ellen will probably be in the same predicament, for the result was precisely the same with her. I may here observe that mamma's fears became certainties, both in her case and Ellen's. Eventually they both left the country together, when staying would have brought on discovery. And, curiously enough, they were both delivered of daughters on the same day. Of both I was the happy father, although Harry had the credit of Ellen's child, but she herself always asserted to me that it was the delicious fuck in the wood that did the mischief. And from the peculiar effect produced on both mothers on that day, I never had any doubt of the real paternity, besides, the child grew up my very image. Mamma's daughter was superbly developed when she became a young woman. She had even a larger clitoris than Miss Frankland, with which she absolutely deflowered her sister's cousin at the age of fourteen. I may also incidently observe that at the age of fifteen I had both their maidenheads, as far as the male sex was concerned. And Harry and I often fucked them together in every way; and my darling daughter with her long and large clitoris has often fucked my bottom, while I was doing the same to her sister, with Harry below fucking her whom he believed to be his daughter. But this belongs to my latter experiences, and has nothing to do with the present period of my life, though, perhaps, I may be tempted hereafter to enter into all the details of my middle age and later experiences.

Dear reader, pardon me this digression. To resume, I slept soundly for an hour, then rose, and strolled in the garden with Harry, who related to me how he had taken advantage of mamma's occupation to steal into Ellen's room. She had been much afraid, the sly pussey, to allow him to enter again, but when once he got within, and she found it did not hurt her, but the contrary, she got extremely lewd, and they had two splendid fucks. Then stealing along to my door to peep as to how we were getting on, we so excited them again that he had another from behind, while she stooped and peeped all the time, for it was when I was fucking mamma from behind, on my knees, and they concluded it would be our last for the present. When they had brought matters to a finish they separated, and mamma had found Ellen fast asleep.

"But, by Jove, Charlie," said Harry, "how splendid mother fucks, I quite envied you, and I shall never rest until I get into her myself; how gloriously she wriggles her backside, and how lusciously she enjoys fucking; to be sure such a mighty prick as yours is enough to stir up every passion; it astonished, and I think made Ellen more lewd, although she is sure she could never take in such a monster."

I smiled at thinking how easily the very youngest of the fair sex deceives us, but I took care not to let Harry know my opinion.

We re-entered for dinner, and spent a pleasant evening, which was the forerunner to the delights of the night. Mamma came as soon as she thought Ellen fast asleep, which Ellen took very good care should soon be the case. In a moment, she was quite naked, and clasped to my equally naked body. I had been expecting her, and thinking over the delights of our last fuck, so that I was rampant before her arrival. She was equally eager for the fray, and at it we went hammer and tongs, and soon brought the first bout to a close, in mutual "ah's!" and "oh's!" of delight. We soaked for some time in the delicious enjoyment. Then mamma scolded both herself and me for our precipitation, saying that we threw away all the luxury and abandon of fucking when we went at it in such haste; it was in that way mere animal instinct, and wanted all the lascivious delight of lubricity and skill in fucking. She said, now that the edge was taken off our appetites, we must begin again with a mutual gamahuche. She rose first to piddle, and allowed me to see the rush of water from her delicious cunt. Then lighting two more candles, she placed two at the foot of the bed, and two at the head, by which we should both have the advantage of seeing all we were caressing. Then I lay down on my back, and she mounted on me, in reverse, thus bringing her bottom down over my face. I thrust my tongue up her cunt, and licked up the delicious spunk oozing down from the inside. Her piddle had washed all away from the pouting lips. Then taking her charming clitoris in my mouth, I sucked it up to its greatest stiffness. I had thrust three fingers into her cunt, and when I found she had thrust hers into my bottom, I transferred them all into her beautiful pink bum-hole. They were very greasy from my sperm coming down upon them when in her cunt, and as she favoured their entrance by pushing out her bottom, all three slipped in, without, apparently, her thinking it was more than one. I was delighted to see how easily it stretched out, for this gave me great ground to hope that I should be able to manage to get my large pego within, which I was fully resolved upon doing, but it required a little artfulness to do so without raising her suspicions that it was no new road to me. She brought matters to a conclusion much as before, and when re-excited, mamma proposed to teach me a new way, which was by her mounting on me, and staking herself on my standing pego. Like others before her, she did not stoop down upon me until she had made herself spend where she was, while I saved myself for further fucking.

When she died off, she sank on my bosom. I clasped her waist with one arm, sucked the bubby nearest my mouth, and reaching round my other arm, I brought my hand over her bottom to the delightful orifice, first moistening my finger with her spending which was oozing out between the lips of her cunt and my standing prick. I thrust my finger into her bottom-hole, and worked it in and out, to her infinite satisfaction. She cried out in the excess of her lewdness—

"Oh! my dear boy, that is just as my dear husband used to do, and it gave me great pleasure, but not near so much as you do, for your dear prick is twice as large as his was, and fills me with an excess of pleasure which was never approached with him."

All this led up to a superb and lascivious fuck, in which we both died away in mutual extasy, with cries of voluptuousness, and then lay soaking in delight until her weight forced me to beg her to turn on her side. We then had a long sweet chat of love. Turning the talk on her suspicions of having got with child at the morning prayers, I remarked that she had had only one child by her husband, and as he had lived many years after Harry's birth, and from what she said, she had continued to be enjoyed by him, it was, therefore, not probable she would now be got in the family-way.

"That appears probable, my dear boy, but then he took precaution not to get any more children."

"But what precautions could he take, and how did he do so?"

"You are a curious boy, but I shall tell you. He used to continue long at it, making me spend two or three times before he did, and then when he felt it coming he used to withdraw, and his prick being all moist, he would slip it into my bottom, and spend there as soon as ever he got the head of it inside."

"And did that give you any pleasure, mamma?"

"He had excited me, and made me spend several times before he did so; and beyond slight irritation I did not feel much pleasure, as he was generally so near the crisis that he could scarce do more than get its head in when off he went."

"Did he ever get it in altogether—and then did it give you pleasure?"

"Sometimes he did when he had drawn it out of my cunt too soon; in such cases he used to pause until by rubbing my clitoris he got me into a renewed state of lewdness, and then the pleasure was peculiar and great."

"Oh, my dear, mamma, you must let me too fuck you in that way, and then you know we shall get no children."

"My darling Charlie, it is impossible that this great big thing could ever get into that orifice, my late husband's was not half your size, and he had great difficulty unless I had already spent three or four times and relaxed all those parts. I should not dare to let you attempt it."

"Oh, yes my darling mamma, you will let me just get its point in and spend there. I should so like to try. We will fuck two or three times first, and then after the third time I shall frig you till you spend first, and so I shall be ready just to put in the point for you to try how it feels."

"But, my dear boy, the least throb on my part will push it out, unless it is in over the nut, and only look what a size it is. I can hardly grasp it, and although it is so velvety it is quite hard. Oh, the dear fellow, let me kiss it, and then do you fuck me again, my darling."

She bent her body, gave me a delicious suck, then

throwing herself on her back, and opening her beautiful thighs, invited me to mount her. Before doing so I also bent and sucked her charming and well-developed clitoris, until she squealed again with pleasure, and begged me to put it to her. I threw myself on her belly, and with one vigorous shove drove my rampant prick up to the hilt, making her all shake again. She was so hotly wound up that she spent with the single shove, and poured a flood of hot liquid over my delighted prick. I, too, would have gone off in two more thrusts had she not thrown her arms and legs around me, and slipping her hands over my buttocks, held me tight pressed against the pouting and greedy lips of her salacious cunt as if she would shove in ballocks, buttocks and all, if it were possible. So keeping it tightly thrust in up to the lowest hair, which lay all crushed between us, I let her indulge in all the delight of perfect conjunction, responding to her delicious throbbing cunt with powerfull throbs of my own highly excited prick. For more than a quarter of an hour did she lie panting and convulsively sobbing in the perfect extasy of enjoyment. At last she drew my mouth down to hers, and thrust her sweet tongue into my mouth; I sucked it, and her hands relaxing the pressure of my buttocks, against her cunt, I began a slow in and out movement that soon renewed her utmost lubricity. Most actively and divinely did she second me with an art quite her own. Fast and furious grew our movements, until, like all things human, they came to an end in a death-like agony of delight, in which my very soul seemed to take flight, and we lay all unconscious, for I don't know how long, enjoying all those exquisite after-delights which a prick soaking in the cunt of a beautiful and lewd woman so enchantingly confers. When we recovered, we rolled over sideways, and still intertwined and conjoined in the sweet priapic bonds, we lay billing and cooing with all those soft loving murmurings and bitings so befitting such moments. At last both were again ready, and longing for the fight. I proposed the delicious kneeling position. She saw at once my object, and said I was a little traitor, who wanted to surprise her bottom-hole.

"But, my darling boy, it is really impossible."

I embraced, flattered, cajoled, and implored her until at last she promised that if I would engage on honour not to go further, she would try and support the entrance of my prick as far as over the nut, but that I must really withdraw it if it was too painful for her. So these preliminaries being arranged, she got into position. First stooping to lick out her delicious cunt, and give a suck or two at her charming clitoris, I brought my eager prick to the pouting and longing lips of her delicious cunt, and after two or three rubs, thrust it in with a rush that made my belly smack against her glorious backside. We then lay quiet, throbbing mutually in the luxury of voluptuousness. I passed a hand under her belly, and frigging her clitoris quickly, made her come in an extasy of delight. I only gave her time for one or two throbs of my prick, and knowing that nothing so much delights a lecherous woman as quick movements almost immediately after spending, I commenced rapid series of thrusts, shoving my prick well up to the hilt every time, and talking grossly all the while, such as—

"Does not that shove make you quiver? There you have it to the ballocks in your lascivious and delicious cunt," &c.

She grew madly lewd, called me her own dear delightful fucker.

"Yes, yes; I feel it is up to the root. I have it well in, my dear boy. Your dear, great big prick, it kills me—kills—kills me—with—joy. Oh! oh! oh!"

She squealed again with all the lewdness of the most delicious spend. She had hardly gone off, and was yet in all the throes of delight when I, too, feeling I could hold out no longer, suddenly withdrew the reeking shaft, and bringing it to bear against the corrugated and beautiful orifice of her bottom, attempted to introduce it. Notwithstanding the fury of my excitement, I was sufficiently gentle to push in without force, and sheathed it over the nut without difficulty or drawing a murmur from dear mamma, who fulfilled her promise, and did her utmost to help me by pushing out her big bum, and offering no resistance with her sphincter muscles. I was so highly wound up that even if I had promised to be content with the insertion of the head, I could not have gone on further, as the access seized me with such killing sweetness that I melted away, shooting a torrent of sperm far up into her entrails, and then losing all power of even the slightest further thrusts. I suppose it was the long holding back to let mamma spend two or three times that had wrought me up to such a high pitch of nervous excitement that when I spent I seemed to lose all power of further advance. This was the first time I ever felt this momentary impuissance, but it was by no means the last; it generally follows the holding back your spending powers in the fuck that leads to it. The delicious throbbings of dear mamma's luscious cunt, which were repeated in her arms, soon reawakened my momentarily dormant powers. My prick had gone down more than usual, so that it was only a soft half stiffness that ensued, but enough to enable me to give it a forward movement, and it slipped almost imperceptibly in quite as far as he could go before dear mamma had recovered from the extasy of her last discharge. As she came to, I continued convulsively catching my breath, as if I were still in that exquisite sensation of half consciousness. I felt her pass her hand between her thighs, and heard her murmur—

"Why, I declare he is up to the hilt!"

Her gentle touch on my cods, which she took in her hand and fondly caressed, made my prick stiffen sensibly. She felt this, and caressed them more until she made it stand as stiff as ever, still imbedded to the utmost in that delicious bottom, which by its increased throbbings, seemed rather to welcome the stranger than repulse him. I pretended now to recover my full consciousness, and cried out—

"Oh, where am I? I have never known such heavenly joy."

She raised her face up from the pillow—

"Why, you naughty boy, you have actually gone in up to the hilt; ah, you have broken your promise; but I forgive you, only don't move yet."

I assured her I did not know how it got there, as I had spent and lost consciousness as soon as ever his head was within.

Here I throbbed, and was met by as delicious a pressure. I passed my hand round her belly, and found her clitoris stiff and excited. I rubbed with the fingers of the other hand at one of her hard projecting nipples. She soon grew madly lewd, and began a side wriggle on my rampant prick. I lay still, determined to let her passions demand movement of my part. I had not to wait long. She begged me to try a gentle movement, I obeyed, and slowly withdrew but a short way, and as slowly returned. Soon her lubricity got beyond all bounds. She begged me to draw out further and somewhat quicker—then quicker and quicker, until we both were in an excess of furious lust, which knew no bounds. We rushed on to the final crisis with mutual cries of agonised delight; indeed, mamma squealed so loud that I afterwards thought she must have been heard. Her pleasure was of the wildest, and when I poured a flood of sperm up her entrails at the very moment she herself was spending, we both fell forward and fainted away. I was too much lost in extatic joy myself to observe this, but lay long a tightly held prisoner engulphed in that most exquisite joygiving aperture. At last I became aware that mamma had really fainted. So drawing my prick out with somewhat of a good pull, for he was most tightly held, and came out with a flop, I rose and brought some water to mamma. I sprinkled her face, and she opened her eyes, which beamed the intensest love upon me. Her lips murmured something, I put the tumbler to her mouth, she drank with avidity. Then looking at me again with the most loving expression, she said—

"My darling boy, you will kill me with delight. Never—oh, never—have I known such joy. It was too much for me, and I fear I am also injuring you. We must be more moderate in future. Help me up, for I must rise. Your last coup requires me to absent myself for a few minutes."

She rose, threw her robe over her shoulders, and left the room to go to the water closet. I hoped that she would not go into her own room and discover how matters were going on there. Fortunately she was afraid of awakening Ellen, and so prevent our continuing bedfellows for the rest of the night. She returned. I had purified myself in the meantime, and now acted as her *femme de chambre*, and laved all the parts.

"My dear boy, we must not do this again for some time, do you know I have passed blood, and was very sore when relieving myself."

We got again into bed. She would not allow of any further fuckings, but tenderly embracing me, and putting my head on her bosom, we soon fell asleep. She awoke me at dawn with kissing me and feeling my stiff-standing pego. She laid herself on her back, and we had two most delicious fucks without withdrawing. I knew that if I did withdraw she would take herself off. Nevertheless, she took most kindly to the second, as it would be our last until we had another opportunity of meeting. She exerted all her wonderful skill and her movements were of astounding agility. She twined herself round me almost serpent-like. Our mouths and tongues were equally engaged, and the final crisis was beyond description exquisite. I tried hard for a third course, but we had already prolonged our sports to so dangerous an hour, for we could hear them opening the lower window shutters, that she gave me a sweet kiss of thanks and tore herself away. I lay thinking over the joys of that extatic night, and then rose and dressed quickly, as we were to breakfast and then walk home, where we were expected at nine o'clock. However, after breakfast, mamma drew me into her sanctum, a house store-room, to give me some directions.

Of course, no sooner was she there, than pushing her towards the table, I canted up her petticoats over back, and gave her a good fuck, getting in from behind. She yielded with a good grace, notwithstanding her protestations that it was not for that she had come, as if it had been for anything else! Oh! woman, woman! how thou seekest to deceive, even when gaining the very object thou hast in view.

Harry told me they had peeped in and seen what we were at but he was not so ready as me, and had not been able to go and do likewise.

We loitered all too long, and did not get back to school until after ten o'clock. The doctor sternly ordered us to attend him in his sanctum at twelve o'clock. We knew what that meant—a good flogging, and then the doctor enjoying the account of our successes. At twelve o'clock we entered the doctor's room, who followed us immediately after. He scolded us sternly for being late, and said he meant to flog us both well for our idleness and, he had no doubt, debauchery. We knew immediately that he meant to lay on. From time to time he was fond of really seriously flogging some one and we now saw that such was his present intention, although we also knew it would end in an orgie, after we had excited him sufficiently by recounting the details of the fucking which he no doubt felt certain had taken place. He made us all strip, and choosing to take Harry first he made me the horse to flog him on. When all was ready, he began by some real sharp cuts on Harry's backside, and then commenced his remarks.

"So, young gentleman, you have been seducing your cousin, have you?"—whack—whack—whack—"and then making that the excuse for neglecting your school." Whack, whack, whack. "I thought I had formerly whipped out all idea about fucking your cousin." Whack, whack, whack.

Poor Harry writhed in real pain.

"Oh, sir, I'll never do it again without your leave."

"My leave indeed!" Whack, whack, whack.

The doctor now laid on for some time most unmercifully until the revolution of pain turned to lubricity, and Harry's cock began to stand, rapping fiercely at my bottom as he writhed under the sharp infliction of the rod. Upon seeing the expected effect, the doctor relaxed his severity, and changing the rod to his other hand, afterwards only tickled the bottom to keep up the excitement. Taking hold of the standing prick, he said—

"So this is the article that has been doing all the mischief."

He frigged it a little, stooped and gave it a suck.

"Ah, yes, I find it still tastes of cunt, and smells the true odour of it; so you have been at it this morning again. Let me hear how it happened."

Here Harry was let go. The doctor seated himself, Harry stood before him, while the doctor in delight, handled his stiff-standing pego.

"Now, let me hear."

"Well, sir, when Charlie occupied mamma—"

"Oh, that is it, is it?" cried the doctor, "we shall have all that out of him, by and by, go on."

"I slipped into Ellen. She made some difficulty for fear mamma should catch us; but I took her and showed her through the key hole, how she was having Charlie into her. Ellen was astonished at Charlie's immense size, and seeing how easily and delightedly mamma accommodated him, she thought that my smaller size could not hurt her, and she let me do it. But I made her scream and bleed when I got in

far enough to reach her maidenhead. She tried to shake me
off, but I was too firmly seated for that, and I fucked her
then, and again before I withdrew. I laved her cunt and
applied some glycerine, and this morning did it again without
hurting her any more. And she liked it so much that afterwards she would kiss and suck it, and made me spend in
her mouth, and then got me up again for a final go."

"Upon my honour, a very pretty affair," cried the doctor.
"Now suck my prick, as she sucked yours."

This Harry did, till the doctor was rampant. He then
made him cease, but ordered me to mount on Harry's back.
I knew I should catch it sharp, as the doctor was just
excited enough to wish to be more so. And preciously he
gave it me—interpolating questions as to how I had accomplished my wicked ends. I told him it was his own
advice to me to let her see my prick, which I did, and the
bait took. Whack—whack—whack.

"And did you act this innocent sin?"

"Oh, yes! do spare me, sir, and don't lay on so hard."

Whack—whack—whack.

"Spare you, indeed! and how did she fuck?"

"Oh, most splendidly, sir."

Whack—whack—whack.

"How often did you do it?"

"I hardly know, sir; we were at it all night, and again this
morning."

"Did she suck your prick?"

"Oh, yes, sir."

Whack—whack—whack.

"What did she think of it?"

"She said it was the finest she had ever seen, and that I
must keep it for her only."

"Well, that will do, now suck my prick, as she did yours."

He was soon excited up to the top of his bent. He made
Harry take the rod, and belabour his backside, and I had to

stoop over the table, while he fucked and frigged me, repeating all the time the account we had given him of our fucking. After he spent, he dismissed us, having gained his object. Shortly before our Christmas holidays commenced, dear Mrs. Dale informed me, while sleeping with her one Saturday night, that she found from the stoppage of certain things, she was in the family-way by this sad rogue of a fellow, taking my large though at the moment soft and inert instrument into her caressing hand.

"Oh, my darling mamma, is it so indeed?"

My prick rose to bursting point at the very idea, and in an instant I was on her, and we ran a most delicious course, in which both died away in rapturous insensibility. Being thus cooled, mamma began to discuss the probabilities, and what ought to be done, if it should turn out as she feared. She explained to me that as yet she could not speak with certainty, but remembering the fainting on the first night, and the cessation of her monthlies, the nature of which she explained to me, little dreaming that I was perfectly au fait of the whole matter, she had every reason to dread that her fears where too well founded. This would make it necessary for her to go abroad, when she would be so far advanced as to be likely to draw observation. But she said it would not do to distress ourselves about that until we were more certain of the event. However, the very idea nerved me to renewed efforts, and again, and again, we rushed into all the extasies of passion in every form and way, especially did I gamahuche and suck up her precious balm, and in like manner she, too, sucked me until exhausted nature laid us both in the lap of Morpheus. We renewed our delightful pastimes when morning light awoke us after our refreshing slumbers. Several times during the Sunday we adjourned to mamma's bedroom for the same purpose, and again had a glorious night of it before separating on the Monday morning. The following Sunday, after another Saturday night of bliss, we all went over to church, which heavy rain had prevented on the previous week, and after service went to the rectory for luncheon. Here, in course of conversation, Mrs. Dale mentioned that business would require her presence in London for some days, and that she proposed starting on the following Thursday, which was the day after our breaking up for the holidays. She said also that she would take her son with her to London. The doctor here observed that he, too, must go to London, to see a gentleman who had some idea of sending his son to the rectory, and if Mrs. Dale could defer the departure until Saturday, it would be very agreeable to him to be her companion on the journey. This was readily acceded to, and my dear aunt, who guessed to what this tended, and who had herself taken a great fancy to Ellen, and longed to embrace her young charms and gamahuche her, chimed in with a proposal that as the dear girl would thus be left quite alone, she would be most happy if she would accept her invitation to occupy the bedroom that opened out of her own room during Mrs. Dale's absence. The latter, who little dreamt of my connection with her dear niece, and thought that the protection of my aunt would be a safeguard to her, jumped at the invitation, and expressed her gratification and thanks for so kind a consideration on my aunt's part. I have not alluded to Harry all this time, but of course, whenever his mother and I were occupied in amorous alliance, he was equally engaged in the same delicious pastime with Ellen. And, I may add, that once or twice I had seized a favourable opportunity of gratifying the little lecherous creature with what she called a feast of my noble prick. She, of course, was delighted at my aunt's proposition as she at once foresaw how she would have me all to herself for more than a week. A single glance from her explained all this; and when, on leaving, she found an opportunity of taking my hand, her pressure of it was most eloquent. So all parties were delighted, for Harry, when we got together alone said—

"By Jove, Charlie, I am so jolly glad; I'll bet you anything

I'll fuck my mother before I come back. You know how I long to be in the delicious cunt that bore me; the moment I heard she meant to take me with her, my cock stood ready to burst."

My uncle, too, who also longed to fuck Mrs. Dale, had his intentions in that direction favoured by the arrangement concluded. The following night, when I was in bed with aunt and him, in the interval of a charming little orgie, and after fucking me while I was in aunt's bottom, and for the moment he could do no more, the conversation turned on the coming journey. He expressed the pleasure he felt at the opportunity it gave him of indulging in a long desired object. The lecherous old fellow also alluded to a future opportunity it would give him of enjoying the younger charms of the niece.

"Of course, you and my dear wife between you will break her in to allow of any action on my part; and, by the way, my dear, I would suggest that you should surprise Charlie in the act, and tear them asunder in pretended rage—that Charlie should seize you, and say he would make you by force a participator in the act, on the pretence of shutting you up for finding fault: you must break from his arms, and fly to your own bed, he must catch you as you try to enter it, and push his great big cock into you, on which you must cry for help, and call upon Ellen to come to your succour; she will come, but I do not judge her right, if she will not rather assist Charlie, by holding you, than otherwise. You must afterwards appear much offended; but it may be safely left to the influence of Charlie's great prick to reconcile you to the incest, then relaxing, as if gained over by it, you can join in their sports."

Thus this admirable man, with his great knowledge of the world and sex, gave us excellent advice, which, as I shall state in the sequel, we followed pretty exactly. Meanwhile aunt, excited by expectation, had taken my prick in her mouth, and sucked it into firmness, then mounting upon me, she began such an exciting action, wriggling her magnificent backside, that it fired my uncle anew. Finding his prick stood sufficiently stiff, he knelt between my legs, and greatly to the satisfaction of my darling aunt, gave her the double pleasure of two pricks fucking her at the same time, one before and the other behind.

My guardian had desired that I should continue with my uncle during the holidays, and I was to leave him altogether at the end of the next half. I did not know his object at the time, but I found that he himself went down to my mother, and stayed for a fortnight, paying great attention to Miss Frankland. He announced his wish that my sisters should go to a first-rate finishing school in London in the summer, and seeing Miss Frankland look somewhat disappointed, he sought an interview with her, and laid himself and his fortune at her feet; expressing a wish that if she accepted him, their marriage should take place on her separation from her pupils. This was too good an offer to be refused, and after the usual grimace of being perfectly unprepared for such a proposal, and desiring to have a day or two to consider it, she accepted the offer. I at once anticipated immense gratification from this connection. I should naturally, when in London, have every opportunity of enjoying that adorable creature, and it will be seen in the fourth volume of these memoirs, to what delicious orgies this connection led. You may be sure that my loved mistress, the adorable Benson, and the no less lascivious Egerton, would welcome so glorious a creature as Miss Frankland, at that time become Mrs. Nixon, and how the Count's eyes glistened, when he beheld her in all the majesty of her superb and hairy form; how the two women gamahuched her splendid clitoris, and how the Count and I strove which should most fully satisfy her lascivious and lustful passions. But all this will be seen in its proper place in the sequel.

Meanwhile the day arrived for the departure of uncle and Mrs. Dale, with Harry. As the coach passed through our village, Mrs. Dale drove over bringing Ellen with her, to leave her at the rectory, as arranged. All the proprieties were duly observed. They departed, Harry going outside, with only the doctor and Mrs. Dale in the interior, I squeezed my uncle's hand, and gave him a knowing look, which he returned, with a meaning wink—and off they went. When we returned to the house, and aunt took Ellen up to the room adjoining her own, with which there was a door of communication, and which, I have before observed, had been made use of by uncle on more than one occasion. When they came downstairs, with kind consideration, for she could see by the protrusion in my trousers the state I was in, aunt said—

"My dear, I have some household duties to arrange, so you must excuse me; meanwhile Charlie will show you our grounds, and amuse you for an hour or two. When luncheon is ready I shall order the large bell to be rung for you."

Ellen had not yet removed her bonnet, and taking up her shawl, we sallied out. You may be sure we lost no time in reaching the summer house, already known to you as arranged for and dedicated to the service of Venus. A fire was always kept laid, which I immediately lighted, but as it was a bright sunny day, and the place looked south, it was not at all cold. While I was occupied at the fire, Ellen threw off her bonnet and shawl, and undid her belt—she wore no stays. I seized her in my arms, and gently laid her on the couch—her petticoats were freely canted up, showing her beautiful belly and now more fully fledged cunt. I stooped and gamahuched her at once. She was so excited that in two minutes she sighed deeply, pressed my head down to the lips of her cunt, and gave down her sweet and balmy sperm. I myself was already so rampant that not waiting to lick it up, I brought my huge pego to the charming orifice, and plunged in one effort up to the hilt, quite taking away her breath. But she recovered herself in an instant, and with all the energy of her younger lubricity, quickly brought us both to the grand final extasy,

in which soul and body seem to die away in a joy too great
for poor humanity to bear. We remained locked in each other's
embrace, and lost to all around for some time. On coming to
our senses I rose, and said we must go to work more lasciviously the next time. The fire having burnt up, and the room
being small, it was already of a pleasant temperature. So
begging Ellen to strip, I threw off my own clothes, and we
quickly stood in all the beauty of nature, admiring each other.
Some delicious preliminaries preceded our next encounter,
which we procrastinated till passion could no longer be restrained, and again we died away in all the raptures of
satisfied lust, and sank once more into the soft languor of the
after-enjoyment. Next we had a mutual gamahuche, and then
a final fuck for the present, as it was time to dress and be
ready when called to luncheon. As soon as our toilets were
finished, I took her on my knee, and told her how I should
steal along to her bedroom at night, so that she must not
lock her door. I told her also that we must be as quiet as
possible, as aunt slept in the next room. She was delighted
with the prospect of having me all to herself for the whole
night, naïvely telling me that I gave her so much more pleasure than Harry did, that I seemed to fill her whole body with
a joy almost too intense, and now that she was to have me
every night, she hoped her aunt would stay away for a month.
Here the dear creature threw her arms round my neck, and
kissing me, thrust her sweet little tongue into my mouth. You
may be sure I reciprocated, and putting a hand up her
petticoats, and a finger up her charming little cunt, was just
about to turn her on the sofa, when my aunt opened the
door, and stopped further proceedings. She pretended not to
see Ellen's confusion, hoped I had amused her, and told us
to return to the house, as luncheon was ready. We, of course,
obeyed. With sharpened appetites, produced by our late warm
exercise, we indulged in a plenteous meal, aunt taking care to
ply me with Champagne, for which, as may well be imagined,

she had her object. She afterwards ordered me to my room, to do the daily task the doctor had set for me and which, as she said, she was to see to the doing of—giving me a sly wink.

"Ellen, my dear," she added, "you must keep up your practice at the piano daily, for an hour and a half at least."

She thus separated us. I went to my room, lay down, and fell fast asleep, but in about half an hour, was awakened by the warm embrace of my glorious and wantonly lustful aunt. She stooped down, and taking my limp prick in her mouth, rapidly sucked it into its accustomed firmness. As soon as that was accomplished, she begged me to rise and undress. She herself had come only in a loose morning dressing-gown, which she instantly threw off, and jumped on my bed, where she lay stark naked, in all the splendid development of her superb form. I was naked in a jiffey, but knowing she would want some extensive fucking, I threw myself upon her cunt, and gamahuched her until she spent twice before I mounted upon her, and introduced my large tool into her longing cunt. Here, also, I played with her, and did not spend myself until she had twice given down her own contribution. This encounter was on her belly, with her magnificent legs twisted above my loins for a fulcrum to her splendid action, for few women could equal her in the delicious wriggle of her glorious backside. After we had soaked for some time in all the extasies of the after-languour. I withdrew, to place her on her hands and knees for the next bout, but took advantage of her position to gamahuche her again into spending twice before I withdrew my insidious tongue. Then turning round, and gazing in rapture on that most noble and massive bottom, which, as I have before remarked, I never saw equalled by any woman, I stooped, and closely embraced and kissed its divine orifice, tickling her into wild excitement by thrusting my tongue therein, so much so that she begged me to fuck her at once. I mounted behind, her hand passed under her belly and guided me into her throbbing hot and longing cunt. I gave one violent lunge, and sent my prick at the first thrust up to the hilt. This so excited the dear creature that in one or two delicious wriggles on my stationary prick, and with a pressure that seemed as if it would nip it off, she spent profusely, squealing all the time like a rabbit. I was very glad to give her so many discharges, without myself being forced to spend, for I wished to be able to do my duty by Ellen at night. Aunt lay for several minutes panting and throbbing on my prick most deliciously, until I could no longer bear to be inactive, although the pleasure of looking down on the glorious and palpitating orbs below me had given me the greatest satisfaction. But now stooping down upon her, I passed one hand under to excite her clitoris, and with the other took hold of one of her beautiful large and hard bubbies, and began manipulating its nipples—a proceeding most powerfully exciting to dear auntie. It awoke all her lust and the dear lascivious creature again spent before I was ready to follow suit. The pause that followed allowed my excitement to subside a little, and enabled me to hold out until her lust recovered its wonted energy. She again, with her pressures and movements, soon compelled me to more rapid action, but this time I determined to enjoy the exquisite delights of her delicious bottom-hole. So when she became very hot, I suddenly withdrew, and, happily, hitting at once on the delicious orifice, plunged at the first thrust up to the cods, taking dear aunt's breath away, but she instantly recovered, and loving sodomy to her heart's core, I could not have done anything better suited to her libidinous passions. It was glorious to see the energy with which she met and responded to my thrusts, her superb buttocks working with surprising energy, and giving me, at each stroke, when I buried my prick to the hilt, the most exciting pressures. Both being so lustfully excited, matters were not long in coming to the final extasy. I felt as if my whole soul was poured into her, when with loud cries of the liveliest enjoyment, I spent with fury, in the very heart

of her entrails. She was perfectly overcome with delight, and
sank senseless on her belly, dragging me down with her, for
her grip by the sphincter was too strong to let anything out
that was within. We both became insensible to everything but
the delicious death-like languor of the after-enjoyment. We
lay long in this trance of joy, and when dear auntie came to
her senses, she begged me to rise, as she must go downstairs. I did so, and when she rose from the bed, she took me
in her loving arms, and kissing me tenderly, thanked me for
the enormous pleasure I had given her, and said no one in the
world was my equal, and that I ought to thank her much, that
she allowed any one else to participate in my exquisite power
of fuck. She gathered up her gown, and left me to dress. I
soon was downstairs, and found Ellen, who looked as if she
expected me to find an opportunity to fuck her at once. But
after the encounters I had already had, both with her and
with aunt, though I had kept myself from excess with the
latter, I felt no inclination to press matters again to a conclusion, especially seeing that I intended passing the night
with her. So assuring her we should be likely to be caught if
imprudent and so lose all chance of night work, she was
satisfied to be quiet and reasonable. Aunt coming in, we spent
the afternoon in pleasant conversation, and a walk together in
the garden. After dinner I fell sound asleep on the sofa. The
two women, each with the same object, left me to my deep
repose, and only awoke me when it was time for all to retire.
Thus refreshed, I was all ready for the night's work before
me. I allowed half an hour to elapse, that all the house might
to be in their bedrooms, and then, with merely a loose dressing-gown on, I stole along to dear Ellen's room, opened the
door and entered. She was already in bed, impatient for my
arrival; she had left both lights burning, as well as a cheerful
blaze from a good fire. I dropped my robe, and was in an instant stark naked, and in her longing arms. Under our mutual
impatience, our first was a rapid course. Then followed a long

enjoyment of the after-languor, and then a more prolonged and rapturous embrace. After soaking in bliss for some time, we rose, and I posed her before the fire, gazing delightedly on all her young charms. The hair on her cunt had become much more developed than before, her bosom too was filled out, even her hips and bottom seemed enlarged, doubtless owing to the fucking she had had since I first knew her, which naturally hastened her ripening into womanhood. I grew very excited by this inspection of her increasing charms, and determined to have a fuck on the rug before the fire. In order to enjoy it the more, I drew forward a cheval glass, projected it forward, and lying down, directed her to move it until I was satisfied I could see all the play of her bottom in the position I meant to fuck her. So lying down on my back, I made her stride across my head and settle down on her knees, and bringing forward her delicious little cunt over my mouth, I gamahuched her until she had twice given down her balmy essence. Then she shifted her position lower down, until just above my prick, which by this time was rampant with desire. I guided its point to the rosy-lipped orbit, and bringing her own weight to bear upon it, she sank delightfully impaled upon the upright stake. I made her rise and fall a few times, that I might enjoy the sight of its entrance and exit. Then gently drawing her down upon me, I folded one arm round her slender waist, and turning my head, found that the cheval glass, inclined forward, reflected as it were from above her beautiful bottom and back, and of course her cunt stretched to the utmost with my huge prick, and above it the sweet little corrugated pink aperture of her bottom. With my free arm I embraced one hip, and bringing my hand round, moistened it with the plenteous spunk of her cunt, and insinuated a finger into the smaller abode of bliss. Her excitement grew furious, and knew no bounds. The action of her backside was glorious to see reflected in its active risings and fallings. I let her do all the work, which enabled me to hold back

my own, until she approached a second discharge, when the
heat of her cunt seemed to fire me with additional powers,
and the action of both our backsides became fast and furious,
and soon brought down the extatic discharge, which instantly
laid us low, panting with all the wild passions we had just
allayed. We lay long locked in each other's arms in the extasy
of blissful enjoyment. Then rising, we embraced tenderly, and
retook us to bed. I would have excited her and myself to another effort, but she begged off, saying that she felt quite exhausted and overcome with the day and night's work we had
already enjoyed. Indeed, I did not wonder at it, for I had
made her spend seven or eight times more than myself. Nor
did I regret her resolution, as I knew the morning would bring
my aunt into the field, and then the two would try my powers
to the utmost.

We slept profoundly, and morning was already advanced
before we awoke. From a displaced chair I saw that aunt had
been in to look at us, so I knew she was on the watch. I threw
the clothes off dear Ellen that I might gaze on all her young
charms. The want of covering awoke her. She lovingly looked
up at me, and throwing her arms round my neck as I bent
over her, drew my head down to hers, and impressed a loving
kiss on my lips. Our tongues interlaced—a hand slipped down
and encircled my rampant and throbbing prick. I turned,
and placing my knees between her legs, was about to penetrate love's bower when the door leading to my aunt's room
flew open. My aunt entered, gave a scream of surprise—well
acted—and cried out—

"Good gracious! What do I see? Who would have thought
it—"

And, apparently to save Ellen, she rushed forward, seized
me by the arm, and with a certain degree of willingness on my
part, drew me out of bed, saying—

"I am horrified beyond measure. How dare you commit
such a sin and crime as to seduce a young girl under my

care? Cover yourself up, sir, directly, and go to your own room."

I boldly declared I would do no such thing; on the contrary, as she had spoiled my sport with Ellen, I was determined she should pay for it herself.

"How dare you talk to me, you dreadful boy?"

"Not dreadful at all, dear aunt, look at this poor dumb thing, and see how he longs to be into you."

Upon this I seized her in my arms as if to throw her on the bed. She made a pretended struggle, during which she gave a tender squeeze to my rampant prick. Then, breaking from me, she fled to her own room, pretending to endeavour to shut the door in my face but taking care to give way and hasten towards her bed. I caught hold of her as she bent forward as if to get into it, and canting up her chemise, the only article of dress she wore, I was into her longing and luscious cunt from behind up to the hilt in one thrust. She gave a subdued scream, and called to Ellen to come and prevent me from violating her. Ellen came, but wisely would only look on while I worked away manfully.

"Ellen, why don't you pull him away—he is ravishing me—and oh, horror!—committing incest."

She pretended to struggle greatly, but cleverly did so to her own profit, by wriggling her backside so as to send me further up into her cunt.

"Oh, Ellen, Ellen, do help me."

"Ah, no," said Ellen, "I shall let him do it, and then you cannot tell upon me."

My aunt seemed greatly distressed at this, and actually managed to shed tears, then buried her face in the bed as if in despair, but all the time most actively seconding me. As the crisis drew near, she raised her head, and said—

"Heaven pardon me, this mere simple schoolboy is exciting me to such pleasure as I never before felt."

She then gave way to all her lubricity, and we brought

matters to a crisis in the utmost extasy of enjoyment. Aunt's head sank on the bed, while the rapturous inward pressures of her cunt soon began to raise my prick to its pristine vigour. She felt its throbs and responded to them, but no doubt thinking that an immediate repetition would betray our previous intimacy, she turned her face and body suddenly round, and completely unseated me, my prick coming out with a plop. She began again to weep, women can do so at pleasure, and to scold me for the dreadful crime I had committed; to do so to her was incest—here followed sob upon sob. I threw my arms round her neck, and kissing her tears away, laid all the blame on that rampant fellow—taking her hand and placing it on my still stiff prick. She drew her hand away quickly, but not before she had given it a gentle squeeze. She told me I was a dreadful boy, and that I must go away and leave her and Ellen to think over what could be done in such an awful dilemma.

Here Ellen came forward, and tenderly kissing her begged her not to send me away.

"I do so love him, dear madam, and I do so long to have him now—it was so exciting to see him having you, that I shall die if you don't let me have him now."

"Dreadful! dreadful!" said aunt. "Why, I thought I was just in time to save you."

"Oh, no, he had slept with me all night, and has often had me before, but he was not the first who had me, so that there was no violation nor seduction."

"Then you must have seduced him, you wicked minx, for a more innocent boy never was known."

Poor Ellen, confounded at the accusation, repelled it as untrue, and said she knew well enough who seduced me.

Aunt for the moment felt this as a home thrust, for be it remembered, she fancied she had had my maidenhead.

"What do you mean by that? I insist upon you speaking out."

Ellen gave way and said it was Mrs. Dale who first had me.
"She had accidentally seen how powerfully Charlie was
armed, and then could not resist teaching him how to use his
weapon. I saw them doing it, and hence I longed for it myself.
Look, dear madam, what a noble one it is. I am sure, if you
had known of it, you could not yourself have resisted having
it, try it, try it once more, and I am sure you will forgive us,
and share our joys."

I seconded this good advice. Aunt seemed to be afraid of
me, and jumped into bed. While she was on her hands and
knees I also jumped up, and catching her round the waist, held
her fast until I could also kneel behind her and bring my
prick into play. With all her apparent attempt at resistance
everything was done in such a way as to facilitate rather than
prevent matters going forward. Of course I was in her in a moment, and then remained quiet for a few minutes to let her
enjoy her inward pressures for which she was so famous. She
had buried her head in the pillow, crying out—

"It is dreadful!—it is dreadful!"

Ellen came and leant over the bed embracing her, and
telling her not to resist, but to take it in freely, and then she
was sure it would give her the utmost pleasure.

"It is that which horrifies me, my dear, I never felt anything
so exquisite in my life before, but then think of the sin—with
my own nephew! it is quite an incestuous connection."

"What does that matter, dear aunt? for I shall call you aunt
too, you are so loveable and so beautiful. Oh, it was such a
pleasure to see him doing it to you and you are so gloriously
fine a woman, I longed to be a man to have you."

She had embraced aunt's splendid bubbies, than which
nothing could more please her, and now she begged to be
allowed to suck one. Aunt gave way, and was delighted. She
slipped the hand next to Ellen down to her charming cunt—
Ellen opened her legs—Aunt's fingers began frigging her.

"Ah, my dear, how I loved to embrace my own sex at your

age, our tongues acted instead of men, and I could still delight in a fine fresh one like this, it would almost reconcile me to what this bad wicked boy is doing."

"Oh, that would be charming!—do let us do it at once. Charlie can withdraw for a moment while I get under you, and while you lick me I can excite you and see the glorious work above me."

"You tempt me much, my dear girl, but what would your aunt say if she knew?"

"But she never will know," said Ellen, who was all the time arranging herself on the bed.

Aunt moved aside to allow Ellen to get under her, who then begged aunt to throw off her chemise that both their bodies might be in close contact. Aunt was longing to do so, yet made some grimaces about it. She at length complied, and striding across Ellen, threw herself with avidity on the delicious young cunt below, and began to gamahuche her *à mort.* I instantly resumed my position. Ellen guided my prick into aunt's burning cunt, then frigged aunt's clitoris, and worked a finger in my fundament, while aunt was so delightfully gamahuching her. We all rapidly came to the grand finale, with an excess of lubricity rarely equalled. We were all somewhat exhausted by this bout, and, as it was getting late, we rose. Aunt pretended to forgive my violating her for the pleasure I afterwards afforded her. She embraced Ellen tenderly, and said she had so enjoyed her person she hoped to renew such a delight. Then taking hold of my prick she kissed it and sucked it until it stood upright, and said—

"I don't wonder, my dear, at your having it when once you had seen it, and I envy Mrs. Dale the pleasure of having first enjoyed such a monstrous thing. If I had known he was so wondrously provided, I doubt if I could have resisted the temptation to teach him how to make use of it myself—my only wonder is how such a little thing as you have got could ever take it in."

Ellen laughed, and said that her cousin Harry had opened the way, or she doubted if ever she could have admitted it, but I was so gentle while getting in, and when once in, it filled up every crevice so deliciously, that she should grieve much if she were refused access to it in future.

"So, dear aunt, I hope you will let him do it to us both. I can do to you what you have just done to me, because before we had him and Harry, aunt and I used to amuse ourselves in that way. Aunt is immense in that particular, she could put it a little way into me, and gave me great pleasure, and she said that I sucked it better than either her late husband or any of half-a-dozen schoolfellows who used to amuse each other; so, dear aunt, you must let me do it to you while Charlie is in me, and then you will do it to me while he is in you. Only fancy how nice it will be."

"Oh, you dear little coaxer, you are enough to seduce an angel."

So all was arranged that Ellen should come from her room and I from mine, and meet in aunt's bed at night. We did so meet, and a most glorious eight days we spent. I showed aunt that I could get into Ellen's bottom-hole, and thereby gave her immense pleasure, and with more reason the same result would occur with her. She gave an apparently reluctant consent, and, that done, there was no bridle to the utmost lubricity that the most wanton lust could devise. Aunt took immensely to Ellen, and gamahuched her *à mort*, while the other repaid her in kind. I did not regret this for it relieved me from too excessive work. Thus we passed a most delightful eight days before the absent ones joined us. Both uncle and Harry had succeeded in their desires. From each I had the fullest details, but as their stories would in some particulars repeat themselves, I shall relate the events in a connected narrative.

Uncle and Mrs. Dale had the inside of the coach to themselves, Harry riding outside. Uncle began by praising Harry;

and then reverting to the time he was first sent to the rectory, and the note Mrs. Dale sent with him; he asked, not without a knowing smile, if the intimacy she had formerly feared had been at all renewed, because he had observed that Harry appeared worn and pale on his return on the Mondays, and was dull and stupid that day. Mrs. Dale seemed somewhat alarmed at hearing of this, probably she began to think that something might have occurred between the cousins while she was busied with me, uncle observed her uneasiness, and, guessing the cause, said—

"My dear Mrs. Dale, if anything has taken place, and anything comes of it, I am a man of the world, and you may rely upon my assistance and discretion to take such steps as may tend to keep it from the knowledge of the world."

She thanked him, and said she would be glad to accept his aid if any unfortunate event should have happened—but she hoped not.

Uncle saw that her fears were excited, so he held onto the subject, so at last she avowed the she feared there might have occurred some passages between the two cousins, for she had foolishly trusted that all thought of that had gone out of their heads, and she might not have taken such precautions as she ought to have done.

"Well, my dear madame, my services are at your disposal in case of any necessity, I am not in reality strait-laced, although, in my position, I am obliged to appear so. I feel certain that my experience would be able to suggest the best way of hushing up the scandal if such should be likely to occur."

Mrs. Dale was profuse in thanks, and the doctor became warmer in his discourse, saying that for such a woman as herself, whom he had long admired and coveted, he would do anything.

"For, my dear madam, though I am in the church, something of the old Adam still adheres to me, and the sight and touch of one who has so charmed me as you have done makes a young man of me again."

Here his arm glided round her charming little waist. He drew her to him, and with some coyness and words of refusal, she yielded her lips to his embrace. His other hand, lifting up her petticoats, sought to feel her beauteous cunt. Again resistance of hand and tongue, but a yielding for all that, and the doctor soon got possession of her lovely cunt. Finding her large and fine clitoris in a state of stiffness, he knew that her passions were excited. So opening her legs, he got between them down on his knees, and as he previously unbuttoned his trousers in readiness and the fresh cunt stimulating his powers, he pulled out his prick fully erected, and quickly established himself up to the hilt within, the lady up to the last declaring she could not allow him, but wriggling her bottom to perfection as soon as she felt the doctor's very fine prick working within her. She then hugged and seconded him, kissing and tongueing to his heart's desire. They soon brought things to the extatic conclusion, to the great satisfaction of both parties.

Of course, after this there was no difficulty in arranging for a comfortable meeting in London. Indeed, it was resolved that they should lodge in the same house and have contiguous apartments. On their arrival in town they put up at one of those large lodging houses in Norfolk Street, Strand, and were fortunate in finding the first-floor bedrooms vacant. The house was a double one, or rather two houses opening into each other. The doctor's bedroom was in the front, and a former door of communication with the back room was locked on one side and bolted on the other. Mrs. Dale took the back room, from whence opened a small room with a bed in it, where Harry was lodged. The doctor had thus easy access when the lady chose to withdraw the bolt on her side. After consultation it was thought more advisable that she should go into the doctor's room, so that Harry might not by any possibility hear any love exclamations that might happen to escape them in the excess of their amorous amusements. Of course, the doctor, who knew all about Harry's great desire to fuck his mother, and that he meant to do so by one way or another in London, communicated his intention of having Mrs. Dale into sleep with him that night, and, therefore, begged Harry to defer his attempt until after the first night, and then the doctor would aid him in his efforts.

The wily doctor fully intended, after Harry had perfectly succeeded, to become the future companion of their incestuous intercourse. Harry's bedroom door had one of those old-fashioned brass locks that were screwed onto the inside of the door, with a brass covering for the bolt at the side—not morticed as is now usual. Mrs. Dale locked her son in after he retired to bed. Harry noticed the circumstance and smiled to think how easily he could foil her but as he had promised the doctor to make no attempt on his mother that night, he went to bed and slept soundly. Next day he provided himself with a turn-screw and a small phial of sweet oil. When mamma was busy at cards, he slipped upstairs and easily unscrewed the brass receiver of the bolt, he oiled the screws and worked them in and out until they went freely and then screwed the covering on again, and felt secure of entering mamma's room whenever he pleased. It had been combined between the doctor and him that by means of gamahuching and frigging, mamma should be put into a state of great excitement without allowing her to be satisfied, so that her passions might be in favour of being fucked, no matter by what prick. For this purpose the doctor was to keep her with him till dawn. At night Harry watched through the key hole, and when he saw his mother pass into the doctor's room, he at once unscrewed the covering, shot back the bolt, and screwed the cover on again. He was thus all ready for any event, and if his mother was astonished at his entrance, he could say he found the door open, and she must have forgotten to lock it. Thus prepared he went to bed and slept soundly. He was awake before seven o'clock, and gently opening the door a little, he could see by the opposite open door, and the the light in the doctor's room, that mamma had not yet left him. He drew on his woollen socks, and sitting where the light flashed through the key hole, awaited his mamma's return, which occurred very shortly after. The shutting off the light by closing the door of communication told him that she had returned to her own room. He heard her sit down on the pot, and the force of the flow of water proved how healthy she was. He heard her rustle into bed. Then throwing off his dressing-gown and socks he opened the door and approached his mother's bed. Being awake, she instantly saw him in the half-daylight that came from the unshuttered window.

"Harry! What on earth brings you here, and how did you open the door?"

"I heard you moving, dear mamma, I could not sleep for the cold. I got up and tried the door, it was not locked, you must have omitted to turn the bolt, but I should have rapped and called to you, if it had not been open. I want you to let me get warm in your nice warm bed, and you will cuddle your poor Harry—will you not, dear mamma?"

"If you will be quiet, and speak lower, for the doctor may hear you, you may come in, and if you turn your back, I will warm you."

Harry lost no time in lying down by her side, and being really very cold, and even shivering, he was glad enough to do as she bid him, and turn his back, and cuddle his bottom into his mother's belly. She said—

"Poor boy, he is indeed cold, now go to sleep in mamma's arms."

Of course, he had no such intentions. Speedily getting warm, he turned his face to mamma, and whispered, in the same tone she used—

"Oh, how I love my beautiful mamma."

Pressing his belly against hers, and letting her feel his prick standing against her mons Veneris.

"Harry! What do you mean by embracing me in that way— don't you know I am your mother, sir?"

He had seized with one hand her beautiful firm bubbies,

and was evidently in full amorous excitement, as she could feel by the stiff pego pushing against her mount of Venus.

"My darling mamma, if you knew how much I love you and how I have longed to embrace your beautiful body."

"Go along, you impudent boy, do you not know it would be sinful to indulge in such sentiments with your mother—leave me directly."

"Oh, no, mamma, I can't, indeed, my own mamma. I mean to possess you, what harm can there be in returning to whence I came."

Here he transferred his hand from her bubby to her splendid mons Veneris, and showed what his words meant. She pretended to be very angry, and endeavoured to push him away, but he held her round the waist with his other arm too well.

"Desist this instant, or I shall cry out."

She really appeared very angry but, nevertheless, did not excite a whisper during all the colloquy before or after. Harry now thought of his best argument.

"Why do you attempt to repulse me in this way, dear mamma? Why should you not let me enjoy your person as much as you like Charlie to do it?"

She gave a start at this home thrust.

"What do you say, you naughty boy? and where did you hear such a falsehood as that? is that one of your friend Charlie's inventions, after all the kindness I have shown him?"

"My darling mamma, Charlie never opened his lips to me on the subject. I speak from what I saw with my own eyes."

"What do you mean? Tell me directly."

"Well, my loved mamma, do you remember the first Saturday night that Charlie and I slept at home: after retiring to my room, I was obliged to go downstairs to the water closet, where I went in my stockings, and without a light, not to disturb you. I was coming up again, when a sudden flash of light shone out in the upper passage. Mounting the stairs, and when my head was on a level with the upper floor, I saw you going towards Charlie's room. I went into my own, but left the door open to see when you would return; finding you did not come back, I crept softly along the passage, until I came to the turning that led to Charlie's room. The light shone through the key hole. I quietly approached. You know the bed exactly faces the door—and there, my darling mamma, I saw you initiate Charlie into what was to him a previously unknown pleasure. Oh! my beloved mother, the sight of your naked charms, of the delicious way in which you were giving him his first lesson in love, maddened me with desire. I was almost tempted to come in upon you and violate you, if you would not consent. It was in that state I remembered that Ellen was asleep in your bed. I ran there, and throwing off the little I had on, I lay down beside her, and began feeling her private parts. She awoke and said—

" 'Dear aunt, do you wish me to do the same to you?'

"Her hand passed down to my erect member, she gave a cry of astonishment. I whispered it was only me.

" 'Oh! you must leave me directly. Aunt can only have gone to the water closet, and will be back directly.'

"She was not to be pacified until I convinced her that there was no chance of your speedy return, so I was obliged to bring her along to Charles's door; we saw you quite naked, rising and falling on the enormous weapon that Charles has. I never before saw it erect and could scarcely believe my eyes; nor was it less wonderful the way in which you so charmingly took it in. It greatly excited Ellen, as well as me. We returned to your room—the fire still burned. I laid her down on the rug before it, and took her maidenhead. She had seen how Charlie's monstrous affair went easily into you, and felt how much less mine was, so she never dreamt of it hurting her, and she let me get fairly within the lips; then, while making her spend, I suddenly thrust it through all impediments, and the affair was done; she gave a scream, as it hurt her, but I had shut the door and none of you heard it. I let her sleep after this, and did not do it again till morning. The next night we again watched your delicious proceeding. Ellen was less sore, and we repeated your example several times. She continues to this day to wonder at the enormous size of Charlie's tool, and is surprised at your taking it in so easily. But, oh, my mother, how my passions have been excited by your glorious charms. What is Ellen compared with you? She did very well to relieve my agony of desire to possess you, when I knew you were better occupied, and that I could not do so—but that is all. It is you, and you alone, my beloved mother, whom I adore, and I wildly long to possess this dear and magnificent cunt beneath my hand."

Mrs. Dale was perfectly flabbergasted at this recital.

"You abominable boy, how dared you to follow me, and be a spy upon your mother, and to make it known to Ellen, too; doubtless you have been boasting of it, and telling others."

"No, indeed, mamma, Ellen and I were on oath that we would never reveal to any mortal the delicious sight we had seen—so you see, darling mamma, that you can fully trust your own boy. Oh, do let me do it; feel how my poor thing throbs."

Here I must give you Harry's own account of what took place.

"I took her hand with very little resistance, and I could feel her fingers gently clasped my prick, before she withdrew her hand.

" 'But no—it cannot be—it would be incest.'

"She twisted her body round, so that her magnificent bottom came against my belly. As she turned, I slipped my hand down, and laid hold of her shift, so that in turning, it left her bottom bare, and sticking out against me. I lost not an instant, and before she had quite settled down, I brought my stiff-standing pego against her delicious cunt from behind, and as it was reeking from her previous spendings produced

by the rector's gamahuching, I plunged it at one shove as
far as her buttocks against my belly would allow, at the same
time dropping my hand from her waist to her cunt, so that
when she sprang forward, as if to turn me out, I met her
clitoris, it was quite stiff, showing her to be really in a state
of amorous excitement. This attack on the clitoris made her as
quickly move back, which double movement thoroughly engulphed me. I lost no time in proceeding to the most active
movements in and out. This was too much for her, she could
not resist entering into the encounter with all the force of her
passions, and we ran a very rapid course, ending in the most
extatic delight, and with sighs of joy we lay clasped together
in all the delicious after-languor. I could feel by her exquisite
internal pressures that her lust was not yet alleviated, and
this nerved me to fresh efforts. After a feigned resistance, dear
mamma passed her hand behind her, and putting it on my
buttocks, assisted in sending me further in at each home
thrust. We were longer this bout, and enjoyed it more. After
the usual indulgence in the after-joy, she turned, and embracing me tenderly said—

" 'Oh, my dear child, this is very wrong, but very delicious.
You must be very discreet, my dear Harry, for if it were
known it would disgrace us both for ever.'

" 'My sweet mamma, do not fear; have you ever seen anything like indiscretion in the last six weeks, although I was
madly longing for you? Oh, kiss me, my beloved mother.'

"The sweetest of kisses followed, our tongues met, her hand
wandered; already she found my pego standing.

" 'My darling, I must kiss it, it is so much more developed
than I could have expected, and as hard as iron.'

" 'Not as large as Charlie's, mamma.'

" 'That is true, my dear; but it is the stiffness, and not the
size, that gives the real pleasure. Of course, when both are
combined, as with Charlie, they are irresistible.'

"Meanwhile I was feeling her cunt: her clitoris, which you know is largely developed, stood stiff.

" 'Mamma, darling, what a size this is. Ellen told me you could put it into her.'

" 'Oh! the bad girl, to tell tales out of school.'

" 'Never mind, mamma, I must suck it while you play with mine.'

"I turned on my back with my heels up—mamma lay down upon my belly reversed. I sucked her clitty while frigging her cunt, and she sucked my prick until we both spent, and each licked or sucked all the balmy sperm that issued from the other. We continued our caresses until my prick showed its readiness for another encounter. Mamma took me on her belly this time, and as soon as I was engulphed, threw her legs over my loins, and, by the most lascivious actions, contributed to our enjoyment. Her glorious bottom heaved in unison with mine, our tongues were interlaced, and at last with sweet murmurs of delight, we died away in each other's arms in the most luxurious extasy of thoroughly gratified desire. We lay long insensible of all around, throbbing in pressures of lascivious delight, which would have soon led to another love bout, but that mamma whispered it would be imprudent to continue, for the sun was up, and breakfast time had arrived. I withdrew from the sweet cunt with great regret, and in slipping out of bed brought my mouth down to it, and gave it a loving kiss and suck, played with the magnificent covering of bushy ringlets, and then tore myself away with difficulty. Thus ended my first possession of my adored and glorious mother, which was followed by night upon night of the most lascivious enjoyment. I returned to my room, and was dressed and downstairs before her. The doctor took an opportunity to inform me that she had excused herself from joining him the next night on the pretence of not feeling well, but in reality it was to have me all to herself for the whole night; and a most delicious night it was. She displayed and exercised her libidinous passions to the utmost. Never before had I such a treat. It was, perhaps, the closeness of the relationship that added to the excitement, but it appeared to me that she beat even the doctor's splendid wife. Oh, she was so loving, too. The way she fondled me in her arms and caressed me was irresistible. I can't tell how often we did it—we were at it all night. The next night, under pretence of fearing to exhaust me, she forced me to retire to my room after two fucks, and locked me in. I had previously been informed by the doctor that he had bespoken her for that night, and he begged me to fuck her first, that the pleasure of gamahuching her might be enhanced. I, therefore, did not do more than make a feigned resistance to her when she told me I must go to my own bed. She said she would let me have one embrace before she rose in the morning but that one was converted into two exquisite spends. The next night the doctor wished to repose, as he purposed surprising me in the morning. I laid myself out for this, and when mamma was asleep I rose as if to piddle. I unbolted the door and shook up the doctor, and then returned to bed. I had agreed with him to make more noise than usual in the final extasy; he was to wait long enough to allow of the after-enjoyment, as if he was taking time to clothe himself a little, and was then to come in with a light. My mother still slept. It was about four o'clock in the morning. I began feeling her glorious buttocks, and, sliding under the clothes, turned her legs apart—she insensibly slipped upon her back, I took her charming clitoris between my lips, and soon sucked it into stiffness. The excitement awoke her—she had dreamed I was fucking her—and so was hot and randy. She drew me upon her bosom, threw the clothes off, and her glorious limbs clasped my loins—her two hands pressed on my buttocks, as if to drive me further home, and we ran a most delicious course, I feigned to be even still more excited than I really was, and almost brayed at the extatic moment of ejection. Mamma herself was too far gone in delight to notice the loudness of my bray-

ing. She lay panting and throbbing on my prick, almost in a
state of insensibility to aught else beside. Her eyes were closed,
so that she did not observe the entrance of the light carried
by the doctor. It was not until he was standing by the bedside, and made an exclamation of surprise, that she was aware
of his presence.

"She gave a scream—though not very loud—and covered
her eyes with her hand. I scrambled off her. The doctor, with
great politeness, begged her pardon for his intrusion, but hearing what appeared to him an unearthly noise, he had feared
she was taken ill.

"Here the usual resource of woman—tears—fell plentifully
from mamma. The doctor most affectionately begged her to
calm herself.

" 'My dear madam,' said he. 'I do not in any way blame you
for this. I am a man of the world, and I know that incest is
practised to a far greater extent than is at all imagined, and
to prove that it in no way offends me, I may at once tell you
that it was my own mother who initiated me into these delightful mysteries. I see that this dear boy looks terribly
frightened at my being a witness to the delight he must have
had; but to put him at his ease, we may as well inform him
that we, too, have indulged in that delicious game. I may
add that this is not the first time I have joined in orgies with
more than one man or woman, and nothing gives me more
pleasure than to embrace one reeking from the arms of another, especially if I have been a witness to the previous encounter. See, my dear madam, how this dear instrument stands
stiff in proof of what I say, and to insure my silence dear
Harry must not object to my enjoying you after and before
him.'

"So saying he dropt off his trousers and jumped into bed.
He was met with feeble remonstrances from my mother at
doing it before her son: but I assured her that I rather preferred to see her at work, as she knew, than otherwise, es-

pecially as she evidently enjoyed it so much. So the doctor forthwith mounted her. There could be no doubt that she enjoyed it equally with him. My cock stood at the sight. I put it into her hand, and she squeezed it lovingly—then stooping I sucked one nipple, and you know how this excites her, and slipped a hand behind the doctor, and after gently tickling his ballocks, acted postillion to his bottom-hole. They ran a most exciting course and died away in mutual raptures. No sooner did he turn off than I jumped up into his place, and in one moment was up to the cods in that overflowing cunt. Mamma feebly expostulated, but the doctor begged her to let him have the pleasure of witnessing the vigour of the youth. I knew that in heart mamma was delighted, for all women especially enjoy having a fresh prick into them immediately after a previous one has been withdrawn."

This is quite true—witness my own dear Benson in our early days; her greatest delight was to have me the instant B. retired, and she avowed that nothing could give her greater pleasure. I knew a lady in after-life whom I and three others used to have together, and no sooner was one off than another was on and sometimes two at once. She used to tell us how she deceived her husband. When at Florence she had eight lovers, and she had had them all on the same night without any of them knowing of the others. She managed it in this way. She made them come—two at ten o'clock, two at half-past ten, two at eleven, and two a half-past eleven. They were put in four different rooms with convenient sofas. She ran to No. 1 in a merely loose robe, which was instantly thrown off. She was a magnificently made creature, the sight of whose charms would inflame any one. She rapidly got two goes from the first without withdrawing. Then saying that her husband would be seeking her if she did not leave him, she rang for her German valet, who used to fuck her himself, and who afterwards confirmed her story to me, who showed my gentleman out of the room. Off she ran to No. 2, told him she had only got away by

letting her husband have a go, and that he thought she had
only gone to the water closet so he must do one good and
leave her. Of course the cunt full of fuck only excited him the
more, and he very soon racked off to her great satisfaction,
and was dismissed, leaving the rooms vacant for the two at
eleven. As there was not five minutes to spare she ran to No.
3, where another lover was waiting. The same pretence was
made as to the last, but as he was largely hung, she got two
coups from him and then packed him off, and in the same way
ran to the others, always with the same story, getting two
coups out of three running, who were the best fuckers, and
waiting with the last until he could do no more.

The same lady told me that once while living at Dieppe
her husband ran over to England for a few days. During his
absence she had four young men to supper every night, and
made them all fuck her on the sofa squabs laid on the floor,
accommodating one in her bottom at the same time. During
the day her landlord, a married man, used to come in and rack
her off besides. At one time she was left alone at Mannheim,
where she made acquaintance with an officer, who introduced
a second, and a third, until she knew eight in all. She had the
whole lot once to supper, and they all fucked her three times
each. She was a wonderfully fine woman, and could take no
end of fucking. Her father had initiated her at twelve years of
age. She was of Greek origin, and actually was hairy and
menstruated at that early age. But all women are rakes in their
hearts, and numbers never encumber them.

During Harry's encounter with his mother, the doctor stood
beside them, and handled Harry's ballocks and acted postillion
to him. Mamma took to it most kindly. The sight again inflamed the doctor, the incestuous idea enhancing the excitement. As Harry withdrew, he begged Mrs. Dale to get on her
hands and knees, to let him put it in from behind. He would
rather have gone in behind but did not think she was as yet
quite prepared to allow that. He only said that the movement

below his eyes of such a fine bottom as hers added to the excitement. He further proposed that she should kneel over Harry's body reversed, so that she might gamahuche him, and he frig her beautiful clitoris.

"You mean to kill me between you," she said, but all the same complied. She sucked Harry's prick and he spent in her mouth, which she swallowed with great gusto, spending herself at the same moment in advance of the doctor. Harry kept frigging her clitoris with one hand, while the other was frigging the doctor's bottom-hole. It was a long bout, she made Harry spend twice in her mouth, while she spent thrice to the doctor's once, all dying away together in the final fuck. They lay long lost to everything, and when they recovered, they separated and retired to their own rooms.

The ice being thus broken, the remaining days were passed in the most refined lasciviousness. The doctor had his way with her bottom, and asked her leave to have Harry's after Harry had had his mother's bottom-hole, while the doctor was fucking her, and had fucked the doctor upon another occasion, the doctor crying out—"Hi, hi, hi!" as if it hurt him, and he was losing his maidenhead. He professed immense satisfaction, when she let him have Harry, declaring that he could not tell whether having her both ways, having Harry, or being had himself, was the greatest pleasure. Mamma declared that to have both apertures filled at the same moment was the most delicious. It was then the doctor said he would try. So fucking mamma in a kneeling position he presented his great backside to Harry and was well fucked. It was after this complete initiation that they returned home, and after such proceedings, the transition to a general entry into our orgies was easily arranged. As they were to arrive to a late dinner, it was resolved that Mrs. Dale should stay the night, and we would see what that would bring forth. They arrived accordingly. Mrs. Dale went to Ellen's room, taking Ellen with her to help her at

her toilet. Here ensued an explanation between them. Mrs.
Dale felt that there must be an explicit avowal on both
sides. She admitted to Ellen that Harry had come to her
bed, and only succeeded in his horrible purpose by telling
her how he and Ellen had seen her operations with Charlie,
and had followed her example.

"And now, my dear Ellen, as there must be no secrets
between us, tell me if you and Charlie have got together."

"Well, yes, we have. You know I had seen how immense
he was, and yet with what pleasure you took him in. So
curiosity made me give way one day that we were in the
summer house, and he slept with me afterwards."

"Does the doctor's wife suspect?"

"Oh, yes, she knows all about it. I forgot to bolt the door
one night; in the morning Charlie made too much noise. She
came in, merely in her chemise, ran up and pulled him off
me, without imagining she ran any risk herself. Charlie
seized her in his arms, and swore he would do as much to
her, to prevent her telling. She was horrified, and fled to her
own room, but had not time to shut him out; he forced the
door open, she ran to her bed, intending to ring for the
servant, he caught her as she had one knee up on the bed,
and was into her from behind before she could accomplish
her purpose. She cried out to me, to come and pull him
away. I went, but told her Charlie was right, as it would
prevent her splitting upon us. I rather think that Charlie's
large proportions gave her much pleasure, for she soon
ceased to struggle, indeed she had her back to him, and his
strong arms round her waist prevented her using her hands.
She cried much afterwards, and talked about the greatness
of the crime. She had then got into bed. Charlie followed,
to coax and console her, and, of course, got into her again.
I thought she enjoyed the second, for her bottom heaved to
meet him. She afterwards accused him of the crime of seducing a young lady, her guest, but I stopped that, by

avowing that my cousin had had me previously. Then she accused me of seducing Charlie, and here, I must implore your pardon, for I let out inadvertently that you had initiated him, for I had seen you having him."

"Oh, you bad girl, how could you be so cruel and imprudent?"

"Well, dear aunt, there is no great harm done. Charlie's aunt was soon quite appeased and regularly joined us after this. She is as fond, if not fonder, of gamahuching me as you used to be; she has grown greedy for Charlie's immense cock, envies your having had the first of him, and says that if she had known of his wonderful proportions, she could not have resisted initiating him herself. She hopes that, through my means, she will become more intimate with you. I have told her of your beautiful clitoris. She dotes on the gamahuche, and vows that she will never be happy till she has done it to you."

This explanation was a great relief to the widow, who knew she was all right with the doctor, and now foresaw that it would be all right with his wife also and they would have complete freedom to indulge in the wildest lubricity. So having dressed, they descended to dinner. The doctor had explained all their London doings to his wife, so that after dinner the three ladies exchanged confidence. Aunt was so eager to see and suck Mrs. Dale's large clitoris that they adjourned to aunt's bedroom, where the doctor discovered them in the midst of their operations. Mrs. Dale was stretched on her back, with extended thighs—aunt, with her head pressed by Mrs. Dale's hands down on her cunt, was sucking at the splendid clitoris, and working some fingers in and out her cunt. They were too intent on their pleasure to notice his entrance. Aunt's petticoats were above her hips, as she knelt. The old boy's cock stood, he advanced, knelt down, got between her legs, and fucked her as she was, begging her to continue her lascivious operations on Mrs.

Dale. When he had finished, he congratulated both ladies on the intimate friendship established between them, said it was the best wish of his heart. He assured Mrs. Dale that his wife was the best woman in the world, and never grudged him a little variety.

"So I have acknowledged my infidelity with you, and it appears my nephew has been taking my place, in my absence. She tells me you instructed Charlie, and that he is monstrous when in erection, as big again as me, or as a certain Grenadier Captain, once a favourite of my wife's. I am curious to see it. She tells me also that he has been sleeping with your charming niece Ellen, who, I must confess, has raised in me a great desire to possess her. Now, my dear madam, if you will consent to invite Charlie to sleep with you and Ellen, I could come in, after you have each had a turn or two out of Charlie, and take Ellen, while you would have Charlie all to yourself. My wife won't object, and I hope you will give your consent."

"Well, my dear doctor, after what has occurred between us, I can refuse you nothing, but I think dear Harry should have some comfort. I suppose, my dear madam, that the doctor has told you of my son surprising and violating me. Your husband reconciled me to his caresses, and I can assure you that without the enormous size of Charlie, he has a charming way that may please any woman. From what the doctor says, you are free from prejudices, why should you be left out in the cold, while we are all enjoying ourselves, why should you not go to his bedroom, and see what he is made of. I, his mother, can strongly recommend him to your favour."

So it was arranged.

During the evening, Mrs. Dale whispered to me to come to them after the domestics had gone to bed. I went and fucked them both three times, twice in front and once behind, the one who was being fucked always gamahuching the other. When I began to tail off, Mrs. Dale arose, unbolted the door of communication with uncle's room, and invited him to Ellen's arms, who was very glad to have a little further experience of another man's prick. Uncle gallantly gamahuched her before fucking her, then begged to see my wonderful prick, pretended to be perfectly astonished at its monstrous dimensions, and wondered how Ellen's little cunt could ever have taken it in. It was a tight fit certainly, but the dear creature liked it none the worse for that. Before fucking Ellen, he begged Mrs. Dale to let him guide my large prick into her. After enjoying our first movements, and being excited into sufficient consistency, he proceeded to fuck dear Ellen; even he had some difficulty in entering, notwithstanding the libations I had previously poured into her, but being once fairly hilted, he declared it was one of the tightest little cunts it had ever been his good fortune to fuck. After this, we proceeded each our way, and with a longer interval, brought matters to the exquisite conclusion, panting and throbbing for some time afterwards.

The doctor now retired, and we arranged ourselves for repose. We were awakened in the morning by the entrance of aunt and Harry. He flew to his mamma's arms, who lay down on Ellen to gamahuche her while Harry was fucking her. Aunt and I coupled in the old-fashioned way. Uncle entered while we were in full operation, and seeing the tempting backside of Harry, scrambled up behind and fucked his bottom. After we had done, aunt pretended to be shocked at his attack on a boy's bottom—a woman's was a different thing.

"Well, then, my dear, get upon Charlie the next time, and I shall fuck your truly magnificent bottom."

And he drew Mrs. Dale's attention to the glorious proportions, not only of aunt's bottom, but of her body, and all her limbs.

"Oh, it is indeed glorious," said she. "I must, my dear

madam, gamahuche you. I have not forgotten the exquisite pleasure you gave me in that way."

"Willingly," cried my aunt, "provided you give me your clitoris to occupy me."

"Certainly, that will suit me admirably; but you must lie upon me, that I may have the pleasure of gazing on that magnificent bottom, and caressing the immense rotundities of your buttocks."

Oh, it was a glorious sight to see these two wanton lascivious women in the full enjoyment of each other. It set us all on fire, and the moment they had done I slaked the fire within me in the capacious but tight cunt of my aunt, while uncle fucked her bottom-hole. Mrs. Dale lay under Ellen, while Harry fucked Ellen from behind, and Ellen gamahuched her aunt, who herself guided her son's prick into Ellen's cunt, and tickled her clitoris, at the same time acting postillion to her son's bottom-hole.

Oh! it was a splendid bout—we were all so excited and it was also the first meeting of us all in one orgie. We all died away in a perfect heaven of extasy, and lay long in the after-enjoyment. Our previous night's work made this the last for the time, and we all separated to seek some welcome repose before breakfast time.

Mrs. Dale remained our visitor for three days, during which we met in the doctor's bedroom every night, and renewed our delicious orgies. Mrs. Dale carried off her son and niece, and I promised to come over to her cottage on the following Saturday, when Harry and I took turn and turn about with the two dear creatures, sometimes fucking one between us two at once. When the school resumed its work, Mrs. Dale and Ellen always dined at the rectory on Sunday and slept there, when we made a general orgie in the old style.

This continued until our midsummer holidays, when I was to leave the rectory for King's College. Mrs. Dale's and

Ellen's pregnancies, daily becoming nearer to the period of parturition, were getting more difficult to conceal. We had long discussions with uncle as to what was best to be done. It was at last arranged that they should leave the cottage as if for a tour on the continent, but in reality should only go to Paris, and take apartments in the house of a good *accoucheuse* in the environs, and remain quiet there till the period of delivery. It was not necessary for them to go before we broke up, and the doctor and Harry and I could accompany them, and after I had seen my guardian on my return to London, I had no doubt of getting his leave, and the necessary means to visit the continent up to the middle of October, when the classes would begin. It all fell out as arranged. Nothing of the pregnancy was visible, thanks to the full robes worn.

We accomplished our journey, found a capital *accoucheuse* in a beautiful neighbourhood, with a large garden. Harry, uncle, and aunt remained with them, while I returned to London. I saw my guardian, who, after putting me through an examination, expressed himself much pleased with my progress, said the visit to the continent would expand my mind, and that he would furnish me with the means. He recommended that I should visit my mother first for a fortnight, and announced that at about the end of that time the girls would come up to London to enter a first-rate finishing school. He further told me he had proposed to and had been accepted by Miss Frankland, and they were to be married at the same time; my sisters were to be bridesmaids, and I could be present at the marriage before going abroad. All this being arranged, I ran down home. My mother was delighted to see me, and thought me grown and much improved. It is needless to say how glad my sisters and Miss Frankland were to see me. They had had no fucking except by tongue or dildo, so you may imagine the fury with which they set upon me the first two or three nights. We resumed all our lascivious operations of former days. My sisters had developed into splendid women, the youngest still the most libidinous. Dear Miss Frankland, on my congratulating her on her intended marriage, lovingly told me that it was the prospect of being near me that had reconciled her to it. We spent a most delicious fortnight, which passed like a day.

I found an opportunity of fucking my old governess, Mrs. Vincent that was. My son was a fine little fellow, toddling about and talking already. His mother loved me as much as ever, and was become a finer developed woman, more amorous and lecherous than she used to be. She said no one could be kinder or more loving than her husband, and she had never been unfaithful to him but with me, whom, as her own formation, she must always love, and would never refuse me anything I asked when it could be safely done. At the sole opportunity I had I fucked her three times without drawing, and finished with a bottom-fuck. I may here mention that a little girl followed for nine months from that period, which she always assured me was mine.

My mother, the girls, and Miss Frankland all came up with me to London. The marriage went off with *éclat*. My guardian made very handsome presents to my sisters, and gave me a gold watch, chain, and seals, together with a handsome cheque for my travelling expenses. He and his bride, whom I fucked just before she went to church, departed for Scotland, to return by the English lakes, for their honeymoon trip. A few days afterwards, having had two or three nights excellent fucking with my sisters, mamma and I conducted them to their school, and left them with tearful *adieux*. My mother was to remain in town for a week until uncle and aunt's return, when she intended to accompany her sister to the rectory and remain there until I returned from the continent. I was quickly again in Paris. We took rooms near the two darlings, where uncle and aunt remained for the week they had yet to stay. We took mamma and Ellen several times to the play, and they slept with us every night. Uncle and aunt left at the end of the week, but we kept on the apartments for the dear women to come to us, fucking them as much as we could. It seemed as if their pregnancy stimulated their lubricity, for we could hardly satisfy them. We had at least always to take them on hands and knees, although neither of them ever showed much in front—their babes lying just between—but, by Jove, their hips expanded splendidly. Dear mamma measured a yard across, and her backside projected almost as much as my aunt's. She loved to be fucked in her bottom-hole to the last. We actually had them both up to the night before the day they were each confined. Nothing could be more favourable than their time. As I formerly stated, each had a little daughter.

On the ninth day afterwards they were both able to rise, but as it would have been very prejudicial to renew our intercourse before another three weeks had elapsed, Harry and I went off for a walking excursion in Switzerland, which we traversed in all directions, with continual delight at the glorious scenery. We did not touch a single woman. When very sharp set we fucked each other, but very little even of that, so that we renovated our constitutions and returned in robust health, ready to do justice to the charms of the two darlings, who had impatiently awaited our arrival.

It is needless to repeat the description of the delicious fucking with which they welcomed us. They appeared more lovely than ever, especially Ellen, who had developed into womanhood. We made arrangements to leave the two darling children in the hands of a healthy wet nurse, and set out on an expedition down the Loire to Tours, Bordeaux, and the Pyrenees, returned at the end of September by Montpellier, Nismes, Avignon, and Lyons.

The two babes were in excellent health. Arrangements were made for their remaining with their foster mother for a year, and we all returned to London together.

We had three nights' delicious fucking before they returned to the country, and promises were made that they would come to town from time to time to renew our orgies. My mother and aunt came up to see me settled in my lodgings, which were taken in Norfolk Street, and I was entered at King's College.

I passed a delicious night with aunt before she left; and ran down with my mother to see her safe home. On my return I found my guardian had returned. I called to pay my respects to his wife. I found her alone, and we managed her first piece of adultery, which, as you may suppose, was not the last. But as this third volume is already a long one, I shall here close it.

The fourth will introduce us to London, and renew the delicious intercourse with Mrs. Benson, as well as with my guardian's wife, and our dear friend MacCallum, as well as many other friends.

END OF VOL. III.

Volume IV
The Romance of Lust

I concluded my last volume by saying that I had taken lodgings in Norfolk Street, Strand, for the convenience of being near King's College. It was at the house of a Mrs. Nichols, tall, powerfully built, masculine, but a kind and motherly looking widow of fifty-two—an attentive and bustling landlady, looking herself to the better cooking, and having a plain cook, who was also a general servant, to help her downstairs, and two nieces to do the waiting and attendance on her lodgers upstairs. The younger was there alone when I entered the lodgings; her elder sister had had what they called a "misfortune," and was then in the country until she could be unburthened of it. She was expected back in about six weeks. Meanwhile, as the winter was not the season, I was the only lodger, and the younger had only me to attend to; her name was Jane; she was but a little thing, but very well made, good bubbies and bottom, which I soon discovered were firm and hard, projecting fully on both sides. She was fairly good looking, but with a singular innocent manner of freedom about her that made me imagine she had as yet had no chance of a "misfortune." In a week we became intimate, and after often praising her pretty face and figure, I snatched a kiss now and then, which at first she resented with an attractive yet innocent sort of sauciness. It was in her struggles on these occasions that I became aware of the firm and hard bosom and bottom.

Up to this time my flirtations were without ulterior object, but the reality of the attractions of these hidden charms raised my lustful passions. I gradually increased my flatteries and caresses, squeezed her bubbies, when I sometimes drew her on my knee and was kissing her, and as at first she resisted my drawing her to my knee, I took occasion to lay hold of her buttocks, which I found more developed than I could have supposed. Gradually her resistance to these little liberties ceased and she would quietly sit on my knee and return the kiss I gave. Her dress was a little open in front, so from feeling her bubbies outside, I gradually got to feeling their naked beauties inside. I now thought I could attempt greater familiarities, so one day when seated on my knee with one arm round her waist, I pressed her to my lips, and while so engaged, whipt my free arm up her petticoats, and before she had become aware of the movement, had got my hand upon her mount, a very nicely haired one. She started up to a standing position, but as I held her close clasped round the waist she could not get away, and her new position enabled me the easier to get my hand between her thighs and thus to feel her charming pouting little cunt. I began attempting to frig her clitoris, but stooping she drew her cunt away, and looking at me with a droll innocent expression of alarm, and with a perfect unconsciousness of the import of her words, cried, —"Oh! take care what you are at. You don't know how a lodger this last summer suffered for seizing me in that way and hurting me very much. I screamed out, aunt came up, and, do you know, he had £50 to pay for his impudence."

I could not but smile at the extraordinary innocence of the girl.

"But I do not hurt you, dear Jane," said I, "and don't mean to do so."

"That was what he said, but he went on in a most horrible way, and not only hurt me very much, but made me bleed."

"It would not be with his hand, you see I only gently press this soft hairy little thing. I am sure that don't hurt you."

"Oh, no! if that was all I should not mind it, it was when he pushed me on the sofa, and pressed upon me, that he hurt me terribly, and you must take care what you are about, or you, too, will have to pay £50."

There was a curious air of innocence in all this; it was evident to me the fellow had got into her, and broken her hymen with violence, and then her screams had prevented his finishing his work. Her manner convinced me that she was really not aware of the consequences, or rather had not as yet really had her sexual passions aroused.

"Well, my dear Jane, I neither intend to hurt you or make myself liable to pay £50, but you will not refuse me the pleasure of feeling this nice little hairy nest, you see how gentle I am."

"Well, if you will do me no more hurt than that I shan't refuse you, because you are a nice kind young gentleman, and very different from the other rough fellow, who never chattered with me and made me laugh as you do—but you must not push your fingers up there, it was something he pushed up there that hurt me so."

I withdrew my finger, and as, at my request, she had opened her thighs a little, I felt and caressed her very nice little cunt, and with a finger pressed externally above her clitoris, I could see that she flushed and shivered on feeling me there. However, I did no more than gently press and feel all her hairy mount and fat pouting cunt; she said I must let her go, or her aunt would be coming up.

The first step was now gained. Gradually I progressed further and further; felt her charming bare arse as she stood before me, got her to let me see the beautiful curls she had got on her cunt, then came to kissing it, until at last she opened her thighs and let me tongue it, to her most exquisite delight. I made her spend for the first time in her life, and soon she came to me for it. I had gradually introduced a finger up her cunt while licking her clitoris and exciting her so much that she was unconscious of my doing it; then two fingers, and after she had spent deliciously, I made them perform an imitation of a throb, which made her jump and ask what I was doing. I asked if she did not feel that my fingers were inside of her sweet Fanny.

"You don't say so. It was there I was so hurt."

"But I do not hurt you, dear Jane?"

"Oh, dear no, it makes me feel queer, but it is very nice."

"Well, now you know that I have two fingers inside, I will use my tongue again against your charming little clitoris, and work the fingers in and out."

I did so, and she soon spent in an agony of delight, pressing my head down hard on her cunt, and crying—"Oh! oh! it is too great a pleasure!" and then died off, half insensible. Another time I repeated this she told me not to forget to use my fingers. Having made her spend twice I took her on my knee, and told her that I possessed an instrument that would give her far more pleasure than tongue or finger.

"Indeed?" said she, "where is it? I should so like to see it."

"You won't tell."

"Oh, no!"

So pulling out my stiff-standing prick, she stared in amazement. She had really never seen a prick, although it was evidently a prick that had deflowered her, for with my fingers I had explored her cunt, and found no hymen there. I put her hand upon it, she involuntarily grasped it firmly.

"This enormous thing could never get into my body, look, it is thicker than all your fingers put together, and only two fingers feel so tight."

"Yes, darling, but this dear little thing stretches, and was made to receive this big thing."

I was exciting her clitoris with my finger, she grew evidently lasciviously inclined, so saying, "Just let me try, and if it hurts you I will stop; you know I am always gentle with you."

"So you are, my dear fellow, but take care not to hurt me."

She lay down on the bed, as I desired, with feet up and knees laid open. I spat on my prick, and wetted the knob and upper shaft well, then bringing it to her cunt, well moistened by my saliva in gamahuching her, I held open the lips with the fingers of my left hand, and half buried its knob before getting to the real entrance.

"Don't flinch, dearest, I shall not hurt." And I got it well over the knob, and buried it one inch further.

"Stop!" she cried, "it seems as if it would burst me open, it so stretches me."

"But it does not hurt you, dearest?" I had immediately stopped before asking the question.

"No not exactly, but I feel as if something was in my throat."

"Rest a little, and that will go off." I slipped a finger down on her clitoris, and as I frigged it she grew more and more excited, giving delicious cunt pressures on my prick, it gradually made its way by the gentle pushing I continued to make without other movements. It was more than half in when she spent, this not only lubricated the interior, but the inner muscles relaxing, a gentle shove forward housed it to the hilt, and then I lay quiet until she recovered from the half fainting state her last discharge had produced; soon the increased pressures of the inner folds showed that her passions were awakening afresh. She opened her eyes and, looking lovingly, said I had given her great pleasure, but she felt as if something enormous was stretching her inside to the utmost. Had I got it all in?

"Yes, dearest, and now it will be able to give you greater pleasure than before." I began a slow withdrawal and return, frigging her clitoris at the same time, for I was standing between her legs. She soon grew wild with excitement, nature prompting her, her arse rose and fell almost as well as if she was mistress of the art. The novel combination of prick and finger quickly brought on the extatic crisis. I, too, was wild with lust, and we spent together, ending in an annihilation of all our senses by the extreme extasy of the final overpowering crisis. We lay panting for some time in all the after-joys. Dear Jane begged me to give her some water, as she felt quite faint. I withdrew, still almost in a standing state, got her some water, helped her up, seated her on the sofa and kissed her lovingly as I thanked her for the exquisite joy she had given me. She threw her arms round my neck, and with tears in her eyes told me I had taught her the joys of heaven, and she should always love me, and I must always love her, for now she could not live without me. I kissed and dried her eyes, and told her we should in future enjoy it even more when she got accustomed to it.

"Let me see the dear thing that gave me such pleasure."

I pulled it out, but it was no longer at the stand; and this surprised her. I explained the necessity of its being so, but said she would quickly see it rise and swell to the former size if she continued to handle it so nicely. It rose almost before I could say as much. She fondled it, and even stooped and kissed its ruby head. We should quickly have got to another bout of fucking if the ringing of the call bell had not brought us to a sense of its imprudence; so after arranging her hair and dress, she hastily descended with some of the breakfast things.

Of course, so good a beginning led to constant renewals and Jane quickly became extremely amorous, and under my instruction a first-rate fucker.

As all my dear friends were not in London, I was fortunate in having such a *bonne bouche* to comfort me. My sisters passed every Sunday with me, and both got some good fucking out of me in every way, without raising any suspicions in the house.

A month after I had taken up my residence at Mrs. Nichols's, Jane's sister arrived. She was a much finer woman than Jane, broad shouldered, wide-spread bosom, which, in after-days, I found had not suffered by her "misfortune," but then she had not suckled it. Her hips were widely projected, and she was grand and magnificent in her arse. Naturally of a very hot temperament, when once she had tasted the magnificent weapon I was possessed of, she grew most lasciviously lustful, and was one of the best fuckers I ever met with. Her power of nip almost equalled by beloved aunt's. Jane was fair, Ann was dark, with black locks and black hairy cunt—a very long cunt, with a small tight hole in it, and above it a wide-spread projecting mount, splendidly furnished with hair. Her clitoris was hard and thick, but with little projection. She also became madly fond of arse-fucking, and particularly liked me to spend therein. This was partly to prevent any consequences leading to a second "misfortune."

On her first arrival Jane was much afraid she would discover our connection and we took every precaution, although I, in my heart, wished this might occur, for as she occasionally waited on me, I grew lecherous upon one whose charms, even covered, excited me greatly. I always flattered and praised her magnificence of figure whenever she came alone to me, but as Jane generally was running in and out, I did not attempt further action. One morning I overheard Mrs. Nichols tell Jane to put on her bonnet and go to Oxford Street on some errand; I knew thus that Ann would attend on me, and there would be no chance of interruption from Jane, so I determined to come at once to the point. We had become on friendly, chatty terms, and when she had laid breakfast I asked her to help me on with my coat, which done, I thanked her and with one arm round her waist drew her to me and kissed her. "Hallo!" said she, "that is something new," but did not attempt to withdraw, so giving her another kiss, I told her what a glorious woman she was, and how she excited me—just see. I held one of her hands, and before she was aware, placed it on my huge prick, that bulged out of my trousers as if it would burst its way through.

She could not help squeezing it, while she cried—

"Goodness, gracious! what an enormous thing you have got!"

Her face flushed, her eyes sparkled with the fire of lust that stirred her whole soul. She tried to grasp it.

"Stop," said I, "and I will put it in its natural state into your hand."

So pulling it out, she seized it at once, and most lasciviously gazed upon it, pressing it gently. She evidently was growing lewder and lewder, so I at once proposed to fuck her, and thinking it best to be frank, and put her at her ease, I told her that I knew she had had a "misfortune," but if she would let me fuck her I should be on honour to withdraw before spending, and thus avoid all chance of putting her belly up.

She had become so randy that she felt, as she afterwards told me, she could not refuse so splendid a prick of a size she had often dreamt of, and longed for.

"Can I trust you?" said she.

"Safely, my dear."

"Then you may have me—let me embrace that dear object."

Stooping, she kissed it most voluptuously, shivering at the same time in the extasy of a spend produced by the mere sight and touch. She gave one or two "oh's," and drawing me to the bed by my prick, threw herself back, pulling her petticoats up at the same time. Then I beheld her splendid cunt in all its magnificence of size and hairiness. I sank on my knees and glued my lips to the oozing entrance, for she was one who spent most profusely, her cunt had the true delicious odour, and her spunk was thick and glutinous for a woman.

I tongued her clitoris, driving her voluptuously wild. So she cried—

"Oh! do put that glorious prick into me, but remember your promise."

I brought it up to that wide-spread, large-lipped, and immense cunt. I fully expected that big as I was I should slip in over head and shoulders with the greatest ease. So you may imagine my surprise to find the tightest and smallest of entrances to the inner vagina I almost ever met with, it was really with greater difficulty I effected an entrance than I had with her little sister, whose cunt presented no such voluptuous grandeur. It was as tight a fit as Ellen's was to me on our first coition. Tight as it was, it gave her nothing but the most exquisite pleasure, she was thoroughly up to her work, and was really one of the most voluptuous and lascivious fuckers I have ever met with, excellent as my experience has been. I made her, with fucking and frigging, spend six times before I suddenly withdrew my prick, and pressing its shaft against her wet lips, and my own belly, spent deliciously outside. Shortly after it rose again, and this time after making her spend as often as before, for she was most voluptuously lustful, when I withdrew, she suddenly got from under me, and seizing its shaft with one hand, stooped and took its knob between her lips, and quickly made me pour a flood of sperm into her mouth, which she eagerly swallowed and sucked on to my great delight.

We should have had a third bout but for the necessity of her going down to her aunt.

I breakfasted, then rang to take away. Again we had a delicious fuck, and a third when she came to make the bed and empty the slops. This third time I begged her to kneel on the sofa, and let me see her gloriously grand arse, and when I had to retire I would show her a way that would continue both our pleasure. So after fucking her from behind, and making her spend far oftener than me, I withdrew, and pushing it up between the lips over the clitoris, with my hand round her waist, I pressed it tightly against her cunt and clitoris, and continued to wriggle my arse, made her spend again as I poured a flood all up over her belly. She declared it was almost as good as if inside.

After this very shortly I proposed to push its nose into her bottom-hole, and just spend within.

With reluctance at first, it ended in her not only liking the point there, but deliciously enjoying my whole prick within, and eventually it was always the receptacle of a first discharge induced by fucking, and a second fuck completely carried on in that more secret altar of lust. She became a first-rate *enculeuse.*

It soon happened that both sisters knew of the other enjoying me, and it ended in their slipping down from their attic, where both slept in the same bed, to my room, and we had most delicious fucking and double gamahuching.

Ann was by far the finest and the most lascivious fuck, but little Jane had a certain charm of youth and also of freshness, which got her a fair share of my favours.

We carried this on for several weeks until use made us careless and noisy.

The aunt, when no lodgers occupied the room, slept overhead, and, probably being sleepless one morning, when it was early daylight, heard our voices, came down and surprised me in the very act of fucking Ann and gamahuching Jane, who stood above her and presented her cunt to my lecherous tongue. A loud exclamation from their aunt roused us up at once.

"Get to bed, you dreadful hussies."

They fled without a moment's hesitation.

Mrs. Nichols then began to remonstrate with me on the infamy of my conduct. I approached the door apparently to get my shirt, for I was stark naked, but in fact to shut and lock my door, and then to turn on Mrs. Nichols, who apparently had quite forgotten she had only her short shift on, which not only allowed the full display of very fine, firm, and ample bubbies, but not falling below the middle of her thighs, showed remarkably well made legs and small knees, with the swelling of immense thighs just indicated.

My stiff-standing prick in full vigour, and if anything, still more stimulated by the unexpected beauties shown by Mrs. Nichols, I turned upon her and seizing her round the waist from behind, pushed her forward, and before she could recover herself I had hauled up her "cutty sark," seen a most magnificent arse, and into her cunt—not without somewhat painful violence, before she could recover from the surprise of the attack.

She screamed out murder, but there was no one who could hear but the girls, and they knew better than to interrupt me. I kept fucking away in spite of cries, and passing an arm round her body, with my finger I got to her clitoris, which sprang out into considerable proportions. My big prick and the frigging of her clitoris produced their natural result. In spite of herself she grew full of lust. I felt her cunt pressures, and knew how her passions were rising. Speedily, in place of resisting, she began to cry, "Oh, oh," and breathe hard, and then most gloriously wriggled her splendid arse, and as I spent she too was taken in the delicious extasy of the final crisis. She lay throbbing on my delighted prick until it stood as stiff as before. I began a slow movement, she made no resistance, except crying out, "Oh! dear, oh! dear," as if in spite of regrets, she could not help enjoying it; indeed, at last she said—

"Oh! what a man you are, Mr. Roberts; it is very wrong of you to do this, but I cannot resist enjoying it myself. It is years since I did such a thing, but as you have done it, it makes me wish you should do it again. Let us change position."

"Very well, but you must throw off this tiresome chemise, or I won't withdraw."

As her lust was so excited, she made no objection, so

withdrawing we stood up; she drew her shift over her head, and displayed a far more splendid form, with an exquisitely fair and dimpled skin, than I could have thought possible.

"My dear Mrs. Nichols, what a fine perfect form you have got, let me embrace you in my arms."

She was nothing loath, flattered by my praise. She laid hold of my cock with one hand, and closely clasped me with the other arm, while I threw an arm and hand round on her truly magnificent arse, and with my other hand pressed on a wonderful pair of bubbies as hard and firm as any maid of eighteen. Our mouths met in a loving kiss, our tongues exchanged endearments. She said—

"You have made me very wicked, let me have this enormous and dear fellow again."

I said I must first gaze on all her beauties, especially on her gorgeous and enormous bottom. She turned herself round in every way, delighted to find that I so ardently admired her.

She then lay down on her back, and spread wide her legs, and called to me to mount and put it in.

"First I must kiss this beautiful cunt, and suck this superb clitoris."

Her mount was covered with closely curled brown silky locks; her cunt was large with grand thick lips and well-haired sides. Her clitoris stood out quite three inches, red and stiff. I took it in my mouth, sucked it, and frigged her cunt with two fingers, which went in with the greatest ease, but were nipped tightly the moment the entrance was gained, and I frigged and sucked until she spent madly with absolute screams of delight. I continued to suck and excite her, which quickly made her cry out—

"Oh, darling boy, come and shove your glorious prick into my longing cunt."

I sprang up and buried him until our two hairs were crushed between us. She held me tight for a minute without moving, then went off like a wild *Bacchante*, and uttered voluptuous bawdy expressions.

"Shove your delicious prick further and harder. Oh, you are killing me with delight."

She was a perfect mistress of the art, gave me exquisite pleasure, and, I may add, proved afterwards a woman of infinite variety, and became one of my most devoted admirers. Our intrigue continued for years, while her age, as is the case with good wine, only appeared to improve her. Her husband was not a bad fucker, but having only a small prick, had never stimulated her lust as my big splitter had done.

We had on this first occasion three other good fucks, which she seemed to enjoy more and more.

As I had previously fucked the girls pretty well, my prick at last refused to rise and perform. We had to stop fucking, but I gamahuched her once more after again posing her, and admiring her really wonderfully well made and well-preserved body. She had a good suck at my cock, without bringing him up again.

At last we separated, but not before she made a promise that she would sleep with me that night, and a glorious night we had. I had the more difficult task of reconciling her to my having her nieces. I used to have them one night, and sleep with her the next.

Ann, as I have said, was one of the lewdest and most lascivious women I had ever known. I had told them of the beauty of their aunt's whole person, and of her wonderful clitoris, and how she liked me to gamahuche it. This awakened the tribadic passions of Ann to gamahuche her aunt.

I, at last, persuaded her to let Ann join us, and both were afterwards extremely glad I had done so, for both were thorough tribades, and lasciviously enjoyed each other, while being fucked by me in turns. Mrs. Nichols too, once she got used to arse-fucking, delighted in it, and we had the wildest orgies together.

Meanwhile, my very dear friend MacCallum had returned

to town. He lived in the outskirts, but had taken a small set of chambers at Lyon's Inn, a sitting-room and bedroom, where he had a complete library of bawdy books and pictures to excite to new efforts passions palled with excess. It was here I took my sisters, and every Sunday we four, stripped to the buff, indulged in every excess the wildest lust could prompt.

At Christmas, uncle, aunt, the Dales, and Ellen all came to town, and taking the same rooms with others that uncle and Mrs. Dale and her son had formerly down in Norfolk Street, we had the most glorious orgies.

I confessed that I had debauched my sisters during the weary months I had been left alone with them, and advised their initiation into our society. Uncle greedily snatched at the idea, so did aunt and Harry Dale, but his mother and Ellen rather discouraged it. However, the majority had it, and aunt went to the school, and took them away for the holidays. I had instructed them to keep up the idea of a late initiation by me, and how much they liked it when done, carefully avoiding the least reference to former freedoms.

They afforded a very effective aid to the wild variety of our orgies. Uncle especially affected them, and was never tired of fucking, sucking or gamahuching their splendid charms. Aunt, whose lech was for fresh young women, was unbounded in her admiration and tribadic use of their bodies.

I made a confident of Harry Dale about our re-unions at MacCallum's, and, with the latter's leave, introduced him to our orgies in the Inn.

MacCallum took greatly to the fine tight arse of young Dale. He also wished to have Ellen introduced. I took occasion to break the matter to her, and in the end she made a delicious addition to those private orgies. In March Mrs. Benson, Mrs. Egerton, and husbands came up to town.

I had written to the Benson, and got a note from her the moment she arrived. I called immediately, and finding her alone, her husband having gone to the city, was received with delight. After flying into each other's arms, nature was too fierce for any amorous preliminaries. A sofa received our ardent bodies, and before one could think, legs were opened, cunt invaded, and a most rapid fuck, too rapid for luxury, was run off. Then while recovering from our first delirium of pleasure, we had time for a few words of mutual praise and admiration of improvements in both; but it was not until I had fucked her four times, and made her spend at least twice as often, that we found time to enter into close converse upon past events.

I had known by letter of the intrigue with the Count, Mrs. Egerton, and herself, and now heard, from her own mouth, more exciting details. She told me how Mrs. Egerton was eager to possess my unusually great prick, adding—

"By the way, she must be alone at this hour. Come along, we may have some fun to-day."

I had not seen Mrs. Egerton for many years, in fact, for long before I had fucked Mrs. Benson. We went. Her reception was all I could wish.

Mrs. Benson told us to lose no time, but to run off at least an introductory embrace when the field was so clear. Mrs. Egerton made no objection; the Benson acted mistress of the ceremonies, pulled out my prick and lifted the Egerton's petticoats, turning both sides to view, and making the Egerton handle and admire the nobleness of my prick, then telling her to kneel and present her fat arse to my lustful gaze, guided my longing prick into her really delicious cunt; and a most excellent fuck we had, which, as Mrs. Benson said, would put us at our ease in an interview she had planned for next day, in which the Count was to join us, and telling me I should have to show my mettle to rival the Count.

We met next day at a quiet house in Percy Street, Tottenham Court Road. The ladies had gone to the Soho Bazaar, leaving their carriage in Soho Square, going out by another entrance in a back street, and driving up in a cab to us in Percy Street.

At an evening call I had made, to be introduced to Mr. Egerton, I had met and been introduced to the Count. We had walked home as far as his apartments, in Berners Street, and arranged to meet in Percy Street, before the arrival of our beautiful and dear friends. Thus we were impatiently awaiting their coming when they arrived.

It is needless to say no sooner had they entered, and the mere embrace and kiss of welcome been given, than they retired to another room, opening into the one where we were, to take off all encumbrances to the wildest lust, while we, too, disencumbered ourselves of all our clothes. We were quicker than they were, and the Count was in the act of handling and admiring the grandeur of my prick when the two beautiful creatures entered in nature's only robe, and well might we exclaim—

"Woman, when unadorned is adorned the most," for two more beautiful women or more perfectly lovely in shape could hardly be seen. Women, too, as voluptuous and lascivious in their passions as any of their sex could be, and it was now our delight to enjoy and satisfy their ardent lust by fucking them in every way, as well as for the first time giving them the joy of having two real pricks in them at once. The charming Benson, as my original initiator in love's mysteries, claimed my first embrace, the Count fucking Mrs. Egerton. We were so placed that each could see the other, and thus enjoy the excitement of the scene. The dear creatures spent thrice to our once.

Then the Egerton claimed me while the Count refilled the cunt I had just quitted.

Again we made them spend thrice to our once. They preferred these preliminary encounters to the more lascivious excesses we were about to enter upon as exciting and preparing their passions for more voluptuous embraces.

Both the dear creatures loved a prick *in culo* from time to time, but as yet they had not had the opportunity of having a prick in each aperture at once.

The Egerton, to whom my prick was as yet a novelty, said she must have it in her cunt while the Count planted his lesser but very fine prick in her arse.

The Count's prick was quite as long, or nearly so, as mine, and even thicker close to the roots, but tapered up to a small pointed knob, so that for the *enculage* he had greater facility, than my huge-knobbed affair, whose head was as thick as any part of it. This difference of formation made the dear creatures both prefer my prick in front while the Count attacked them in the rear. They generally each got two, with me below and the Count above. But, although it was at first somewhat painful when my huge prick took the rearward side with the Count in front, they soon got accustomed to it, although invariably beginning, after our preliminary fucking, with the Count first *in culo*.

The Egerton, as I said before, made her first trial of two pricks fucking her at once, by having me below her. I had laid down on my back, she straddled over me, the Benson claimed the place of conductress to the instruments of pleasure, and, first giving a suck to my prick, she guided it into the delicious cunt of her friend, who sank down upon my stiff-standing prick, deliciously impaling herself thereon, and went off in a voluptuous discharge on feeling its huge head engulphed to the utmost; she rose and fell upon it in an upright position, until she had spent a second time, and had brought up her passion to the wildest rage of lust, then falling into my longing arms, she called out to the Count to shove his prick at once into her arse.

The Benson had, meanwhile, sucked and moistened the Count's fine prick, making him as eager as the Egerton to be into her beautiful arsehole. The Benson conducted it to the divine entrance of that rapture-giving receptacle, which he

entered at first with little difficulty, but as the thickening of
his prick by its further entrance began to stretch the tender
folds between our two pricks, the Egerton cried out for a
momentary pause, as it was producing the strange sensation
that one prick alone produces in the earlier stage of sodomitic embraces.

The Benson came to her aid by desiring the Count to withdraw about half the distance he had gained and having
whipt up some warm soapsuds she well wetted his lower
shaft and then he more easily recovered lost ground, and
gained a complete lodgement within the tremendously
stretched affair, for as I have said, the lower part of his
shaft was thicker than I could grasp.

The Egerton felt as if the two apertures were about to
be torn into one, and cried out for a few minutes' cessation.

We both lay still, beyond the involuntary throbbing of our
pricks, pressed as they were against each other, for the
at-all-times-thin membrane dividing cunt from arsehole was
now stretched to the fineness of gold leaf, and to our sensations did not appear to exist at all.

These double throbbings soon stirred up all the wild
lubricity of the Egerton's nature, first showing itself in the
responsive inward pressures of the delicate widely stretched
folds of both receptacles, then increasing in fiery lust, she
cried out for us to begin gently our first movements. We drew
in and out in unison together, at first slowly, but the Egerton
finding that we were producing the most excessive delight to
her double-gorged receptacles, cried out—

"Oh! oh! It is heavenly; fuck faster, you angelic fuckers.
Oh! faster, faster. Oh! oh! it is too much."

She spent in such an agony of extasy as to faint clean
away.

We were not aware of this, not having ourselves spent as
we had only paused to let her enjoy her most heavenly discharge to the utmost. Then, first with throbs, and then with

in and outward movements, we soon recovered her from her trance of excessive joy. Her passions were more violently stirred than before. She wriggled her arse convulsively sideways, she raved in the grossest bawdy terms, and so excited us that we all three came to the final crisis in wild cries of the grossest lust, and died away in an agony of bliss, so overpowering that we lay, almost insensible, soaking in the sacred vases in which were compressed our well-satisfied pricks. Meanwhile the Benson, wildly excited by the scene enacted below her eyes, sought relief by kneeling beyond my head, for we always fucked on the floor with mattresses spread widely around; she then backed her splendid arse over my head, and brought her cunt to my mouth, and I had gamahuched her continuously until my own delicious spending annihilated all power of movement for the time being.

The Egerton, in the agony of her pleasure at the moment of the last spend, had fastened her teeth on the glorious arse of the Benson before her, and bit so hard as actually to draw blood and make the Benson spring forward with a sudden start and cry. But we were all too lost in the extatic joys to even hear the cry of pain she uttered.

At last the Egerton gave signs of returning life. The Benson had risen and was eager for her turn, but Mrs. Egerton implored that she might have once again a taste of these more than heavenly joys while both pricks were still engulfed within her and thus avoid the pain of entrance.

This was so reasonable that the Benson yielded with a good grace.

The Count, to indemnify her, begged her to stride over our two bodies, so as to bring her delicious cunt to his mouth, which, as he was kneeling, was just at the proper level; so he gamahuched, and embracing her splendid arse, postillioned her at the same time; thus we were a chain of delight.

This bout was drawn out to great length.

The Egerton must have spent half-a-dozen times, and when we both at last jammed our pricks up in the ferocity of lust, making all three give down life's essence in an almost killing extasy, she really fainted quite away, and so alarmed us that we withdrew to use such remedies as were at hand to bring her to; even then she was quite hysterical. We laid her in the bed; she was relieved by a copious flood of tears, which she assured us were those of joy at the exquisite and over-powering delights we had conferred upon her. She begged us now to gratify the Benson with the same extatic joys we had bestowed upon her, and she would be a quiet and delighted spectator of our doings.

It was now my own loved Mrs. Benson's turn to experience the inexpressible delights of the double junction. From her love of my splendid splitter, of which she had taken the first sweets, and which had been initiated in her deliciously adulterous cunt into the divine mysteries of love, and the still more sacred and secret joys of the second altar dedicated to the worship of Priapean unutterably sensual raptures; from this circumstance and the constant use of the rear receptacle practised by her husband, whose prick was a very fine one, the initiation into the *double jouissance* was less nervously effected than with the less used arsehole of the more delicate Egerton, but at the same time two such pricks operating at once made her wince a little before we were fairly en-gulphed to the cods, the banging together of which in their close proximity added greatly to the stimulating of our lust.

The sweet Benson lent herself most readily to the work, and seconded us by her art in wriggling her arse and the delicious cunt and sphincter pressures; enjoying herself at once and more rapidly than the Egerton, she got four deli-cious discharges before our somewhat more sluggish senses would allow us to come to the grand final crisis, which seemed to stimulate the divine Benson to a point of raving lust, which showed itself in cries of the grossest bawdy;

shouting to us to shove our pricks in further and faster, calling us all the loudest blackguard names she could put her tongue to—absolutely roaring as the final discharge seized her in the very same instant that we poured floods of sperm into both interiors, she then sank, annihilated by the excess of the voluptuous delights conferred upon her, but lay throbbing and pulsating in all the after-joys of the utmost venereal satisfaction. We lay long in this delicious inanition of such voluptuous excesses.

The darling Benson exercised her delicious "nippers" in both orifices, which soon had their expected effect, and shortly the flesh gave symptoms of its "resurrection" to mundane joys, after having passed through the heavenly delights of Paradise, truly rising from the most delicious graves in which they were lying so exquisitely buried. Like her lovely predecessor she was eager for more, and if it were possible our second course was superior to the first, at all events it was longer drawn out, for the previous draughts on our slackening appendages made the further delivery an effort requiring longer pumping, and thus swelled the amount of pleasure by lengthening the process before arriving at the grand final crisis.

The Benson, much more ungovernable in her passion than we were, must have spent six or seven times in our last effort, and died away in, if anything, greater abandon than in our first course, and eventually sank completely overcome by the entire satisfaction of her raging lust for the time being. We, too, both wanted a respite, so we all rose.

The two dear creatures when once on their legs found instant necessity to evacuate their rear receptacles of the double cargo taken in, and disappeared for a few minutes.

We all purified ourselves and well laved everything with ice cold water to reanimate them the sooner. We then sat down to a stimulating refreshment, in which we at least all drank a bottle of Champagne apiece, in the midst of delightful and exciting bawdy wit and obscene stories, in which our darling *fouteuses* showed a witty proficiency.

In half an hour we began to take up our positions. It was my turn to take them in the rear, but both begged off for that day. The pause for refreshment had given time to make them feel sore after the great stretching they had undergone for the first time, so my turn was delayed for three days, that being the usual delay in their orgies to prevent suspicion by too frequent absences, but not excluding any opportunity that might occur for a rack-off in the mean time. So we only each fucked them once and closed our exquisite orgy for that day; parting with every expression of fully satisfied desires, and the warmest kisses and embraces.

The Count and I walked to his apartments to refresh ourselves there with hot tumblers of toddy; whiskey being a great favourite of his, and, in his opinion, the best restorative after our exhausting efforts with the two insatiable creatures.

He congratulated himself on my accession to these orgies, as being a great relief to the burden he had had in satisfying both in both ways when all alone with them.

However, the Count was an indefatigable and an unwearied fucker, but two such insatiable cunts often had tried his powers to the utmost, and was more than he liked to do at the interview, so he had found whiskey toddy a remedy at once efficacious and agreeable. I myself with my private excesses at home was glad to know so pleasant a restorative. The Count and I became the most intimate and attached friends; through him I perfected myself in Italian, and not many years after this, passed some happy months with him in Italy after he had been amnestied, returned to his country and recovered part of his once large property, but of that hereafter.

I called next day on my adored Benson, who had developed into a glorious woman, more lovely and lustful than ever.

We had but a moment to ourselves, and could not use it for amatory purposes but as we both had much to relate we agreed to meet at our house in Percy Street the next day.

This house was taken furnished for love purposes only, and merely an old woman was kept to take care of and arrange matters when we were gone; it was held in the Count's name but paid for by the two fair users of it. They had latch keys each, and the place was kept ready for everyday use.

The dear libidinous Benson avowed that she used it for other lovers unknown to the Count or the Egerton; paying the old woman liberally, she had all her own way.

We met there the next day, rushing into each other's arms, and then assisting in the undressing we had three exquisite fucks, during which the delighted Benson spent seven times, and then we could have a long and uninterrupted talk over old times, and my after-doings. I told her all, and how the Vincent, my elder sister, Miss Frankland, my aunt, and Mrs. Dale had all thought me an innocent, receiving his first lesson in their delicious cunts, and how true and wise had been her sage counsels. She listened in wonder and delight, drew from me descriptive pictures of our conjunctions and thrice interrupted my narrative to have a delicious fuck to calm the excitement raised by the lascivious descriptions of my acts with all those most glorious women. I told her also of my intrigue at my lodgings with the two sisters and the Count.

My description of the latter set her off in raging lust, and produced another most excellent fuck. But afterwards she told me I must find other quarters in some place where Mrs. Egerton and she, or either of them, could call and receive comfort without observation.

I told her I was inscribed for chambers in the Inner Temple, which I had reason to believe I should get in a week or two. This much pleased her, and it will be seen that I succeeded in getting just such a set as exactly suited the great object in view, approachable without being under the observation of others; commodious and agreeable, where all that the dear Benson wished to be added to our set were brought together, and the wildest orgies of the most insatiable lust were carried on.

My description of my aunt, of Mrs. Dale, and especially of Miss Frankland, now Mrs. Nixon, excited all the tribadic passions for which the dear Benson was so famous.

Her clitoris, which was formerly prominent, was more so now, and she dearly loved to gamahuche her own sex. In that way she took a great fancy to my sisters, especially Eliza, who had all the same instincts very decidedly pronounced. So we had the prospect of the most consummate orgies in near view, and most gloriously in the end we realised our wildest expectations.

In men we were more restricted; the Count would only consent to have Harry Dale and my uncle in any orgy of which he formed part. He was nervously timid about his sodomistic tendencies being known to many, and only yielded on account of the relationship and the closer ties of Harry Dale and myself, who eventually shared my chambers, and we lived together, so that perforce he was obliged to put up with his presence.

He soon came to delight in having Harry's prick in his bottom when fucking others at our orgies. It will thus be seen that the Count's timid exclusiveness shut out from these family orgies my dear and esteemed friend and master MacCallum More. However, in a certain sense, it was an advantage, as we had at least the pick of the young ones, in my two sisters and Ellen, who wanted very little persuasion to join our Lyon's Inn orgies. And our excellent friend had some of his own set, both male and female, to meet us either with one, two or all, for we could not always manage to have the whole of the dear creatures together. *En revanche*, dear MacCallum had several youthful ganymedes, whose tight young bottom-holes were a great solace when cunts were altogether absent.

We thus had two distinct and separate sets of orgies, which had all the natural effect of novelty, and by exciting comparison, making us turn from one to the other with renewed passions and power of enjoyment.

As my sisters could only come on Sundays, that was our exclusive day, and we made an entire day of it, but I, in the end, persuaded Ann to join our orgies with MacCallum, and she proved a first-rate addition in every way.

I have already stated that she was of a most libidinous temperament, and developed into one of the most lascivious and lustful of women one could possibly find, and as she had rare beauties and splendour of form, she was made to raise the most raging lust in man or woman, for she, too, was as fond of tribadic indulgencies as my aunt or the delicious Frankland. Her position as a servant prevented our introducing her to Ellen or my sisters. As a matter of worldly prudency it was best not to trust her with the knowledge of their complying with all our lustful demands on their charming persons.

The Count, myself, and our two charming lovers met on the appointed day to renew our delicious orgies. After both of us had fucked each dear creature came the *double jouissance*.

We took the adorable Benson first, that the scene of our erotic sports might stir the lust of the darling Egerton to a greater heat. It was my turn to lay my offering on the secret altar of Priapus, while the Count filled her cunt with delight.

As I have before said, the arsehole of the Benson was much more used that that of the Egerton, whose husband never dreamt of such a horror, as she would call it. Mr. Benson, on the contrary, delighted in it, and seldom passed a night without paying his devoirs to that delicious aperture. So, although it was but the second time she had indulged in the *double jouissance*, yet her lust enabled her to take in with greater ease my big prick in her arsehole, with the Count's fine prick in front, than when our parts were reversed. She revelled in the wild fury of raging lust, created by the glorious extasy of having a prick in each aperture—screamed with wild cries of heavenly joy, spent furiously, and eventually died away in an overpowering and indescribable felicity. She soon recovered her senses, and begged for another bout before withdrawing. Of course there was immediate compliance and another more soul-killing encounter was run off with the usual death-like termination.

I had continuously gamahuched the Egerton who straddled over the two bodies below her, and brought her delicious cunt to my mouth, while my arms encircled her beautifully formed and cream-like coloured buttocks, at the same time acting postillion with two fingers to increase her lustful gratification.

We purified ourselves after this, and drank some Champagne, then standing stiff at the prospect of now possessing the lovely body of the Egerton, we took up the same position as before, the Count under, in cunt, the Egerton above, with her deliciously fair arse exposed to my embraces first, and my big prick afterwards.

The adored Benson gave it a suck first, and well wetting the knob, guided it to the narrow entrance of love's secret bower. Its head was soon housed, and although still creating strange feelings, the previous day's attack had made the entrance more facile.

With little halting we drove on to the first delicious discharge. The second bout was all divine pleasure, and ever after the delicious Egerton enjoyed it completely.

These delicious orgies with these two lovely women were indulged in on every third day.

I became a favourite with both their husbands, thanks to a kind of sheepish innocence that I had the power of putting on.

At the same time as my education had been well attended to and as I myself was fond of study, attentive to my college instruction, and anxious for a knowledge of foreign languages, I had become fairly proficient in German and Spanish, and well read in French and Italian. The latter was perfected by the Count's friendship, as we were much together and spoke nothing else. Perhaps it was this which led to a greater friendship for me on the part of Mr. Egerton, who was an excellent Italian scholar. His wife's intrigue with the Count had also perfected her, so that when we all four dined together Italian was the only language spoken among us.

The dear Benson, too, was a perfect mistress of the Count's tongue, as well she might, having it so often in her mouth; and as it is a soft language that lends itself to love and lust, it became ours in all our orgies.

The delicious Frankland, now Mrs. Nixon, returned to town with the spring. By that time I was established in my chambers in the Inner Temple, and had them simply furnished, but with every accessory for love's combats in couples, or in the wildest orgies. The adorable Benson inaugurated and dedicated them to the service of holy mother Venus and her son Cupid, as well as the more lustful Eros.

The Egerton and the Count afterwards came to consecrate them to the worship of Priapus, and we had a most delicious orgy on that sacred celebration.

It was on this occasion that those two wild lustful creatures insisted on seeing the Count and me in conjunction together. The Benson guided me into the Count's bottom, while he was in the bottom of the Egerton, and the Egerton conducted the Count into my bottom while I was luxuriating in the delicious arsehole of my adored Benson. It satisfied a longing desire on their parts to see man with man, and did not displease either the Count or myself, who, in our secret hearts, had each wished to possess the other.

The Count was a powerful and very hairy man, and had an especially very full hairy arsehole, which to me was wildly exciting.

In that I differed from my dear friend MacCallum, who

loved bare-arsed youths with no hair there, telling me that
coarse hairy arsed men rather disgusted him, and although
in his wide sodomitic experience he had had such, it was
with a certain repugnance that went against the grain.

In that I differed from him entirely, the hairier and the
coarser a man's arsehole was the more it excited me. In that
respect the Count was exactly to my taste. He was very
hairy all up the chink of his arse, and had a very coarse skin
and an almost black arsehole, so deep a brown it was, the
very sight of which always drove me mad with lust.

He as much loved me from another cause. His great letch
was to frig a fine prick while buggering the possessor, hence,
as he had never met with so fine a one as mine, he was
insatiably fond of being into me and frigging me at the same
time.

We thus had two points of private attraction, that made us
become the closest of friends, but we did not let any of our
dear female participants know of the mutual joys of which
they were not participants.

The superb Frankland, now my guardian's wife, also came
alone to my chambers, and we had a renewal of all our
wildest experiences. She told me it was such a comfort to her,
for although her husband, Mr. Nixon, was very loving, and
did all he could, still it was nothing but exciting her to long
for others, especially for my own huge prick, of which she
never knew but that she had been the first initiator of it into
love's delicious recess in either sacred grove.

So fresh and eager as she was for the fray you may easily
imagine the wild excess we indulged in, sucking, gamahuching, fucking, and buggering. I cannot tell how often in every
way her exciting and glorious body carried me away to an
excess beyond anything I could have thought myself capable
of.

When fairly exhausted, and we could uninterruptedly talk
over all that had occurred since I had left my mother's house,
she heard in full detail, for the first time, all my adventures.

I had given her, at the time of her marriage, a hint of how matters had gone, yet without any details, which now she was voracious to hear. I told her of my aunt's and uncle's apparent seduction of me, nor did I hide our goings-on with young Dale, and my after-possession of Ellen and his mother, who was the last to believe herself my seducer, for as I told the delicious Frankland (I can never bear to call her Nixon), I had followed her sage advice, and up to the Dale had played off the innocent game with perfect success; but now that I was a man I threw all that overboard.

"Indeed," said she, "and who have you been throwing it overboard with."

I laughed at her ready taking of me up, and then went on to a full confession of all my intrigues.

She did not like my having taken up with the two servants, the nieces of my late landlady, thinking it derogatory in one endowed with a prick that any lady would be too glad to possess, but she was very much struck with my description of the superb body and wonderful lubricity of the Nichols.

It excited her much, especially when I told her that she had given me the idea of her near approach in body and wantonness to herself.

It will be seen hereafter to what a closer alliance with the Nichols this led. Pressing her enquiries, I acknowledged my intrigue with the Benson, Egerton, and Count. This evidently excited her lust, as I could see by the wild sparkle of her eye. It led to an immediate and delicious fuck, and when recovered from its extatic finish, to closer and more searching enquiry as to how I got into such intimacy, but I had expected this somewhat jealous scrutiny, and was quite prepared for it. I led her to believe they had been here nearly all the winter. I told her my mother had desired me to call and see the Bensons as friends of hers. I had done so. The Bensons quickly observed how largely I was furnished, very soon gave me encouragement, of which I did not want much after the late intercourse I had had with herself, aunt, and Mrs. Dale.

Thus matters came quickly to their natural conclusion. She was perfectly astonished at my powerful weapon, and as she and her dearest friend already shared lovers, I was quickly introduced to her friend Mrs. Egerton, and they had me together, and let me into the secret of their intrigue with the Count, which was followed by my initiation into their orgies.

My praises of these two ladies, and my saying how glorious it would be for her to make a fifth, and my description of the exquisite body and the tribadic tendencies of Mrs. Benson, fired her wild imagination, and woke up all her tribadic lusts, and it ended in her begging me to give a luncheon at my chambers to the Benson and the Egerton, that she might be introduced to them, more especially as they really moved in a society somewhat higher than Mr. Nixon's connections, although, in point of wealth, the Nixons were far superior.

The little luncheon came off most agreeably. The ladies all took to each other most warmly; seeing which, I boldly broke the ice, and telling the Benson and Egerton that dear Mrs. Nixon was my first initiator in love's mysteries, and as had both of them, the wisest thing we could do would be to throw away all restraint and have a jollification all round. To set them at their ease—for there was a momentary hesitation —I pulled out my prick at full stand, and said—

"There's a prick worthy of all your exquisite cunts, and one, too, that has enjoyed them all, and been enjoyed by every one of you. So throw away all hesitation and let him enjoy you all again. Who is to have it first?"

They laughed, and all approached and handled it, inter-changing their opinions upon its being the very finest one that any of them had ever seen.

"Ah, now," said I, "that is just the thing, you are at once put at ease, then let us do it with ease; strip is the word, and let us have it luxuriously."

They laughed, kissed each other, and said the dear fellow must have his way, and all at once proceeded to undress.

The glorious and wonderfully hairy body of the Frankland perfectly astonished them, and raised their tribadic passions to fever heat, especially the Benson, who threw herself on that glorious form in an extasy of delight, more especially as the Frankland's passions being excited, her long red clitoris stood out from the dense black mass of hair which covered not only her belly and mount, but all down and around her cunt. Nothing would satisfy the Benson but an immediate mutual gamahuche, for, with true tribadic instinct, these two beautiful and libidinous women divined their mutual letch for that particular lascivious inclination, and at once proceeded, one on the top of the other, to wildly gamahuche each other. The Egerton and myself seized the opportunity of having a delicious fuck together, which we brought to a conclusion before the others had satisfied their immediate desires.

The Frankland, who at first was under, was now above, and as she knelt and pushed out her stupendous arse to bring her cunt over the Benson's mouth, the sight of its hairy arsehole roused my desire to fuck it, and my cock responded instantly, so kneeling behind her, I introduced it to the well-known receptacle, and to her infinite additional delight, sodomised her to perfection. This was another means of putting them all at ease, and I fucked and buggered them all until neither handling nor suction could get my prick to raise his head again.

You may easily imagine after this how delighted they were to make the glorious Frankland a participator in our orgies with the Count. Nor shall I forget the wild gaze of surprise and lust when the Count first beheld the splendid and hairy form of the glorious Frankland when she entered the room in all the dazzling splendour of her perfect nakedness. These two natures were made for each other, both salacious to a degree, both vigorous in body and untiring in the most libidinous excesses of the wildest lust. Both hairy to a degree, showing the meaning of that vast display all over both their bodies. They were instantly attracted to each other, flew into the closest of embraces, and sinking on the floor where they met, two strokes were racked off before they came to a state of more moderation, amenable to our general operations. It had been all the same an exciting scene to us.

The Benson was madly stimulated by the sight of the Frankland's superb body; her long red clitoris, not satisfied with the double rack-off with the Count, appeared only to be more excited, and stirred the whole soul of the adorable Benson. She threw herself in reverse upon the Frankland before she had time to raise herself, seized with her mouth the wonderful clitoris, called upon me to fuck her from behind, and then with fingers up arsehole and cunt worked furiously. The dear Frankland responded on the fine clitoris of the Benson, and postillioned me at the same time. We ran off two bouts in this delicious position, and then with more regulated passions rose to form more general combinations.

The Count had fucked the Egerton while we were engaged above the divine Frankland. Our first pose was suggested by the Egerton, who had been as yet less fucked than any. She had been also greatly taken with the glories of the Frankland's superb body, and especially struck with her extraordinary clitoris, and had taken the curious letch of wishing to have it in her bottom-hole while riding St. George on my big prick. We all laughed at her odd choice, but agreed at once, especially the Frankland, whose greatest letch was to fuck very fair young women with her long and capable clitoris. A fairer creature than the lovely Egerton could not be found. The Frankland admitted that in her inmost heart she had longed thus to have the Egerton from the moment she had first seen her, and her delight and surprise at finding the dear Egerton had equally desired to possess her, fired her fierce lust with increased desire. I lay down, the Egerton straddled over, and feeling the delight of my huge prick when completely imbedded, she spent profusely with only two rebounds. Then sinking on my belly she presented her lovely arse to the lascivious embraces of the salacious Frankland, whose first act was to stoop, embrace, kiss, and tongue the beautiful little pinky aperture, wetting it with her saliva, she brought her fine long clitoris, stiff as a prick, and plunged within. The letch that both had taken for the same indulgence lent enchantment to the act, and their wild imaginations created an excess of joy that the smaller size of the Frankland's clitoris, in comparison with the dimensions of our longer pricks, might not have led one to suppose possible.

Twice we indulged in this excess, the women going off half a dozen times to my once.

I had aided the Frankland by using a double dildo, which at once filled both apertures. This excellent instrument was an invention of the Frankland, which she had suggested to a Parisian dildo maker, and had had it made in two or three sizes. It became very useful in our orgies, as from disparity of numbers an odd couple were left out, when the *double jouissance* was in operation, and then the two outsiders, with tongues and dildoes, could gamahuche with great satisfaction.

During our tribadic junction, with the Egerton fucked by the Frankland in the arse, the Count had first fucked and then sodomised the Benson to their mutual satisfaction. We all rose, purified, and refreshed with wine and biscuits, while discussing what our next move should be. The Count had not yet had the Frankland *in culo*, and suggested, as it was her introductory meeting, that the greater honours should be conferred on her on this happy occasion, so I was to fuck her while he enjoyed her in the rear quarters. The Egerton and the Benson should use double dildoes to each other, or in any other way amuse themselves.

This was a most exquisite encounter, and with such unutterable enjoyment that we hardly paused between the first and second, and it was not until we had deluged thrice both interiors that we withdrew. The delighted Frankland had never ceased spending, but so vigorous a nature could easily have taken twice as much; but the other dear creatures had now to be conciliated.

The Count next took the Benson in cunt while I blocked the rear aperture, and the Frankland once more enculed the Egerton, who dildoed herself in cunt at the same time; all of us running two courses. We then rose, purified, and refreshed. When our pricks were ready it was the Egerton who took me in front and the Count behind, and the Benson, who had grown lewd on the Frankland's clitoris, was sodomised by her and dildoed by herself. The Egerton still suffered a little in the double stretching, so that we ran but one exquisite bout, enabling us, whose powers began to fail to be re-excited, to finish with the *double jouissance* in the glorious body of the Frankland.

We carried this on until the midsummer holidays, when at their desire I introduced the Benson, Egerton, Frankland, and the Count to my uncle, aunt, Mrs. Dale, Ellen, and Harry, and we had some glorious orgies in my chambers.

The splendour of my aunt's arse captivated the Frankland and the Count. The latter soon got into young Dale's arse, which he did one day when arriving for the very purpose half an hour before the appointed time of all meeting. I was present, and was so excited at the sight that I seized upon the Count's arse and delightedly astonished him by giving the double enjoyment.

It was after this, as Harry remained to live with me, that he was introduced to our general orgies, and thus we occupied all the dear creatures at once, and most voluptuous and lascivious meetings we all enjoyed, the Count occasionally giving us a private visit.

Meanwhile Ellen had been put to the same finishing school where my sisters already were, with permission to go

out with them on the Sundays, when we always had a delicious orgy at our dear friend MacCallum's. He, like the Count,
had taken a peculiar fancy for the tight young arsehole of
Harry Dale, without altogether deserting the women, especially my sister Eliza, whose delight in rear sports was
supreme, and she never would be fucked but when she had a
prick in each aperture, preferring mine in her cunt with
either Dale or MacCallum operating in the rear.

Knowing the hours when I could not be interrupted by any
of my lady friends, I did not neglect the superb Nichols, but
had her and Ann to come together for an hour and a half,
from half-past nine to eleven A.M., and most delicious fucking
I had with both. I had equally initiated them into the mysteries of rear delights, and both took it with great gusto. Upon
finding this I gradually descanted on the exquisite delights
of the *double jouissance* with two male pricks, filling with
extasies indescribable the two apertures at once.

When once I had excited their desires on this point, I
mentioned my dear friend MacCallum More, as one in whom
we could all confide, and with some little hesitation obtained
their consent to introduce him. I had already mentioned the
matter to him; told him he might think the Nichols too old,
but she was gloriously superb in body, and so extraordinarily
well preserved that her body was twenty years younger than
her face and her lust and fucking powers were far superior
to a woman of twenty-five. Besides, I hinted that he might
persuade Ann, and perhaps her sister Jane, to join our Lyon's
Inn revels.

We met by appointment on a given morning. I advised
MacCallum to come sooner, and when the women came,
under the pretence of his not being able to join us that
morning, I would get them stript, and when all was ready
he should appear in buff, and so break any *mauvaise honte*
they might have at first undressing before him.

He was wonderfully struck with the superb body of the

Nichols, and, as the stranger, we gave him his choice. He clasped her in his nervous arms, devoured her with kisses, and incontinently laying her down on the mattressed floor, proceeded to fuck her in the good old English fashion, with legs and arms around her body. Ann and I gazed for a little on the splendid action of her aunt's arse, and the evident way in which she milked the teat as it withdrew each time he heaved his arse to re-enter with exciting vigour. We could hold no longer and each ran a course of extatic delight ending in all the frenzy of lust to die inanimate the next instant.

Our charming partners had spent repeatedly during our encounter. They wanted an immediate renewal, but Mac-Callum suggested a change of partners and of position, that is to say, fucking them on their knees with their splendidly developed buttocks turned up but taking them in the cunt.

This change was rapidly effected. We placed ourselves in such a position that each could see all the action of the other. It was a splendid fuck, and as our edge was taken off we drew it out a considerable length, giving the dear recipients the opportunity of spending four or five times to our once.

After recovering from the soaking after-joys of this delicious encounter, we had some champagne and some smutty talk, as well as outspoken praise of their splendid power of fuck; feeling their cunts and they our pricks, till renovated and renewed, we arranged for further action. As it was their introductory lesson in the double enjoyment, the splendid Nichols had, of course, first choice. She chose me for cunt, and to his intense delight, our dear friend for the rear attack. Ann was to straddle over her aunt and me, and be gama-huched both in cunt and arsehole by our friend. We had no difficulty in hilting ourselves to the cods in both apertures, but so excited was the Nichols that with the mere throbbings of our pricks on completely housing ourselves, she spent, squealing like a rabbit. We gave her time to fully enjoy it, and then commenced a slow, regulated movement, which quickly drove the Nichols into a state of furiously raving lust, and again she spent in an almost killing agony of delight, screaming with excess of extasy. Again we paused to allow of the utmost enjoyment, but renewed when her delicious cunt and arse pressures announced a return of craving appetite. These pauses enabled us to bring on seven overpouring discharges on her part, until she was quite exhausted, especially when we both came together in an excess of joy that ended in perfect inanition, on recovering from which we relieved the Nichols of the double cargo within her.

She had already almost strangled me with her embraces in the unutterable joys I had procured her. Rolling off on her side she drew MacCallum also to her, to embrace him for the intense gratification he had afforded her. We again refreshed the inward man after a purification and laving with cold water, as a restorative. Then Ann took up her position in her turn, for she, too, wished to try the novel experiment with the smaller prick in her arsehole.

The Nichols felt exhausted for the moment, so lay on the sofa and enjoyed the sight of our three persons in all the delirium of raging lust and sodomy. The experiment enchanted Ann as it had overpoweringly enchanted her aunt. She, too, spent seven or eight times before joining us in our soul-killing discharge. The Nichols had laid still for about two thirds of the time this bout continued, she then rose to straddle across Ann and me, and was about to present her magnificently large cunt to be gamahuched by MacCallum, but he begged her to turn her bottom to him and heave it well up, while resting her hands on Ann's shoulders. He then could first contemplate and handle her huge superb buttocks, then transferring his hands to her clitoris and cunt, he licked and tongued the grand aperture of her arse—rough, brown, and corrugated, just my taste.

We had a most glorious bout, ending in all the extatic

joys of spending and after-delights. Ann was as greatly gratified with the *double jouissance* as her aunt had been before.
We again laved and refreshed, and closed this most delicious
orgy with MacCallum first in the Nichols' cunt, with my big
and doted-on prick in her arse, which, now she was used to it,
pleased her more than ever.

In the same order we double-fucked Ann, although she expressed her greater gratification of MacCallum in her arse and
my splitter in her cunt. Again we gamahuched them both,
as time would not allow of our resurrection, then they left us.

My guardian, at his marriage, had bought a house in
Portland Place, but the lease of its then tenant only expired
on the 30th March this spring, and before being occupied
it had to be entirely new painted and decorated, so that July
was nearly at an end before they could comfortably take up
their residence in it. Meanwhile they had apartments at a
hotel near Hyde Park corner.

When once they were completely housed, which was not
the case until the middle of August, my guardian desired his
wife to send the carriage for the girls every Sunday morning.
Hearing that Ellen was their intimate friend, she became
included in the invitation. This put an end to our Sunday
orgies in our friend MacCallum's chambers, much to our
mutual regret.

As far as Harry and I were concerned the ever thoughtful
and delicious Frankland came to our aid. Pretending that the
girls must need walking exercise, she always after luncheon
proposed they should walk down to their brother's chambers
in the Temple, take him and Harry as their further companions up to Kensington Gardens or the "Zoo," and bring
all back to dinner.

As my guardian always took a siesta on Sundays after
luncheon, for being too old to fuck his wife every night,
Saturday night, or rather Sunday morning, when he had
nothing in the way of business to trouble him, was dedicated

to two or three hours of extra dalliance with his adored wife. She told me he was very amorous upon her, could not do much fucking, indeed, she thought his efforts that way were even more than he ought to do at his age, but he was never tired of gamahuching her and posing her in every attitude when stark naked; of course she lent herself to every wish of the old man, and had, even after great persuasion, which only her love and attachment to him could have even made her consent, allowed him the honours of her beautiful arsehole. This requiring, as he said, an extra firmness of prick, she further did him the extra favour of toying and sucking his prick up to the utmost stiffness. So she had made him absolutely adore her, and she could turn him round her little finger. Her word and will was law, so she could do as she liked.

She told me on several occasions that she thought he was exerting his erotic powers to too great an extent, and that she did all she could to moderate his excitement, but all to no purpose; he was infatuated with the glorious charms of her body, or what is called *cunt-struck*, perhaps the strongest passion that can seize on man and dangerous for a man of advanced years. Well, his Sunday afternoon's siesta was long, and left the Frankland at liberty to come to my rooms with my sisters, where strip was the word, and fucking in every variety followed.

I soon found we must have other help; the pace I was going at was beginning to tell, so with the consent of the darling Frankland I made a confidant of the Count, and asked him to join our Sunday's orgy. You may imagine with what joy he accepted, for apart from his delight in seeing me in incestuous connection with my sisters, their young charms, especially Eliza's, had great attraction for him, and then the Frankland, so similar in lust and temperament. We had thus most delicious orgies every Sunday afternoon, until the end of October of the following year, when my sisters had finished

their schooling, and I, too, had left college, entered at the
Middle Temple, and had been for three months in a con-
veyancer's office, reading up previous to being called to the
bar.

It was then that Mr. Nixon's health gave symptoms of
serious disturbance, and his doctor recommended him to pass
the winter in a warmer climate. His wife suggested the advantage travelling would be both to the girls and myself; she
had only to express the wish to have us all together, and we
were warmly invited to join them.

We passed through Switzerland, Milan, and Florence to
Rome, where we took up our residence for four months.

The Egertons and Bensons happily spent the same winter
at Rome.

My rooms were in an adjoining palace to where Mr. and
Mrs. Nixon and my sisters resided, there not being accom-
modation for me. I thus had a charming entresol of five rooms
all to myself; one of which looked on and over the Tiber, and
was in no way overlooked. To this room we constantly resorted for orgies.

The Egertons had passed some winters in Rome, and she
had two or three clerical lovers, and these had introduced
two others to the Benson on her former visits, and all had
been accustomed to general orgies. You may imagine the delight of these priestly debauchees when they found themselves introduced to our circle of three fresh cunts, and such
splendid ones, and all without any mock-modest prejudices
but up to every excess of lubricity. So to five women we thus
had six men, and eventually a very handsome young priest,
debauched by the others, joined our party, and we carried on
the wildest and most extravagant orgies of every excess the
most raging lust could devise. We made chains of pricks in
arseholes, the women between with dildoes strapped round
their waist, and shoved into the arsehole of the man before

them, while his prick was into the arsehole of the woman in his front.

These holy fathers had immense resources in the way of infinite variety, stimulating to excesses of debauchery that very soon brought the rod into requisition.

We all from time to time enjoyed the double coition, the women invariably so at every meeting.

These holy fathers had all very fine pricks, but none so large as mine, and many of them loved to have my prick in their arses when opportunity offered. In such delights the winter passed rapidly away.

In the spring Mr. Nixon's health seemed very precarious, and we moved to Naples, where from necessity our extreme indulgence in venereal excesses was much curtailed.

In May we returned to England, but poor Mr. Nixon was evidently fucked out. The Frankland told me that the more his health failed the more lewd he seemed to grow. His passion for gamahuching her cunt had increased, and even his prick seemed to gather new life as life ebbed away, for hardly a night passed without his fucking her, at night in the cunt, and at morning, in full daylight, kneeling and feeling her splendid arse, he took her in the rear aperture. He and she too felt it was killing him, but his infatuation was over-powering, and he declared if it did kill him he could not die a happier death. In fact a month after we returned he had an apoplectic fit actually when his prick was spending in her arsehole. He lived but a month afterwards. He left all his property to his wife absolutely, with legacies of £2,500 to each of my sisters, and 1,000 to me.

This sad event cast a gloom for some time over all our pleasures.

The Frankland took my sisters to reside with her, but all went down to spend the first three months of mourning quietly with my mother. She, too, took ill when we were with her, and died before the three months were up. This drew me down to home, now mine, and the dear Frankland continued to stay with us for two months longer, and then left for London. We three orphans remained for all that winter in our old home, settling a variety of things.

My sisters now with their succession to some £600 apiece, the £1,000 left them by our uncle, and the £2,500 by Mr. Nixon, and the £400 which I promised them as a marriage present, and with their great beauty of form and face, for both had grown into remarkably fine young women, became very eligible matches.

Many country families sought us out after the first three months of our mourning, and several offers were made to the girls. They were both somewhat fastidious after the life they had led, but eventually both were married. Mary to a very nice fellow, who proved, as she told me, a first-rate fucker. He got her with child, and they had a son, a fine boy, in the tenth month of their marriage. She was very happy, now and then coming to see me, and getting a jolly good fuck from my renovated prick, for now that he was lying fallow, my somewhat exhausted system was getting quite recruited.

Alas! poor Mary lost her husband by cholera in the second year of their marriage. He had a handsome estate, and left her well off, and sole guardian to his son, who grew up a very fine fellow, and when at puberty became the solace of his widowed mother, who had initiated him into all love's mysteries.

Eliza was not quite so fortunate as her sister in her husband; he was a good sort of man who, one would have thought, would just have suited the hot temperament of Eliza, well and powerfully built, and with an air of being a man of erotic passions; but he turned out to be of a languid unimpassioned nature, who could not imagine any other manner than simply mounting on a woman's belly and fucking her once a night, and with no conception of using either preliminaries or aids to her passions. So that he left poor

Eliza only in a state of excitement instead of giving any satisfaction to her lascivious nature. She did, eventually, work
him up to good night and good morning, but for her full
satisfaction she used too seek elsewhere, and even to content herself with the embraces of a man servant, who, if not
good looking, proved to have a splendid and powerful prick,
and nearly daily gave her comfort. She also occasionally came
to me, when she had both apertures well exercised, and left
me much comforted.

She never had any children, and so managed her intrigues
as never to be found out.

I returned to London in the spring, and was called to the
bar.

I went the western circuit for odd assizes, and then abandoned the bar as a profession.

Harry Dale, with more perseverance, as well as greater
necessity for exertion, continued in the profession, was duly
called to the bar, and eventually became a rising and successful barrister, and at this period of our old age is now a distinguished judge.

But to return to our earlier days.

Harry and I carried on our intrigue with the Nichols and
Ann, aided by our dear friend MacCallum. Also from time
to time with the Benson, Egerton, and Count, to which generally the darling Frankland brought her exquisite charms to
intoxicate us with pleasure.

This delightful reunion was sadly affected by the loss of the
Count, who received an amnesty—I think I before have said
he was a political exile—returned to his own country, and we
never again had his delightful aid in our sadly shortened
orgies.

The Count and I met in a future year at his old castle on
the hills of Pied, of which I shall have much more to say on a
later occasion.

It was a sad loss, especially for the Egerton, who dearly

loved the Count. He had been her first lover, indeed, her initiator in the real mysteries of Venus. It will be remembered that her husband was one of those old insensible natures that think it is only necessary to hastily "piss their tallow," as Falstaff says, as quickly as they can, and leave a poor woman just sufficiently excited to be madly anxious for a thorough good fucking. It is these insensate cold-blooded husbands who raise, without satisfying, their wife's erotic passions, and drive them perforce to seek salacious comfort in other arms.

Oh! how many women if only fucked with some regard to their own naturally lewd feeling, would have never committed adultery or made a scandal. Many are the women who have told me, with tears in their eyes, of the cold insensible conduct of their husbands, who, never fucking them but when their sluggish natures felt the want, then turning upon them without the slightest preparatory handling or embracing, mount, shove it in, give a few in-and-out movements, spend, and then withdraw, just as they have done enough to excite their poor wives' passions without satisfying them, and thus leaving them a prey to inordinate longing that forces them to seek the relief to their passions the selfish brutes of husbands had only raised without allaying.

I remember an intrigue I had with an Italian Countess. Her husband, a tall and very capable man, was an extreme bigot, who thought it deadly sin to indulge in any caresses or carnal excitement, or even for his wife to expose any naked flesh to raise concupiscent ideas, so she had to have her nightgown closed up to her throat, with long sleeves and skirts, in the centre a slit through which he performed his duty when in want of relief to himself. He never kissed or embraced her body at any time, but lay like a log by her side, with his back turned to her. When his own passions prompted him to fuck, which was very seldom, he was naturally quite ready and rapidly finished his coup. He used to turn to her, waken her up with a shake, cry out, "Marietta, porgemi il vaso generativo" (Marietta, reach me the generative vase), upon which she stretched herself on her back, he got on her without lifting her petticoats or feeling her cunt, but opening the slit, pointed his prick to her cunt, thrust it up to the hilt, and being himself in want of spermatic relief, in a very few strokes spent, just staying in long enough to "piss all his tallow," and then withdraw, turning his back again to sleep, leaving his wife just sufficiently excited to have enjoyed it, and thus left her madly longing for the satisfaction he did not afford. She said he was quite capable, too, of giving satisfaction if his bigotry had allowed him. We used to fuck at a tremendous rate, and I always commenced with a "Marietta, Marietta, porgemi il vaso generativo," and then proceeded to fuck and laugh like mad.

Of course, irritated as her hot passions were by her booby of a husband, she resorted, not only to me, but to whomsoever she could get to satisfy the cravings of her irritated cunt.

The Bensons and Egertons again left in the autumn for Rome.

The Frankland, not yet out of her year's widowhood, did not go much into society, and we saw much more of her than before. She came at least three times a week to my chambers, when Harry and I gave her the comfort she so much required; first each fucking her singly twice over, and then three double-pleasure fucks, with change about in the apertures: finishing off with a mouth fuck from one or the other, and a double gamahuche.

About once a week the amorous and delicious-fucking Nichols with Ann would come of a morning, when we managed to send both away satisfied for the day.

When winter drove our friend MacCallum home from his fishing, we renewed some excellent orgies at his chambers, where Ann, and afterwards Jane, occasionally came. By the way, Jane's arse had developed in an extraordinary manner, and became one of the most exciting delights of our orgies at MacCallum's. He also now joined in our morning encounters with the Nichols and her niece.

At Christmas time the Frankland, Harry, and I all went down by invitation to the Rectory, where uncle welcomed with great delight the glorious and exciting Frankland. Mrs. Dale and Ellen joined our party. Dear aunt positively devoured me with her caresses, and before I was shown up to my room, had drawn me into her little room downstairs, had a suck at my prick, leant her body on the table, stuck out her immense arse, and had me into her cunt for a rapid rack-off; but this only excited me to an immediate renewal, for the touch and sight of her splendid buttocks instantly produced a stiffness, she herself in the middle of my movements in front, drawing my prick out of her cunt and guiding it into the inviting entrance to the secret altar of Juno and of Venus Callipyge. Both courses were run off at a gallop, and were a momentary allaying of the insatiable salacity of my most lewd and lascivious aunt. She then next conducted the Frankland, I can never call her Nixon, into her bedroom, under pretence of showing her to it. She no sooner had her there than up went her petticoats, and aunt glued her lips to the wonderful clitoris of the divine Frankland, and using fingers up both apertures, made the Frankland quickly give down her first offering to the obscene god.

As soon as aunt's tribadic rage to possess the Frankland was thus abated for the moment, she allowed Mrs. Nixon to remove bonnet and shawl, but then as quickly demanded and obtained a double gamahuche. The Frankland the more readily consenting as she knew aunt had taken the keen edge off my lecherous appetite, and she would revel in the thick raging sperm I had shot into both orifices. These preliminaries settled, we were able to be much more tranquil all the afternoon.

The Dale and Ellen came to dinner; I slipt into their room when all were dressing for dinner, and had a delicious rack-off in both their lecherous and longing cunts. Uncle had equally enjoyed the tight favourite arsehole of Harry Dale, he having conducted him to the well-known summer house for that purpose as soon as we arrived.

We could all thus peaceably enjoy the good things set before us, and during our wine after dinner exchange accounts of all events that had passed since last we met, and they were varied, for Mr. Nixon's death and legacies to my sisters and myself were subjects of congratulation, while the death of my mother was, on the contrary, one of condolence and sympathy.

By ten o'clock we all broke up, but with the whispered request to all to repair to aunt's bedroom half an hour after the household had retired. We were all too interested in the delicious orgy there to take place to fail. Blazing fires in both that and the adjoining room had been kept up all the afternoon; plenty of lights were burning so as to illuminate all sides at once. We all met in mere night wrappers, and as soon as we were assembled and the word given "off," they were thrown aside, and we all stood in nature's lovely nakedness. Aunt, in her eager and lascivious inspirations, flung herself on my naked body, drew me to the bed, and had me into her longing and delicious cunt at once, and with legs and arms thrown round me, was instantly pressing furiously forward, notwithstanding the remonstrance of my uncle, who wished to arrange a general plan of operations so as to include all at once. Aunt's voluptuous eagerness produced a rapid discharge on her part. Seeing this, while she was in the momentary extasy of spending, he was enabled to drag me from her arms, fortunately before I had weakened my powers by spending for a fourth time that day. Aunt, too, was now in a condition to listen to reason, and bring her ideas of our after-combinations into play.

As we had brought the Count with us for a week's stay, we were just four cocks to four hens; so we could couple in the first instance on an exact equality, it being necessary by previous good fucking to bring the women's passions up to a boiling heat of lust to make them enter into our greater excesses with all the wild energy of the most salacious lubricity. Aunt had taken a great fancy to the Count when up at midsummer.

Uncle was most lecherous on the glorious Frankland. I took most readily to the luscious and lascivious Dale, who was equally eager to repossess the prick which she firmly believed she had initiated into all the joys of cunt, and a most delicious fuck we had, she spending furiously and frequently to my once.

Harry was equally pleased to pair off with his loved cousin, whose maidenhead he had undoubtedly taken.

The women would gladly have had each fucker run a second course without drawing. But both aunt and uncle opposed this, as both more exhausting and less variety. So aunt chose me, uncle took the exciting young cunt of Ellen, Harry turned on to his mother's cunt, from whence he had originally come into the world, and the Count got the glorious Frankland, of whom he was never tired. This course was more prolonged by the men than the first, with the object of somewhat allaying the insatiable lust of the women by making them spend infinitely oftener than their fuckers.

We so managed matters that we all came together or nearly so, and the women followed suit at the last final crisis, which was ushered in with wild cries of lust, and then a sudden overpowering silence fell on all as they lay panting in all the after-joys that follow the extatic discharge of life's essence.

We rose for a general embrace of our naked bodies, then a romp, and a mutual slapping of arses and seizing of pricks and cunts, a very exciting game, which soon brought evidences of renewed vigour in all except poor uncle, who required a longer pause and an extra excitement before he could indulge in a third encounter.

The Count took the delicious arsehole of the Frankland, who begged for me as her fucker. Aunt got Mrs. Dale under for a double gamahuche, while Harry crammed his prick up aunt's arse. Uncle enjoyed a delicious gamahuche with Ellen, who sucked his limp prick all the time without any success.

This was a delicious bout for us all, and ended in heavenly raptures.

Our second double couplings were: myself in my aunt's cunt, which incest stimulated uncle to a stand, and he took to his wife's arse while her nephew incestuously fucked her cunt. The Count took to the delicious and most exciting tight cunt of the Dale, while her son shoved his prick into his mother's arse, to her unspeakable satisfaction. Ellen and the Frankland amused themselves with tribadic extravagances.

This bout was long drawn out, and afforded inexpressible extasies to all concerned. And after the wild cries and most bawdy oaths that instantly preceded the final extasy, the dead silence and long after-enjoyments were drawn out to a greater length than before. After which we all rose and purified, and then took refreshment of wine and cake, while discussing our next arrangement of couples.

Uncle had, fortunately for him, managed not to spend in the last bout; he, therefore, was still capable of entering an arsehole, and he chose the delicious arse of the Frankland to receive this final offering, for after that he was done for that night. I was below engulphed in the exquisite cunt of the Frankland. The Count fucked Ellen while Harry was into her behind. Aunt and Mrs. Dale mutually gamahuched and dildoed each other. This, too, was a long-drawn-out affair and ended in perfectly convulsive extasies and cries of the wildest sensuality that our most salacious passions could prompt.

I then took my aunt's arse while the lecherous Dale was

underneath gamahuching and dildoing her, and by putting the Dale close to the edge of the bed, the Count stood between her legs, which were thrown over his shoulders, and thus he fucked her, having taken a letch to fuck her cunt, which was an exquisite one for fucking: her power of nip being nearly equal to the Frankland, and only beaten by aunt's extraordinary power in that way. We thus formed a group of four enchained in love's wildest sports together.

The Frankland was gamahuched by uncle while having Harry's prick in her arse, Ellen acting postillion to Harry's arse while frigging herself with a dildo.

The closing bout of the night was the Count into aunt's arse, my prick into the Frankland's arse, Harry enjoying an old-fashioned fuck with his mother, and Ellen under aunt to dildo and be gamahuched and dildoed by aunt. We drew this bout out to an interminable length, and lay for nearly half an hour in the annihilation of the delicious after-joys. At last we rose, purified, and then restoring our exhausted frames with Champagne, embraced and sought well-earned sleep in our separate chambers.

I slept the sleep of the just, and awoke late to find aunt sucking my stiff-standing prick at the very instant it was filling her mouth with a deluge of creamy spunk. She sucked up to the get all out, and in doing so brought him up to the scratch again, so jumping out of my low bed I made her kneel on it, stick out her enormous arse, and licked her reeking cunt until I could stand it no longer. Then bringing my huge prick I plunged in a single vigorous thrust up to the very top of her cunt, and made her squeal and spend with that alone. Pausing to let her enjoy it, I recommenced and ran a delicious course in that most exquisite cunt, and would have done so a second time, after a pause of extasy, if Harry Dale had not rushed into the room to say that all were impatiently awaiting me to sit down to breakfast. Aunt just stayed to give a final suck to my prick, and then vanished.

I hastened to wash and dress, having sent Harry off to beg they would not wait for me.

On joining them the sly jokes they cut at my apparent laziness proved that they knew of the cause of detention. I looked at dear aunt, and at once saw by the air of gratification on her dear plump face, that she herself had been boasting of her exploit, for it was all her own doing.

Being Sunday, we all went decorously to church. The doctor gave us a very unctuous sermon on the goodness of virtue and chastity. It was a really fine sermon, and delivered with an unction that forbade the possibility of supposing that the preacher could be in reality the very reverse of his doctrine. It much pleased some of the country families, and one or two with their wives waited for the doctor leaving the church, to compliment him on his eloquence and admirable teaching. The flattered doctor ended by inviting two rather distant residents to luncheon at the Rectory, so that we formed a numerous party, all on our best behaviour. It was quite edifying to hear the pious and virtuous remarks of the admirable Frankland, and the no less virtuous and correct Dale. It gained them the *entrée* into the exclusive set of both these high country families, and eventually led to an excellent marriage for the dear little Ellen. So much for the success of dissimulation. Vice playing the part of virtue, and succeeding to perfection. So goes the world. One thing is certain, that on this occasion it enforced chastity, in one sense at least, that we had no opportunity of practising vice that afternoon. The charming Frankland-Nixon made a great impression on the wives as well as husbands, to be sure it was well known that she was a very wealthy widow, and they may have had some design of securing her for a son, nephew, or at least having the chance at it. She thanked them with that grace and charming ease of manner which so distinguished her and made her so captivating, excusing herself from visiting, during the first year of her widowhood, anywhere but among family friends, and as her late husband was Charles Roberts's and his sisters' guardian, she considered his family as almost her own. They hoped to have the pleasure of seeing her some future day.

The whole visit passed off very pleasantly, and left us only an hour for a stroll in the garden and time to dress for dinner. It will be recollected that the doctor was a great exacter of full evening dress at dinner, as tending to keep up proper appearances.

We met at the accustomed hour at night in aunt's room, in the full dress of Adam and Eve before they munched the apple.

This night was dedicated chiefly to sacrifices to Venus Apostrophia, for the doctor commenced by having the Count while he was fucking his wife, and when able to get his fine old cock in for another go, would only again have it in my arse, while I was doing the same to aunt's glorious immensity with the Count below fucking her.

That was the end of poor uncle's powers for that night, but he gamahuched all the women at the finish of their encounters with us three men. We gave them all the *double jouissance*, while those unoccupied carried on their own little game with tongue or dildo.

It was again a night of most exquisite enjoyment.

The following and remaining nights of our visit brought into requisition the rod before uncle could get his dear old prick to stand, and myself tailed off on the next Sunday night, the last of our visit, so that uncle seeing what he called the laziness of my prick, seized the rod, and gave me as sound a flogging as ever he had done in my schoolboy days. The fact was that he had been longing to renew on my arse his letch for giving a really severe whipping. He had already by dint of the same punishment fucked the arses of the Count and the divine Frankland, and was now so excited anew that his prick stood as stiff as ever it did; and my red excoriated arse excited and renewed his very fine prick; but first I insisted upon moving to aunt's arse, who at the moment was having a last fuck from the Count, and this incestuous group closed our orgies on this occasion, for we left for town the next day.

After breakfast in the morning I slipt into the Dale's room, and had a parting fuck both with her and Ellen. Harry came in while we were at work, Ellen under the Dale gamahuching her, and I above administering a rear adieu. Harry stopped us for a moment until he could withdraw Ellen and take her place, that he might have a parting fuck with his loved mother, who thus had the two pricks she most loved in the world into her together. We drew our pleasure out to the utmost length our lust would allow of and spent in the most extatic joy that poor human nature could support.

Aunt had gone to the Count's bedroom at the very time we were meeting in Mrs. Dale's. Notwithstanding which, her insatiable cunt made her draw me into her sanctum downstairs for a final fuck at the last moment of our parting.

Harry Dale staying behind to pass a week at home with his mother, the adorable Frankland, the Count and I returned to town together. On the journey up we agreed to dine at Very's in Regent Street, and have a comparatively quiet night all together at my chambers, which we did, luxuriating in having the glorious naked body of the delicious Frankland between us. After we had each bedewed both her front and rear orifices with our life's balmy essence, we slept soundly till morning, when we renewed our double offerings on those glorious and delicious altars, then breakfasted.

This was the last occasion but one of our having the Count, whose time for departure to his own country was drawing near.

He left that day on a visit to a family in Scotland, whose son and heir was really the fruit of his loins.

On his return some fortnight later we again passed a

night with our exquisite friend the Frankland, and being both fresh from the country, we administered so many delicious coups to both apertures as quite contented her salacious love of prick. We parted next day with our loved friend the Count, but not for the last time, as I shall relate in its proper place—a delightful visit we paid to him in his old ancestral castle, and an after-recontre with him and his sister in Turin.

I saw my loved Frankland to her home and left town myself the same afternoon for my home in the country, to arrange for various repairs and alterations required on the property.

I took my dear friend MacCallum with me. We spent a pleasant ten days, varied with a visit first from one of my sisters and then from the other, for two nights each, and jolly nights we spent fucking in every way.

Mary's belly was up, but she declared it only made fucking more delicious than ever to her, still more with the *double jouissance,* in which she preferred the smaller prick of Mac-Callum to mine in her arse.

When Eliza came she stayed a third night, and taxed our powers to the utmost; she was such a glutton for fuck on this occasion, declaring that her husband's want of power, as well as tact, left her more lewd after his fucking her than she was before, so that she had been forced by the excess of her unsatisfied lust produced by her husband to have recourse to the fine prick of her footman, a powerful young fellow, otherwise very plain, and not likely to inspire jealousy to any husband, but with whom she rarely could do more than get a rack-off in a hurry, which was far from satisfaction sufficient for her hot passions. It was this that made her revel with such insatiable desires in the possession of our almost untiring pricks. Differing from Mary in her love of rear-fucking, it was my big prick she loved best to have in her arse, while MacCallum's lesser shaft satisfied her less exacting cunt. She was certainly one of the lewdest creatures ever made, wildly lascivious and full of variety. She had the most engaging ways with her, and could raise a prick from the dead. She was a worthy pupil of the Frankland, and had all the love and longing for prick, and cunt too, that our deliciously insatiable aunt was so famous for. She grew older, and becoming one of the most desirable women, I never tired of fucking her in both orifices whenever the opportunity presented itself.

I returned to town just in time to have a parting orgy with the Count and the Frankland in my chambers, which I before said was a night of the wildest orgies.

MacCallum was called to the country by the illness of some of his family, and was absent for six months, so I was left with Harry to have occasional orgies together with the Frankland three times a week, and with the Nichols and Ann or Jane once a week by way of variety, but as they only came for a morning visit, these were not exhausting encounters, so that we lay comparatively in fallow, till the return of the Benson and Egerton, when they and the lovely Frankland taxed us to the utmost twice or thrice a week.

Thus time progressed. The Frankland had been a widow for nearly two years when she proposed to travel for two or three years without returning in the interval to England. She wished me to accompany her, and made a most surprising and unexpected proposition to me.

She said, "Charlie, my own darling, I love you more dearly than ever. It is true I am considerably older than you, but you are now twenty-five years of age, and, therefore, a full-grown man. I wish to endow you with all my great wealth, and I offer you my hand in marriage. Do not suppose I want to monopolize this dear prick." (We were in bed naked, and had just concluded a most exquisite fuck.) "No, with our love of variety we will still seek it out, but as husband and wife we can do so with perfect ease and safety; whereas if not married and travelling together we should be compromised at every city we stop at. What say you, my darling Charlie?"

Here she threw herself on my bosom with loving eyes upraised to mine.

"Say, beloved of my soul! Why, look how the very idea has raised my prick to instant life. If anything in the world could delight me more than another it is your generous noble offer. To dedicate my life to the woman I love more than any other is a joy greater than I can express. I thank you from my soul, adorable creature as you are. Oh! come to my arms as my future wife and let us revel in the glorious idea."

Such was the way in which this happiness was conferred on me, which endured for long years, although, alas, my widowed heart now all hopelessly ever regrets that most lovable of women and best of wives. Oh, what happiness it was as long as I possessed her.

We were married in a few days after this by special license. The Benson and the Egerton were present and Harry Dale was my best man. We adjourned to her house, now ours, to breakfast. They also stayed to dinner and slept at our house, that we might celebrate our marriage with a parting orgy, for we announced to our friends that in marrying, so far from renouncing our orgies, we meant our union to promote ever varying ones, and that on our return we would renew the exquisite ones we had so often enjoyed with them.

Harry and I did all we could on that happy occasion to satisfy three of the finest women in the world, whose delicious power of fucking was never surpassed and rarely equalled.

Oh! we had such a delicious night. As to the women, their amorous gamahuching of each other was ever renewed, and was most exciting to see.

After breakfast that morning they stopped to see us off, and threw old slippers after us for luck.

We posted down to aunt's for a day and a night on our way to the continent.

They were, of course, delighted with my marriage as bringing great wealth into the family, indeed, my darling presented aunt with a cheque for £1000.

Mrs. Dale and Ellen came over, and we had another delicious night's orgy, in which all exerted themselves to the utmost.

We parted from dear aunt and uncle, Mrs. Dale and Ellen, after luncheon, and posted down to Dover; slept at Birmingham's Hotel, where we had our real first night's fucking all to ourselves, enjoyed it in moderation but in every endearment that two lovers could devise.

We crossed to Calais next day.

The sea was smooth at first, but we found it after passing the Foreland very rough. My dear wife suffered severely; fortunately I myself never felt better, and was thus able to devote every attention to the dear sufferer. It left her even after we landed with nausea and a severe headache, so that night at Devaux's Hotel we slept each in one of the separate beds in the same room, as is usual in French hotels, and indeed in continental hotels in general.

My darling wife was far from feeling well next morning, but fancied that posting on to Abbeville would rather tend to recovery than otherwise. We accomplished this easily between breakfast and dinner, found a very comfortable hotel with very fair cooking and excellent wines. My wife enjoyed her dinner, and felt something like herself after it. We slept together by bringing the two beds side by side, but only took a single fuck before sleeping, and next morning a double one.

We spent the day at Abbeville, wandering through its quaint streets and seeing its fine unfinished cathedral. The following day we posted to Amiens, visiting its very beautiful cathedral, posted the following day to Beauvais, again slept, passed next day there, and on the following day posted up to Paris, and drove to Meurice's Hotel in the rue de Rivoli.

We had previously written for a set of rooms *au premier,* overlooking the Tuileries Gardens, with orders to have dinner ready at a given hour. We arrived just in time to change our travelling costume and to sit down to a luxurious dinner. Here, as we had ordered, our bedroom contained a proper large bed for both to sleep in. This hotel being much used by the English was furnished with French taste but English comfort.

The dilatory manner of our journey, the agreeable breaks we had made at different interesting towns had quite restored my beloved wife to all her accustomed health, energy, and lubricity. The comfort of the bed, the stimulating cheer, and the excellent wine also nerved me to meet her utmost lasciviousness, and we had a night such as we used to have when I first had her in my mother's spare bedroom.

We recalled those happy days, and revelled in every lascivious act of the hottest lust. My adored wife excelled herself, and I myself was fully up to the mark; we fucked ourselves to sleep, with prick left soaking in her deliciously tightest of cunts, so that on awaking in full daylight I found my cock stiff standing in her cunt, which was giving it most delicious pressures, quite involuntarily, for the darling was not yet awake. I roused her by gentle movements, and the frigging of her long delicious clitoris, so that she awoke to joys of which we never tired. On this occasion natural wants compelled a temporary withdrawal to relieve our distended bladders. We found that it was already past ten o'clock, so she smacked my bare bottom and sent me off to my dressing-room, that both might get ready for breakfast, for which our appetites were already craving. I slipt on a dressing-gown, went into our sitting-room, rang for a waiter, and ordered breakfast to be got ready immediately, so that by the time we were dressed it was on the table all smoking hot, and we sat down and did full justice to it.

We spent several days in visiting the wonders of Paris.

I had heard of a famous bawd residing at No. 60, rue Richelieu, and another, Madame Leriche, in the rue de Marc, where they had rooms, from which, through cleverly arranged peep-holes, any operation in the next room could be distinctly seen.

Madame Leriche's girls were instructed to get the finest men they could see in the street, to bring them in, and there to pretend to be so struck with their beauty that they would not be content without having them quite naked, stripping themselves also. When quite naked they caressed their pricks, waltzed round the room, taking care to stop exactly opposite each hidden opening, and there caress, handle, and show the standing prick to any looker-on, eventually fucking in such a position as all peepers could fully see and enjoy.

The fun of the thing was the perfect unconsciousness of the men as to the purpose of all these gyrations. They took it proudly as a homage to their virility, and the power of their charms over their new conquest, and were doubly lustful in consequence, little imagining it was all a well-acted scene, got up for an exhibition to please others, and show all their virile gifts. Sometimes both man and girl were very attractive, and I used to fuck my loved Florence while in the act of peeping.

The place where we sat to see was a small narrow room, with just space for a couch on one side and two chairs at the end, next to each peep-hole. Three other similar narrow rooms looked into the same operating room.

One day we had an exciting fuck from the exhibition of a very fine man fucking his girl with a splendid prick. We were kneeling on the couch with my prick soaking in the quietude of the after-joy. We heard a scuffling with suppressed bawdy exclamations on the other side of the thin partition next to us. We, too, had made use of bawdiness. I had whispered to Florence how deliciously tight her hairy cunt was, and how splendidly her enormous arse moved below my eyes as I fucked her.

We now discovered that the couple next to us had overheard us, for we could just hear her ask if her arse's movement and size pleased him as much as their neighbour's seemed to have done.

"Oh, yes, my angel, you wriggle your immense arse to perfection, and your cunt is almost too tight."

"Then fuck on with your splendid prick as hard as our neighbours were at it." A happy thought seized me. I put my finger to my lip to give the hint to Florence, slipped out into the passage and peeped through the keyhole, which commanded the whole of the narrow room. I beheld a handsome man fucking a superbly stout woman, kneeling with her head down low, but towards the door. Her arse uncovered and held aloft was a remarkably fine one, wriggling indeed to perfection.

I slipped back, described it to my dear wife, and suggested our speaking to them through the partition as soon as they were done, to avow that we had heard all their goings-on, as they had ours, and to propose that we should form a *partie carrée*.

Florence jumped at the idea, just as their sighs and shaking of their couch against the partition announced the grand final crisis.

We allowed them some minutes for the after-satisfaction; we then heard the lady beg him to do it again as she felt his cock was stiffening within her cunt.

"No wonder," said he, "when your delicious tight cunt is giving me such exquisite pressures."

We thought this a happy moment, as they were both in a state of lasciviousness; so tapping at the partition, and raising my voice just sufficient to be clearly heard, I said—

"You have been following our example, and seem as lustful as we are, suppose we join parties and exchange partners. I am sure you must be two desirable persons, and you will find us worth knowing. It will be a novelty exciting to all, and will lead or not, as it may be, to a further acquaintance or just a momentary caprice. What say you?"

A pause and a whisper was followed by—

"Eh! bien, nous acceptons."

"Come to us, for I am half undressed," cried the gentleman.

We rose and went in unto them, even in a biblical sense. My slight peep had given me an idea of two handsome persons, but a full view proved them to be eminently so. He was still up to the hilt from behind. She lifted her head to look at us on entering, but left her splendid arse exposed, and did not for the moment alter her position. We handled and pressed it. The gentleman feeling my wife's arse cried out to his dearie—

"Here's an arse equal to yours."

Meanwhile, as I stood by her side feeling hers, she slipped her hand into my flap, and in answer to his exclamation, said—

"There's a prick bigger than yours. Oh, I see we shall all be delighted."

She rose and pulled out my standing prick to show it to her husband, for like us they turned out to be a most salacious couple of married people.

My wife laid hold of the husband's prick, and declared it to be a very fine one, and a delicious variety which was always charming.

I proposed, as the room and couch could only accommodate one couple, that I should take his wife into our room, and leave mine with him, and as the two couches were close to the partition between, we could excite each other by our mutual sighs and bawdy exclamations. This was at once agreed to.

We all of us stripped to the buff; my new companion was magnificently made—very much of my aunt's figure, with a splendid arse, although not so enormously developed as dear aunt's. Her cunt was delicious, a grand mons Veneris, sweetly haired with silky curls; her pouting cunt had the true odour, and was very tight, and her pressures and action left nothing to desire.

I gamahuched her first—her clitoris was well defined and stiff. Her bubbies were superb, and stood firmly apart, face charming with lovely and lovable blue eyes, full of the sparkle of lust; lips red and moist, inviting a tongue.

We indulged in delicious preliminaries; she had a good look at my prick, declared she had thought her husband's could not be beaten, but admitted mine was longer and larger. She sucked its head. Then lying back on the couch she begged me to mount on her belly, as she liked to commence in that pose. I mounted upon her, got my prick gradually up to the crushing of the two hairs, and then alternately tongue-ing her sweet mouth or sucking a nipple of her lovely bosom, ran a most delicious course, making her spend thrice to my once.

Our other equally occupied couple had evidently got a course ahead of us, and were changing into the position in which we had first fucked our wives.

We, too, followed in the same attitude, and really the fine arse of my *fouteuse*, her naturally small waist, seen to perfection in this position, and her noble shoulders beyond could hardly be excelled, and were most inviting and inciting. I plunged with one fierce thrust up her reeking cunt, and by the very violence of my attack made her spend on finding it up to the cods, giving me at the same time a cunt pressure al-most equal to my loved wife's.

She was so delightful a fucker that I fucked her thrice more before drawing out of that exquisite receptacle.

On comparing notes afterwards I learnt that my wife's fucker had just done as much, and though not so cunt-satisfying a prick as mine, the variety and novelty gave it an extra charm that more than made up for any diminution of size.

We were thus all mutually delighted with our change of partners. An acquaintance begun so delightfully led to a warm friendship and a constant interchange of these most agreeable refinements, including every variety of the gama-huche and *la double jouissance* to all parties.

We all went together to witness some rear-operations between two men, for which the old bawd's house, No. 60, rue de Rivoli, was quietly known to be the rendezvous. I made a first visit alone to see if it would be worth our while; had an interview with the old bawd, a bold masculine woman of a certain age, who must have been very desirable in her younger years, for even now many who frequented her house finished off in her fully developed charms. Her habit being, as I was told, to come in to the man after one of the girls had left him to purify herself, and herself to lave his prick from mere love and excitement of handling a prick, and from long practice she had an art of doing it in a way to raise another perpendicular, which led to its being allayed in the full-blown charms of the bawd herself.

I was shown into her sanctum, and there I told her that I knew she could arrange an exhibition of sodomy. I said that I only wanted to see the operation, as it appeared to me impossible, and I should like the two fellows to be well hung and good looking, if such she could procure.

"I have the very thing for you under my hand if you can wait a quarter of an hour."

As that exactly suited my purpose I said I would.

She rose, rang the bell, and when a tap came to the door, went out and gave some orders. When she came back she said to me, "I have some very fine girls, all entirely without prejudices, would you like to have one up? I have them of all ages, from twelve to twenty-five; and also one or two handsome boys to have in company with them, to excite the slower powers of elderly men or those who like such additions."

I thanked her, but told her my only object at present was to see an actual scene of sodomy. So to occupy me she opened a small cupboard, and took out some bawdy books, admirably illustrated. The examination of these was exciting; her experienced eye detected the effect in the distention of my trousers, the extent of which seemed so to astonish her that she laid her hand upon it, gave an exclamation of surprise at its size, and said she must see so noble a prick, unbuttoned my trousers, and pulled it out. She handled it charmingly and looked so lewd that I don't know what might have happened, for I had already slipped a hand up to an enormous big and hard arse, when a tap came to the door, and a voice announced simply that all was ready. This at once recalled me to myself, although the bawd would willingly have made me before adjourning to the other room.

She said, "What a pity not to let me have this magnificent prick into me. I wish the fellows had not come so soon, I am certain I could have got it if we had not been interrupted, and I can tell you you would have found me as good a fuck yet as the finest young woman you could meet with."

I laughed, and to quiet her, said, "We may have that another time, for you are a very fine and desirable woman." With this placebo she rose and accompanied me to the room where the two men awaited us. They were two tall, good-looking young men, evidently *garçons de cafés*, a class much addicted to this letch, and acting as paid minions to those wanting them.

They naturally concluded that such was my object. They were already stript, and both their very fair pricks were nearly at full stand. They each turned themselves round, and asked which arse I wished to operate on, and which prick was to operate upon me.

The old bawd, whose interest it was to induce me to *have* them, handled their pricks with great gusto, and pointed out the firmness and attractiveness of their arses, bid me feel how hard they were, as well as the stiffness of their pricks and the rough crispness of their ballocks.

I felt them, and would gladly have had them both, but I knew they had an infamous habit of *chantage,* that is of denouncing to their gang well-to-do men who were got within their meshes, and go where he would in Europe he was sure to be waited on and money screwed out of him by threatening to denounce his practices; so shaking my head and refusing to let the old bawd pull out my prick, which might then have become too unruly, I firmly told her she knew I only came there to see what the operation was like, and had no idea of having my own person handled by them.

A mutual glance of disappointment was exchanged between the bawd and them, but they put themselves at my disposal, and asked which was to be the recipient and which the operator. I pointed out the largest prick as the operator. They drew a sofa into the best light, and one knelt on it, presenting a very tempting arsehole to his fellow minion; after moistening it and spitting on it, the old bawd, with apparent relish, guided the prick of the other to the aperture, and it glided with all ease into the well-accustomed receptacle.

I was seated by their side with my eyes on a level and close to the point of junction. A very exciting scene, for he went up to his cods, and fucked right earnestly while the recipient wriggled his arse to perfection, and seemed really to enjoy it. They spent with cries of joy in great delight, it excited me very much, and the observant old bawd could see my prick bounding within the confinement of my trousers.

Hoping to overcome my reluctance to take part in the programme, she stimulated them to change places, and the recipient became the operator, and the other the recipient. I was awfully lewd, but resisted even that; after they had done I gave them a Napoleon apiece in excess of the price paid to the bawd, and left them to dress, and retired with the bawd to make other arrangements.

On shutting the door and entering the corridor I perceived at once some doors opening upon small rooms adjoining the operating room, I guessed their destination; on attempting to open one the bawd seized my arm in great alarm, and said—

"You must not go there."

I smiled and said, "Oh, I understand, come along."

When once more in her sanctum I said, "I see you have had peepers watching the operations, so it is well I resisted any complicity in the action, but the discovery that you have the peep-holes already simplifies my object. I have come here to report upon the effect of this scene of sodomy. A friend who dares not do as much requires such a stimulant to enable him to fuck a woman he much desires to have, and who is my mistress. Now it so happens I want very much to fuck his mistress, and we have made a compact that if this scene is likely to excite him, we are to come to your peep-holes, and while he is thus enabled to fuck my woman I shall fuck his. I am thus explicit that you may know our real object. I suppose that now the witnesses to our operations to-day have left, so let me see the rooms that I may judge how far they will suit and which will most favour our object."

The old bawd complied directly, but still longing to have my big prick into her, pulled her petticoats up to her navel, showing an enormous mons Veneris, thickly haired, and turning round a still finer arse, said, would I not like to assuage my excited prick in one or other of her really splendid attractions.

I said not at present, thank you. And tightening my trousers over it, showed her that it had quite drooped its head, and was no longer in the humour.

She undertook to raise it very quickly, but I politely declined, on the play of want of time, to thoroughly enjoy so splendid a woman.

With a sigh of disappointment, for the size of my prick had evidently raised her lewdness to fiery zest, she led the way. Two or three of the peeping rooms were too small for four, but one was arranged for a *partie carrée*. I made an arrangement for the second day from then, and requested, if possible, to have four buggers together, to do it in various positions, and once at least in a chain of three pricks into the arses before them at the same time; I paid in advance half of the high price we were to pay, and fixed the hour of one o'clock in the afternoon, in order to have plenty of daylight to see and thoroughly enjoy all the excitement.

I left but allowed the old bawd just on going away to take out my prick and give it a suck by the way of allaying a little the great desire she had for it. She doubtless expected to raise such a heat as would compel my passions to satisfy her, but I had now sufficient command of it to keep it down.

Our grand scene of sodomistic encounters took place as arranged, the De Grandvits, as our new friends were called, and ourselves, with a basket containing two bottles of champagne, biscuits, and glasses, betook ourselves to No. 60, and were installed in the chosen chamber some five minutes before the arrival of the sodomites. We saw them undress, slap each other's arses, and feel each other's pricks to get them in fighting order.

The old bawd was there and lent an effective helping hand where wanted. They all declared it would much assist their operations if she would strip and let them see her flitting round and aiding in their efforts.

She knew herself to be much more attractive in body than face, and complied directly, and really added much to the excitement of the scene.

They began by coupling in threes, so that one after the other held the delicious position of middle man—be fucked and fucking. The spare fourth fucking the old bawd, much to her gratification and ours.

The first outsider was now placed in the middle, and the previous recipient became his attacker in the rear, while the previous rear-fucker became the recipient of the outsider. The late middle man, instead of fucking the bawd, buggered her to her apparent satisfaction.

This was just what I wanted, for we had not as yet in our *parties carrées* with the De Grandvits indulged even in bottom-fucking the women, but this, as we afterwards found, was equally indulged in private by them as well as ourselves. Now we enjoyed the sight of the old bawd wriggling in delight with loudly uttered exclamations of pleasure at having her bottom well fucked, for it was the largest prick of the four and a very fine one that was into her arse.

We had already racked off in the cunts of each other's wives at the first display.

"Let us try that," whispered my wife to De Grandvit, "it appears to give the old woman vast delight."

It was what De Grandvit had been longing for in his inward soul. At the proposition of my adored wife his cock sprung into its utmost stiffness. She knelt on a chair before a peep-hole. De Grandvit brought his fine prick, which he had moistened with his spittle, up to her delicious hairy arsehole and with very little effort housed it to the hilt.

At the whispered wish of my darling Florence he did not press to a rapid conclusion, but drew the fuck out to a most exciting length, and to an extatic ending in which they had great difficulty in suppressing exclamations of the delight afforded.

I had followed the lead given, the delicious big arsed De Grandvit had, like her husband, a long previous wish to be so fucked, and from practice of that divine coition had no difficulty in taking in with vast pleasure my bigger prick.

We both ran two exquisite courses in their delicious arseholes, and then separated that all might see the grand finale of the four sodomites each in the arse before him, and the fourth front man into the immense and magnificent arse of the old bawd. This ended their exhibition.

I should add that all in turn had either fucked or buggered

the old bawd to her infinite gratification both in person and purse, for she claimed afterwards and received a good additional douceur for the extra sight of her own fine body, naked and in double action.

When they were dressed she got out the liqueur bottle and gave them all a dram and a biscuit. We, too, partook of our champagne and biscuits while discussing the charms of the scenes just witnessed.

My darling wife chimed in with the remark of how much more the middle man had seemed to enjoy it than the two outsiders.

I added a remark that I had heard that such a position was the *ne plus ultra* of delight.

"Then why should we not try it?" said the glorious De Grandvit.

"I quite agree with you," said the husband.

"Who shall begin?" I thought, as the idea of trying it was first suggested by his wife, she ought to have her own idea first realised in her magnificent person. I would fuck her while he went into her arse.

This was immediately adopted. I lay down on my back, the delicious De Grandvit mounted on me, rose and fell, and spent before she stooped on my belly and presented her splendid arse to her impatient husband, who for some minutes knelt prick in hand behind her. With gentle care and well-moistened prick he got housed at last in his wife's delicious arsehole, and then slowly at first, but more energetically afterwards, we ran a most exquisite course.

As no one was now in the adjoining chamber, no restraint was put upon our lascivious exclamations. The De Grandvit was in such a delirium of extasy that she screamed again and died away in absolute annihilation of all sense but that of the utmost satisfied lust.

My darling wife had straddled across us and been gamahuched deliciously by De Grandvit while *enculant* his wife.

We next changed the venue; he fucked my wife while I plunged into her glorious arse; the De Grandvit straddled across the others, was gamahuched by me as her husband had gamahuched my wife. This course, too, was run in an extasy of enjoyment to all concerned, and ended our orgy on that occasion. We arranged our dresses, finished our champagne, called up the old bawd, satisfied her demands, and thanked her for the exciting scene she had procured us. On asking her, she admitted that the other peeping rooms had been occupied by couples, and that one elderly gentleman had had two of her page boys to operate and be operated upon while the scene before him excited him to the necessary extent to take a part in it himself. He had just left, having stayed to listen to our proceedings and had told her the two gentlemen had in consequence of the scene witnessed initiated the women into the *double jouissance,* and the excitement of listening and hearing had enabled him once more to get into the handsomest boy, and have the other in him.

She hinted that we ought to come again, and have the boys in, for she said the gentlemen, that is ourselves, would find an immense additional pleasure in letting the boys penetrate their bottoms while they were into their ladies in both apertures.

We laughed, and said we should consider her offer, but for the present we were fucked out.

We did not forget the bawd's proposal of having a boy to fuck us while *enculant* the dear women. A hint to my darling wife brought this out at our next meeting. After the dear creatures had both enjoyed the *double jouissance,* my wife said to Madame De Grandvit—

"We are really quite selfish, here are our two loved husbands giving us the unutterable joys of the double junction, and yet not enjoying it themselves. You remember how the old woman at No. 60 spoke of the raptures the addition of her boys would be to the bottoms of our husbands while administering the double coition to us. Why should they not try the same on themselves, and give us the delight of seeing them in all the extasies their double embrace confers upon us? We know how they delight in being postillioned, which shows how much they would like the real thing if they dared avow it. It is for us to break down the barriers of prejudice and false shame. Here, Charlie, let me dedicate your bottom to the lust of our dear friend De Grandvit."

My beloved wife was at the moment handling the prick of De Grandvit, and whose full-standing stiffness showed he was ready to face any difficulty.

I pretended a fear of its size being too great to allow of entrance into that narrow path of bliss without great pain to the recipient.

"You can never know that till you try," cried my darling wife.

In all this she was only acting a part prompted by myself, for I was most anxious not only to have De Grandvit into my own arse, but was longing to be into his great, coarse, hairy, corrugated deep-brown arsehole. In this I differed greatly from our dear friend MacCallum, who loved the delicate unfledged arseholes of youths, while to me it was necessary to be the very reverse of the fair sex, whose arseholes in general are of a delicate pink with puckered-up charming little orifices, which, of course, have their charm; but when with men to me it was twice as exciting to find them like my dear friend the Count's, quite contrary to those of the fair sex. Dark-brown, roughly corrugated, and coarse hairs all round them were the arseholes that raised all my lust, and made sodomy a delicious contrast to merely fucking the arseholes of women; such an arsehole as I most loved to fuck was M. De Grandvit's.

I had suggested to my wife to tempt him with mine for the sole object of getting into his. He bit at the bait, so I shoved my prick into his wife's arse, my wife conducted his prick into my delighted bottom. I made some affected grimaces, but of course took him in with the greatest ease. My darling wife had acted postillion to him, and had frigged his wife with her other hand, so we ran a delicious course of the wildest lust.

As we had already served out our wives too many fucks one trial was sufficient for the moment. De Grandvit was in extasies at the delight I had afforded him, especially as he appeared to be revenging the affront I gave to him by being into his wife *in culo*.

My adored wife, with her happy art of handling and exciting a prick, nonetheless willingly that she was getting it up to go into her own hungry and delicious arsehole, soon brought De Grandvit to the necessary stiffness.

I wanted no other stimulant than the expected satisfaction of a letch I had long had to be into his fine, rough, hairy arsehole. As soon as he was fairly hilted in my adored wife's splendid bottom, his better half took my prick in hand, put it into her mouth to suck and moisten it, and then guided it into that narrow abode of bliss I so longed to possess. It really was the first time De Grandvit's arsehole had ever been penetrated by a prick, although he had long wished for such an experience; there was therefore some real grimacing, for mine was not a prick of the ordinary dimensions, that might penetrate any arsehole, but a prick of the biggest, so I was obliged to be very gentle and make frequent halts.

My darling wife was obliged to exert all her delicious means of keeping his fine prick in her arse at full stand by cunt pressures and her delicate handling of his ballocks; at last I was fully engulphed, and pausing until all strange feelings had subsided, a gentle movement and my darling wife's admirable seconding enabled us to end the course in the wildest extasies of the most delicious delight, and to sink on the broad back of my splendid wife, completely annihilated by the most exquisite joys of satiated lust.

Once this delicious practice had been indulged in, you may be sure it did not end with a single experience, but was thereafter the *bonne bouche* or finish of all our after-orgies.

My beloved wife, whose eye for a capable man was infallible, had observed a genteel, tall, good-looking young German waiter in the hotel, who looked superior to his place. He turned out to be the son of a wealthy hotel proprietor at Frankfort, who had sent his son to Meurice's in a sort of apprenticeship, to learn how a large Parisian hotel was managed. In such a situation they receive no wages and have even in general to pay a premium for the privilege—this practice, which is general with German innkeepers, accounts for the number of genteel-looking waiters that are met with in the large hotels of great capitals, and who are found to be of superior education and information when spoken to in a friendly and familiar manner.

This was eminently the case with our friend Carl. My wife had taken rather a fancy to him, not at first erotic, but observing that after she had talked to him familiarly that he began to be very deferential to her and with a certain manner that she, with the instinct of a woman, saw at once arose from amorous admiration. Casting her eye downwards she detected the effect produced in his trousers whenever she was kindly civil to him. She increased her familiar conversation, which evidently allayed any fear he might have had, and she could soon see by the increased bulging out of his trousers, not only that he was growing more lewd upon her, but that he was evidently very well furnished.

Learning that he was the son of a wealthy father, well educated, only now placed in the position of a servant, in order to know, by obeying, how to command, and also to gain the experience which large and well-frequented hotels alone could teach how best to conduct his own hotel hereafter.

She told me all about it, and thought he might be moulded to our purposes. Even if not she had taken a caprice to him so that in any case it would be a gratification to her to possess him.

So I lent myself to aid her by purposely absenting myself either at breakfast or luncheon, under pretext of going to take one or the other with bachelor friends.

As Carl was told off to especially attend upon us, and no other servant ever came near unless rung for, my wife had easy opportunity, and with her practised skill in seduction, had him into her on the second day.

He proved an admirable stallion; grew passionately lewd on the splendid person of my wife, and became in fact cunt-struck upon her, probably the strongest bond that can entangle a man. It becomes an infatuation that makes him the slave of the cunt that has attracted him. There are few men of hot temperament who have not experienced this over-mastering infatuation, and they know that even supposing the object becomes perfectly unworthy, unfaithful, abusive, and with every vice indulged openly before them, they may wince, they may thoroughly despise her, but the chain holds them fast in adamantine bonds, which neither the persuasion of friends nor their own knowledge of the perfect unworthiness of the object can tear asunder.

Such became the fate of Carl, and my wife moulded him, with all her wily skill, to our lascivious purposes. When once under her enchantment, I made a run over to England on some urgent matters—purposely leaving the field open—my wife completed her conquest, had had him in every way, had postillioned him, and wormed out of him that at college he had indulged in sodomitical practices with young students like himself; but knowing how prejudicial it would be to him in his profession, he had weaned himself from the habit with men, but dearly loved the *enculage* with women, and doubly adored my wife when he found her extraordinary and exquisite talent in that way. She also, after much apparent hesitation, in answer to his eager and continual questioning, admitted that her husband was much addicted to worshipping her bottom, and had taught her its divine use. She even cautioned him against any imprudence on my return, for she said she had her suspicions that I had a letch for men, and if I discovered their liaison, would be apt to avenge myself that way.

"Oh, if he would still allow me to possess your enchanting person he might make what use he pleased of me."

This was the point aimed at from the beginning. My wife wrote to me, and we arranged that I should announce my return for a certain morning, and that she should have Carl to sleep with her the previous night.

I arrived in the middle of the night, walked into the room, found him in bed, played the angry husband, swore I must have revenge, and that as he had cuckolded me I must avenge the affront in being into his person.

He objected, for form's sake, but said he would yield to anything if I would not drive him away from the adorable Madame.

"That will depend upon the manner in which you satisfy my desires."

"Oh, do what you like, dear sir, if only you will allow me to love Madame."

"We shall see, we shall see; let me look at your prick. Oh, a good size, even when down. Let me see it at full stand."

My wife here interfered, and said Carl was so good that she was sure he would prove a satisfaction to me. She took his prick in hand, and with her art of handling a prick, had it at full stand in a minute and asked me if she could possibly have refused so handsome a prick as that. And, indeed, it was a very fine one.

Carl was a very fair young man, with a most beautiful and satiny skin. His prick was exquisitely white, and the blue

veins showed themselves coursing through in a most tempting way—it was seven and a half inches long, by quite six in
circumference, was thick up to the vermilion nut, although
gently diminishing from the roots, the glans was smaller than
the shaft close up to it; a hollow, like what you sometimes
see in the neck of a bottle, ran all round the edge of the nut,
and thus made it a head to the shaft. My wife declared that
its shape gave her great pleasure in both orifices. It certainly was a very attractive prick, and now that it was at full
stand I made him lie on his back on the bed, took it in my
mouth, sucked and frigged it until he spent in an agony of
delight.

I then made him turn over on his belly, that I might admire his ivory-like buttocks, which I caressed and kissed in
every way. My wife slipping her hand under his belly soon
recovered the stiffness of his prick. I now desired him to kneel
that I might be into his bottom.

His exquisitely white buttocks, marble-like in polish, hardness, and coldness to the touch, were most attractive to
women as well as to me.

While thus kneeling with head low, and the chink between the buttocks well spread open, his exquisite small,
pink, corrugated arsehole with almost invisible fair, short
ringlets around it was truly lovely and exciting.

As a rule, I like to fuck a rough, hairy-arsed man, but I can
all the same appreciate the delight in such an exquisite arsehole as Carl possessed. To me also it had the attraction of its
first possession. When thus first fully diplayed to my delighted eye, I flung myself on my knees, kissed and tongued
the exquisite and delicious orifice, and speedily got furiously lewd upon it; and rarely have I fucked an arse more
deliciously incentive to sodomy.

"Oh, poor fellow," cried my wife, "you must let this fine
object (his prick) be housed in me first, and then he will
less feel the introduction of your large instrument."

I immediately consented, on which he cried out in delight—

"Oh, do what you like with me, as long as your adorable lady will permit me to possess her."

"Well," said I, "see, her cunt is reeking with your spunk, so I will first bathe my prick therein, to make it go easier into your arse."

We took up kneeling positions. He filled the delighted cunt of my wife, and presented his really beautiful arse to my raging lust. I humoured the entrance a little, but once within over the nut, I plunged recklessly forward, somewhat too roughly, for it made him wince, and he would have escaped from me if he had not been doubly imprisoned. The pause I gave him after being fully engulphed calmed the strange sensation, and we gradually increased our movements until both died away in excessive delight, especially to him, for it was his first experience of *la double jouissance*, and it gave him such exquisite enjoyment that he begged me not to withdraw, but to run a second course. My darling wife thinking it would increase his lewdness if she changed his prick from her cunt to the more divine orifice, withdrew it, and placed it in the grove sacred to the secret rites of Priapus.

He enjoyed the extasies of paradise on this last occasion, and we all fell on the bed completely overcome by the soul-killing joys of the discharge, and lay soaking in all the after-pleasure for some time, until my darling wife begged us to relieve her of our overpowering weight. We rose and purified ourselves, and then I posed him standing up, admiring the really fine proportions and beauty of his handsome fair form. I sucked his prick until it stood, and then told him he must give me the pleasures of the middle, which he was so highly praising as the utmost exquisite enjoyment he had ever experienced.

My darling wife was delighted. She got on her knees. I

entered her delicious cunt in the first bout, and I quickly housed Carl's prick in my arse.

We ran an exquisite course, and then a second with only a change of my prick to Florence's arse instead of cunt. Carl was after this obliged to leave us, as the morning was getting on.

I sent him away the happiest of men by telling him as long as he placed his arse at my disposal, he should have my wife always at the same time.

Thus we had secured another fine prick to our general orgies. We told the Grandvits of our fortunate *trouvaille*.

Monsieur made some difficulty about his being a servant, and the fear of discovery of our orgies through his indiscretion; but hearing that he was much superior to a servant he consented to his introduction.

After they had seen and admired him, they expressed their extreme satisfaction at the result of his joining us—for both Madame and Grandvit loved to have him into all their orifices. We could now fuck both women at once, and the double pleasure could be given to either sex without there being any outsider.

Every third night they slept in our hotel, and that night we never ceased conjunctions in every variety, with pauses for refreshment, purification, pleasant bawdy talk, fun, and frolic.

For a month longer this delicious existence lasted, and then it was time for us to proceed southward. We parted from the Grandvits with much regret, but promised to return in the spring and visit them at their country house. I may here add that we did so, and enjoyed our visit to the utmost; and, in the second year of our absence, they accompanied us into Germany, where at last we left dear Carl. He had begged us to let him go as my valet with us to Italy.

His intended stay in Paris was within a month of its termination; he wrote to his father that the opportunity of travelling through Italy under the offer we had made was too advantageous to be lost. His father consented, and thus for eighteen months he was our constant companion and participator in all our lascivious conjunctions.

Carl accompanied us to London on our first return home, and resided with us for three months. I told the Benson and the Egerton of our good fortune in discovering him, and the exquisite addition to our party of us and the De Grandvits he had been.

They were instantly alive to the delight of possessing him.

I had continued the occupation of my chambers in the Temple, in which Harry Dale still resided; it was there we erected our altar to the Apostrophian Venus, and held our orgies.

Carl delighted our old friends, who were never tired of having him one way or another, while Harry or I administered to the *double jouissance*.

A new prick to a woman is like a fresh cunt to a man, and for the time gives additional zest to the lust which rages in us. So it is with the darling Benson and the lovely Egerton. They revelled in the possession of Carl. They knew they could only have him but a short time, and they made the most of him.

My beloved wife, with that kindly consideration for every one which distinguished her, quite abandoned Carl to these two dear insatiable cunts, and contented herself with presiding over our orgies, dictating new and exciting poses to our two friends, leaving Carl and me to their embraces, and consoling herself with a fuck now and then from Harry Dale, when we two were simply fucking each his dame. She told them, "I can have Carl and Charlie whenever I like at home, so must leave them to you for the three months that Carl can only give us."

We met thrice a week. My wife used to drive to the dear creatures and take them up, the husbands being much gratified at the affection shown by my wife to them, and never having the slightest suspicion of the object my wife had in taking them out. As to our own servants they knew the chambers belonged to their master, and they knew we lunched there, but they never imagined their mistress would take ladies to share in their master's embraces. So that we carried on our intrigue in perfect safety and impunity.

It was a sad day when we left with Carl, who never again returned to England. Our darling companions had become much attached to him, and parted with close embraces, and with bitter tears bade him adieu.

We parted from him at Frankfort, where his father, retiring to a country life, left him proprietor of a capital hotel, to which in after-years we often resorted when going to and from the German spas, and always stayed some days to renew the orgies we all so loved. His love for my adored wife's cunt endured for ten or twelve years, when an advantageous marriage softened it, perhaps more through the jealousy of his wife who, suspecting, caused us to desist from using his hotel. He had also got a family of a boy and two girls growing up, which completely ended our acquaintance.

To return to the time of our conducting him to Frankfort with the Grandvits, they afterwards accompanied us in a tour in Switzerland, but left us at Sion, when we turned our steps across the Simplon to Italy.

We were invited by our friend the Count to visit him for a month at his old castle in the hills of San Giovanni, overlooking all the ground of Bonaparte's earlier battles in his first Italian campaign.

We followed the right bank of Lake Maggiore to Arona and Allessandria, and thence by Acqui gained the castle of the Count on the hill above. It was situated in the midst of glorious scenery. From the summit of a hill near the glorious line of the Alps could be seen Monte Rosa, Mont Blanc, Mont Cenis, Monte Giovi, and thence round the Apennines, while the Gap leading to Savona gave a view of the sea, the southern suburb of Genoa, and the line of coast leading to Spezia.

It was a glorious view, and we often directed our steps to the summit from whence it was seen during our month's stay with our loved and delightful host.

His old castle was only partially ruinous, but quite habitable. However, his father had built a comfortable house in the garden, at the base of the rock.

The castle crowned a perfect perpendicular detached mass of rock, half round which rushed a mountain torrent, the approach being a very steep zigzag with now ruinous defences, a very steep and difficult ascent. It is true from a low entranced cave at the foot a secret stair led up from the garden, of which I shall have more to say in relating some incidents of the Count's earlier history, as confessed to us in our close and intimate intercourse.

We were warmly welcomed by our dear friend, who, leading us to our rooms, had a rack-off of his waste steam in the ever delicious cunt of my loved wife, who, it will be recollected, had a great penchant for the Count, when she used to prefer him at our Percy Street orgies. When the Count retired, I plunged my excited prick into the balmy bath he had prepared for me in my wife's cunt, fucking her fast and furiously the instant he retired, a change she loved above all things; this calmed us for the moment, and enabled our waiting for night.

We had expected to find a young sister of the Count with him but at our orgy at night he told us that since his return home he had had this sister, and that in fact at that moment she was staying with an *accoucheuse* at Turin, and he expected to hear of her delivery by every post. We congratulated him on finding so delicious a bit of incest to his hand on his return to his country.

"Ah!" said he, "it is much more delicious than you think."

"Indeed, how is that?"

"She is my own daughter as well as sister."

"What a delicious idea!" cried I, "what a cockstand, and what a fuck it must have been to you! But you must have had your own mother to bring about such a delicious result. Do let us hear all about it, my dear Count, it will excite us all to renewed efforts, as incest always does."

This conversation occurred during a long pause we had made in our first night's orgy when quietly seated after purification, restoring our powers with Champagne and some slight refreshments prepared by our host for the occasion. We had already had three hours of the most delicious fucking in every possible combination, being all, especially the Count, fresh and in excellent order for a thorough excess. So we all were glad of a respite, and listened to the exciting story of the Count's delicious double incest. As we did not hear all at that sitting, I will finish an account of our doings, and then give a connected narrative or sketch of that strange intrigue, and some other of his earlier escapades, merely adding that his account of his affair with his mother set us all off in such an excitement of lust, followed by such an excess of fucking in bouts of *double jouissance,* in which not only my adored and most lascivious wife came in for her full share, but both the Count and myself enjoyed the double bliss in our turn. We carried on to such an excess that we were quite knocked up, and were so overpowered with sleep the next evening that by common consent we quietly went to bed, and deferred till morning any fresh deeds in the fields of love and lust.

We found this so refreshing to our powers of fucking that we regularly adopted the system of lying fallow the earlier portion of every other night.

We passed a most agreeable time with walks and rides through the lovely scenery, and explorations of the old castles. The Count himself had two, but the one immediately above his house was by far the most interesting and was the original seat of his ancestors, wild robber barons of their day; and many a black deed was reported in the traditions of the peasantry around.

The castle, although in a valley between the hills, stood on a high perpendicular isolated rock some hundred· and fifty feet above its base; it was crowned with a very high building to make up for want of space at the foundation, and had besides a very lofty and bold round tower, rising high enough above the sides of the valley to serve as a lookout beyond them. The habitable part was reached from the main gate by a steep stair, at one of the landings was a trap door opening upon a profoundly deep shaft; tradition said that this was a trap for personal enemies, who, on pretence of reconciliation were invited to the castle; on passing over the trap it opened, and they were precipitated to the bottom. It was the common tradition of the peasantry that wheels with scythes attached chopped them to pieces at the bottom.

It is a curious fact, and one showing how tradition may preserve a truth where least expected. Our friend the Count for six months lay hidden in the secret recesses of this old castle at the time a price was set on his head for treason. This had led him to all sorts of explorations, in which he had discovered many hiding places.

Knowing of this tradition about the cutting up of bodies at the bottom of this deep shaft he got his two younger brothers to let him down by a long cord, and really found the remains of machinery and wheels with rusty blades attached.

After he had finally escaped, a more regular search was made, and it was discovered that a communication with the torrent on a former higher level had let the water pass underneath the castle, and turn a water wheel which cut up the bodies and made them float away by the outlet. Human skulls and bones were found, singularly verifying the truth of tradition.

At the time the Count was a fugitive hiding therein, the

old apartments were used as a granary to store the rent in kind of his father's tenantry. As there were suspicions of his having taken refuge here, the place had been two or three times ransacked by the police without their discovering him—thanks to the ingenious hiding places he had discovered. But for this very reason every precaution had to be taken, and no beds, bedding, or plates, knives, chairs, or tables were there; he slept on the corn, spread three feet thick on the floor, or sat on it when tired. His mother, with provisions under her petticoats, would saunter in the garden, and, when unobserved, slip into the low cavern and ascend by the secret stairs, and seated on the corn by his side, would wait until he had done, to take everything away, and leave not a trace of any one being provisioned up there.

These details are explanatory of what follows.

The Count had been one of the Royal Guard for two years at Turin, and being a handsome young fellow, had as much fucking at command as he could wish for. When shut up for months in his asylum the passions that had been kept under by constant gratification began to torment him; from the loopholes of the castle he could see the peasant women working on the mountainside, and, in stooping, showing their legs even up to the bare skin, and this used to drive him mad with desire. He did not frig himself, but at night stole down to the garden, secured a large pumpkin or two, took them up to his retreat, cut small holes in their sides, and then thrust his stiff-standing prick into them, forcing the hole to the size of his prick, and then working the pumpkin with both hands till he spent deliciously; he used to get six or seven fucks in these artificial cunts, then throw away the finished one on the torrent side of the castle. This was so far a relief, but his lust grew fiercer every day, and on one occasion became uncontrollable.

His mother, who had married at fifteen, was now a fine ripe woman in her thirty-sixth year. One day, after setting down the things she had brought up, she lifted her outer gown that she might not show she had been sitting on corn; the Count was already seated much below her body on the low corn. His mother accidentally on this occasion drew up all her clothes, showing the whole of her fine arse, and in stooping backwards to seat herself all her fine hairy and gaping cunt was visible to his lower sight. This was too much for the Count, in a moment his prick sprang to the fiercest stand, he instantly unbuttoned his trousers; his mother finding she had brought her bare arse onto the corn, leant over on the side opposite to her son to tuck her petticoats under her arse, but the Count seized her round the waist with one arm, with his body pressed on her already bent body, forced her quite down on her side and was into her cunt up to the hilt, he thrust it up so fiercely as not only to make her shriek with surprise, but also with pain. She struggled to be free, but was held down with all the energy of his ferocious lust. Very few thrusts in and out were required to bring down the first rush of his sperm; this lubricated her cunt, his prick never yielded, but stood as stiff as ever, and with hardly an instant's pause he recommenced a more delicious action than the previous one. His mother, however, was much distressed in mind at the first horror of the incest, but being a ripe woman of hot lubricity, could not feel a fine prick deliciously belabouring her cunt without having her lust excited in spite of herself. As all pain of the unprepared forcing of her cunt had passed away, and the plentiful rush of her son's spunk lubricated all the passage, she soon could not control her passions, and seconded him with an art which left nothing to desire. His long deprivation fired him to unusual efforts, and he fucked her five times before he withdrew.

When she sat up she said, "Oh! Ferdinand, what have you done! How could you do so? Violate your own mother. It is dreadful."

The poor Count, seeing her much distressed, burst into

tears, threw his arms round her neck, and weeping told her he could not help it.

She patted his head, and said. "Poor fellow, poor fellow."

On this he lifted his head to kiss her. She, too, wept, and they mingled tears and caresses together; this almost instantly restored his prick to its pristine stiffness. He bent his mother back on the corn, and although she resisted a little, and said it was too dreadful his wanting to commit such a sin again, she opened her legs when he got over her, and did not prevent his pulling up her petticoats.

He was into her this-time-well-moistened and really longing cunt, for her passions were now become lascivious.

Thrice more did he fuck her, each time more delicious than the others, and in all seconded by the most splendid action of his mother's arse, and the most exciting pressures of the inner folds of her really delicious cunt.

At last she left him, but after so delightful a commencement every day saw a renewal of these delicious encounters.

His mother proved an adept in every resource of lust. Being a splendidly made woman, and salacious in the extreme, when once she had given way to her lubricity, she indulged in every whim of lust. She always, after a few days' fucking, came very lightly dressed, with no stays or other encumbrances, so that they used to strip and fuck at ease in every way. The Count assured us that much as he had since enjoyed some of the finest women, never had one given greater pleasure than his delicious, lewd, and salacious mother, doubtless the fact of it being incest added to the usual gratification given by a ripe, well-made, luscious-cunted woman.

After the first week of their delicious encounters, his mother said to him, "My dear Ferdinand, we are very imprudent, you may get me with child if we do not adopt precautions. Your father does not wish to have any more children, and takes care not to get them."

"How does he prevent it, my dear mamma?"

"Well, dearest, he goes slowly to work, and while he has it in me rubs his finger on the point where you are now feeling (he was gently rubbing up her clitoris, a well-developed one), until he has made me enjoy it several times, and when he finds he is about to discharge he suddenly withdraws it, and pushes the head of it into my bottom and spends there. You must do the same, but you must not put all this long thick fellow in. Oh! come to my arms, my son, you have excited me until I must have it immediately."

Upon which the Count mounted and fucked so deliciously that with arms and legs round his body and loins, devil a bit would she allow him to withdraw, but spent with him most extatically, and quickly called for more, so that it was not until the third time of his being about to spend, that throwing her fine legs high in the air, and bringing her arse with a heave well up, and taking his prick out with her hand, she guided it to the delicious smaller orifice, and as all was reeking with the previous discharge, slipped it in, not the head only, but the whole shaft. She cried out, "Not so far, not so far," but as he began shoving in and out she quickly got excited, and wriggled her arse with all her accustomed skill, and spent deliciously again as he shot his spunk right up into her incenstuous entrails.

He passed a hand between their bodies to press a finger on her clitoris, this made her cunt throb, which was felt by his prick, and quickly sent him up upon another delicious enjoyment of the tight recess of obscene lust, and a second most exquisite and luscious course was run, equally to his mother's as to his satisfaction. Then he withdrew to relieve her body of the weight she had so long sustained, they mutually embraced their naked bodies, and sweetly conversed on the exquisite joys they had just participated in. His mother declared his father gave her nothing like the lascivious joys she received from his dear son. They toyed and kissed until, handling his prick with skill, she got two more delicious fucks, one in each receptacle, and parted for the day.

By the second month she discovered that what she dreaded had happened. Her son had got her with child; she wept when she communicated this unfortunate result, but the Count, like me, always stood fiercely at a woman's tears. Several splendid fucks followed, all in the cunt—the mischief was done, and precautions were no longer necessary.

His mother abandoned herself to him with a greater excess of lust than she had ever yet done, and fucked with an excellence, vigour, and energy that drew from him eight discharges in a wonderfully short time. The fact of his having put a baby into her appeared to stimulate both their passions. She declared she never in her life had enjoyed fucking more. They used the grossest bawdy terms in their intercourse, as if it was one barrier more broken down between them, and made their incestuous love more exciting and a greater destruction of all natural ties between them.

Before parting they consulted about how best to fix the parentage on her husband.

He was a man of fifty-five, and, therefore, past the ardour of passion—taking even his fucking coolly—and, therefore, more difficult to hoodwink.

She knew that he awoke with a cockstand, although that did not always lead to a fuck. Upon this they founded their hopes, and at last arranged she should drug his coffee, and when still asleep in the morning she should handle his prick, get him up, turn her bum, put it into her cunt, work him gently, make him spend which would awake him, hold him in, pretend she herself was in the acme of delight, but on coming to her senses, upbraid him with having spent inside.

This all happened as planned, he did awake on spending, but his wife exerted such unusually delicious pressures upon his delighted prick, that he got so excited as to fuck her again, and she took care he should spend inside a second time; she pretended to be carried away by passion as much as he was. But remonstrating afterwards upon the imprudence of what he had done, especially in having so excited her that she could not help spending at the instant he did, which made it more dangerous. She did not know how it was, but she had never before seemed to receive such pleasure from him as he had given her that morning.

"Well, my darling, it is a curious coincidence, but you never seemed to me more delicious or more lasciviously excellent in your fucking than you did just now. As it is but once let us take more care in future, and hope nothing will come of this little and delightful imprudence."

But of course there did, as the Count related to us, and seven months after this morning fucking my mother gave birth to a daughter. "I had already been in exile for five months when this event came off, I had letters from my mother after she got about and for some years afterwards, telling me that my sister was a beautiful child, and growing up *the image of her father*, underlining those words for me, to put the true construction on them. Poor darling mamma, she died four years ago, and my father followed her two years later. I never saw either of them again.

"Before I escaped from Italy I had passed five months in the constant possession of my beloved mother. As her pregnancy advanced her salacious avidity for my embraces seemed to increase. She was insatiable, but with such variety of charm and art that I never failed to answer to her call. Every refinement and excess of the wildest and grossest lust was practised by us.

"My father possessed a small collection of the grossest bawdy books; my adored and salacious mother purloined from time to time the lewdest, we read and excited ourselves in the realisation of the wildest and grossest scenes therein depicted.

"My mother was an instance of a woman getting once out of bounds and then stopping short of no excess, and became boundlessly corrupt. There was no horror we two could possibly commit that we did not indulge in.

"My father, when once the pregnancy was undoubted, was less reticent of his fucks. My mother at my request used to stimulate him to fuck her just before coming up to me, so that I used to shove my prick into the paternal sperm, sometimes in her cunt, and sometimes in her arse, and eventually used to lick it up before fucking her either way. The incest of her son upon the immediate fuck of her husband was, she said, the most stimulating to her excessive lust of anything I could possibly do.

"My father was obliged to go to Turin for ten days; it was the time of new moon, when nights were dark. My mother used to put on a dark cloak and come up to me; we lay down on her cloak, and, stark naked, gave ourselves up to the wildest lust until dawn, when mother slipt away to the house and left me well inclined to sleep until she returned with my food.

"Oh! it was a happy time, its combinations of solitude and incest, combined with my lusty youth, for I was only nineteen years old at that time, made me be constantly at her call, and she never went away before her excessive lust had been satisfied for the moment. Had circumstances permitted her to stay with me longer than she usually did, she would have got more frequent fucks out of me; at night, when she could come, she got ten and sometimes eleven discharges from me, and probably herself spent twice as often. I was indefatigable.

"In all her after-letters to me she constantly avowed grief that she had lost her most loved son; that she was inconsolable, punning on the *con* in the word, which is French for 'cunt.'

"Various allusions of that sort were in all her loving

letters. Often and often when I have been slack in fucking a woman, and my prick not answering when called on, I had only to conjure up some of these scenes with my mother when my cock would spring to the stand instantly, to the immense satisfaction of my momentary *fouteuse,* and it is so yet, a thought of her reanimates it at once."

Here my adored wife slipped her hand under his dressing gown, and found his prick standing fiercely, she seized it, and pretending to be his mother, cried out—

"Come, oh, come! my beloved Ferdinand, into your own loving mother's arms."

She fell back on the couch, he got between her legs, kneeling on the floor, having thrown off his robe, exhibiting his fine hairy arse—one of those I so dearly loved. The sight fired my salacious prick, so kneeling behind, I guided it into his arsehole, and while he fucked my adored wife, I sodomised his superb arse. We ran two delicious courses, then my wife took me in her cunt, while the Count buggered his supposed mother, for that stimulating idea was kept up. A second fuck followed in the same pose, with both her apertures filled to satiety.

This concluded that delicious orgy; we had a half night's rest the following night, as usual, to recruit, that we might better enjoy a perfect excess on the subsequent night.

It was in this way we kept up our powers, and only near the end of our visit had we any occasion to apply the birch, and that to no great excess.

It was in the middle of the second night that the Count continued his recital of the result of the intrigue with his mother. His sister-child, for she was both, was born in his first year's exile. Beyond his mother's description of her, that she was growing up a beautiful girl, the image of her father, meaning her son, the Count, he had no other intelligence of her. She had just turned eleven when her mother died; for two years after that sad event she kept house for her father.

He then dying, the second brother took possession of the property. As the state had deprived him of all civil rights, the property was given up to the brother. On his return, after being amnestied, the Count had to go to law with his brother to get back his property. His sister-daughter, who had been unhappy with her brother's wife, gladly left them to keep house with the Count. She was then in her seventeenth year, splendidly developed in bosom and bottom, lovely and lustful deep-brown eyes, the very image of her father, although she only knew him as her brother. The recollection of the fierce joys he had had with his own and her mother, drove him wild with lust to possess the incestuous fruit of his intrigue with his own mother. He used of an evening after dinner to have her sit on his knee while he related his adventures abroad, intermingled with kissing and toying. He praised her splendid bubbies and felt them; he said he could not believe that her immense prominence behind was real unless he felt the bare skin. With little resistance this was permitted once, then indulged in, until from less to more he got to feeling and frigging her cunt, while he put his own standing prick into her caressing hand. There could be but one end of this. He took her maidenhead, and then she crept into his bed every night. He initiated her into every excess of venery, and ended by getting her with child. It was concealed as long as possible, and then, on pretence of a visit to a friend at Turin, to see some fêtes, he conducted her to an *accoucheuse,* and left her there until her parturition was over.

I may here mention that just five weeks after that event came off we met them at Turin, on our way home from Venice. She was a beautiful girl. The Count introduced us as old friends, with whom every thing could be done in common.

We stopped a fortnight, and initiated her into all the mysteries and extravagancies of the wildest lust, and she proved so apt a scholar that she almost equalled in action and enjoyment the greater experience of my beloved wife.

The Count had taken apartments at Turin for the winter, and finding his sister-daughter so facile a pupil he intended getting up a *partie carrée* to continue these delightful orgies. His child was a lovely fruit of double incest, and gave promise of being a lovely woman. Her mount was charmingly plump, and the pouting lips of her delicious little cunt were already lust-exciting. The Count hoped he would be able to fuck her when old enough and promised me a participation when the time came.

I may here add he had her always to bed with him, and his sister-mother every morning, and in the bath with him.

She grew up admirably developed. From between seven and eight years old he gamahuched her delighted cunt; at eight began rubbing his prick on her clitoris, and by nine had gradually stretched it that he could enter nearly his whole length, and spend there.

We long knew each other, and he always said he was practising the lesson my adored wife Florence had instructed him in, when relating to us the incidents of her earlier days, and of her gradual violation by her own father.

I shall defer this story that I may at once describe the after-fate of this beautiful child, whom I and my wife have since often enjoyed between us, when she was entrusted to us by her father.

After a visit to us in England he left her to perfect her English for six months with us. We certainly perfected her erotic education while she perfected herself in English by her own ready talent for language, for although only in her sixteenth year, she spoke five languages perfectly, besides all the local dialects of Italy, which differ greatly from each other. Her stay with us was much prolonged, for at the time she was about to leave us she proved to be with child by me. In due course of time she was safely delivered of a daughter.

Her father, who came over to take her home after the advent, ceded the dear little object of my connection with her mother to my wife's prayers.

We had no children of our own, and she would adopt her. The Count, who in his heart was delighted at the proposition, left her with us. He afterwards had a son by this beautiful and charming daughter and granddaughter of his at one and the same time.

It is now long years ago, and that son legally adopted is now Count in succession after his father's death.

We paid many visits during these years to each other, during which the Count related to us some of the episodes in his life, which I give in his own words—

"You ask me to relate my first experiences. My earliest initiation into the secret mysteries of love's recess was rather a curious one, and one which ended very disagreeably for the fair nun who sought to teach me the gentle art of love.

"You must know that after Bonaparte's first conquest of Northern Italy, when he had turned the Alps by the Savona depression, and by the battles of Montenotte and others in that neighbourhood, gained the interior plains and carried all before him, Piedmont was annexed, and after the then French fashion, all church property was seized. Monks and nuns were turned loose in the world, with a promise of small pensions which never were paid. A nun of a convent in our neighbourhood was one thus thrown on the world. To sustain life she opened a little school for boys and girls of tender age. The neighbouring gentry, willing to assist a worthy creature reduced to poverty by no fault of her own, sent their children to her for primary instruction; my mother had taken a great fancy to Sister Bridget, as she was called, and I was sent to her school. I had just entered into my twelfth year, but was a fine grown boy of my age, and I can remember that my prick when standing in the morning had already shown proofs of fair development, which gave promise of its future prominence. I think I was the biggest boy in the school, all the others being two or three years my juniors. I was in perfect ignorance as to the relation between the different sexes. The nun seemed to have taken a fancy to me, she used to embrace me with her arms, and kiss me with very pouting lips, and I could feel that she seemed to suck in my breath. She made me stand very close to her in repeating my lessons, her arms or elbows, apparently by accident, were always pressed against the spot where my, at first insensible, prick lay hid. Without knowing how it came about, these sort of accidental pressures at last excited it to stand, which she, no doubt on the watch, was delighted to perceive. Seeing how she could now excite it to the point she wished to arrive at, she said aloud one day—'Fernandino, you must stay to repeat that lesson after the school rises. You want a little extra instruction which I cannot give you while occupied with all the class.' I thought this a kindness on her part, but her object was very different. When all had gone and we were left alone, she desired me to come nearer, the elbow played its usual game, my cock stood, she pressed harder against it, then cried out, 'Dear me! what is that hard thing in your trousers? let me see.' She unbuttoned them, put in her soft hand, and drew out my prick. 'How curious that is. Is it always so?' 'No, not always.' 'When how comes it so now?' 'I don't know, but sometimes in moving to show me my lesson your elbow touches it, and it gets into that state.' All this time she was handling my prick in the gentlest and most exciting manner, indeed she very quickly produced the spasmodic joys of heaven thus brought down to mortal man, of course with only the nervous result. This was all that was attempted the first time, when she told me to button up, saying that it was a very bad thing to encourage that habit, and I must be prudent and not let others know of its being improperly hard and stiff.

"This sort of thing continued for a day or two. Finding I

had said nothing about it to any one, she proceeded to effect her grand object. I was kept in as before. She excited me as usual, and soon had it out stiff-standing. 'Now,' said she, 'I will initiate you into love's mysteries. I see you are discreet and can be trusted; lie down on your back on this school form.' I did so. She lifted my shirt, my trousers were already down on my legs, she felt the shaft and appendages, then kneeling by my side she sucked it deliciously until it felt as if it would burst. She then rose and straddled over the low form and my body, pulled her petticoats up to her navel, and to my great surprise showed an immense thick mass of hair, covering the whole of her lower belly. Guiding my prick to the entrance of her cunt, she gradually engulphed the little object by letting her body descend upon it. I felt a certain smarting of pain in her first movements, and my prick partially softened, but quickly regained all its stiffness by the pleasure she gave me by her up and down movements on it. I went off as before in a paroxysm of choking delight; she, too, spent, for I was conscious of a stream of warm liquid flowing on my cock. She tightly held me where I was, and by cunt pressures quickly brought it up to full stiffness again, and a second delightful paroxysm followed.

"After this I fairly shrank to nothing, and dropped out. On rising I saw that there was a wetness streaked with blood all over my cock and cods; boylike, the sight of blood frightened me, and I began to cry, she wiped it all off, and skinned back my prick to wipe under it but here the raw surface made it painful, and even drew a show of blood; previously my foreskin had been attached to the projecting edge of the nut, her action of sinking on it had torn it off and forced it down on the shaft, doubtless this is the maidenhead of a boy, and hence the first smarting pain and the slight loss of blood that followed. She tried to detain me that she might get some warm water, which she told me would put it all to rights. I was too frightened, and ran off home crying all the way, and like a stupid lubberly boy, sought my mother and told her all what Sister Bridget had done and showed how sore she had made my cock. My mother, enraged, ran at once to the school, where in a back room Sister Bridget resided—berated her well, and in her anger let it all out, so that the poor woman lost all her scholars, and was reduced to perfect poverty. However, a young Count in the neighbourhood, who had been long trying to have her, now persuaded her to accept his protection; she had the wisdom to make him settle indefeasibly a pension upon her, so as to be safe from future abandonment. I, of course, soon regretted the stupidity of my conduct. As soon as cured of the slight soreness of my cock, my imagination recurred to the pleasure her handling and sucking had given me, and the delicious paroxysms she had produced, but, alas! all too late. However, now I was awakened to the true use of a prick, and our women servants and the peasant girls in the neighbourhood, who knew of my affair with the nun, gave me encouragement, and I fucked them right and left, in the fields, under the bushes, in stables or lofts, and carried on this for a year; but at last I was discovered by my father, and sent off to college at Savona. Colleges in Italy have schools attached for younger students like your King's College, in London.

"Here I found a youngster but six months older than me, the son of a friend of my family. I told him the story of my affair with the nun. We used to get leave to go to the water closet from different masters, so as not to be supposed to go together by design. From feeling our cocks and frigging ourselves until we spent, which we both now could do, my friend suggested that I should put it into his bottom, which a young usher in his first school had taught him to do. He was a plump, good-looking lad, with wonderfully large buttocks, and with an arsehole which from the usher's practice, whose cock was full grown, was so widened and sunk in that it

really looked more like a vulva than an arsehole. By this
time my cock was nearly as large as it is now, notwithstanding
it entered up to the hilt without difficulty, and I used to fuck
him most deliciously. It is a curious fact that he liked to be
the recipient, and to be frigged by me at the same time. Although he got into my arsehole a few times it was merely
from curiosity; his letch was to be fucked and frigged. While
at college together this quite satisfied us, and we never sought
the dangerous intercourse of the strumpets of the town, and
so avoided the horrible diseases that so many of our fellow
students suffered from, many for all their lives after. For
years this agreeable intercourse lasted, and was only cut short
by my exile.

"Meanwhile, on my return home for the vacation, I had
not forgotten Sister Bridget, and longed intensely to renew
my acquaintance with her. I easily discovered her abode;
meeting her one day she scowled at me, and turned off in
another direction. But I found out she had a favourite walk
in a lonely direction. I hid myself until she approached too
near to get away, seized her hand, implored her to forgive
the folly of a mere boy, who had ever regretted his ignorant stupidity, but who was now a man, and longed to
prove his devotion to her. Here I had unbuttoned my
trousers with the other hand, and pulled out a very fair prick,
at full stand.

" 'There!' cried I, 'see how the recollection of the paradise
I lost grieves him to the heart, let the poor dumb creature
plead for me.'

"I placed the hand I held upon it, she grasped it tightly—

" 'O! Fernandino, I always loved you, and but for your
indiscretion should have had you all myself for months.' I
threw my arms round her neck, our mouths met in a loving
kiss, her tongue darted fire into my soul. I drew her, a willing
participator, into some side bushes. She sank on the ground,
her legs fell apart; I lifted her petticoats, her rich fleece and

palpitating cunt were irresistible, I flung myself upon her, gamahuched her until she spent twice, and then fucked her three times before I withdrew. I would willingly have continued the delicious junction, but that she implored me for prudence' sake to rise. We parted, but not before arranging for other meetings, which took place in woods and barns, wherever most convenient. Her protector going for a week to Turin during one of my vacations, I was admitted to her room at night by climbing the roof of an outhouse, and then stark naked we indulged in every excess. She was hot and lewd to the utmost, a splendidly made woman, with an insatiable cunt when once our sports began. She was, as I before mentioned, most hairy, had a well-developed clitoris, and fucked with as much pleasure in the rear attack as in her tight delicious throbbing cunt. She loved above all things to gamahuche a prick, sucked it most charmingly, but with greater art licked around the hollow below the nut, and down the under side of the prick, with an occasional lick of the ballocks, all in so exciting a manner that no matter how often I had fucked her, she was sure to get another and another. This charming intrigue continued until I went to Turin.

"During my connection with Sister Bridget I learnt the whole history of her convent life. She was forced to take the veil by her family, much against her will, for she even then felt the prickly sensation of desire, making her cunt throb at the idea of coition with the male sex. She quickly found a friend with similar desires, but more experience, who first taught her all the art of tribadism, and then confessed to having connection with the youngest father confessor. This priest came once a week to confess the nuns, to confess their liaison, and to let him inflict what penalty he liked. He told her he would flog her, and then punish her where she sinned, which, in fact, meant putting his prick into her cunt when in a kneeling position. This sort of thing was done to see if she took it in with gusto, and when it was found that was the case, their hour of confession was a scene of every excess, stark naked, for neither wore aught but the frock of monk or nun. This delicious indulgence lasted until the dissolution of the convent, and you know the rest."

Another recital of the Count much amused us. The Count was admitted at seventeen into the Royal Guard, where each private was born a gentleman, and held the rank of sub-lieutenant in the army. Here he had many intrigues, and took the maidenhead of a charming and beautifully made girl, who was being brought up for the stage as an opera dancer, for which she showed early capacity. She proved a great success when brought forward. She dearly loved our friend, and was supposed to be faithful to him, although she had developed excessive wantonness and lubricity under his able tuition. His flight and exile separated them.

Years afterwards he met a lovely, magnificent, fully developed woman, splendidly attired, walking in the Regent's Park. He did not recognise her, but was looking at her with longing eyes, when suddenly she seized him by the arm, and exclaimed in the patois of Piedmont, "Ces tu si! Buzaron." (Is that thou thyself, Buzaron). This latter word is a familiar expression of carnal affection, but, literally, is "big bugger."

Their intercourse became of the warmest, she was now a first-rate *danseuse*, very highly paid.

The Count had first had her, she really loved him, and in London stuck faithfully to him, for love alone, for she never would accept even the smallest present. She, of course, had plenty of splendid offers from noblemen, but as long as the Count would have her she was faithful to him. When, which a knowing woman's tact senses, she saw a falling off, she released him, and, although never refusing her person to him, took to others as well. She was a very lovely bird, and used to relate the erotic experiences of her previous years. Many of these were most amusing, but one in especial showed the ardent nature of her temperament. She had accepted, when dancing at Genoa, an eligible offer from the Lisbon Opera proprietors, and had to take passage on an Italian brig; she was the only passenger, and her berth was in the same open cabin as that of the captain and mate. On the second day out the captain showed signs of wishing to have her. She was already longing for a fuck, to which she had been daily habituated on shore, so she lent herself most willingly to his desires; from him to the mate, and eventually to all the ship's company, without any jealousy of captain or mate; for the system in those days made captain and crew all equally interested in the success of the voyage from the terms of their agreement.

The captain, mate and carpenter were owners of the vessel. The crew of a boatswain and four picked men received food, mostly dried fish, but no wages. They were entitled to a certain share of the profits of the voyage, and thus were interested in its success, and on very different terms of intimacy with the captain to what ordinary sailors could be.

The voyage lasted six weeks, and during all that time she had every man in the ship into her every day, and from fair front-fucking had eventually satisfied them in both apertures, and often had had one in each orifice, and sucked a third to spending point, which she deliciously swallowed; she had even taken the *prémices* of the little twelve-year-old cabin boy, and she declared that she never enjoyed so complete a satisfaction of her excessive lascivious lust as in that happy voyage of six weeks' duration.

The Count, who had split his sides with laughter as she recounted this extraordinary indulgence in every enjoyment of lust, related in the amusing patois of Piedmont, told us that notwithstanding such excessive indulgence in both orifices, and by pricks, many of which were of immense dimensions, not the slightest appearance of such ample stretching could be detected on the closest examination, and that in either orifice she could almost nip your prick off. One of those exceptional constitutions and splendid forms that no excess injures, and who are ready for any number of pricks and reducing them all to inanition, while she remained as ready as ever to recommence the utmost excess of lust as soon as any one set had exhausted themselves.

As a sequel to the Count's confessions, I shall here give my adored wife's account of her early life in the form of a narrative, for when it was told to me it was interrupted by various lustful encounters produced by the lascivious and exciting nature of her revelations.

She was the daughter of a Greek mother, married to a high clergyman of the Church of England, a man of great erudition, who had taken the highest honours at Oxford. When Fellow of his college he was tutor to a great nobleman's son, had travelled for years with him, and hence his wide acquaintance with the languages of modern Europe. In Greece he had fallen over head and ears in love with her mother, had tried to seduce her, and, failing that, married her. He was a man of most lustful propensities, her mother was of a beauty most attractive and exciting to such a man, having lustrous and most lustful eyes, extraordinary wealth of hair, which when undone reached to her heels; thick and meeting eyebrows, and a well-defined moustache, all enough to drive a sensualist like her father mad. So failing all other means to have her, he married her, and, as far as she could afterwards learn from him, was in all voluptuously lewd, carnal acquirements, every thing the wildest imagination of lust could desire. It was from her mother she inherited all that deliciously haired body, and from both parents her intensely lascivious passions. She lost her mother just as she had attained her eighth year. During her mother's life she had generally crept into their bed in the mornings to have a cuddle, and had often been a witness to the fucking of her mother by her father, and had, at other times, played with his prick until it stood, and even made him spend with her toyings. She owned to a sense of sensual gratification in this, but at that early age without any idea of the possibility of its being put into her. She always accompanied papa to his bath, and he invariably dried her and finished by kissing her mount and her cunt, and without tongueing it.

After her mother's death he always had her to sleep the whole night with him, and when in her ninth year he had commenced by gamahuching her clitoris, which even at that early age he declared gave promise of exceeding in projection the fine one with which her mother had been provided.

In this manner he soon awakened all the latent lubricity of her nature. Afraid to force an entrance at that early age, after exciting both her and himself, he used to rub his great prick between the lips of her cunt, and against her clitoris, until worked up to spending point, when he transferred his prick to her mouth, and spent therein, he having taught her to practise that voluptuous and delicious method.

It was naturally impossible to stop short *dans un tel beau chemin,* and it ended by his first getting the knob of his prick into her small tight slit and spending there, gradually forcing his way further and further in, until she, driven mad by such excitement, felt the utmost desire to have it into the deepest recess of her longing cunt, and begged him to shove it in harder and further.

With such a spur to his passions, unable to control himself, he burst through all obstacles, and completely deflowered her, giving her greater agony than she expected, which was subsequently completely alleviated and converted into the most exquisite sensations. Once he had fairly fucked her, he continued to do so constantly until the age of puberty, which declared itself by the coming-on of her monthly courses even before she was twelve years of age. Already an extensive moss-bed of sable silky short curls adorned her mount and body.

At this period her father told her he must take precautions against getting her with child; at first he drew out and spent in her mouth, which she dearly loved, but becoming lewd on her bottom-hole, which he constantly fingered, he declared it was too much derangement of position to get it into her mouth, and suggested merely driving the knob into the arsehole, and spending therein, which he could do by her merely heaving up her arsehole as high as her cunt had been, and so entering without any change of position on his or her part. Of course it soon came from the knob only to the utmost length of his prick in her arse, and gradually she came so to like it that often the entire encounter of three or four coups was delivered in her arsehole to her infinite satisfaction; and thus her father enjoyed the first fruits of every aperture in her body.

He it was that instructed her so deeply in classic literature as well as modern languages, but always choosing such lewd works to carry out her education, such as Meursius and Suetonius in Latin, Athenæus with his supper conversations in Greek, especially drawing her attention to his chapter on boy love, Boccaccio and Casti in Italian, the uncastrated editions, the adventures of Casanova, and the hundreds of other French bawdy books, with the most exciting illustrations of all these works and many others besides. The lecture on them always led to good fucking in one aperture or the other, practising the particular description that excited their lewdness.

He thus depraved her mind that she soon longed for other experiences than all he could give, and she cast about for an *aide-du-con.* This she first found in their young and handsome footman, who proved not only discreet, but completely up to his work, and uncommonly well furnished.

They occupied in every voluptuous excess the hours papa had to attend to the extensive and rich parish of which he was the rector. I must tell the rest in her own words; she said—

"Continued immunity in our excesses led to excessive incautiousness, and caused the discovery of our intrigue by my father, who appeared shocked and distressed at the discovery, but he was quickly reconciled, as it ended in his having the youth himself, and his introduction into our incestuous orgies, in which he both fucked and was fucked by my father when not giving me the exquisite delight of having both together. And for five or six years I had but these two charming satisfiers of my lust.

"At this period a beautiful youth of fourteen, the son of a younger brother of my father, and, consequently, my first cousin, came to live with us. He was an orphan, left by his mother under the guardianship of my father. I was some three years his senior and he took to me as an elder sister, was very loving in that character only, and used to embrace and kiss me most affectionately. I, for my own part, soon began to have other feelings.

"On his first arrival, in grief at the loss of his only surviving parent, he feared to go to bed alone, so I used to accompany him, and help to undress him. He was all innocence, his mother, up to her recent death, had done the same, so he had no *mauvaise honte*, and I helped off his shirt and helped on his night-gown, and even witnessed his diddling before he got into bed, which I tucked him in and kissed him before leaving.

"Of course with my then complete knowledge and practice of every art of lust, I could not but look for and discover all his secret charms, then always in a state of repose, but promising a future development. I grew lewd upon him one morning, after an orgy with papa and the footman, who had not altogether satisfied me. I was tempted to go along to my cousin Henry, to waken and cuddle him, knowing that he would probably awaken with a cockstand, as usual with youths, and even men.

"I slipt along, and at once saw, as I expected, for only partially covered with the sheet, the prominence of his prick was unmistakable. I gently removed the sheet, and was delighted to see that his instrument, insignificant enough when down, was of a very respectable volume when erect, and quite capable of giving any woman perfect satisfaction from its excessive hardness. I gently took it in my hand to feel it, it throbbed at the touch, and felt like a piece of wood in hardness, with a velvet covering.

"I got into his bed by his side without awakening him, taking care to pull up my chemise so as to let him feel the contact of my bare skin. I pulled the sheet over us, took him in my arms, and woke him with a kiss.

"He was surprised and delighted at finding me by his side, but as yet had no idea but that of cuddling and caressing me. In throwing my arms around him I had taken care to pull his night-gown up to his loins, so that his naked body pressed against mine as we embraced.

"In apparent surprise I cried out what is that pressing so hard against my body; at the same time moving my hand and laying hold of it. It throbbed violently to the touch. I threw the sheet off to see what it could be.

" 'Dear me,' said I, 'how is this? What a change! it was not like that when I put you to bed last night. How has it become in this strange state?'

" 'It is so, dear cousin, when I want to pee in the morning, and goes down afterwards.'

" 'Then jump up and pee, and I want to do the same.'

"He took the pot and piddled. I took another and piddled, standing with legs wide apart, and holding the chamber pot partly between and partly under my thighs, so that he could perfectly see the whole of my cunt, and the flow of water from it.

"He stared with astonishment; it was really the first time he had any knowledge that women were differently formed down there than he was.

" 'How funny,' cried he, 'you piddle from a chink, and have no doodle. I should like to see it nearer.'

"I told him I should lie down on my back on the bed, and he could look as much as he pleased, but he must never tell any body what he would see, because it was a great secret.

"He promised, of course. I lay down on my back, having first thrown off my chemise, stretched wide my legs, told him he would see better if he knelt between my legs, some slight distance from the object to be seen.

"He got up and began a close examination, admiring the immense quantity of hair I had already got, opened the lips, caressed what he called the little doodle, my clitoris, which was rampant with lewdness. I told him to feel inside with his middle finger; he pushed it up—I nipped it, to his astonishment, so that he could hardly withdraw it. Nature, unknown to him, acted her part; his cock, which had gone down after piddling, stood stiffer than ever. I laid hold of it, and said—

" 'How comes this, Henry? You can't want to piddle again.'

" 'No, no, but I feel queer all over, I don't know why, and it seems to have raised my doodle as you see.'

" 'If you will keep it secret I will show how it comes about.'

"He promised that he would never, never, tell any thing I should teach him. So I said—

" 'Come to my arms, lie down on my belly, and I will teach you. There that is it.'

"His cock beat fiercely against my cunt. I passed my hand down, guided it into my longing cunt, then placing my hands on his buttocks pressed down and forced his charming shaft up to the hairs of my longing cunt, foaming with my father's and the footman's sperm, so that he slipped in with the greatest ease; but no sooner was he hilted than one of my exquisite cunt-pressures made him cry out with unexpected pleasure, while I spent with the delicious conviction that I was enjoying the first fruits of a beautiful youth. I told him how to move in and out, nature did the rest the moment he knew what to do. A very few thrusts brought down his first tribute on the altar in the exquisite recess of Venus, the voluptuous goddess of love. I joined in the delicious discharge.

"Once experiencing the joys of coition the dear boy fucked

me five times before I could get him to withdraw, and it was only the fear of discovery that induced him at last to get off me. We had a delicious cuddle, and I promised to come every morning I could do so with safety. Impressing upon him the absolute necessity of secrecy and caution, if he wished to have any repetition of the delightful lesson I had given him, I returned to my room gratified beyond measure in having taken a maiden tribute. Women who have the luck of such good fortune alone know the exquisite delight of initiating a virgin prick into love's mysteries and our longing cunts.

"We carried on this delicious intercourse for months before it was discovered, but use begets want of caution, and my father at last discovered it. Poor Henry thought himself happily excused by allowing my wanton parent to take possession of his bottom while fucking me. My warm embraces enabling him to support the great and curious pain and pleasure attending a first penetration of that delicious narrow aperture, dedicated to the obscene god. It ended in his complete initiation into our orgies with the footman. His addition to the orgy enabling more complex and lustful combinations than two men and a woman alone could indulge in.

"My father, who lived quite up to his income, died and left me with a very small capital at his death, which happened after the coming of age of my cousin Henry, to whom I had become violently attached. Indeed, it was my first love, and had all the devotion and ardour of that passion. He had a small independence, and we lived together for two years after my father's death, secretly sleeping together.

"The interference of relatives who, without suspecting our real sensual intercourse, preached upon what the world would say, &c., induced me to undertake a governesship, for which the great instruction I had received from my papa more than fully qualified me. I saw the reasonableness of this, and also thought it was more likely to strengthen Henry's love than otherwise. But the parting was a great trial. He had

grown a fine man, with a superb prick, although far inferior
to this monster," laying hold of mine at the moment stand-
ing-stiff and wanting but her touch to make me bend her
back and fuck her off hand, so exciting had been her recital.

She resumed after this episode, by saying her system of
teaching was eminently successful. From time to time she was
comforted by interviews with her loved Henry, besides satisfying the lust of both the father and sons of the families she
lived with, teaching and taking the maidenheads of several
youths, but in none receiving the gratification her loved
Henry had given her, until, as she flatteringly said, she had
the good fortune to enter our family and find such a jewel as
I possessed.

She had occasionally found girls of such a warm temperament that she was induced to initiate them into the art of
gamahuchery. It was in this character of instructress that she
had first used the rod to the bottoms of her pupils, and it was
seeing the erotic effect produced on them as recipients that
first gave her the letch of being herself birched. After this she
had had a vast variety of youths, fathers of families, and
old worn-out patients, whom she birched into action.

From one situation to another she had arrived at ours;
since which time I knew all her doings.

The Count's son and my daughter meanwhile grew up to
puberty. We watched their progress with great interest.
They were both initiated in all love's delicious mysteries by
their respective parents.

My lovely little Florentia, for we christened her in my
adored wife's name italianized, which became familiarly
Entee, was a great comfort to us. From childhood she
always came to cuddle us in bed before we rose. She was so
beautifully made that we used to strip her naked and kiss
her whole body, which always gained my dear wife an extra
fuck, especially after she reached her tenth year, when her
form was rapidly developing into puberty. Being from infancy
familiar and accustomed to be always stript by us, she had no

shyness; indeed she became so exciting that often I grew rampant and fucked my dear wife while she was present. She grew to like to see us do it, and used to play with my big cock, and bring him up to the scratch. It ended as it was sure to end, in my gradually toying with her from one excitement to another, until she was completely fucked in her thirteenth year.

Ten years after that epoch I lost my beloved wife, and would have been quite inconsolable but for the sympathizing endearments of this darling child, who became so necessary to my existence that twelve months after my adored wife's decease I married her. She was a perfect Italian beauty, and no one supposed she was other than an orphan adopted by my late wife.

Now, in my old age, she is the comfort of my life and the mother of my beautiful son, whom we have named Charley Nixon, in memory of both my first adored wife and my guardian, through whom he will inherit great wealth. The dear little fellow is now eighteen years of age, handsome, well grown, and very well furnished, although not so monstrous in that way as his father. His dear mother has initiated him in every delight, and he has all the fire of lust that his old father had before him. He often comes to us at night, indeed, it is the only thing that enables me from time to time to get a cockstand and a fuck at his mother. To see them in all the agonies of lust, fucking furiously before my delighted eyes, so excites me now and then, for, alas, it has come to be a gratification few and far between. But occasionally to suck up his young sperm after the excitement of their love combat produces a stiffness for my beautiful wife to mount upon me and then have our charming son to put his prick into her bottom for this, too, is necessary to my failing vigour, and the contact of his vigorous young prick against the thin filmy substance separating us feels as nothing. I am long in spending, and his delighted mother gets two and sometime three delicious discharges in her arse before my lazy prick deluges her cunt with my incestuous sperm.

We are thus a happy family, bound by the strong ties of double incestuous lust. It is necessary to have these loved objects to fall back upon, for alas! all the earlier partakers of my prick are now dead and gone. Aunt and uncle, the Dales, the Nichols, my beloved Benson, and her friends the Egertons.

I have already mentioned the Count's death, and both my sisters have left me alone, and I should have been a dreary and solitary old man but for my beloved wife and son, who solace me and replace the void in my heart I should otherwise have so sadly felt.

I shall here end this long tale of my erotic life.

A curious event has happened lately, the divorce of a Mr. Cavendish from his wife for adultery with the young Count de la Rouchefoucalt. The details brought before the court were of the most scandalous nature, especially the letters exchanged between them when the Count had to go to Rome, where he was attaché to the French Embassy. When the husband's counsel handed up the letters with the sworn notary's translation, he remarked that he thought they were too horribly scandalous to be read in court. The judge scanned a few of them, and, addressing the counsel said—

"I am perfectly of your opinion, my learned brother, I shall take them home and make a point of them in my address to the jury."

It will be seen that they were of such a nature that doubtless the old judge, who was no other than my dear old chum Harry Dale, gave his wife two or three extra fucks on the strength of the lust produced by those exciting and extraordinary lascivious letters from a young man of only twenty-one years of age, showing quite as early an initiation into all the luxury of the utmost depravity as any of my own details of my early experiences with my darling old aunt.

Some of the letters are a string of imaginary events as to how far they could carry their imaginations. The Count constantly alludes to the inferiority of his descriptions to those given in her replies. Alas! as he possesses those exciting replies of the lady, they cannot be got at, but from his descriptions, and the remarks on certain gross familiarities, it's evident she was gifted with as lascivious and lustful a temperament as either my aunt or the divine Frankland.

A chance threw these interesting letters into my possession, and I can assure the reader they are the veritable sworn translations of the letters found in Mrs. Cavendish's davenport when it was broken open by her husband, and produced on the trial. The Count had evidently dreaded such an event, and it will be seen he constantly implores her to destroy his letters as soon as read. But, with the infatuation of her sex, she kept them to furnish the sole evidence by which she lost her place in society and became a lost woman. It is added that she was a woman of forty-five, and the mother of several children, but it is these randy voluptuous matrons who have the most attractions to a young man who feels flattered and is proud of, as he thinks, conquering a woman in a good position in society. It is evident enough that she was no tyro in every depravity of lust, and probably had passed through many hands before he gained her. He appears to have been really cunt-struck, which, as I have before observed, is one of the strongest infatuations that a man can have.

END OF VOL. IV.

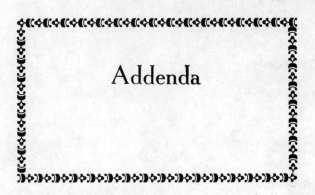

Addenda

LETTERS
Produced in the Divorce Case
CAVENDISH
v.
CAVENDISH AND ROCHEFOUCAULT.

rome, *Saturday*
August 6th, 1859, 10 o'clock.

I tried last night, my angel, to write you a half sheet, but it was as much as I could do to read your letter a second time, and it was only by making a great effort that I was able to write a few lines. However, this morning I will try and continue, in order to reward you, not for that one which you have deprived me of from pique, but for those bewitching ones which I have lately received.

I have just received your letter 17, begun August 3rd, 11 o'clock at night, and bless you for the idea of addressing it to Pal. B., it is infinitely preferable, and there is no fear of any risk ("indiscretion" in original) either now or later.

I am delighted when I think of the pleasure you derived from what I sent you the other day. I only decided upon it in fear and trembling. I do not understand what you mean by letter direct to Albert. If you do not send it per Embassy bag I should not have it here till Monday; you would have done much better to have put it in the parcel. All last night I slept very badly, no doubt in consequence of a presentiment I had that I should not receive a half sheet, and that you were annoyed at my going to Albano, and I thought of a mass of things as disagreeable as they are painful. Of your birthday, for instance, the 1st of October, which will be an opportunity for II * to make you a present in return for the set of studs which you gave him on his birthday, when you, no doubt, will give him something.

As to your brown cloak which II gave you, &c. &c., I request that on your birthday when he makes you his usual present, whatever it may be, you accept it and say, "I thank you," and, without even looking at it, put it upon the table, immediately speak of something else, and when he has left the room, put it away out of sight without ever speaking of it again, or appearing to know what has become of it.

I have just been interrupted for an hour and a half by M. de Fiennes—very agreeable is it not? You must forgive me if I am unable to write to you at length; what I have said to you above is for the future, but the past is over since he has those studs. I forbid you to give him something in future, unless you cannot possibly do otherwise; and, in that case, you must give cigarettes or anything which does not last. I will see what is to be done about your shawl, was it not II who gave it to you? Thanks, my treasure, to walk so far from II; it is so good of you to give up to me that walk, which I hate when you take it with him.

Ah! new projects again, but let us hope these will be the last, how I pity you. You were so well you told me two days ago, and now you are already obliged to take some powders—it is II system. Nice health you seem to have; you have good reason for believing that the regimen you have hitherto followed is a good one, it succeeds so well! Poor

---

* II stands for her husband.

darling, I can comprehend how uncomfortable these frequent agitations must make you. I suffer from them so often myself.

I will make you some drawings later. I have not the time to-day. Those uncertainties of your mother are terrible. Oh, yes, I am in despair at that departure, particularly before my lot is decided, and knowing, as I do, that you are unhappy. But, my child, do not fear to let it be known in every direction that you cannot endure II, and that you have taken a disgust to him. Do not hesitate to give the true reasons when you refuse to do anything, simply, "Yes, or No, the hand, but with . . . . it is not necessary. I can dispense with it, nothing of that sort is necessary." And then, when that has produced the desired effect, add, "We can only live under the same roof upon those conditions, for sooner would I go away altogether than that it should be otherwise." Speak in this manner; it won't answer very well at first perhaps; but he will soon get accustomed to it, "How do you do?" in the morning, and "Good night," at night. Then gradually get into the way of saying "Mr. C." when talking of, or speaking to him. You may be told it is not the custom. Answer you don't care, it is not the custom to be such an idiot as he is. Ah, you are too sad, poor child, all that is charming, and all our superstitions. Moreover, one must think of what has been, not of what will be, and compare it with what is. The progress is very delightful and consoling.

Do not be unhappy about my horse, he did not go very well, and then I do not care about driving in a carriage when you are on foot.

I have made two drawings, one prettier than the other, and I have had a copious emission.

Mrs. S. has made no tentative overtures towards me. She is often that way inclined, and with everybody. Be calm then; but, after all, you are perfectly so, only you pretend to be otherwise. God bless you for speaking so often of your pretty rose-coloured silk stockings. I like them so much, and adore you for wearing them, although it is not the custom, above all in the day time. Doubtless it is very coquettish, pretty, and wondrously exciting. Even only to think of them gives me an erection. And that rice powder! how divine you must look. It is to be hoped that the powder in your hair will not give ideas to II and embolden him—take care. Thanks for thinking so often of me, my idolized angel. Adieu, my good, my best treasure, I love and embrace you tenderly. I will have my revenge, for I, too, had prepared a half sheet, but will not send it till to-morrow.

ROME, *Saturday, for Sunday's Post*
August 6th, 1859, 2 o'clock.

I wish to give you a little surprise, my own dear little darling, in sending you this letter, which you will receive with a half sheet upon which you had not reckoned on Tuesday morning, so as to supply the place of Sunday's post. It was to give you this little surprise, and in no way of retaliation, that I did not send a half sheet in my letter of this morning. It was very unkind of you not to send yours upon the pretext that I was at Albano, but you will have been ashamed of it since. Besides, even supposing that I had been there, I should not have committed any indiscretion with your envelopes, which are so excellent, and, if one had felt inclined to do so, your letter was sufficient to make me indifferent to it. I suspect you of not having prepared what is necessary, I shall be sure to see if it be so; to-morrow's letter ought to contain two.

I continue your letter 17, and I perceive with rapture that you have had a thick cream-like emission of enjoyment. How delicious it would be in my tea. How I should like to send you some like it also. It is a good thing that my letter to the little girl was successful. Will you tell Madame de Delmar that I am sorry to hear that she is suffering, particularly as her ordinarily detestable disposition only becomes more thick and more execrable. Suppress this latter part if you think it better.

Ah! you think that Madame Salvi has played her cards well, and in what way, I ask? You are too bad, too implacable. I do not like that in you. I have told you that your suspicions wounded me, and I think you can believe me when I tell you that I have completely changed my conduct in that respect. Besides, what can I possibly do. I am very uncomfortable here. The Abdol don't want me; besides, the Duke has given me to understand that I ought occasionally to go and see his wife, and the Borgh bother me with all their children.

Thanks, my good angel, for the letter Des Pierre. If it be decided that you leave, I shall go for a few days to Civita—sad and mournful consolation. Why do you tell me that you will go barefooted when I go to see you. I am quite of your opinion that your feet are only too delicious. The costume rather disgusted me than otherwise, without, however, producing any effect upon me. To-morrow I shall pay the Duchess de Grano a visit, and since it seems to put you out, shall not return again to Albano.

Heaven knows that the pleasure is not great, and that I care very little for it. The other day I did not even find it any cooler there. The Duchess of St. Alban's leaves on the 20th for Schwalback and England on account of the apprehensions about war—another subject of uneasiness for me—such is life. I can go and live with the Duchess de Grano and Salvi. No one would say anything about the one, and not much about the other, whatever you yourself might say, but that annoys me exceedingly, and disgusts me, and I dare not do so with you. You might, however, have been my ambassadress, see what it is to be so seductive, so graceful, so pretty, so kind and gentle. Just fancy, dearest, that I have not answered Madame Rudiger. I must really do so to-day. She is a person one must be careful with.

I have always this phrase before my eyes. "I prepared a divine half sheet yesterday evening, but dare not send it!" Very agreeable, and very kind of you! well, I do not complain.

They have been so heavenly during the last three days, and mine are so shameful. How nice it is for me to think that I should have sufficient influence over you to get you to sit perfectly naked at my table. Long ago might you have had that influence over me, and even have enforced requirements more depraved, and more degrading than that if you had wished it, and with what rapture! Adieu, my angel, what a happiness to give you this trifling pleasure.

When I shall have undressed my adorable little mistress it will be nine o'clock, she will be mad with desire, delirious from passion and rapturous exactions (exigencies), her maddening look exciting me in the highest degree will arouse all the strength I possess, and enable me to exhaust her so completely that she herself will attain the height of happiness; the greater the refinement and delicacy of my caresses the greater will be your happiness, the more languishing will your eyes become, the more will your pretty mouth unclose itself, the more will your tongue become agitated, the more will your bosoms, firm and soft as velvet, become distended, and their nipples grow large, red, and appetizing; then will your arms grow weaker and then will your angelic legs open themselves in a voluptuous manner, and then seeing ourselves reflected on all sides in the mirrors, shall I take you in my arms in order to excite you (*branler*, frig) with my hand, whilst your little rosy fingers will similarly excite me with vigour, and I shall suck your divine nipples with passion. When the agitation of your little legs, of your lovely little bottom (*derrière*), of your head, and those murmurs of pleasure (*rugissements*) prove to me that you are at the point of emission, I shall stop and carry you to a piece of furniture made to sustain your head, your back, your bottom, and your legs, and having near your cunt (*con*) an opening sufficiently wide to allow my body to pass erect between your legs; then shall I fuck (*enfiler*) you with frenzy with my enormous and long member, which will penetrate to the mouth of your womb; being squeezed by your pretty legs, which will bring me closer to you, I shall wriggle (*remuerai*) my strong pretty member, which you love, with more vigour than ever; my private parts (*organes males*, testicles) will touch your little bottom, and this contact will provoke such an abundant flow of the essence of love in your little cunt that I shall be as if I were in a bath.

How I fear to leave off there! But we shall see. Do not write to me by the night post, it is useless! It is true that when I am near you in a carriage I have difficulty in remaining quiet. Oh, no, do not alarm me by your insatiability, mine is much greater than yours, there is not the slightest comparison to be drawn between us in a physical point of view, but as far as our moral nature and heart is concerned we can rival each other, and I am very happy on that account.

1:40. I was most annoyingly interrupted by the luncheon bell, and afterwards I played a game of Fourreau (a game all the fashion at Verteuil), and here I am again. I have just refused to accompany my father and mother in a drive in the neighbourhood, so that I shall be able to write to you more at length, unless, indeed, I write to Fallenay.

You tell me that you like the little costume, but that is all you say, and you give me no details as to the colours, the length and shape. I will believe my treasure, my jewel, that your bosoms will be white, swollen and soft as velvet, and it is very nice of you to tell me that my hands will have difficulty in holding them and putting their ruby lips to my mouth.

You are quite right in saying that you will develope my virility, it is you who have made my member what it is now. I repeat, on my word of honour, perhaps you will not like to hear these details, but, nevertheless, I shall say it, you are the first woman in the world who has stimulated that essence which flows from my prick (*queue*), which your kisses have rendered so pretty, and it is you who have plucked the flower of my virginity. Never have I had (*baisé*) any other woman, and whatever may be the misfortunes to which I may be destined, it will always be an immense and ineffable happiness to me to think that I have given and lost it through the luscious draughts you offer (*par tes délices*). It is, and it will be, perhaps, the greatest blessing, and the only consolation of my life. But before God it is a great one, and my enjoyment has not been such as one can expect to find in this world. I do not believe that he who had the madness to rob you of yours was as pure as myself, and as for voluptuous pleasures, if there be any greater than that which I know, I promise you never to learn or seek it, although I don't require this at your hands. I do not wish to have any other woman spoken of, they all disgust me, even to look at them. You know it, and you know that there is nothing, absolutely nothing, in you to disgust me, but all that belongs to you maddens me, and I love and adore all; it has become a madness, and you know it; for when you are kind you give at least the idea by letter of that which you would not do if you had the slightest doubt.

You know that I have sucked you between the legs at those delicious moments when you made water, or when you had your monthly courses, and that my happiness will be complete when you will allow me, and when circumstances will allow you, to let me lick (*passer la langue*) at that ineffable moment when your little love of a jewel of a bottom has just relieved itself. In you every thing appears different and pure, the purity which reigns in your every feature, the excess of refinement which exists in your whole body, your hands, your feet, your legs, your cunt, your bottom, the hairs of your private parts, all is appetizing, and I know that the same purity exists in all my own desires for you. As much as the odour of women is repugnant to me in general, the more do I like it in you. I beg of you to preserve that intoxicating perfume; but you are too clean, you wash yourself too much. I have often told you so in vain. When you will be quite my own, I shall forbid you to do so too often, at most once a day, my tongue and my saliva shall do the rest.

If it is necessary let the doctor cauterize you (*toucher*), that is to say with his instrument, and mind he does not fall in love with you; I bet he has never before seen anything so seducing, so pretty, or so perfect. It is to be hoped that the irritation does not proceed from the size of my member.

You did quite right to go to the play, and I regret sincerely to have spoilt the pleasure you had in going, it shall not happen again.

As to the place George had, that is perfectly indifferent to me.

Ah! you think that the portrait was done afterwards. You are not sure of it, but it is a matter of no moment, my much loved one. I shall not be the less happy to have the photograph if you are good enough to give it to me, not too much in miniature. I shall be very grateful for it.

If I said that Galitzin was clever, I was wrong; he has a kind heart, and is very fond of me. Now that he has lost his mother, I shall be more kind to him. He is a person one can depend upon; his letters are silly productions. Those Russians have always the imagination easily excited.

Yes, my father has always the same answer. Thanks for your obliging offer of gloves, my mother must settle about it.

I shall still have lavished the following caresses upon you, angel of my delight, were I a little calmer. I had a dream, such as it was, about it last night, and only remember it just now by way of explanation of my mad excitement of this morning. I saw you as I was asleep, you were by my side frigging me with your fingers of love, and you heard me say to you, "I see you there." You are as lovely as Venus, your lusciousness and lasciviousness are at their very height, your body is completely perfumed with your urine, in which I forced you to bath yourself for my enjoyment, so that I might lick you. You have painted the most seductive parts of your person. Your shoulders are white, your rosy bosoms reveal themselves through a rose-coloured gauze, trimmed with bows of the same hue. Your thighs, as well as your navel and your heavenly bottom, are revealed through a heavenly gauze, your legs are clad in rose-coloured stockings. The sperm flows; but how much I needed it! This is true, for my testicles were swollen in an alarming manner.

Oh, my child, my pretty little mistress, if you only knew how much I suffer from the excessive heat, and the privation in which I live! Without exaggeration, my testicles are enormous. My member is as large, straight, and stiff as my arm. I am mad from desire for you. I had the unhappy idea of going to bed again. My mind was full of a dream I had had, and of which you were, of course, the subject. Then I thought of the caresses which you would have been obliged to submit to, and at last, in consequence of your yesterday's half sheet, so pretty at the beginning and at the end, but yet quite beside the question, and found myself engaged in the act of rubbing myself with frenzy, and of stroking myself and of frigging my prick (*la pine*) until I was exhausted, before I could discharge the merest drop; that was too much for me, and now I desire you like a mad man. If a delicious half sheet does not arrive by the Embassy bag, I know not what will become of me. I have had an emission. I am saved. I shall feel myself so relieved. You have forbidden my going with other women. You are determined that I shall not have a discharge with any one but yourself, and that I have fucked (*baisé*) no one but you. Oh! how I must love you.

It is two o'clock in the morning, I have violated and well worked you, kissed, frigged, licked, and sucked you, obliged you to yield to my desires, the most debauched, the most shamelessly degrading during the whole of the afternoon. All the afternoon, too, I have got you to suck my member and my testicles. I have made you pass your tongue between my toes and under my arms. I have compelled you to paint your body, to drink my urine. I was almost on the point of getting you sucked and licked by a pretty Lorette, perfectly naked, between your legs, and to make you piss into her cunt in order to make the depravation more debased than ever. I have had discharges from jealously. I have discharged at least forty times; and when, after having left you to go to my club, I returned home, and finding you fast asleep from exhaustion, I awakened you and insisted upon your frigging me with your rosy fingers, all the while licking my several parts. You implore me. You are wearied, but I am intractable. You must do it in order to excite you as much as I am myself excited. I suck your breast with frenzy. The sucking that I have given your bosoms, and the fear you have lest I should fetch a young girl to violate you with her breasts in your cunt, filling your womb with her milk, excite your senses, and then you hear a voice whose sound alone so pleasingly tickles your womb, saying to you, "My pretty mistress, I implore you to abandon your (?) to me. I will love you so fondly. I will be too kind and gentle, I am so handsome, I will do all you can possibly wish. I know so well how to have and suck a woman, my member is enormous, it is beautiful, rose-coloured, large, long, hard and vigorous. Yield yourself to me."

Tell me if you like this one.

When you are ready you will call me so that I may come and say my daily "How do you do?" You will begin by taking my —— out of my trousers, then half opening your gown, you will lift up your pretty chemise with one hand, and will pass your other arm, soft as satin, round my neck. I shall embrace you tenderly, then I shall lick your snow-white shoulders, your bosoms, which seem to be bursting from the imprisonment of your rose-coloured stays embroidered with lace. I shall lick between your legs, over your divine little bottom, your nymph-like thighs being at that moment on my knees; then you will place your angelic little feet, with your stockings on, one after the other in my mouth. After this you will send me into the dining-room, in order to get rid of the servants, and, by this time, filled with an amorous and impassioned languor, each of your movements breathing forth the frenzy and voluptuousness of passion, you will come and join me. There will be only one chair, and the table will be laid for only one person. We shall each of us have only one hand free, I the right, and you the left; then you will sit upon my left leg, which you have found the means to make naked; you will have unfastened your gown in such a way that it will hang down behind, and your right hand will caress and stroke my enormous prick, which you will have taken between your legs without putting it into your angelic cunt, whilst my left arm will wind itself round your lovely waist in order to bring you still nearer to me.

After breakfast, which will have lasted till half-past twelve, and which will have given you strength, we will go into the little rose-coloured boudoir. I shall place myself in a low narrow chair, and as I shall be very much excited by your enchanting looks, my enormous member will come out of its own accord from its prison, and you will sit astraddle upon me, introducing, with the greatest difficulty, my pretty and vigorous prick into your pretty girl-like cunt, when wriggling about from sheer enjoyment you will stop its movements every time I tell you I am on the point of discharging, so as to increase my desires and my transports of happiness. Then in half an hour's time you will get up and place yourself upon the sofa, whilst I, at your desire, shall slip off all my clothes; then you will get up from the sofa and take off your dressing-gown, only keeping on what you have underneath. In my turn I will stretch myself on the sofa, getting every moment more delirious with passion, for your dress, betraying the delicious outlines of your figure, without revealing them entirely, will render me almost beside myself, and will make my prick so long and so stiff that you will hardly be able to sit on its point without being fucked, in spite of its size, which will force from you sighs and murmurs of rapture. At last, when once seated, fucked by my manly and powerful prick, you will throw yourself backwards. I should lean my enraptured legs against your bosoms, in order that you might lick my feet, while you would pass your amorous and divine legs, softer, whiter, and more rose-tinted every day, over the whole breadth of my chest, placing your tiny goddess-like feet in my mouth. As our desires would augment at every moment, you would allow me, would even ask me to take off your garters, your pretty stockings, and your slippers, in order to procure me the luxury of licking every part of your body there, and of realising in the most perfect manner the intense enjoyment arising from the contact of the most delicate, the most woman-like, the most voluptuous member of your body. My hands would frig your little love of a member, my manly prick would kiss your celestial womb, and my thighs would caress your delicious bottom. When I have worked you in this way for hours, ceasing every moment you were on the point of emission, I should, as I withdrew my member, let you at last discharge, and then an immense stream of love would flow into my mouth, which suddenly and as if by enchantment would find itself in the place of my member while your bosoms would be covered with that white essence of which you are the only source in my eyes (I had never known it before Homburg), and which would escape from my amorous member.

Every day after dinner, reclining voluptuously on a couch, you would snatch a few moments of repose while I was taking off all my clothes. When I had finished, and when I, filled with love, had shown myself to your contemplation, you would give up to me your place upon the sofa, and assuming the most seductive, the most coquettish, and the most graceful attitudes, would come and play with my member, whose vigour would arise solely from the sight of your pretty costume, which, I am convinced, would render you more delicious than the most graceful fairy. You would love me so deeply that I should cease to have any power of will, you would have exhausted me, sucking me completely dry, nothing would remain in my prick, which would be more full of desire, more enormous, and stiffer at every moment. My languishing eyes, gentle as love itself, surrounded by large dark blue circles caused by your look, your tongue, your bosom, your cunt, your member, your heavenly little bottom, your legs, your fingers, and your angelic little feet would tell you how complete was my happiness, my intoxication, my extasy, and my faint, exhausted but happy voice would give you the same assurance, would murmur with rapture in your ears—"Oh how I love you, my lady love, my divine little virgin, caress me yet once more, again, still again, it is a dream. Thank you, oh, thank you and yet again. Oh I am in heaven, do not pause, I implore you, suck me harder than ever; lick me well; oh! what rapture; ask me what you will, it shall be yours. You are my mistress, no other but you in the whole world can transport me in this way. Frig me with your knees. Oh! oh! oh! I am going to discharge," and my half-opened mouth would prove to you my enjoyment, and the thirst I had for the bliss you could confer.

Then, more full of passion than ever woman lover had ever been, and enraptured as you listened to my voice, so completely beneath your sway, listening only to your own love, you would raise your little coquettish petticoat, and pressing your dear little loves of calves more closely together, for you would be on your knees, resting upon my little blue veins, you would frig me in this manner, with greater vigour than ever, sitting down every now and then upon your fine little heels, in order the better to release my beautiful prick, perfectly straight and rudely swollen and inflamed with passionate desires, from between your divine thighs, as soft as satin, and as white as snow, to better introduce the wet tips of your lovely and velvet like bosoms into the seductive little hole of my member, whilst my knees raised slightly behind would gently caress your bottom, so as to give you some little satisfaction in your turn; and at last, unable any longer to retard the moment of emission, you would bend forward, resting upon both your hands, to increase my desire, and keeping yourself back a little distance from me, while your petticoats would now cover my head, and act almost like an electrical conductor upon me, you would intoxicate me with the perfume exhaled from your legs, from your member, from your cunt, from your bottom, and lastly, you would slack my thirst and complete the celestial transport by pissing, with eager rapture, between my burning lips some of that woman's nectar which you would alone possess, and which, emanating from you alone in the world, is worthy of the gods. It would be half-past eight.

You cannot form any idea of my excitement at this moment. I hope you will like this, and will answer me prettily. Am I sufficiently in love? And do you believe there will be another woman in the whole world beside yourself for whom I shall have any desire? Oh, how wild is the longing that I have for you at this moment; and this nectar I have spoken of, from whom else could I care for it, could I endure it even, whilst from you what mad delight! Tell me, do you believe this? You know it perfectly well, I am sure; these are not mere words. Tell me that you will piss into my mouth again when I ask you. I am now going to try to sleep, but what chance of doing so with this love that consumes me. I must await your pretty letter of to-morrow morning, for it is that alone which will excite the flow and stream.

At half-past eight you would like to conform to the usages of this room of mirrors, and as your desires have become greatly inflamed by my own state, and by the soft and sensual temperament of our bodies, you would ask me to undress you, in order that, being completely naked, I might the more easily overwhelm you with my most passionate caresses. I should then strip you of every thing, except that in order that your feet might not come into immediate contact with the looking glasses upon which we should be walking, I would slip on your feet a pair of tiny little slippers, with little silk soles, at a distance they would hardly be visible.

Some one is coming. Adieu till to-morrow.

And larger and stouter than that of my little darling, and so indifferently shod with shoes. (Their boots are pretty.)

Adieu, my angel, I finish this so as to be enabled to add a few lines to the picture—it is late. I love you with all my soul, with love, respect, and adoration. Nothing yet has been heard about de L. R. It is very bad weather, and my father is still no better.

I would take you for a drive either in a pretty barouche or in a phæton, your toilette would be beautiful but simple. I would only insist upon your wearing a veil, for my love and happiness would render me somewhat egoistical with regard to others. We should not be serious all the time of our drive, for at every instant I should steal a kiss, and your feet would be resting on mine.

We should return home about half-past five to dress for dinner. You would change every thing, and without paying any attention to what our servants might think, I should put on a loose pair of trousers, prettier than what I had worn this morning, but, like them, opening in the front. As for you, my own love, I should insist upon your dressing yourself as a ravishingly pretty little *danseuse,* with some little difference, however, in my favour. Your hair would be in curls, falling all round your head, upon your beautiful naked shoulders. You would crown them with a pretty garland of flowers, such as I like for Aimée. You should wear a light-coloured muslin dress, very low and very short, up to the knees, your arms bare, and the skirts exceedingly full (the body of which would be transparent, and refine and reveal the divine shape of your angelic bosoms), your legs, perfectly naked, would be visible amongst a mass of folds of muslin, and would be covered by little open-work stockings of rose-coloured silk, fastened at the instep by bows, like the dress, and on your tiny virgin feet you would have little satin shoes, without soles. To pass into the dining room, so as to avoid catching cold, and also prevent the servants revelling in the sight of my treasure, you would envelope yourself from head to foot in a long veil. During dinner I would try to remain tolerably quiet so that you might eat and strengthen your-self for the evening, which would be a fatiguing one. Our servants would have directions not to enter until we rang; during each course you would open your veil, and turning towards me (for you would be on my right hand), you would place your pretty legs across mine; immediately my manly prick, which your love would render daily more and more delicious, would display its vivacity, and you would caress it with your lovely satin-like calves, your chair enabling you to do this, being tolerably large, with only one arm on the right, while mine would be much lower, that would not fatigue you much, and this is what you would say to me, "Am I not bewitching and delicious? Do you not think me voluptuous? and regard me as your mistress, holding you under my entire subjection? I am very happy to please you this way." And I should answer, "Yes, I am your slave; you give me the greatest enjoyment that can be had; there is not a woman in the world who possesses the attractions you have; you make me do anything, you are the queen of voluptuousness, of enjoyment. No one knows how to make love as you do." At last at the dessert you would glide gently upon my lap, allowing your petticoats to flow behind. I should suck your bosoms, for as the servants would be getting their own dinners, I should have thrown your veil quite off, and you would then appear enveloped in all your many charms. Then I should give you your dessert, which would consist of a biscuit moistened with that white essence which you alone in the whole world have known and know how to produce in me, and for my reward you would allow me to make my wine for dessert. I would then place my wine-glass between your legs, opened voluptuously wide, and you would let that delicious urine flow into it. The intoxication that this fragrant liquor would produce would be the signal for my most passionate caresses.

You would begin by placing yourself astride me, and I should thrust with the greatest difficulty my virile member between your legs. In this position we should leave the dining-room, I carrying you along by the stiffness of my member, while every step I took would make you wild with excess of enjoyment. We should go into a pretty boudoir, the floor of which would be completely covered with looking glasses, and filled with furniture intended by their shape and softness to augment the voluptuousness of our embraces. No costume whatever would be put on in this room. Nudity alone would have a right to remain there. There would be pieces of furniture to excite the senses and whereon to recline, others enabling us to suck each of our members, to lick, to frig, to kiss, to enjoy, to complete our performance, to discharge, to fuck, in one word, to supplement and promote the extremest refinements of the most celestial and most perfect of all enjoyments.

The continuation on some future occasion. My fear of exciting you will depend somewhat upon my letter of this evening or to-morrow, and particularly upon the frank and sincere reply for which I ask you for the day after to-morrow.

Send me back the beginning.

You cannot have the faintest idea of my dread when one of these sheets is on its way.

Why do you trouble yourself to pay so much attention to style and writing—that takes time. I never read mine over, and that is so much time gained.

ENGLISH TRANSLATION OF THE LETTER WRITTEN BY THE COUNT ALMOST ENTIRELY IN CYPHER

Here is the response of my heart, my beloved adored one. Thou shall have it as soon as I shall dare to send it to you.

Thou shalt belong to me entirely one day, perhaps in eighteen months, and then here is the existence which you shalt have the grief to be compelled to lead.

In the apartment which I depicted to you the other day, and with the toilette that I require of my beloved lady, my lady mistress is to render herself every day between eleven o'clock and noon.

She will find there thy loving husband, all fresh and in every respect desirable (*gentil*), clothed in a dressing-gown of very light texture.

From noon until three o'clock this is the programme.

At noon thou wilt stretch thyself on thy easy chair, thou wilt loosen a little thy girdle and open thy pretty dressing-gown. I on my bent knees at your side shall lick you with my tongue, while my arm shall encircle thy divine waist and thy two naked arms shall encircle my neck; afterwards softly widening thy virgin legs thou will cast aside all that which hides from the eyes, and you will place me between those divine legs.

Successively I shall lick with voluptuousness thy neck, thy shoulders, under thy arms, thy breasts. I shall suck with force those chaste little bosoms, which by their swelling would desire to escape from the pretty little rose-coloured stays; then passing to thy intoxicating cunt, I should suck it with such an amount of frenzy that thou wouldst discharge for the first time in my mouth.

This done it will have so much excited me that, taking thy place, it will become your turn to mount between my legs, and licking all my chest thou wilt finish by frigging with passion my prick, which will become longer and straighter than ever.

As soon as thou shalt feel the enjoyment coming thou wilt cease, in order to lick the parts adjoining.

At one o'clock thou wilt want to make water, then my mouth adhering between thy legs, thou wilt allow me to swallow all, then lying down again on thy little belly, I shall lick with fury thy bottom so voluptuous, and thy delicious legs.

Afterwards it will be thy turn to continue thy caresses upon me.

At two o'clock both of us elevated in a supreme degree, lifting up thy little chemise in front we shall do the business, that is to say, that surrounding me with vigour with thy legs, thou wilt make efforts in order to fuck thyself (*enfiler*), but my member will be to such a degree enormous that we shall have all the trouble in the world (the delights corresponding to the efforts). At last, once entered thou wilt procure, by my movements and my pauses, such enjoyments that I shall hear you uttering the softest murmurs of thy voice, and so that thou wilt wriggle thyself on my ravished prick which will still further augment thy transports.

Thou wilt enjoy thyself thus three times. At the third time I shall suck thy breasts with such passion that thy eyes depicting a heavenly languor and a divine abandonment, thou wilt empty out upon me thy delirium-causing seminal fluid.

That will last until half-past two o'clock, then we shall sleep together thus until three o'clock, and at three o'clock thou wilt go to dress thyself in order to go out or to receive visits.

Behold, the following part shall come to you if the commencement pleases you.

Mem. The commission herein is returnable in Paris, 24th June, 1866.